W9-CLV-531

YO-YO

YO-YO

by Diane Balson

WILLIAM MORROW AND COMPANY, INC.
NEW YORK 1976

Grateful acknowledgment is made by the author for the use of the following:

Definition of a cell. By permission. From *Webster's New Collegiate Dictionary,* © 1975 by G. & C. Merriam Co., Publishers of the Merriam-Webster Dictionaries.

"Good and Bad Children," "Foreign Children," both by Robert Louis Stevenson, from *A Child's Garden of Verses,* published by Charles Scribner's Sons.

Four lines from "COPPER KETTLE" (The Pale Moonlight). Words and music by Albert F. Beddoe. TRO — © Copyright 1953, 1961 & 1964, MELODY TRAILS, INC., New York, N.Y. Used by permission.

Definition of a Capybara. Quotation from *South American Mammals* by John Leigh-Pemberton, published by Ladybird Books Limited, Loughborough, England.

Six lines from *The Soldier's Guide,* Department of the Army Field Manual FM 21-13. Department of the Army, June 1952.

Printed in the United States of America.

1 2 3 4 5 80 79 78 77 76

Library of Congress Cataloging in Publication Data

Balson, Diane.
Yo-yo.

I. Title.
PZ4.B199Yo [PS3552.A4715] 813'.5'4 75-25723
ISBN 0-688-02979-5

Book design: Helen Roberts

For the memory of my father, Boris Michel Balson
and for Glee Zusi

Thanks and love to all the people who encouraged and helped, especially: Stephen Bennett; Helen Brann; Carol Hill
My family: Elizabeth Balson; Maurice, Danielle and Michael Baroni

Anything awful makes me laugh. I misbehaved once at a funeral.

—CHARLES LAMB in a letter to Southey

I

The city is moving. I noticed it just yesterday. Or maybe the day before. No matter. The buildings tremble and waver in the gray, dusty light like reflections in a funhouse mirror and the pavement rolls and heaves. Is this how it begins? Or ends? Is this what makes women in Tenafly, New Jersey, or Lake Forest, Illinois, run naked through dark suburban streets screaming, "HELP ME. SOMEBODY PLEASE HELP ME." And when they reach the police station (they always head for the police station) do they receive the help they so urgently require—the rubber hose, manacles, rape ("No, it's *my* turn, Joey, for Chrissakes, wait your *turn*") on the cellar floor? It is an interesting question, but one that I do not feel like exploring, at least not at the moment.

This afternoon, lying on my bed as the children shrieked and fought and watched television, I looked into a patch of light on the ceiling and saw a cell. Nucleus, protoplasm, semipermeable membrane, and all. When a friend called awhile later I mentioned this, casually, and she said, "Ridiculous. Nobody can *see* a cell; they're micro*scopic,* for

Christ's sake. You're just upset. You'd better get your ass together, take some Librium. Have you called Nina Farrow about a job yet? I gave you her number two weeks ago; have you called?" No. I have not called Nina Farrow about a job. Yet. Ah, but I know. I *know*. The cell was there. Just to be sure, however, I got out the dictionary and looked it up.

Definition of a cell: a small usu. (usu., notice, usu., not always) microscopic mass of protoplasm bounded externally by a semipermeable membrane, usu. including one or more nuclei and various nonliving products, capable alone or interacting with other cells of performing all the fundamental functions of life, and forming the least structural aggregate of living matter capable of functioning independently.

Yes, it was a cell all right.

Yesterday I went to see Mother. I walked thirty blocks. I had to walk because I could not get on a bus. Oh, I have had problems before. Perhaps, you will say, I am simply upset, that Mother's incarceration (breakdown, crack-up, psychosis, neurosis, paranoia, bout with lunacy?) has simply intensified my problems, brought them more sharply into focus. Perhaps. For now even walking alone is not easy. I am much better off holding onto a shopping cart, dog's leash, child, but they do not admit children under sixteen in the hospital (rest home, mental institution, retirement hotel, school for exceptional non-children?) although I've often wondered why; it might do them good, especially Kate. Taxis are better than buses, but what with the rent, children's tuitions, cost of food, I feel guilty about spending money on taxis. Subways I gave up on a long time ago.

Memory: Nine and a half years ago while standing on the 86th Street platform of the Lexington IRT, the man next to me who'd been calmly reading his newspaper folded it neatly, took off his glasses, set both glasses and newspaper down on the platform and jumped into the path of the oncoming train. The train ground to a shuddering halt. Most of the body was under the train, but the impact sent one hand flying up from the track. The hand landed at my feet. It was wearing a watch, a heavy gold one, which seemed to be intact and still ticking away. The little finger sported a star sapphire ring. The next day there was a short notice on the forty-third page of *The New York Times,* wedged in between the lengthy obituaries of J. Carleton Van der Voort, a retired State Supreme Court Judge, and Jeremy F. Woods, M.D., a retired surgeon:

> Dr. Manny Gerber, D.D.S., retired, of 102-34½ 111th Street, Rego Park, Queens, jumped or fell to his death yesterday morning from the platform of the 86th Street Lexington Avenue IRT station. Service was halted for an hour.
>
> He leaves his wife, the former Trixie Tussig; two daughters, Helene and Lynette, and three grandchildren.

"Just look at that, girls! Your father! Right between a Judge and a Surgeon! Both retired, too, just like Papa. Isn't that a coincidence? Isn't that *something?*"

"Yeah, Ma, really something."

"Listen, I have to go home now and breastfeed Arnold."

"Breastfeed? Who breastfeeds anymore? The sitter hands him a bottle, I'm free. Could I be secretary to one of the best CPA's in Forest Hills, in the entire *borough,* maybe, if I breastfed Adam? Answer me that!"

"You want a kid who sucks everything in sight for the rest of his life, Helene? *Go* ahead. *Be* free. *Have* a career. *Don't* breastfeed. *Let* a sitter hand him a bottle. But don't tell *me. I know what I'm doing.*"

(Lucky, lucky Lynette.)

"Girls! Girls! And Papa hardly cold in his grave."

Should I have telephoned the widow Gerber and *The New York Times?* After all, that "jumped or fell" leaves things a little . . . nowhere, doesn't it? (And what the hell was he doing at Eighty-sixth Street at eight-thirty in the morning anyway? Why couldn't he jump on his own goddamn turf?) No, in retrospect I think I played it safe by leaving the widow Gerber, *The New York Times,* Helene, Lynette and Papa (pieces of Papa, actually) in peace. Or nowhere. Whichever term seems most apt.

I bring up Manny Gerber, D.D.S., retired and deceased, only because it fascinated me then, still fascinates me, that not a single person on the platform seemed to think much out of the ordinary had happened but me. One woman looked at the hand, gave a short, stifled scream, and went on eating a pumpernickel bagel. A few men shook their heads, sighed, looked irritably at their watches (now they'd have to take the local, be late for work), but my reaction—nausea, uncontrollable shaking, deadly pallor—seemed sadly overdone, out of place. If I had not been pregnant with Kate I might have remained hidden for days in the womb of the iron girder into which I'd retreated, but an old woman in a purple coat with a black fox collar finally noticed me and my bulging belly and led me upstairs onto the waiting local, all the while soothing, "There, there, dear, no reason to be upset. On your way to work? Better to go on to work, no reason to go home, you'll be fine in a minute, just fine. Pregnant, are you? Musn't upset the baby. I worked until my seventh month with the last one, killed in the war, blown up by a grenade he was, what month are you in? Third time I've seen this happen; I don't know what gets into people, jumping off platforms, mixing things up. Oh, I saw what he did. They'll say he fell or someone pushed him, but he jumped. Standing right next to him, were you? Then you saw too. Fell? *Hah.* He *jumped. Some nerve.*"

Note to the ecology-minded: Hey, want to *really* mix things up? Sabotage the system? Think bodies! Yes! Bodies tossed in front of trains, cars, buses, trucks. Bodies hurled into the nose cones of moon-bound rockets. Parachutists sucked into the engines of 747's, with maybe a skydiver or two to liven things up. Clean air! No more fumes! Ecology and population control all in one!

Still a little shaky but propelled by my protector in purple, on I went to work, suddenly feeling very gutsy and full of drama—"Look at her, having a baby, the man standing next to her jumps (falls? Was pushed?) to his death under a train, but does a little thing like a disembodied hand get her down? Not her! Not this girl! *This* girl goes on to work, keeps functioning, uses her energies in a positive, productive way, gets the job done. What a sweetheart! What a girl!"

Anyway, ever since Mother was "put away" last month, it is often the same with buses. Here is what happened the last time I tried to ride the 79th Street crosstown: I deposited my token (like everyone else), sat down next to the door (always next to the door, *just in case*), opened my newspaper. Then it began. People separating into eyes, arms, mouths, heads, hands, ears; all those *parts* floating, writhing, quivering, glistening in the moving molecular air. A total, I remember vaguely from elementary school math, is supposed to be the sum of all its parts. Not only did all those parts not add up to any definable total, but they were moving besides. I got off at the very next stop.

Now before I go on, let me say that I know all about anxiety attacks. I have even sought professional help. One shrink was convinced that my problem (at the time limited to subways, Ford station wagons, and parades) was due to what he called "overbreathing." You start out by being a little anxious, a little dizzy, he said, which makes you breathe faster. The faster you breathe, the more anxious and dizzy you get. To test out his theory (the more he talked the more turned on he got; he was positive that he, Jordan Morgan, not even a real shrink but only a Ph.D., had found THE ANSWER) he suggested that I pant for fifty seconds, oh, all right, if I felt silly he'd do it *with* me. So we sat there over-breathing, panting together in a companionable way, pant-pant-pant-pant-pant, our tongues hanging out like two horny St. Bernards. That's right. At the end of the fifty seconds Dr. Morgan was so dizzy he had to lie down on his black vinyl couch, while I felt about the same as before. I never went back to Dr. Morgan, but I hope he has that session on tape. I'm sure he does; one day he left his closet door slightly ajar and I could see a tape recorder revolving merrily away, next to a bottle of mouthwash and a half-eaten tuna on rye. What I mean is, what I'm trying to say, I hope he lies on his black vinyl couch (tears, spills, and sperm wipe off at the touch of a sponge!) and masturbates to the tune of it. I hope he plays it at parties. I hope he plays it for his wife (I know he has a wife—God, she looked like an insect, all pointy—because he kept a picture of her prominently displayed, for protection I suppose, but he didn't need it, on his desk): "See Janet, I can *too* get it up once in a while; just listen to *this!*" I hope, in effect, that those fifty seconds, although they did nothing whatsoever for me, have changed Jordan Morgan's life. For the good. I am nothing if not altruistic.

But I do not think overbreathing is my problem. Nor do I believe that Manny Gerber's hand has caused some sort of transit trauma. No, I think my problem is something worse, or something bigger, something better than a simple anxiety attack. That last time when I looked around the bus, at the sweating blonde reading a recipe for sweet-and-sour meatballs made from Spam whose head was approaching the pale-pink fingernails of a blue-haired lady of a certain age whose well-shod feet were in slow motion moving away from the elbows of a crisp young man with four pens in his pocket whose collarbone was tentatively mating with the luscious buttocks of a ten-year-old in gray flannel slacks and school blazer whose green eyes were revolving toward the glossy mouth of a cute little teeny-bopper in recycled jeans, I wondered, I asked, I ask still: People! My fellow Americans! (Yes, even you three slouched like a ribbon of stale licorice across the back seat of the bus, you nodding Puerto Rican in drag, you two macho blacks with combs in your fro's.) Do you notice? Do you see what is happening? And if you don't notice, do you notice that I notice? And if you do notice that I notice, will you rise up in one bloodthirsty moving throng and nail me to a neon cross? Duck me in a frozen pond? What sensuous delights await me once you find me out?

I felt . . . conspicuous. I felt like a sequined whore at a DAR meeting, a mountain mama on the designer floor at Bendel's, a Junior Leaguer who has walked into a Forty-second Street porno flick by mistake: "Oh dear, oh *dear,* Bitsy said to meet her at this terribly quaint, divine, new, very *in* little restaurant in this sort of *slum;* I must have gotten the address wrong; my *that* looks interesting, oh well, as long as I'm *here,* as long as no one *sees* me . . ." I felt the way I did when Kate was very small and I took her to a birthday party, not for one of her nursery school friends but a party for the son of someone I'd worked with. All the parents and relatives were sitting around eating fruit Jell-o and ice cream and angel food cake and there was Kate in the Florence Eiseman pinafore my mother had bought her, and her straight blond hair and perfect nose, and they knew we were somehow, I don't know, *different,* and I very acutely knew that they knew. One of the old men, the grandfather of the little boy, I think, finally came right out and asked me, "Are you Jewish?" Just like that. *"Are you Jewish?"* The whole room was suddenly very quiet. You could have heard a blob of Jell-o drop on the wall-to-wall beige carpet. And when I said, or rather mumbled, "Uh, no. Well, I mean, I don't *think* so. I mean, we're not *anything,* really," he gave the room a knowing look. Aha. Ahahaha*ha!* You *see.* I knew it all the time. Thought you could fool *us,* did you? Christian cunt. Bitch. Whore. Get out of our party. Go back uptown where you came from.

But which way is uptown, grandaddy? And do I take

the local or the express? "It's not my fault," I wanted to cry. "Don't you see? *It's not my fault.*" Or is it? *Is* it? My fault? Is this how it began, or ended, with Mother?

She has a look of eager anticipation, of ecstasy, on her face when they take her upstairs for shock; she races ahead of the nurse—shock it to me, baby, I deserve every volt, every jolt, give me pain, lots of pain, in the starry skies above. More, more, more! Wham! Whoopee!

"I didn't mean to do it!" she kept screaming the night she thought the S.P.C.C. was coming to take her baby away, the night my father called me and I called one of my ex-shrinks, the tall gray one, not Jordan Morgan, not the white-haired Viennese, not the motherly endomorph (a mistake, the tall gray one, but who do you get on a Sunday night in New York City when your mother is fending your father off with a knife?). She'd been carrying the doll around with her for weeks; she refused to put it down. My father ignored the doll, pretended not to notice, until the crib and layette—dear little pink booties, hand-smocked dresses—arrived on Saturday. By Sunday he decided he'd had enough ("You're just being silly, Allison; just stop this silliness. How about going away for a few weeks, Acapulco maybe, you've always liked Acapulco. Jesus, what that altitude does to my breathing, all right never mind I'll suffer, anything to make you happy") and tried to take the doll away. My father is not what one would call terribly aware, but the knife-wielding business that followed . . . only a table knife, but still . . . scared the shit out of him. Which is why he called me. Even after he agreed she might possibly need a little "rest," however—checked her into the hospital, signed all the forms—it wasn't until he finally noticed the locks and screams and crazies that the truth blazed upon his balding head.

Moment of Truth for Dear Old Dad: "Jesus Christ. This is a *mental* hospital."

That's right, Daddy dear. That's exactly what it is!

My mother is still carrying the doll. They cannot get her to put it down. *The best psychiatric brains in the country and they cannot get her to put it down.* Hang in there, Mom. Hurray! They also cannot get her to take off her toe shoes. Somehow, during the phone call to me, my call to the shrink and the time the ambulance arrived, she had the presence of mind to pack her toe shoes. They are the shoes she wore when she had a minor part in a musical comedy extravaganza in the thirties. There is a picture of her, on toe, looking very beautiful and clutching the backdrop curtain for support, in my parents' living room on the gleaming grand piano, along with a silver bowl of roses (changed every other day), a large vermeil bird, an ivory elephant with a menacing tusk, a lump of jade, two heavy silver candlesticks, and a photograph of my brother (the one my father doesn't talk about) and myself at the ages, respectively, of two and ten.

Here is an account of yesterday's visit. All visits seem to me the same—each a keyless capsule, insanity locked in position. Yesterday, as usual, my mother and I sat in the "day room" (Is there a "night room"? An "afternoon room"? A "morning room"? Keep 'em moving, that's the main thing!) drinking coffee out of paper cups. The paper grated on my teeth like chalk. My mother was wearing a print silk dress, a great deal of lipstick, and a bright red wig, the same wig—funny, wonder where she got it, cheap Dynel, not at all her style; she has box after box of soft blond wigs, falls, and wiglets from Saks tucked away in her closet at home—in which we delivered her to the hospital. She would not speak to me; she has hardly spoken a word all month. At first I kept on talking about anything, anything—about Andrew, the children, the weather, the dog—but eventually I gave up and stared down, as I often do, at the puppet store across the street. Ten puppets hang in the front window. Their faces are huge, bigger than any puppets' faces I have ever seen, but their bodies are tiny, grotesque. There must be a draft. Every half hour or so the tight-bottomed homosexual who runs the place has to dash out and untangle the puppets' strings. The strings only tangle up again, though.

In a telephone booth at one end of the room, near the door, a fat brunette of about sixty-five, wearing a sleeveless orange muumuu upon which black herons danced, was sobbing into the receiver, "I love you, darling. I'll always love you. Kiss the children for me. Tell the children this business trip will be over soon. Tell them how much I hate leaving them, how much I miss them, but this trip is so important to my career. Sometimes a woman has to think of herself. Don't you think so, Robert? Don't you agree? Sometimes a woman has to think of herself."

"Shiyitt," said a massive black nurse. "*Business trip.* Shi*yitt*. She don't have no job. She don't have no husband. She don't have no children. She don't have no *nuthin'*. Since that fat old sister, fatter'n she is, brought her in day before yesterday, that old girl just stay in that telephone booth talkin' to *nobody*."

I was one of three visitors. My companions in sanity were the mother of a pretty young woman who cannot stop crying and the daughter of a woman about fifty who cannot stay awake. Most of the patients and nurses, as usual, sat motionless in front of the television set. Yesterday, however, an event occurred that shook the sameness. A TV special preempted the usual soaps: Evel Knievel successfully completed an indoor motorcycle jump over seventeen pick-up trucks. A few patients smiled; one old woman even clapped and kept on clapping until a nurse reached over and casually swatted the old woman's hands with a rolled-up copy of the *Daily News*.

The announcer was beside himself, shouting, practically jerking off into the microphone. He asked Evel if he had any advice, anything at all to say, to the boys and girls of America, to all those hundreds of thousands of motorcycle enthusiasts who had just watched this fantastic jump.

Evel Knievel looked straight into the camera. In his red, white, and blue jump suit and cape he looked very honest, very sincere. Something about his lean, sensitive face reminded me of James Dean in *Rebel Without a Cause.*

Evel spoke directly to the boys and girls of America, to all those hundreds of thousands of motorcycle enthusiasts who ride and joke and mess around, and the advice seemed so important I wrote it down on a piece of paper napkin. What I wrote was:

Always wear your crash helmet.

And there was more.

I also wrote:

When you're out on your motorcyle, with your crash helmet on, remember—Somebody Up There is looking out for you.

(Somebody Up There sure is looking out for Evel.)

The pretty young woman who cannot stop crying stopped crying, looked dazedly up at the ceiling, and then began to cry again.

My mother suddenly got up and did a series of wobbly châiné turns around the room. At the door she ran into the tall gray shrink—he puts in an appearance every day, for appearances' sake, no therapy, she's too old, beyond therapy —and ended the series with a sweeping curtsy at his feet. Her doll dangled from one hand. Her hands were shaking, she was shaking all over, she is emaciated, she must be down to eighty pounds. She straightened up, walked to the refreshment table, pointedly took a chocolate-chip cookie from the huge platter next to the coffee urn, looked up at the shrink for approval. *See Daddy what a good girl I am I cleaned my plate am I pretty do you love me now Daddy do you do you?*

"How's my favorite girl? Overeating again?"

Favorite! She smiled, bit into another cookie. A bright slash of lipstick came off onto her front teeth. Her caps, however, looked fine. After her second shock treatment my father noticed a slight unevenness of the upper left incisor and immediately spoke to the shrink about it—("That kind of an investment, a man has to protect his investments, thousands those caps cost me")—and the shrink agreed to take special precautions.

"Still carrying your baby, I see. Going to let me hold her soon?"

"Maybe," my mother said coyly. "Maybe."

"That's my girl! See you tomorrow!"

Bastard. I hate this shrink, hated him during my own short period of treatment, now hate him more than I have ever hated anyone in my life. In the beginning, after the initial confusion, I brought in another psychiatrist, a good man, a good doctor, for a consultation, who said to my father:

"Your wife, Mr. Thulin, is not a commodity, a stock or bond that you are buying or selling. She is a living human being. You cannot think of treatment simply in terms of which process is fastest. Personally I feel that shock therapy is . . ."

"But shock works fastest! They told me that. Shock works fastest! I want her out of here. My wife is not crazy. I want my wife out of here, away from all these crazy people!"

So shock it is. And as my father points out, every chance he gets, I am not paying for my mother's hospitalization; I have no right to interfere. In any case, my mother *prefers* this hulking six-foot five-inch gray god in his Peal shoes and suits from Brooks. "Wishy-washy," was her sole comment after the consultation with the other, good psychiatrist. "Wishy-washy."

Usually I do not interfere. But yesterday, paying the bills or not, I was determined to find out what was going on. I followed the tall gray shrink to the door, caught hold of one flap of his lightweight herringbone tweed.

"I would like to know how my mother is doing. I'm

very concerned about her. She seems so . . . vague. She won't talk to me. She doesn't remember. I talk to her about . . . things and . . . she won't talk to me. She doesn't seem to remember."

"Oh, they're all like that at first," he said airily. "Most of it comes back."

"But . . . she's so thin; she can't be eating anything. She seems just the same. She doesn't seem any better, any better at all. She seems just the same."

Please, please, somebody do something. My mother. My mother in this room with women sobbing, we used to have tea parties together, sugar water tea in tiny china cups, and when I could not sleep she used to read to me. She read:

> Children, you are very little,
> And your bones are very brittle;
> If you would grow great and stately,
> You must try to walk sedately.
>
> You must still be bright and quiet,
> And content with simple diet;
> And remain through all bewild'ring,
> Innocent and honest children.

My mother. You are shocking away her brain.

But the shrink was in a hurry to be off. "Look, she's better; she's doing fine. Calm down. Think you're the only girl whose mother has ever had shock treatments?"

"Think you're the only girl who's ever had a baby?" they said when I went to the hospital to have Kate, and they strapped me to a table and shot me full of Scopolamine.

"But I thought I was going to have natural childbirth; I did all the exercises, the breathing, we talked about it, you said . . ."

"Just lie back, honey, just relax, this shot is standard, something we give all our girls, just something to relax you you . . .

"Let's induce, why not, hell, she's here. I have to get up to Cornell to see my kid. Why the hell did the water have to break today; she isn't even due for another two goddamn weeks. Shit. Oh well, Allen can handle it. She'll never know the difference."

I can hear you. You do not know it but I can hear you. My body is inert, leaden, not my own but I can hear you. I open my mouth to scream but there is no sound. Kate still has a forceps' mark, faint but visible, near her eye.

I took my mother's hand, a hand so dry, thin, fragile it felt like the body of a frightened bird, all bones, fluttering sinew, dry, threaded skin.

"Mother?"

"The thing is . . . the thing *is,*" she said finally, with tears, the first tears I have seen her shed in a month, in her eyes, "that really, no matter what anyone thinks, I didn't mean to do it."

"What is it, Mother? What is it you've done?"

There was a long silence.

"I can't remember," my mother said.

A nurse trundled a cart dotted with little paper cups filled with pills, bleached votive candles, offerings to an unknown god, through the room, signaling the end of visiting hours. When I gently released my mother's hand and placed it in her lap she did not notice. She did not say good-bye. When I looked back she had not moved.

After I passed the manic with teased black hair and sooty false eyelashes who paces up and down the hall saying, "Very funny very funny I can't stop this walking up and down I can't stop talking I'm a manic you see I'm a manic I'm tired so tired but I can't stop walking I can't stop talking," I ran into the old woman who waits for me, the one whose private nurse fusses over her, ties shiny pink bows in her beautiful snowy hair. She is very old. I would avoid her if I could, but there is only one exit, and she waits for me there. Every time I leave we have, word for word, the same conversation.

"My dear," she says, her strong, ring-laden fingers tightening on my arm. "You simply must get me out of this place. They are keeping me here against my will. You must reserve a first-class cabin for me on the *Mauretania* immediately so that I may rejoin my son in London. My son is awaiting my arrival."

Her nurse gives me a knowing wink.

"I will, Mrs. Chisolm."

"You won't forget?"

"No, Mrs. Chisolm. I won't forget."

"Did I tell you my name? I don't think I've told you my name. Chisolm. Mary Chisolm. C-h-i-s-o-l-m."

"I think you've told me before, Mrs. Chisolm."

"You won't forget? My son is waiting, you know. My son is waiting."

"No, Mrs. Chisolm. I won't forget."

What if I did? Reserve a cabin, I mean? Oh, not on the *Mauretania,* of course, but on the *Elizabeth II?* Or a seat on a plane? What if I got her out? What then?

Then she'd be out and I'd be in. That's what then.

My husband says I should not visit Mother so often. It exhausts me, I am nervous afterwards, he says. Perhaps he is right. Today, for example, it is half past three, the two younger children are still in their pajamas, the dog has not been walked, we are out of milk, fruit punch, orange drink, ginger ale, raisins, apples, pretzels, cookies, and glancing up at the bedroom ceiling I see that the cell is still there. A reaction to yesterday's visit? Possibly. But something draws me to the hospital, the puppets, the manic, the crying young woman, Mrs. Chisolm, my mother, the others, as if somehow these things hold an answer to some vital question, a question I do not feel like exploring. At least not at the moment.

II

A question, however, that I obviously must explore. And soon. For I am slipping away from all the things that hold me, have held me, to the earth before: clean linoleum, dusted tables, vacuumed rugs, shopping lists, polished silver, bathed children, fresh towels, balanced meals, ironed clothes, neat closets. I am sleeping too much too, twelve hours last night; I went to bed before the children did. And there are other signs: I am eating and drinking too much (alcoholics, I've heard, rarely overeat, so that is some small comfort, or perhaps simply another sign that I am some sort of aberration, mutation, for I am always hungry).

Another sign: I have returned to the reading matter of my childhood. This morning at eleven A.M. I fixed myself a martini and six peanut butter crackers, snuck into Kate's yellow and white room, the only neat room in the house, took a book from her alphabetically arranged yellow bookcase, went back to bed and read, from cover to cover, *The Little Princess,* by Frances Hodgson Burnett. At Kate's age I took that book out of the school library over and over, until I was given my own copy the Christmas I was ten.

Kate has that same copy. She keeps all the books I saved for my phantom children, but she does not read them. Kate does not read *The Little Princess, The Secret Garden, Ballet Shoes, The Poor Little Rich Girl.* Anna will, I think, if she ever learns to read, which seems doubtful, but not Kate. No, Kate hardly reads at all although she does well, far better than I did, at school, but when she does read it is Nancy Drew, or *Teen* magazine, or books that ask and answer questions like: "When did the Ice Age end?" "Who were the first people to chew gum?" "What was the origin of the hat?" She is always sending away for things, too, instructions on how to make mobiles out of shell macaroni or jewelry boxes from Popsicle sticks. I do not understand her very well, I do not think I like her much, my eldest daughter, so blond, so perfect, with her scores of friends, all of whom look exactly like her, her secret clubs, file cards, collections of china animals, ornamental dolls brought back from my parents' trips. When I cry or go into one of my rages—smash plates into the sink, throw cups to the floor—she stares at me coolly, then turns away. But she will obviously turn out, function best, will Kate. Anna is, I suppose, what might be called "difficult," in that she is hypersensitive and cries easily when she is frustrated or hurt, which is often. But when I lie on my bed she comes and touches me, offers to get me a glass of lemonade, a cookie, or to massage my feet with her own special bottle of pink hand lotion. I think in some ways we are very much alike, I think we understand each other, Anna and I, but then again, she is only seven; I may be projecting. Or perhaps she does not really understand at all but, like Andrew, only accepts what she cannot, or does not want to, understand. "He's either unconscious or made of steel, being able to live with you," a friend once said. That may be true. I do not know what kind of man my husband is. Another question consistently in my mind lately is: after thirteen years of marriage, shouldn't I know?

The baby, the boy, Nicholas, the four-year-old accident I could not abort ("Think of it as a tumor, a growth," they said; I even made an appointment at an abortion clinic but could not go through with it), I do not really know anything about except that until several months ago he slept exactly six hours a night, could climb out of his crib before he could walk, is into everything from kitchen cupboards to my makeup, and that I love him in an overpoweringly physical, intense way that I never loved the girls. I love to towel his warm, sturdy body after a bath, feel his fuzzy head against my breasts when he climbs into bed with me in the morning, watch his strong, short legs running. He still wanders, but not as much as he used to. And he is sleeping more regularly. Last summer even the fifteen-year-old mother's helper was exhausted; she fell asleep several times at the beach, the girls told me. I was so afraid Nicco would wander off, run into the water—he did that, all last summer; he'd run into the water and just keep going—that I let her handle the girls and mostly took care of Nicco myself, not that I blamed Zibby for falling asleep, she was as tired as I was, but I knew that no matter how tired I was, I would not fall asleep while watching Nicco. On the beach or anywhere else.

Once when Nicco was about six months old and I took him to the pediatrician for a checkup, I worked up enough courage—for the first and last time—to speak to Dr. Carroll about Nicco's lack of sleeping, hyperactivity, and other related problems. Here was Dr. Carroll's reply:

(Sigh.) "Look, Mrs. Calder, I see children every day with leu*kemia,* children with menin*gi*tis, children with cerebral *pal*sy. There are children up there at the hospital right now, *dy*ing. All any normal woman wants is her behind sewn up properly and a healthy baby. You've got both. You're lucky. Don't complain."

Lucky. People are always telling me I'm lucky. Or to take a Librium.

I have only two questions about Dr. Carroll's statement. Did he mean that I am not a normal woman? And how did he know the condition of my ass? He'd never seen it. Unless, of course, he'd called the last obstetrician, the good guy, the one who delivered Anna and Nicco, to find out. No, no. That's too paranoid. Even for me.

Anyway, since Nicco has started nursery school, he has calmed down a great deal. He and Anna go to school in a crumbling brownstone in the West Nineties where the children wear ragged jeans and work shirts and swear with gleeful abandon, even at Nicco's age. When I take Anna and Nicco to school and stand amongst the frowsy mothers in wrinkled slacks and stained suede jackets, I feel less conspicuous, less out of place. Anna told me excitedly last week that her group was studying the Netsilik Eskimos, not as they are now (having been exposed to the civilizing processes of guns, government schools, liquor, the English language, and hard rock) but as they were. "Do you see the difference, Mommy? As they *were*." Anna does not know who George Washington was, or the capital of the United States, or who invented the light bulb, but she knows a great deal about the Netsilik Eskimos. As they were. I suppose that is why I love the school.

Kate stayed on at her girls' school with its rows of shiny desks, starched white blouses, knee socks, plaid jumpers, and mothers in pale wool coats who reluctantly appear on nanny's day off, the same school that said of Anna after three months in first grade: "She is not working up to grade level. She cannot read. In mathematics, for example, she is unable to make a one-to-one relationship. Perhaps you might eventually wish to consider a less pressured school, a school where the standards are not quite so . . . high." I was eventually more than happy to so consider. But Kate flatly refused to leave. Just because we'd moved, she said, just because Anna was retarded (Anna is far from "retarded"; I think she is bright, far brighter than Kate), she didn't see why she had to go to some "second-rate" school. And when I talked it over with Andrew, he said, "Well, if she's happy there and doing well, why not let her stay?"

He does not think much of Anna and Nicco's school, I know. But he does not say so. Just as he said little about my insistence on moving to the West Side. Yes, the apartment is larger, and we could never have found so much space on the East Side at a comparable rent. Yes, the building has a certain old-world charm. ("There isn't even a doorman," Kate said, sniffing, as she looked around the huge marble lobby with its vaulted ceiling, carved paneling, mirrors.) And these are the reasons I give—space, reasonable rent, charm. But they are not the real reasons. I think I insisted upon moving to this neighborhood although, no, *because* I am frightened by it, and within that fear lies a strange fascination. I am fascinated by the screams that drift up at night from the Eldorado Hotel that houses a variety of pimps and prostitutes; the giant black who stands in the middle of Broadway, his arms upraised, proclaiming, "I am the new God of Israel"; the one-legged Chinaman who sits on the corner saying fuckfuckfuckfuckfuck all day; the hunch-backed midget behind the cosmetics counter of the drugstore where the druggists mix up prescriptions as they sing old show tunes; the red-faced Irishman who directs imaginary traffic on a blocked-off play street where no children play—stop, go, stop, go; the restaurant across the street where they monthly change the facade: first a thatched roof, up, down. Then a stucco effect, up, down. Then painted bricks, up, down. Right now it is green shingles. Tomorrow? Who knows! The day there was a gas explosion and manhole covers went flying like giant pot lids into the air and flames streaked toward the sky it all seemed perfectly normal, right.

I am fascinated, too, by the perverts in the park; the shabby Russian ladies who sit on benches in the hazy sun and talk of Minsk and Pinsk; the dog shit heaped in mounds, some large, some small, coiled in varying patterns everywhere: in the playground, on the grass, under the benches, behind the trees. Yes, the dog shit fascinates me most of all.

"What would you like for your birthday, honey?"

"Dog shit."

"Dog . . . shit?"

"*Yes.* A big, Bonwit-wrapped, flowery-papered, shiny-ribboned box of it. Any kind would do: Dalmatian shit, Poodle shit, Pomeranian shit, Corgi shit, Spitz shit. Or failing that, giraffe shit, llama shit, squirrel shit, raccoon shit, chameleon shit . . ."

"But . . . *why?*"

"Because I'd like to fill the bathtub with it and sink down up to my eyes. I'd like to wear it to a fancy dress ball (the kind of charity affair that ended my mother's committee work—"Jesus Christ, Allison, something to keep you busy, occupy your mind, stop this moping around, but $150 for a goddamn *mask?*"), and there I'd be amongst all the Cleopatras and Marie Antoinettes . . ."

"And what did *you* come as, dear?"

"Dalmatian shit."

"Ooh. How *original!*"

Dog shit I can understand. Dog shit I can relate to. Perhaps in dog shit, or in any kind of shit for that matter, I can find the answers I seek.

Enough, as my father would say, of this silliness. I am not really mad. Yet. I still know there are certain rules, certain amenities to observe. Outwardly, at least, I play by the rules. As I see it, playing by the rules of our time, there are several ways a woman is supposed to be able to get her ass together. (Of course in other times, other places, there were other rules: Churn that butter! Tote that bale! Keep your knees together! Roll bandages for our brave young lads in gray! Win the vote! Wear a veil! Bind your feet!) Eliminating for the moment the more mundane rules like organized religion, psychiatry, tranquilizers; predominantly coastal phenomena like TM, Scientology (Is there a Midwest? I've never quite believed there was.); reactionary rules like Buy a new hat! Hire a sitter! Get your hair done! and the more extreme directives like Death to the male chauvinist pigs! the new rules seem mainly to be the following:

Open marriage
Sexual freedom
Sisterhood
Freedom from stereotyped male-female roles
A meaningful career
Honest communication
Financial independence
One, or at the most two, children; preferably no children at all

Some of these rules, obviously, overlap. But perhaps I should consider them (aside from the last; too late for that) not necessarily in order, but one by one. Something bothers me, however. I have heard and read about women who've gotten it all together—women who've had triplets, head ad agencies, write best sellers in their spare time; women who live alone in sleek, plant-filled duplexes, earn $35,000 a year and have more lovers than they can handle; women who communicate honestly with their husbands and describe each extramarital affair freely, in delectably graphic detail—but I have never actually *known* one. The last woman I knew who tried to have an affair (not even an affair; she just slept, twice, with a twenty-two-year-old Navajo silversmith she'd met at the beach in East Hampton) wound up with a black eye, a separation, and a custody battle that is still going on. She is presently living, minus children and alimony, in a studio apartment in a semi-tenement on West Eighty-first Street and working as a salesgirl in Gimbel's East. You may think I am exaggerating. I am not. I will even tell you her name: Alexandra Johns. Her husband, a corporation lawyer with a huge firm, will almost certainly win the custody case; he's got money, power, and the judge—a cranky old bastard who won't let his own wife get a driver's license and has a two-year-old-type temper tantrum if dinner isn't on the table the minute he gets home—on his side. When Alexandra's husband found out about the "affair," he took his shotgun from the rack (just like in the olden days!), loaded it, left their sprawling redwood and glass weekend retreat overlooking the ocean, and went out hunting. Indians. Or rather, one Indian in particular. The drums must have sent out a message: the terrified Navajo beat it back to Gallup on the next Greyhound bus.

Another bedtime poem remembered from Mother's nocturnal readings:

Little Indian, Sioux or Crow,
Little frosty Eskimo,
Little Turk or Japanee,
Oh! don't you wish that you were me?

You have seen the scarlet trees
and the lions over seas;
You have eaten ostrich eggs,
And turned the turtles off their legs.

Such a life is very fine,
But it's not so nice as mine:
You must often, as you trod,
Have wearied *not* to be abroad.

You have curious things to eat,
I am fed on proper meat;
You must dwell beyond the foam,
But I am safe and live at home.
    Little Indian, Sioux or Crow,
    Little frosty Eskimo,
    Little Turk or Japanee,
Oh! don't you wish that you were me?

Terrified Navajo: "Shit no, Mama. I've got enough problems of my own."

No, the few women I know intimately seem just as confused, just as unhinged as I, and their tentative forays into liberation usually end in disaster.

And something else bothers me. Suppose by some miraculous accident I do get my ass together by following the new directives; will there suddenly be a whole new set of rules, leaving me revolving in limbo once again? What about those pitiful women who followed the rules of the fifties, baked their own apricot-banana bread, produced 3.5 children, put their hubbies through college, kept their hands off other women's husbands? Their children are gone, bread is too fattening, their husbands screw every bright young bird they can get their hands on. "But I followed the rules," say their bewildered eyes, dulled brains, sagging bellies. "What happened? What went wrong?" "Outsider. Parasite. Extraneous object," says the world. "Why don't you fuck off? Why don't you *die?*"

Ah well. Maybe, as usual, I am simply looking on the dark side. I do attract—besides dogs, men (have I mentioned that I attract men? Only sexually, of course, but one can't have everything), members of esoteric sects who hand out leaflets on Broadway, and other people's children—neurotics. Especially of the female variety. Or perhaps the phrase is redundant. So having looked on the dark side for the greater part of my life, I think I will give these new directives a cautious try, start life anew from a solid outer base. Or from nowhere. Whichever term seems most apt.

It is now almost Easter. I will give myself until Christmas. If the new directives have not worked by then, I will return to the summer home of my childhood, walk down the beach to a hidden area of dunes and tangled grass where at fifteen I was initially, and amazingly well, considering our ages, fucked by a sweet-faced Italian boy with blue eyes and a funny nose, and shoot myself in the left (not to be "different" in an adolescent sense but simply because I am left-handed) temple. The shot will leave (I have already decided), a neat, small, bloodless hole. No gas ovens, oceans, or overdoses for me. I have learned from my predecessors' mistakes. I dislike mess and the risk of failure.

III

But where shall I begin? I have outwardly played by the rules, yes, but I have never had very much respect for them, no matter what they were. I have even broken them occasionally, when no one was looking. When Kate's present school, Anna's ex-school, called me in for a solemn conference because Anna refused to stay in line at lunchtime—she didn't push ahead or linger, she just stood to one side, waiting, which left a gap in the line—I was delighted. Anna may have the courage I never had, to break the rules with everyone looking on.

I am in a box. Every hour on the hour a bell rings, the door to the box opens, and I am let out to dance: chaîné, pas de chat, preparation, pirouette, arabesque. My ankle wobbles in the arabesque. The bell rings again; the dance is over. It is time to return to the box. I return, but something has gone wrong; the bell keeps on ringing, ringing, the door opens and shuts, opens and shuts.

I wake up with a start. The telephone is ringing. It is Elly. Elly lives downstairs, is seven years older than I am, forty-one, but doesn't look it, has gray-blond hair cut in a Sassoon except she doesn't go to Sassoon but to a cheaper place between Broadway and Amsterdam. Elly wears granny glasses and no bra. She is bright, bitchy, vulgar, tender. I have never, really, had a woman friend before. We moved in June, but the children and I were away all summer, and I only met her in September. How can two women become so close in only six months? On the East Side I knew almost no one; I did not know who lived behind those shiny black doors neatly spaced along an endless red-carpeted hallway. I did not know the few mothers who took their children to the park. We were embarrassed misfits, outcasts; nannies bunched in stern, ethnic groups ruled the playground. Elly is part of what lately has kept me together, or maybe we keep each other together. Yes, Elly may be a good place to begin because right now, although all I have said is "hello," she is asking:

"Liza? Liza, are you all right? You sound . . . I don't know . . . weird. What's going on up there?"

"On? Up here? Nothing whatsover is going on. Up here. I am a normal woman. I polish my faucets. I scrub my toilets. Elly . . . did you know? You can actually see cells. I'm looking at one right now. I'm lying here and it's all there, the nucleus and everything, moving, right up on the ceiling. Why don't you come on up and look at it? We could just lie here together, looking at it. If you're not doing anything, I mean. If you don't have anything important to do. Like scrubbing your toilets."

There is a short silence.

"Terrific," Elly says. "You really sound terrific. I'll be right up. I'll have to bring the kids though; Justin is *working*. He says. And I have an extra one today; Natalie, do you know Natalie, no that's right, you've never met her, Natalie's maid is sick and I'm keeping Charlie."

"Charlie. Is that the one who's afraid of dogs?"

"Yeah. Better lock up old Max. If he throws up like he did the last time, I consider myself responsible."

Soon the doorbell is ringing frantically. There are tremendous clattering sounds drifting in from the front hall, so I take one more look at the cell, say good-bye, get out of bed, and answer the door. Elly, wearing embroidered jeans, a striped jersey, and brown suede clogs, is pushing three children in front of her and saying, "All right, all right, I *said* they could come down for supper, didn't I? If you'll just leave us *alone* for a minute, go watch TV, I don't *care* if it's bad for your eyes (to her eleven-year-old), I don't care if you go *blind.* Oh God, not you, Charlie, I didn't mean you, don't cry, just *fuck off* for a few minutes, will you?"

"God," she says, dropping into a kitchen chair and kicking off her clogs. "This vacation shit is incredible. Christmas, then a week in February for God knows what, now *Easter,* who the hell celebrates *Easter?* We're paying about five thousand dollars in tuition and the little fucks are home about three quarters of the year; one more day and I'm going to *kill* one of them. Maybe both of them. *Christ.*"

"Is risen," I say. "Do you want coffee?"

"I'd rather have a drink. Oh shit, never mind, make it coffee, it *is* too early. I've gained another pound this week and Justin's after me every goddamn minute. Do you know, I think he's actually been measuring the gin? He drinks as much as I do. More. *Christ.* Do you have any cigarettes? Oh, thank God. That too, he's after me about that all the time too. Try to do anything with a husband that works at home half the time. At least Andrew isn't here, following you around all day, *watching* you. No, no, just black. My *diet.*" She takes a long sip. "Is something special wrong, your mother or something, or just the whole general shit?" she asks carefully, taking in the sink full of dishes, the soggy paper filled with dog pee on the kitchen floor, the open jar of peanut butter on the counter. And I begin to cry and cry as if I will never stop, and Elly pulls my head to her warm, sagging breasts and rocks me back and forth like a child. "Oh yeah, baby. Oh baby, I know, I know," she says softly. I continue to cry; Elly's jersey is wet with my crying.

"Do you want a drink?" she asks after a while. "Do you want to be alone? Do you want to talk about it? Just tell me. Tell me what you want."

Kate's combed blond head appears around the kitchen door. She looks at us with distaste. "I was going to get everyone some juice, but I just remembered that we don't seem to *have* any juice and all the glasses seem to be in the *sink* so I guess we'll have to *wait,*" she says, twitching her crisp skirt.

"Are you a paraplegic?" I shriek from between Elly's protective breasts. "Did you ever think of washing a glass yourself? Did you ever think of drinking water for a change? Get out of here. Get away from me. Don't ask me for one single goddamn thing. Just get out."

"Do it. Fast," Elly says.

Kate retreats.

"Little shit," Elly says. "I'd like to give her a good smack."

"You can't," I say, sniffing.

"Why not? Who says?"

"I don't know. Spock. Gesell. The school shrink. Somebody."

"Listen, remember I told you about all the trouble we had with Marilyn last year? You know what the accountant—we had to have an accountant this year, our tax is so fucked up—you know what the accountant said when he saw all those bills for the shrink? 'You people have got to be crazy,' he said, 'spending that kind of money on a shrink for a kid. A belt is a lot cheaper.' "

"A belt is a lot cheaper," I repeat. I stop crying and we both begin to giggle, and now I can't stop giggling.

"Listen, listen to me now," Elly says. "I'm going to

get all these kids out of here. I'll give them supper early and you take a bath and lie down, no, don't lie down, just take a bath and get dressed and take a Librium, and then when Andrew gets home you can both come down for a drink, why don't you do that? You could meet Natalie; she's coming by around six to pick up Charlie. You'd like Natalie, you really would. Well, parts of her might get to you, but she really has guts. She's divorced and here she is with this kid and she's opened her own p.r. thing, agency, and she's doing fantastically well; she must earn a goddamn fortune. Liza. Liza? Are you listening to me at all?"

I stop giggling. "Yes. But I'll have to get those two dressed. They can't go downstairs in their pajamas. Andrew will think I'm inefficient. Not functioning. Crazy or something, like my mother. Not that he'd say so. But that's what he'd think."

"Oh shit, leave them in their pajamas, what's the difference? He'll just think that you're *terrifically* efficient, that you've gotten them ready for bed *early* so that we can have a drink in peace."

Suddenly she remembers the reason for her visit. "Say, what was all that business about a cell? Were you just kidding around or freaking out or what?"

I lead the way to the bedroom and we stand for a moment, hand in hand, staring at the ceiling.

"Christ," Elly says in awe. "The goddamn thing really is there, isn't it?"

Max, the dog, has been locked in the bedroom as per request. Max is a neurotic, aging Schnauzer who does not like to be locked up in the bedroom or anywhere else. Elly and I look down and notice the trail of pale yellow vomit at exactly the same time.

"Oh God," Elly groans. "No, I *said* I'd do it. Get me some paper towel."

After Elly has left, gathering all six children up like

a great billowing sail (with Kate protesting; she does not like Elly), I take a long hot bath, a Librium, wash my hair, shave my legs, put on makeup, a pair of clean jeans and a blue sweater, do the dishes, straighten the kitchen. I even remember to take two small steaks out of the freezer and put them on the counter to defrost. A peaceful dinner, just the two of us for once; no children whining, squirming, fighting, spilling food. On an impulse I set the table with linen napkins, wine glasses, candles. By the time Andrew comes home, letting himself in silently with his key, I am much better, and that fact annoys me. My pain, anguish, imminent (probably) suicide should not respond to such reactionary rules: apply makeup, spray on perfume, wash the dishes, clean the sink. How dare these shoddy rules work for me, an unusual, sensitive, creative person! Am I going backward instead of barreling on ahead? And yet, it's true, I do like certain aspects of housework: polishing furniture, arranging flowers, watering plants. I get a heady power high out of neatly arranged food cupboards: "Get in line you package of macaroni! Stand up straight you box of Oreos! Keep it quiet in there you bag of potato chips!" "Yassuh, Boss. Yes *Ma'am!*" And I cannot think clearly if my hair is not clean. Can the solution be as simple as a bottle of Breck?

"You look better. You look very pretty," Andrew says as he hands me a small bunch of daisies and hangs his raincoat, which he wears even on the sunniest spring days, on a wooden hanger in the hall closet. Better. Does that mean he has any idea of what's been going on? He does not look better, he looks exhausted, but when I dutifully admire the daisies and tell him so, he just shrugs and smiles his funny smile.

"Where are the children?"

"Downstairs at Elly's. They're having dinner there. Elly asked us down for a drink, as soon as you got home, she said."

"Okay. Do you want to go right down?"

"Why don't you change first? You'll be more comfortable."

What I really mean is, I cannot stand Andrew, or any man, in a suit. And Andrew's suits run to plain dark blues or grays. The husbands of the women I know are mostly art directors or copywriters who wear bleached jeans or corduroys to work, but Andrew is a lawyer with a conservative firm. He has to wear suits, he says matter-of-factly, for the same reason that he has to keep his hair short and wear shoes with laces. I suppose that's true; I just wish it bothered him more. But when I can talk him into putting on a pair of jeans and a work shirt, as I usually can, in the evenings, I almost love him again. His whole face changes; he looks more like Nicco—the same gray eyes, light brown hair, wide mouth. None of the children look like me, and only Nicco looks anything like Andrew, and even then not much.

I follow Andrew into the bedroom, light a cigarette, and sit in the flowered chair near the night table. The daisies, still wrapped in their stiff white paper, lie forgotten in my lap.

"Shouldn't you put them in water? They'll die, you know, if you don't put them in water."

He'd much rather I didn't watch him undress. Funny, considering how marvelous he is in bed; all his hang-ups dissolve once the lights are out. But out of bed Andrew is a man of closed doors, caution, whereas lately I am always leaving the bathroom door open so that the dog, children follow me in. I scatter signs of myself everywhere—used Kotex, cracker crumbs, empty glasses, a hairbrush on the dining room table, a frayed bra on a doorknob. He doesn't like my signs, he doesn't like my watching him, too bad, because I love his square, slightly heavy body, so clean, his broad shoulders, his short, strong legs. I love the hairs scattered on his chest, downy, soft like feathers when I brush my lips against them. I take one last look, sigh, and go to the kitchen where I arrange the daisies in a cut-glass bowl, make myself a gin and tonic, and stand at the window, staring across town. The heavy violet air is shimmering; to the north a curious cloud formation, tinged with red, hangs over Yorkville like a large drooping hat. Yorkville. Easter cakes and chocolate bunnies. Beyond confectionary counters in tearoom dimness fat German women with pink cheeks and spreading thighs gobble pastries. There are no Easter cakes or chocolate bunnies on Broadway. The one concession to Easter I've seen is a dusty plush rabbit (on special at $2.99) in the drugstore window.

Andrew comes up behind me so quietly I jump. "Ready?"

I slowly finish my drink. I want him to see that I've been drinking. Why? What *do* I want? Screams of recrimination? A slap in the face? Insults? Gaining weight. Old. Getting old. Drink beginning to show. Slight lines at either side of my mouth, subtle gashes, a portent of things to come. In repose my face crumples, descends into sadness, sags to the floor like a sopping sponge. But the other day I discovered that these lines are not lines of sadness, but of laughter. Do sober women laugh?

"I saw the table. It looks awfully nice. It'll be nice, won't it, to have dinner alone together?"

It is almost a plea. I rinse my glass and set it on the drainboard. "Yes, it will be nice. I'm ready now; let's walk down."

Although Andrew does not ask why, and I do not volunteer any information, we walk because right now I cannot face the particular Stefan (there are six in help in the building, all named Stefan) who is on the elevator from two to ten. Stefan II hates everyone—Jews, Puerto Ricans, Protestants, Japanese, Chinese, Indians, dogs, cats, hippies, blacks, children, women. Most especially, I think, women. Or maybe Jews; it's a toss-up. He is not sure about us. Without Kate I can usually pass for almost anything, due to my mixed heritage—Italian and Swedish on the paternal side, English on the maternal—but luckily Kate's uniform confuses Stefan II: only Catholic schoolchildren, he believes, wear uniforms. So he treats us with wary courtesy. (Thank God he's off on Sundays; he'd wonder why we weren't heading off to mass with the girls dressed in pink organdy, their hair in huge floppy bows, and Nicco in a suit, tie, and tiny fedora, which, of course, he'd remove as soon as he passed through the sacred portals.) Just to be on the safe side, however, I am always careful to say "Merry Christmas" or "Happy Easter!" If indicated I would be just as careful to say, "Cuba, Si!" or "Happy Year of the Rat!" or "Aux Barricades!" Courage I have none. Courage is for the sane at heart. I just want to save what's left of my own ass.

Stefan II loves to stand, immobile and sneering, as female tenants struggle in and out of the elevator with bags, babies, shopping carts. The other day he watched Marcia Plunkner from 4B, wheeling one child and balancing another on her hip, drag three heavy bags of groceries down the hall to her door and when she'd gone, shut the elevator door with a flourish, turned to me and said:

"See pork roast? She always have pork roast on top of bag. Know *why* she always have pork roast on top of bag? So no one *know* she Jew. Jew no *eat* pork roast. But *I* know. I know she Jew. That why her little boy always sick. Because she no believe in God. Right, lady?"

What I said was: "mm."

What I thought was: "You bulging Slavic bastard, I'd like to wrap those great hanging donkey's balls of yours around your neck like a coil of kielbasa. I'd like to stab you in your heaving Eastern European gut. I'd like to kick you in your baggy, squared-off ass. I'd like to spit in your slit-eyed, sneering potato face. I'd like to . . ."

Oh God, why couldn't I have said that? Will I ever be able to say something like that? Or forget "say," will I ever be able to give some son of a bitch a good kick in the ass? Joyfully, without fear or guilt? If I thought I ever could I'd die right now, happy.

When we reached our floor what I said was: "Thank you, Stefan."

What Stefan II said was: "Your welc."

Elly, looking harried, opens the door and ushers us in. From the dining room come shrieks, sounds of a cartoon show, and deafening piano chords.

"Hi Andrew. Hi love. Listen, I'm going in there right now and tell them to shut up; this is insane," she says, brushing her bangs off her forehead with a sugary hand. There is flour all over her jeans. (Bad sign.) "For some ungodly reason they all wanted to make *cookies,* but they took off in the middle of the whole goddamned thing and left me with the whole shit. No, no, go ahead, have a drink, Justin's in the living room. I just have one more tray to take out and then I'm done." She darts back to the kitchen, stopping at the dining room door to scream, "Shut *up*." From the kitchen comes a great clanging of tins and a muffled, *"Shit."* I would like to go in and help, but at times Elly is better left alone. I know she is furious . . . at herself for letting the kids talk her into baking cookies, at Justin for lolling in the living room . . . furious because her jeans are too tight, she's probably already had a drink and her striped jersey has a large dribbling stain of Hawaiian Punch straight down the middle. In a moment she will reappear with a lavish assortment of hors d'oeuvres. Like me, whenever Elly is tired or mad, she cooks.

Justin, a tall, slim, graceful man with curly gray hair cut in a sort of Afro gestures us into the living room.

"Hey. Natalie, you know, Charlie's mother, isn't here yet. I hope she removes that kid soon; Elly's about ready to freak out. Man, that kid has widespread problems. Not your kids; your kids have been great, but that Charlie. Jesus. I try to talk to her about it, why do you have all these kids over all the time when you know you're going to freak out, I say, but try to tell her anything when she's this freaked-out. What'd she tell you upstairs today, that I'm a bad-ass old man? Well, I *worry* about her. 'I love you, I care about you,' I told her. But does she believe me? No. Just because her old man beat her up all the time she doesn't think I care about her. 'I'm not your old man, I'm me,' I told her. 'You just want me to live up to some fucking *image,* you only married me for my fucking legs *anyway,'* she said. 'What was ever so great about your goddamn legs? It's *you* I love,' I said. And then she cried. Jesus. What can I get you? Martini? I think we have some Scotch, too. Or maybe a beer, Andrew?"

I want (naturally) a martini; Andrew accepts a beer. I wonder if nondrinkers have any idea what incipient alcoholics go through. Elly's mother-in-law, who drives Elly wild when she visits (the last time Elly came upstairs in hysterics because Mrs. Buck had insisted on getting down on her hands and knees and taking all the old wax off the kitchen floor with a razor blade) *says* she understands, but I'm not sure. That last time I calmed Elly a little, took her back downstairs, and sat with her through several martinis. We were on our third and just high enough to be feisty when Mrs. Buck, her dewaxing chores finished, peeked in and asked if we wanted some homemade lemonade. We declined. "Do you know why I want to drink gin instead of homemade lemonade, *Mom?*" Elly said. "Because I can't stand life sober, that's why." Mrs. Buck looked thoughtful for a while and then her faded blue eyes lit up a little and she said, "Well, dearie, I can understand that. I guess it's the same kind of yen I have for candy. Candy really gets me over the hump, you might say."

I don't know. I could pass up a Milky Way, a Reese's Peanut Butter Cup or a Mounds bar any day, but vodka, gin

—anything, I'm not fussy, the only thing I don't drink is rye but I probably would if that's all that was around—a very different cup of juice. And yet, Mrs. Buck does have a problem. She nibbles and sucks all day long: chocolate-covered cherries, peanut brittle, caramels, sourballs, peppermints. "That *noise,*" Elly moans, gritting her teeth. *"That sick little nibbling noise, like a demented chipmunk; it's going to drive me out of my mind."*

Like Mrs. Buck, although the source of our problem is different, Elly and I are concerned about one aspect of our addiction: the calorie count. Not that we're ruining our livers, blotting out our brains (some sadist once told me that several brain cells die, irrevocably, with each martini), but that we're gaining weight. We compare the size of our bellies as we pour, sighing, jiggling flaccid flesh up and down, squeezing it between our fingers, groaning, finally laughing. But we're not really kidding. We want to be thin.

I look at the pale-green martini that Justin has handed me. I can hardly wait to finish it and start on another. I love to look at the frosty glass, hear the ice cubes rattle, smell the juniper ("Just lay there by the juniper, while the moo-oon is bright; watch them jugs a-fillin', in the pale moonlight," Joan Baez used to sing, and oh Joanie, you sang so well back then; you filled me with more protest than any protest song ever could), dip and roll my tongue in the stinging cold, feel the first swallow thud and spread in the pit of my stomach.

Am I an alcoholic? They keep changing the rules. Sometimes it's one out of twenty questions (Do you drink to forget your worries?), sometimes two out of ten (Are you less efficient when you drink? Do you ever drink alone?), sometimes three out of five (Have you ever had a drink before noon? Do you drink because you lack self-confidence? Is drinking jeopardizing your home life?), so it's hard to tell.

"Hi there. My name is Liza. I am an alcoholic"

"Hello, gang. Liz is the name. I am an alcoholic."

"How do you do. My name is Elizabeth. I am an alcoholic."

"Hey, people. My name's Betsy. I am an alcoholic."

"Um. 'Lo. My name is Beth. I am (gasp) an alcoholic."

No, I could never go through with it.

I love Elly's apartment. While our own is mostly neutral—some good pieces but nondescript, boring—Elly's is a riot of color, plants, antiques. Justin is an antique dealer; he runs his business from the apartment. Except for the plants and a few basics, like beds, the scene is constantly shifting; everything is for sale: paintings of stern-looking farmers holding pitchforks, tables, chairs, blanket chests, weather vanes, huge merry-go-round horses made of wood, their faded paint scabrous and peeling. When we came back from the country and Elly invited me down for a drink, we were sitting in the living room, me on a chair and Elly on the floor, and a short, shrunken man wearing a black Homburg came in and said (in a sinister Greek accent):

"I have come to pick up my rush-bottomed, ladder-back chair."

"Could you get up, Liza? That's his chair you're sitting on," Elly said.

I got up. The Greek handed Elly a check.

"You give to Justin, yes?"

"I give to Justin. Yes. I'm sorry he couldn't be here himself but he had to go to an auction. And come back again soon, Mr. Zurbas. Justin has a new shipment coming in next week."

The short, shrunken Greek picked up the rush-bottomed, ladder-back chair, bowed, and slunk out the door.

When they recently sold the largest merry-go-round horse, the younger child was inconsolable. It had been in his room for five months. Like selling your kid's favorite teddy bear, sort of.

Elly appears looking grim, holding a huge platter of hors d'oeuvres (I was right)—guacamole, corn chips, red caviar, slim rounds of French bread topped with chopped mushrooms, celery remoulade, cheese, crackers—and slams it down on the coffee table.

"Easy, baby, easy," Justin says. "That's sold, you know. Mifflin's coming to pick it up Wednesday."

"Easy," Elly snaps. "Don't talk to me about easy. Mifflin can stick the goddamn thing up his ass. Easy." She lights a cigarette, inhaling deeply and exhaling smoke in short, angry bursts, turning to me and speaking as if we were alone in the room. "I work, right? Oh, but I only work part-*time,* forget the conferences, forget the lesson plans, forget the mothers so that half the time I don't even get home until two, so that every day I'm supposed to come home to all this *shit,* the goddamn kids, the food, the laundry. You know what he said to me last night? 'You're on vacation,' he said. *Vacation.* Some vacation. He said he'd give the kids dinner last night so I could get ready to go to a lecture, this very important thing on early child care I wanted to go to, and I bought the fucking food, I put it all out for him, and you know what he did? He boiled the frozen French fries. Boiled them. In water. Do you know what that *looks* like? Boiled frozen French fries? Cook? Oh no. This brilliant person, this very *with* it forty-five-year-old hippy who listens to the Band and Grace Slick and all that, who turns the volume up so goddamn loud I can't even *think,* who forgets his sick little middle-class background—his mother starts oatmeal cooking the night before; the goddamn crap tastes like glue—oh no. He can't learn to cook. Why the hell didn't *she* show him how to do some of these sick little middle-class things, like cooking, like boiling water even?"

"Well, she must have shown him that," I say.

"What. Shown him what."

"How to boil water. I mean, if he boiled the frozen French fries he must know how to boil water."

"Look, don't *you* start. You know goddamn well what I mean. We both work; we're supposed to have this equal marriage and everything, right? So sometimes he vacuums and he always leaves these little balls of dust all over the floor. Or he cleans out the bathtub and forgets to rinse it so that there's Ajax all over everything. *Men. Christ.*"

"Oh Elly," I say, laughing—I shouldn't but I can't help it. "Come on. You can't blame the whole thing on Justin. You can't blame the whole thing on men."

"Why not?" Elly says fiercely, puffing smoke. "Why *not* blame the whole goddamn thing on men? Who's left? The Russians? Even the Chinese are out." Then, inexplicably, she starts to laugh. "Oh God," she says between gasps. "You know what else he did? He *lost* the shoulder lamb chops. I mean it. Just as I was about to leave he shut the broiler door so hard that the goddamn lamb chops shot out the back of the broiler, behind the stove. We had a hell of a time fishing them out. 'They're gone,' he said, just as I was about to leave. 'What do you mean, gone?' I said. 'They're just . . . gone,' he said. 'They were there a minute ago and now they're gone.' We had to . . . wash them off and everything."

I can't stop laughing either. Justin chuckles and then throws back his head and roars. Andrew looks at us all warily, and dips a corn chip into the guacamole.

"Very good, Elly," he says.

Well, that's safe. You can't go wrong complimenting a woman on her food, can you? Can you? *Can* you? Now I'm getting as angry as Elly was a moment ago.

Charlie appears and tugs at Elly's skirt. He wants juice. He wants a cookie. He wants his mother. He says all the other children are being mean to him. He makes a spastic dive for the corn chips, eats one, upsets the rest of the bowl on the Oriental rug and throws himself into Elly's lap, sobbing. His shrieks reach a level of acoustical pain I would never have thought possible. Elly looks at me over his head, and raises her eyes heavenward.

"For Christ's sake, Justin, make me another drink," she says as she carries Charlie off to the kitchen, murmuring soothing words of comfort. I follow her down the hall.

"Elly, wait. Elly, did you ever get to the lecture?"

Still holding Charlie, she rummages in the refrigerator for juice. "What lecture?"

"You know, the lecture. The early child care thing. After Justin lost the lamb chops and everything."

"Hey, could you get me a glass? One of those little ones, on the second shelf. Oh. No, I didn't go. It was so late. It was probably boring, anyway; all those things turn out to be boring."

Our eyes meet for a moment, and then she turns away. "Well it's true, they do. They do turn out to be boring," she says. "Go on back and have another drink; he'll calm down faster if no one else is around. Charlie, it's all *right*, I'm telling you. Mommy will be here soon."

In the living room Grace Slick is singing and Justin and Andrew are talking about the Civil War; it is their sole topic in common. I am very hungry. I load celery remoulade onto a whole-wheat cracker—great, just enough mustard, Elly really is a good cook. Justin pours me another drink, gesturing, still talking. The windows with their rusty guards are flung wide open; river air, dank, smelling of fish floods in. From the street below comes the sound of a smashing bottle and then a guttural laugh, like a cat in heat.

"Mother," Kate says, appearing from nowhere. "It is almost eight o'*clock*. Could we possibly go *home?* They all want to watch this program that I don't *want* to watch, and there's another program on at eight that I've been waiting all *week* to watch, that I *have* to watch, it's part of my social studies homework, as a matter of fact. I have to hand in a two-page *report* on it."

"Maybe we should, Liza," Andrew says, setting his glass carefully on a coaster and getting up. "It is kind of late."

"I don't know where the hell Natalie *is,*" Elly says, settling herself on the floor with a quieted Charlie in her lap. "Don't go yet; I really want you to meet her."

As if on cue, the doorbell rings. Charlie, jumping out of Elly's lap and racing down the hall, screaming, "Mommy!" slips on a toy truck, falls, and cries violently.

I have finally met her. The Liberated Woman. The Woman Who's Got It All Together. Back from Elly's (we sent Kate on up alone to watch her TV program), I am pleasantly high but functioning very well, far better, in fact, than I would be functioning cold sober. Andrew puts the children to bed and I efficiently mix salad dressing, shake lettuce in a wire basket, sauté the steaks, and think about Natalie. Natalie. Still beautiful at thirty-six. Long nails, glossy black hair sleeked back in a bun, perfect figure. (She goes to an exercise class three times a week.) Her own publicity firm. Travel. Child. Many lovers. Her current favorite is a rich businessman who adores her but, she said, daintily fitting a cigarette into an onyx holder and lighting it with a gold lighter (she smoked one to my eight), she's not ready to marry yet. If ever. My God, if I were alone with a child, much less three, I'd be terrified, but not Natalie. I believed her, I admired her and yet, somehow I didn't like her very much. She made me feel so inadequate, so old (although of course I am actually younger), so settled, so dull. And I didn't like the way she treated Charlie—brushed him away from her Pucci print lap as if he were a speck of dust, a crumb, an ash.

Andrew and I face each other across the dinner table. The candles flicker and pulse; it is easier to talk in the near darkness.

"What did you think about what we were talking about downstairs?" I ask. "What Natalie was saying, and Elly, about freedom and all that?"

He shrugs, puts down his fork, picks it up again and goes on eating. "I don't know. I don't like women like that, though."

"Why not? Did she frighten you?"

"Not frighten, no. I just didn't like her. Did you make a different dressing? It's good."

"No, it's the same. Funny. Neither did I."

But my complicity does not make him expand. Later, as we are getting ready for bed, I try again.

"What would you do if I ever had an affair?"

In his striped blue and white pajamas he looks about twelve years old. He considers.

"Openly, you mean? You'd tell me all about it, the way Elly was saying?"

"Yes."

He answers with a question. "How would you feel if I did? Have an affair?"

"If you ever had an affair," I say, suddenly turning bitchy as I climb into bed and pull the sheet up over my shoulders, "I'd have to *find* you somebody."

IV

Why have I never had an affair? During my childhood Mother was always having "affairs"—one with the butcher at Gristedes kept us supplied with excellent meat during World War II—but her liaisons seemed to end above the waist: smiles, soulful looks, an erotic phone call or two. I mean the real thing. Why have I never been able to jump into bed with a man just because I feel like it, enjoy fucking for whatever it's worth without laying on such a weighty load of values? Why does sex seem so *important* to me, miraculous, something to be taken very seriously? It is the same kind of feeling I had when the children were born; all the other women in the maternity section, even first-timers, seemed to take the whole birth process quite casually, but for me, having made another human being out of nothing, from nowhere, those tiny fingernails, those feet on the ends of infinitesimal legs, those eyes on either side of a nose . . . incredible.

I have been thinking over this problem, if it is a problem, for some days now and one answer that comes to me is: Andrew and I are good in bed; it is the one constant high in our relationship. Sex, the old story goes, is supposed to mirror all other hang-ups. We seem to be hung up everywhere *but* sexually. Most women (I have read) have an affair primarily for the fucking part. What I want, lying in bed at three o'clock in the morning in that strange, semi-sleeping state between the dark and the daylight, letting my fantasies run free, is not laughing Allegra or Edith with golden hair, not so much an instant fuck, as a friend. Male. With this friend I talk, take walks in the park, sit on a bench by the river, hold hands in a midnight drive-in, go to bed. Of course, go to bed. *Too.* But not *only.* Not *primarily.* Which is strange, because to most men I apparently send out magnetic waves of being a marvelous fuck; men are drawn to my crotch as moths to an eternal flame. Considering my age, encumbrances, and the fact that I am not beautiful, I am propositioned often, I do not lack for offers . . . from total strangers, the husbands of my friends, fathers picking up their children after a day of play, maître d'hotels, dentists, pediatricians, shrinks, podiatrists. Perhaps it is a matter of confidence; I have always attracted men. At the age of five I had a boyfriend who brought me candy; at seven another who saved his allowance to buy me flowers. By the time I was fourteen I looked pretty much as I do now—short but long-legged; the same full breasts, rounded hips, tousled dark blond hair curling around a face that is noticeable only because the eyes are large, brown, and slightly uptilted at the corners. Not a beautiful face. But even at fourteen, something pulled them in—both men and boys. At that age, the men terrified me. "Tell him I'm only four*teen;* tell him to go *away,*" I'd beg my mother as I fled to crouch behind potted palms in hotel lobbies from Saint Thomas to Antibes, leaving her to deal with vacationing pursuers who ranged in age from twenty-one to thirty-five. (She was delighted to deal.)

"I'm sorry, I feel terrible, I know you're not like that,

the type of girl to go all the way, it will never happen again, I swear on my mother's grave," said my blue-eyed-Italian-of-the-dunes . . . until Andrew my first and only fuck. Unfortunately, he kept his word, although we subsequently did just about everything else. I would slowly lick the salt off his hot brown back; we would roll over and over in the sand until our bodies were coated with it and then press our moving bellies together. He would suck my nipples gently, his thick lashes brushing my breasts; I would tentatively massage his throbbing penis. We came all the time. But no fucking. And I wanted to. Also no fucking with the tall dark boy from Iran who went to Dalton, with whom I wintered wetly on a brocade sofa under a unicorn tapestry. For two years I promised tearfully, and seasonally, to marry them both. In both city and country, I kept my mouth shut. In both sets, fucking was looked down upon. Fifteen-year-old girls did not fuck. They "made out" on the back seats of cars, under bushes, on living room couches when parents were out for the evening. But did not fuck. Or so they said. So I said too. Those were the rules.

The Iranian boy graduated from Dalton and went back to Iran, after a dramatic scene at the airport in which we cried in each other's arms and talked about the grandiose wedding we would have in Teheran after we both finished college. My father cried too; he was all for it. (Why wait, the kid was loaded, wasn't he?) That summer, my seventeenth, was dull. The Italian boy took a job with a construction company and was often so tired after work that he fell asleep in my lap after we'd parked on some dark dead-end street. I read movie magazines, cried a lot, and gained weight. In the fall I went off to college and in November, at a dreary dance in Cambridge, met Andrew. Used to being turned on by more exotic types, at first glance he seemed terribly straight—silent, serious, Working His Way Through—but I was bored and hated college and was sick to death of giggling girls and dormitories, so I danced with him a few times. We walked across the freezing black grounds. A small animal, a squirrel or a rabbit, darted in front of us, and I was startled; Andrew put his arm around me. Through the lighted windows far away I could see couples, moving, dancing. Within minutes we both knew what it was we were after. And we were right.

I am good in bed with Andrew, yes. But Andrew is the only man I have slept with since I was eighteen. The question is: *Am I really good in bed?* Maybe it is time to find out how good I really am, although the thought vaguely disgusts me, like too much gin and creamed herring on a hot summer day. "But how do you know if you've never *tried* it? You're just *afraid*. Let me help you get over your *hang*-ups," wails my coterie. But they do not appeal to me, these lumpy podiatrists, balding shrinks, paunchy papas. Shouldn't a man you go to bed with have *something* about him that appeals to you, even if it's only one ear? (Or is that simply a cover for my *hang*-ups?)

And there are other practical problems which, to all of you out there, happily fucking up a storm, organ to organ, minds and souls be damned, may seem absurd, but still bother me. Exactly where do you go to fuck? A seedy hotel? A Queens motel? A Long Island boatel? Before our marriage Andrew and I did it anywhere, but now at thirty-four I'm used to being freshly showered, perfumed, unrushed, with clean sheets, wine, music playing. His own bed? Your own bed? (That's too much for me.) Do you carry a suitcase, or is that outré? How do you avoid being seen by people you might know? When do you fuck? On his lunch hour? After five? (and if so, where do you leave the kids? And if you find a sitter, how do you explain your absence?) What happens if your husband (or wife) finds out? Who uses what? I have tried every single brand of birth control pill on the market;

all of the cases are decorated with cameos of sweetly pretty, serene-looking women in white. The pills do not make me serene. They send me into a psychotic depression.

"Life is too short to be depressed," the kindly obstetrician said as he wrote out a prescription for the last batch. That is true. But positive thinking has no effect at all; one pill and I rampage around the house sobbing, ravaged, wanting to die. But not to fuck. And I have never been able to use a diaphragm. I was fitted for one, but the few times I managed to get it into position I became totally frigid. The idea of being the one who's forced into taking "precautions" turns me off, my basic theory always having been, "You want to fuck me, baby? Then *you* figure it out." Even if I could use a diaphragm, and I'd have to get a new one, the one I have was fitted after Anna was born, to further my own questionably pleasurable future ends, do you walk around prepared at all times? I'd never dare risk using nothing, even though I know with absolute certainty when I ovulate: I can feel the egg wending its sure-footed way down; my ovaries swell and twinge. Can you ask a semi-strange man to use a condom? Wouldn't that turn *him* off? (Point in his favor: Andrew is not turned off. He's so turned on, so ever-ready, he'd wear a Baggy tied up with one of those cute little striped ties if he had to.) But as I ramble on, even I can see that these are mechanics, not the crux.

"Baby, I can't exist on one fuck a week," my last propositioner, the short fat father of one of Nicco's school friends, recently told me after having spent an hour in my kitchen drinking beer and analyzing, in boring detail, his wife's sexual "problems." Is that my fault? That his wife only consents to one fuck a week? Somehow lately I feel that it is.

V

Today something important happened. I will set it down carefully, leaving out nothing, and perhaps by so doing see a pattern, a path. What I very definitely need right now is a path.

Today my father and I were allowed to take Mother out for two hours, the first time such an outing has been permitted. I try to plan my visits to Mother so that they never coincide with his, but when he called last night and asked me to come along, I felt a strange kind of pity, and agreed.

The day began well enough. It was a freakishly hot day, Saturday, the day before Easter. Things began to revolve on the way to the bus stop, but I was able to get on the bus, and stay on, by clutching the pole tightly and repeating sternly to myself: "My name is Liza. I am thirty-four years old. I am a female human being. It is 1974. I have three children. I am on the crosstown bus." Et cetera. Like that. The stick-to-reality ploy doesn't always work, but today it did. I felt almost pulled together as I briskly headed for the hospital elevator. (Not self-service, luckily. One test a day is enough.)

We had planned to take Mother to lunch but had

forgotten to look up a suitable restaurant in the area, some dark, discreet place where we might have lunched unnoticed. So we wandered up and down Second Avenue peering into what turned out to be singles' haunts. Young couples sat under Cinzano umbrellas, sipped Bloody Marys and played with each other between bites of eggs Benedict. The three of us, a short thirty-four-year-old with tousled hair, a dapper man of sixty-eight wearing black-and-white checked slacks, a red blazer, and white patent leather loafers, a terrified, painfully thin woman carrying a doll (they'd apparently been able to talk her out of the toe shoes)—no, we could not have carried it off; we would not have fit in.

"I want to go back," Mother said suddenly. "I have to be back on time. They'll be angry. They'll send someone looking for me. I have to go back."

My father immediately began to argue. A good lunch, a little fun—he'd just thought of a place across town, we'd get in a cab, he said—was all she needed. Besides, she'd only been out with us for half an hour; what would the hospital think? But she insisted, and when we reached her room with its yellow spread and curtains, its sick sweet smell of roses, her shaking lessened and she breathed more easily. "She's tired, just tired," my father kept saying to anyone who passed by. "The heat, it's too much for her. The heat makes her tired." But that wasn't the reason, of course, I knew—and so, for once I think, did he.

After Mother had fallen asleep (pretended, to get rid of us), my father was still hungry, so he ignored my feeble protests (I didn't want to go to lunch; I wanted to go home.) and hailed a cab. Soon we were settled in a corner booth of a cool restaurant farther west, half empty because of the hour. He was, as usual, waved in as if he had OIL emblazoned across his burnoose. He either under or overtips, is rude to waiters, talks too loudly, complains, sends orders back and yet . . . when he is in a room the air is charged, electric. In looks and general aura he is far more Mediterranean than Swedish; actually he is not really Swedish at all. His father, a gentle, reticent bookkeeper whose family settled in America in the 1800s, died when he was eight and he was raised by a domineering, histrionic—although I must say, colorful—mother from Ventimiglia.

As a teen-ager his manners embarrassed me; even today his patronizing little byplay with the smiling hatcheck girl (she seemed to enjoy it) made me cringe. Thank God I wore something decent, a pale beige pants suit, shoes with heels, makeup. Above all, makeup. My father gets terribly incensed if "his" women are not impeccably groomed, with their heads held high, their lipsticks on, and happy smiles on their happy faces. That's me and Mom—red-lipped, high, and grinning. Saves trouble. (But is trouble worth saving?)

I ordered a Bloody Mary; my father a Dubonnet on the rocks. He sat, one hand dramatically pressed to his forehead (a troubled man in agony, Agony, do you understand?), his eyes shut. But he must have been squinting at the menu because he officiously summoned the waiter and without consulting me ordered hot hors d'oeuvres for two and was heading on into the minestrone when I stopped him—I can't stand minestrone; beans drive me wild—and held out for no soup and the plat du jour, veal chop Marsala. I always order the plat du jour; if it's the special of the day they want me to order it, don't they? Saves trouble, keeps the cook happy, the waiter will love me. I also asked for another drink, a martini, mumbling something about nerves. (Nice girls don't drink.) Across the room an interesting-looking man, sort of—slim, dark-eyed—was eating. Alone. He looked up at me from time to time, smiling faintly. Did he think I was out with an old roué, I wondered? Or did he see the resemblance: the same dark eyes, the (I'm told) sensuous mouth, the wavy hair? My father sank back in his chair, both hands now over his eyes. He rarely leans forward; his top hair is thinning. He uncovered his eyes, shuddered, and bit into a seeded breadstick.

"I cannot tell you what this is doing to me," he said. "This whole thing is going to kill me."

"Oh Christ," I thought. "Here we go."

He covered his eyes again and I used the opportunity to signal the waiter for another martini.

"Now Dad," I said comfortingly. "Lots of people . . ."

The hors d'oeuvres and my drink arrived.

"Don't lots of people me!" He worked his fork into a baked clam. "Me! Why did this have to happen to *me!* My *wife.* Jesus. You spend your whole life breaking your balls, giving your family everything they want, anything I always said, the most expensive shoes, dresses from Bendel's, wigs, her hairdresser's bill alone, do you know what that cost me, forty dollars a week and that's not including color, and now *this.* My wife. My wife in a lunatic asylum."

"Dad, it's not exactly . . ."

He reached for another breadstick, finished the clams, ate the last shrimp and five fried pepper strips, snapped his fingers at the waiter, and began spooning up minestrone.

"And the office, what can I tell them at the office? That my wife is locked up in a loony bin? Nuts? Waiter, get me some grated cheese. She's away, I tell them. Off on a trip. A *trip.* No, not that out of a jar, freshly grated I want. Trip. *Jesus.*"

"Daddy, why don't you . . ."

The waiter cleared and I waved my hand over my empty glass. The waiter winked, just slightly. My father ordered a bottle of wine.

The sort-of-interesting-looking man was really interested by now, staring at me openly. Could he hear our conversation? I hoped not. His face—narrow, rather delicate with high cheekbones and an aquiline nose—appealed to me. His hands, however, I noticed as he inexpertly wound spaghetti with clam sauce around a fork, using a soup spoon for balance, were small. Small hands have always made me shiver; how could I stand them crawling, inching like a centipede, over my body?

"It's now or never; nobody's perfect," I told myself grimly, gulping gin. I was completely soused; the red and gold room revolved like a crazily listing carrousel. But I had made a decision without really having made a decision. This whoever-he-was was to be my passport to sexual freedom. Why today? Why this man when so many others had eagerly conveyed their availability? Who knows? Who ever knows? The fight I had with Andrew this morning over going to visit Mother, the smell of dying roses in her room, the heat, the gin, my father's presence, Kate's remark that my new pants suit made me look fat—all rational reasons. All equally irrational.

My father began to cry. Large tears dripped off his distinguished nose onto his osso buco. "Not only that," he said. "Not only that. Everybody else has a son whose hair is too long, they complain about it all day at the office, and me! *Me!* After Harvard, graduate school, everything, I have to have a son with a shaved head, no hair at all, just a tiny little braid down the middle of his head, a *braid,* like a goddamn *fairy,* who dances around on street corners in an orange nightgown all day and eats *grain.*"

"Daddy, if David wants to be a Hare . . ."

My father picked up a large bone in his hands and gnawed on it hungrily. "Grain," he said, still snuffling. "Like a horse."

"Dad, you can't control . . ."

"You know what I regret most of all? You know what I really regret? My mother. My mother raised me to be a Catholic. A good Catholic. We went to mass every Sunday right from the time I was two, no matter what my father said. And then after we got married your mother talked me out of it, it wasn't nice, she said. Nice. Some nice! Her family, a bunch of poets, of lousy drunks who never did a day's work in their life, and who took care of them, paid for their funerals, me! Just because they're Episcopalians, just because they got here on the *Mayflower, before* the *Mayflower,* she says, they think they know everything. Listen, if David had been raised as a Catholic do you think he'd be out there with no hair, dancing around? Thank God Mama isn't here to see it. Thank God."

"Daddy, I don't think that would have made . . ."

But there was a sudden light in his eyes as he mopped up the last bit of sauce with a chunk of bread and removed a piece of gristle from his mouth.

"But you," he said proudly. "So pretty. Married. A family. A good husband. At least you turned out right."

Oh my God.

He blew his nose and beckoned for the menu.

"Have some rum cake."

"I really don't want any, Daddy."

"Come on, have some rum cake. Good for you. Have some with me. I feel bad enough. Don't make me feel any worse."

I had some rum cake.

I glanced over at Sexual Freedom (Stephen Fine? Sam Fox? Some Fuck?) who was waiting, timing his departure with ours. He looked back at me boldly, raising his eyebrows. I inclined my head imperceptibly, but he perceived. It was all happening. Just like in the magazines!

"But is this safe?" I immediately asked myself, through the gin-wine haze and all. "Will I be enticed to a hotel room and brutally murdered? Horribly mutilated? Sadistically beaten? Raped?" (Well, isn't that what I'm really after?)

At the door I fended off my father's persistent efforts to get me safely into a cab, saying (stupidly, I should have known better) that I'd rather walk home through the park.

"You should know, Liza, the park, even in the daytime it's not safe! A girl like you shouldn't be walking through the park alone, and those side streets! That's asking for trouble. Andrew would say the same. Well, all right, if you promise just to walk over *to* the park, not *through* it, and take a cab from Fifth I guess it's all right, but call me the minute you get home. I'll take this one." He raised one finger and a checker pulled up out of nowhere.

"You're sure you don't want to come home with me, have some coffee or something?"

"I don't think so, Dad. Not today."

"I know, I understand. You probably have a lot to do for tomorrow. I'm bringing up some nice things for the kids, I stopped in at Schwarz. You know, at times like this a man really wishes he had a dog. The apartment, it's so quiet. Every night she helped me do the crossword puzzles. A woman like that, always running around to stores and to the hairdresser and everything, you wouldn't think she'd know so many words, words I don't know even. But she does."

He laboriously climbed into the cab and wiped his eyes.

"Do you think she liked the roses? I think she noticed them today. I bring her a new bunch every other day. It's funny, how fast they die."

I shut the door for him and patted his arm through the open window. Huddled into a corner of the cab, he looked shrunken, suddenly, older.

"It's going to be all right, Dad."

"Listen," my father said, his eyes still damp. "The only way a man gets any peace is six feet under. And even then you never know."

The taxi departed in a trail of exhaust.

Behind me the hand of Sexual Freedom was beckoning. And what a hand! Still, standing, he was much taller than I'd expected and not bad. Not bad at all.

"Hi," he said. "Want to go back in and have a brandy at the bar, or would you rather go someplace else?"

I opted for the bar; seemed safer.

"Hey, who was that old guy? Not your father or anything?"

"No, not my father."

Two brandies later and we were very jolly. "Baby, you have great tits," he kept saying solemnly, as if taking an oath. His name, it turned out, was Marcus Taylor; he was a manufacturer's representative in town for a convention, the first time, he told me, puffing up visibly, that his firm had asked him to represent them.

"I don't know how all you people live here," he said, taking my arm and steering me firmly toward Fifth to try to find a cab. "I just don't understand it, how all you people can live here."

I could easily have filled him in, but every time I tried to speak, giggles exploded from my drunken mouth like floating comic balloons. The dusty, stunted trees, the dog shit in the gutters, the shining buildings seemed to be laughing along with me; they shook with laughter. My heel caught in a crack in the sidewalk and Marcus steadied me.

"Maybe we should forget about this for the time being," he said nervously. "You could always give me your telephone number or something. Maybe you should go on home and get some rest."

No, Marcus, rest was not what I needed, although I don't blame you for having been frightened, I was drunk as a coot and I suppose you'd read terrible stories about what happens to out-of-towners who pick up drunken ladies in the Big City. I might have lifted your wallet or cut off your balls. But you didn't have to worry. No, what I needed (or thought

I needed) was a gigantic prick pulsing up inside my body, reaching so high and stretching so wide it filled all the crevices. And since no other prick was available, Marcus, the rest was up to you. Enough to scare the shit out of any normal, red-blooded American male.

When we reached the hotel Marcus looked furtively around the huge lobby. Men wearing brown shoes and little plastic badges pinned to their lapels were dashing around slapping each other on the back and saying, "Hiya, fella!" or "Sure is hottern' hell out there!" (There really is a Midwest after all.)

Marcus swallowed hard; his confidence was melting faster than the chocolate ice-cream cone held by a small child sitting on a suitcase by the registration desk.

"Maybe . . . do you think we should take separate elevators? I mean, maybe it wouldn't be too good an idea if someone saw us together. There're a lot of other guys here from Cincinnati who know me, good guys, but well, you know."

I knew. One thing was sure, however. I was safe. No one I knew would ever be caught in this Disneyland lobby. Even the plants were plastic.

The room was not bad. Horrible, but not bad. Spotless, brand new, two single beds, a small refrigerator, laminated walnut chests and night tables, drapes and spreads printed with green and orange foliage that looked like elephants' ears. Marcus switched on the radio and drew the drapes. The minute I undressed and lay down on one of the beds, the one nearest to the door, I was cold sober.

"Look, dummy," I said to myself. "You've got the clean sheets, the music, you can even take a shower. What the hell do you *want?* Grow *up.*"

It didn't work.

"Marcus," I said from beneath a shaking mound of bedspread. "I think I'd better go home."

He was having none of that at this point, however, and creepy white, covered with small black hairs and wearing polka-dotted boxer shorts which he soon removed, nostrils flared like a bull's, he made a dive for me. And so, to the tune of "In Your Easter Bonnet," we began. Or rather, he began. Marcus's personal theme song was, "Screw the preliminaries! Let's get the ball rolling!" (Which, considering those hands, may have been all for the best.)

Admittedly, I have not been acquainted with many pricks, but I have never felt a prick that small. It felt like a pencil; there must have been two inches of free space on either side of what I have always considered a fairly standard-size vagina as it pumped rhythmically away.

"Marcus," I gasped from between clenched teeth. (I clenched them so hard that I later had to have an entire inlay replaced.) "Do you have anything?"

He stopped pumping.

"What do you mean?"

"You know. *Anything*. One of those *things*. I'm not wearing anything. I'm not on the pill and I don't have anything *in*."

"You don't?"

"No. I *said* I didn't. Do you *have* anything?"

"Well, gee, no. I thought *you'd* have something."

"Well I don't. And I'm fertile, Marcus. Very fertile. I had three children like . . . bing. You'll have to use something. If you want to go through with this you'll absolutely have to use something."

On the verge of tears, he looked at me.

"But I always thought . . . oh, never mind, okay, wait a minute. Let me see if Jack has anything."

He withdrew. Jack, he'd told me, was his roommate, away for the day on a larkish trip to the Statue of Liberty. I lay back and waited. Marcus returned.

"Thank God. Gee, I haven't used one of these in years. Hope I remember . . ."

"You'd better."

". . . well, here we go."

As in the dentist's chair, I tried to go into a trance and think of other things. "As long as he doesn't touch me I can stand it; if he touches me I'll kill him," was my final thought as Marcus approached the end of his exertions—what seemed like the end, anyway; it was hard to tell. The program of Easter music drew to a close and a sole rickety female voice began to sing "Oh beeootifull, for spaa-cious skies, for am-ber waves of grain." I began to laugh so hard I nearly dislodged Marcus' frail member.

"Hey," he said. "What's up?" (Nothing, friend, especially not you.) "What's going on?"

I dressed quickly.

"You have great tits, baby," Marcus said, all confidence again now that the ordeal was over.

"Thanks. Good-bye. I hope you enjoy your stay in New York."

"Could I have your number? Could we see each other again? I'll be here another week."

"I don't think so," I said, hurriedly brushing my hair. "But thanks anyway."

"Hey wait. Want to see a picture of my kids?" He picked his jacket up off the floor, fumbled in the pocket, and produced a photograph of three dark, sharp-faced, snaggle-toothed children, all of whom looked like ferrets.

"Very cute. Adorable," I said. "Look, I have to go now. I'm late."

"Did you say you had kids too? That's really, I never thought . . . what do ya do, keep 'em in the country or someplace?"

What *is* this asshole *talking* about?

"Well, here then. Is that right? Is that okay? And thanks. It was really great."

At the elevator door I looked down into my clenched fist. Two tens and a five. Twenty-five dollars earned by fucking the father of three ferrets.

I collapsed into the dusk. Lights were going on all over the city; they streaked before my eyes like shrieking trains racing through the night toward California. I was soaked with sweat. My dizziness was so intense I could not even hail a cab, so I walked all the way home, up Broadway, moving with the moving throng, smelling fried chicken and pizza throbbing out in hot, greasy waves from take-out restaurants, music blaring in my head, blaring "where am I? Where am I?" I sat down on a bench at Seventy-second Street and lit a cigarette. I don't know how long I stayed there, minutes, hours. During the last few blocks my feet were so sore that I took off my shoes; no one noticed, no one cared. And when I got home Andrew grabbed me by the collar and began shaking me back and forth, once knocking my head against the wall, asking me over and over, "Where have you been? Where the hell have you been? Your father said you left hours ago, he's been calling here every hour, we've been frantic. Where the hell have you been?"

I was so stunned I couldn't speak; I had never seen Andrew's face so furious. Then I started to cry. I buried my face in the coolness of his shirt and he put his arms around me and kissed my head, my face, my neck, whispering, "I was so worried, Liza, so worried. I thought something terrible had happened to you."

"It did," I wanted to say. I had an overwhelming desire to tell him everything that had happened, "It was so funny," I would say, "I was drunk and there was this man whose kids looked like ferrets and he had the tiniest prick you could imagine and . . ." analyze it, laugh about it as we lay in bed together, our legs touching, sipping wine. But how could I tell him? It would either kill him or he would kill me. My head still hurt where it had been knocked against the wall.

"I went to see a movie and then just walked around for a while," I said finally. "I should have called but Mother, seeing Mother, the whole thing upset me, I guess."

"You see," Andrew said, "I knew it. That's just what I said. You musn't see her so often, Liza, it upsets you too much. You've got to think of your own family; the children were worried about you too, you know. Anna didn't go to sleep until about ten minutes ago. And we've got all the Easter baskets to set up; we have to hide the eggs."

We arranged the Easter baskets, hid the eggs, and then I ran a tepid bath and soaped my defiled crotch thoroughly, just in case. No nasty little ferrets swimming around in my semi-Waspy belly. And then Andrew and I went to bed and made love, which was fantastic, hugged each other, and fell asleep. For fucking there's no place like home.

So much for sexual freedom, honest communication, financial independence, and a meaningful career. Not forever. But at least for the moment.

VI

A red-haired dwarf wearing a strapless purple bathing suit is cutting away my lifeline with a shining silver scalpel.

"But will I live? Will I live?" I cry.

"The cancer must be removed," the dwarf replies.

I am not reassured. I have nothing against dwarfs or even female doctors, but what the hell kind of doctor wears a strapless purple bathing suit during a major operation?

I wake up suddenly with a mild hangover—I drank too much again last night—and the uncomfortable sensation that someone is pushing me out of bed. Someone is. Nicco is fast asleep between us, stretched straight out crossways, his feet pressing hard into the small of my back, his head buried in Andrew's stomach. It is the Tuesday after Easter; vacation is over, although why all the private schools in New York City have Easter vacation before Easter I've never been able to understand. Easter itself was pleasant enough; my father came laden with bags of outrageously expensive toys, I baked a ham, the children hunted for eggs. We have not mentioned my disappearance of Saturday. We have simply gone on, Andrew in his silence, me in my dizziness, barely speaking, hanging in, hanging on. Outwardly. For the fact is, I am worse. "Big deal, Idiot," I say to myself, trying to get out of the range of Nicco's feet, "so your mother's in a nut house, you get fucked by a guy with a prick like a pencil, your husband won't speak to you, and your eldest daughter hates your guts—is that any reason for going mad?" Maybe. Maybe.

Thinking of the morning ahead of me, of getting all three children dressed and off to school, I groan softly and pad barefooted out to the kitchen in my nightgown which, as Kate pointed out several days ago, has a large tear down the back, to start the coffee. No one is awake. The silence is deafening; it rings in my ears. Outside the air is heavy, gray-green; the sky looks like rain. I will have to take Anna and Nicco to school this morning, a fifteen-block walk (I can already see that I am not going to be able to face a bus today). On Tuesdays Andrew usually does, but today he has an early morning meeting downtown. Kate just has to be put on the 79th Street crosstown. (Better her than me.)

A family of roaches, the same family I noticed yesterday, is out walking on the stove—daddy, mom and the kids, all three of them. Daddy looks up, his antennae waving; it seems to me he is smiling. He knows me, knows that I will not hurt his family. And why, after all, should I? If you can't be a tiger be a kitten; if you can't be a human be a roach, all cells, cells all, in the end. I have never minded roaches, but Andrew is revolted by them; every roach is a silent reproach for having moved to the West Side. Of the few times I have ever seen him angry, at least three have been over roaches. He jumped up and roared when one tiptoed across the dining room table one evening and lovingly eyed his pot roast. I felt so sorry for that terrified roach that I would have gladly cut up an entire tiny meal—pot roast, gravy, carrots, onions, and potatoes—and set it out for him on a doll's plate. Enjoy, roach, enjoy.

I am setting cereal bowls and glasses on straw place mats when Anna stumbles into the room, her face crumpled with sleep, and puts her arms around my middle. "I love you," she says, and stumbles away again. She is the only person I know who is able to do that, to say "I love you" without hesitation or caution, and mean it. She always wakes soon after I am up, even at three or four in the morning as I have been waking lately to smoke a cigarette or stare out the window at the sky or the building across the street. No matter how quietly I move about, she senses that I'm awake and comes to me to be sure I am all right, and reassured, goes back to sleep again.

"I love you too, baby," I call after her.

Raindrops splatter suddenly against the pane, startling me. The coffee has begun to percolate. I turn it down and rummage in the hall closet for boots and raincoats, scraping my hand on a forgotten skate. On my way to the bathroom to wash my face and brush my teeth, I glance in at Andrew. He is still sleeping, one arm thrown across his face. He mutters something, cries out a word I cannot understand, pulls his pillow to his chest and cradles it in his arms, burying his face in it. A wave of tenderness, almost a pain, tightens my chest. I put my hand gently on his shoulder.

"Andrew? It's seven. You said you had to get up early today."

He sits up, rubs his eyes, looks at me as if he had never seen me before.

"Andrew, are you awake? Were you having a bad dream?"

"No, not at all," he says politely. "Thanks for remembering to wake me up."

Everyone is sleepy; the morning seeps in and weighs us down like fog. Even Kate, spreading marmalade on her toast, is quiet. She is not wearing the blouse she insisted I iron the night before, which, after a small fight, I ironed.

Nor has she mentioned the cake I baked for a book party her class is having today; I had to run out at five yesterday to buy the ingredients because she'd forgotten to tell me about it earlier. After a few stirs of batter she went in to watch TV, leaving me to mix, bake, and ice. I suppose that is why we fought over the blouse, and why she is not wearing it, but I decide to say nothing.

I am glad the children are going back to school; it has been a long vacation. But what shall I do today? Kate's school, ten-thirty meeting; brush dog; food shop; vacuum; buy plant vitamins, my list reads. Is that a day? And what about all the other days stretching before me, making beds, turning down beds, sleeping in beds, making beds; washing clothes, folding clothes, putting away clothes, wearing clothes, putting clothes in laundry bags, washing clothes; buying food, cooking food, eating food; setting tables, clearing tables, washing dishes, putting away dishes . . . I must stop. I must stop thinking. My hand is shaking as I pick up my coffee cup.

"Don't be sad, Mommy," Anna says suddenly, her gray eyes worried. A short piece of hair, a pale frond, sticks straight up at the back of her head. In passing, I kiss her chubby neck and smooth her hair.

"I'm not sad, baby. It's just the rain. Nicco, you're going to upset that bowl. Finish up now; it's almost time to get ready to go."

"I found a blueberry!" Nicco yells excitedly. "I win!" He is happily eating the most revolting-looking cereal I have ever seen, a cereal he begged me to buy—bright blue pellets mingled with desiccated blueberries that spring to life at a splash of milk, or so the label says. Would that I were a desiccated blueberry; one splash and there I'd be. Sprung.

"You don't win anything for *finding* them, stupid," Kate says, having decided to take her chances. "You have to send in a *box*top or something."

Nicco begins to cry.

"That's enough, Kate. Go get into your boots and raincoat."

"Nobody *else* is in their boots and raincoat. *You* aren't in your boots and raincoat. Why should *I* be in my boots and raincoat?"

Andrew looks up. "Do what your mother says, Kate."

Kate bursts into tears.

"You always say do what *she* says," she sobs. "You never say do what *I* say. You're always on *her* side. You're never on *my* side. How do you think Nicco is ever going to *learn* anything if nobody ever bothers to *teach* him?"

"One, two, three!" Nicco yells through his tears.

"There, you see? *I* taught him that, he wouldn't even *know* that if I hadn't taught him. *Somebody* has to teach him that you don't win anything for *finding* blueberries, that you have to send in a . . ."

"Kate, please, just please get dressed. Everyone get dressed; your boots and raincoats are out in the hall." My head is aching. When we are ready I stand uncertainly at the doorway to the dining room. "Well, good-bye," I say finally. I cannot think of anything else to say.

"Good-bye. I'll be leaving in a minute. I'm sorry about the meeting, about not being able to take them, I'll take them tomorrow. Try to have a nice day."

"You too. Try to have a nice day." I am almost crying; my throat aches from the effort not to cry.

The morning Stefan, Stefan I, is kind. He lets Nicco close the elevator door saying, "Big boy now!" and smiles, exposing a gap and a glinting gold tooth.

"And for God's sake," Kate says as I put her on the 79th Street crosstown, "when you go to the school meeting, wear something decent." Before my hands can close around her throat, the doors swing shut and the bus pulls away from the curb.

When I get back from walking Nicco and Anna to

school I am soaked; my hair sticks to my forehead in muggy strands; even my underwear is wet. I undress, wrap myself in a cotton robe, and heat up the coffee. I do not have to go out again; I cannot go out again. A bus brings Nicco back at twelve-thirty, Anna at three. Spaghetti will do for dinner. Oh but God, I have to go out again. That damned school meeting. Tears and rain mix in salty furrows down my face; I cannot swallow, I am gasping for air. The red-faced Irishman who directs imaginary traffic screamed at me when I tried to cross the street against his directions, and then would not let me cross at all; I had to circle the block.

Why do I care? Why do I care so much about everything? Every morning I think, "Today will be different. Today I will be calm, I will not smoke, I will not drink, I will not eat peanut butter, I will get my ass together . . . and every day something happens to send me right back into gin, cigarettes, and peanut butter.

I light a cigarette. Somehow it is worse with the children gone; I cannot stand them when they're here, I cannot stand it when they're gone. I dial Elly's number and then replace the receiver, remembering that she went back to work today. Work, is that an answer? Elly spends every morning in a paint-splattered smock teaching other women's four-year-olds how to string blocks and grow plants from sunflower seeds. Another friend, a potter, sits in a peeling basement studio making piggy banks; the studio's shelves are lined with row upon row of pink pigs with flowers on their heads and butterflies on their tails. Still another friend, an artist, fashions angels from dough and sells them to department stores at Christmastime.

Work. I too once worked. It seemed a very liberated thing to do in those sad days. Every single girl I knew married while still in college and spontaneously, it seemed, gave birth. After our own marriage we visited these couples, Andrew and I, taking seedy trains to White River Junction or New Haven or Cambridge where the husbands were still in graduate school, spending weekends in tiny apartments in old houses owned by ancient widows, eating meat loaf and drinking Gallo wine, dutifully admiring smelly infants. It was bliss to come back to our own neat, quiet New York apartment with its small fireplace and off-white walls. Andrew had finished law school and found a job with his present firm. I worked in an advertising agency, first as a secretary, then, due to the efforts of the copy chief I worked for, as a junior copywriter, and spent my days behind a glass partition dreaming up vital, scintillating copy about a then-popular tranquilizer (later taken off the market when it was discovered that its side effects included addiction, blood clotting, and deformities in infants). "Are you anxious, bored, depressed?" my copy read. I guess they were: the tranquilizer sold and sold. The artwork featured a forlorn-looking woman sitting on a flowered couch, vacuum cleaner at her feet, head in her hands. Not exactly the career I'd planned, but I knew I was lucky to be writing at all—the agency frowned upon women writers. Or women anything. The only woman in a real position of authority was a lesbian who'd recently undergone a mastectomy: she headed up a baby food account.

But I liked the people I worked with. The upstairs crowd, the account executives, took their work seriously; they would spend hours sitting around a polished conference table discussing whether or not to have my forlorn-looking-woman-in-need-of-a-tranquilizer seated on a flowered couch or a plaid couch, whether or not the copy should read "anxious" or "nervous." They looked down on us, the creative semi-drunks who took nothing seriously. My co-workers were as on their way to madness as I, writers and artists who despised their work and more, themselves, for doing work they despised, who drank their way through three-hour lunches, staggered back to the office, and stared at the walls of their cubicles thinking creative (?) thoughts until five when they could leave and begin drinking again while waiting for the 6:15 to Westport. In between, however, they, and I, often worked our asses off. And sometimes, as they say, paid the price. One man finished up a presentation on prophylactics upon which he'd worked for forty hours straight, climbed to the top of the Plaza fountain, stripped, and naked as a worm began to masturbate (he must have set a world record—those heavy ejaculations just kept on coming), sending semen into the fountain in wide, shooting arcs, all the while shouting, "I have sinned! I have murdered! I have sent babies, innocent fetuses to a watery, bagged death in the Hudson River, East River, sewers, gutters, toilets, pipes. I now make restitution! I will stay here jerking off until I die. My sperm live! Take! Eat! Drink of my body! Do it now, now, now, while the little bastards are still warm!" His shouts and laughter rang through the square. Heads appeared from hotel windows; a crowd collected. A few brothers and sisters took him up on his offer, jumped into the fountain and let water (and presumably sperm) flow into whatever orifices were available; one girl even took a big, refreshing gulp. It took four policemen to get Willie down. He was "put away" for several months, conned his way out of Happy Farms in Rolling River, Connecticut, and is now, I recently heard, the head of an orphans' home in Arkansas. Wherever he is, I love him.

So I worked. Knowing full well that not every girl gets to be a junior copywriter at the age of twenty-two. And although hating the work, enjoying my life: the freedom to meet Andrew for a drink after work, the frequent dinners in small French restaurants, concerts, movies, galleries, being able to make love when we woke at noon on Sundays. But then the Mystique, as Betty Friedan would say, began to get to me. My friends kept asking what was *wrong,* here I was twenty-*three,* why wasn't I *pregnant,* had I ever thought of *adoption?* I began to cry every time an Ivory soap commercial with a darling chubby baby being laved and loved by its beaming mum came on the telly and what the hell was I doing, writing about some crummy pill when I could be belly-large, fulfilled, being, doing, what (everybody said) I should be being, doing. The old Catch-9. So one night (that's all it took), we forgot about prophylactics and just plain fucked. And that was Kate.

I call another friend. Then another. No answer. No answer. Of course! They are all at a party together, having fun, without me. Okay friends, fuck you, go ahead, *have* a party without me. I begin to cry again and start another list: brush dog, vacuum, buy plant vitamins, make new friends—and sit staring at the list until the hissing noise of the coffee boiling over forces me to get up. Outside it is raining even harder; it is coming down in torrents. Will the school bus carrying Nicco home crash into a car, truck, street light? I thought I would worry less with each child, that my fears of car crashes, rapists, muggers, kidnappers, drownings, perverted babysitters, hit-and-run accidents would lessen. I thought I would become like all those healthy, sane other-mothers who send the kids off to Food City with two-page shopping lists or to Loew's 83rd for a four-hour kiddie show without a qualm. No such luck. If anything, my fears are worse. If one of the children is as much as minute late I panic; I walk around the apartment like a caged animal, smoking one cigarette after another, waiting for the telephone call that will inform me of death, mutilation, abduction. My rituals are also worse; every time I leave the apartment I carefully check each gas burner, each ashtray, kiss Anna's dolls, Nicco's stuffed animals, step across lines on the parquet floor, go back to checking the gas burners—soon I'll never leave the apartment. Maybe I could set up housekeeping under the bed, make myself a nest in the closet, wrap myself in swaddling clothes and lie on the fire escape. "They found the babe wrapped in swaddling clothes, lying on the fire escape," the newspapers would say. Oh my God, what will happen? What will happen to me? Keep busy. How do you keep busy when you're paralyzed? I want to lie here stoned; I wish I had some grass, some Quaalude (too bad David's a Hare Krishna now—he used to keep me well supplied).

I dial Andrew's office, but his secretary crisply informs me that he cannot come to the phone; he is still in the meeting. Who do I call now, Dial-a-Prayer? Rap-a-Minute? The Weather Lady? Poison Control? (Or can you only call them after?) That crazy Christian Science practitioner?

"It's all in your mind, dear."

Of course it's all in my mind; where the hell else would it be, my asshole?

"Our revered leader, Mary Baker Eddy, has said . . ."

Forget about Mary Baker Eddy for one goddamn minute and listen to *me!*

I could always check into Bellevue but, as Elly once remarked after visiting a friend there, "Shit. If all you're going to do for ninety days is walk around carrying a shopping bag with all your stuff in it, why not go to Broadway and save a lot of trouble?"

On the counter I notice a tattered piece of lined paper with a smiling red and yellow flower and underneath, a child's scrawled kisses. Oh Anna.

I pour another cup of coffee, pick up the newspaper, and turn immediately to the obituaries. Miriam Kashinsky, spinster, is dead at the age of seventy-two, leaving a sole survivor, a nephew named Fred. Harold Leighton is dead at the age of forty-five, suddenly (suddenly, what does that mean: heart attack, murder, automobile accident?). And at the bottom of column two, John Santangelo, aged three, drowned in the family swimming pool. Dead, they are all dead, everything, everyone is dead—Camus, Jackson, two Kennedys, Plath, Arbus, King, Bruce, Dean, Socrates, Joplin,

Hemingway, Croce, Monroe, Hendrix, Piaf, two young boys who headed South and joined another, a girl who stuck a flower in a guardsman's rifle. Bodies blown to bits, dead bodies lying twisted in front of smoking hovels and a naked child on fire runs screaming forever in my head down a narrow road. Dead Israelis, dead Arabs, staring ribs, gas chambers, bayonets, guillotines, electric chairs, get dressed, get dressed. I dash to the bathroom. My face leers crazily in the mirror; each eye is swimming in a viscous river. I look at my hands. My skin, such a tenuous covering. It seems ready to burst, explode. I vomit black coffee into the wash-basin. I am choking, strangling on my own vomit.

Dear Sylvia Plath: I know that your writing leaves you little time for correspondence, but do you think an oven is really better than a . . .

Baby, I don't know, I tried just about everything going. Just do *something,* that's all.

Dear Diane Arbus: Do you feel your affinity for freaks had anything to do with . . .

But I took damned good pictures, didn't I? Too good! That was the problem. Too good!

Dear Marilyn Monroe; I know you're very busy rushing around to premieres and galas and all that, but would you say that your sudden elevation to the status of world sex symbol might possibly have contributed to . . .

Honey, just putting on my makeup alone took two hours. And then my hair, the exercises, watching my weight, getting dressed up all the time . . . I guess I just got tired.

Dear Edith Piaf: Excuse me, Madame, for addressing you in English (perhaps Monsieur Camus might translate) and for asking so personal a question, but looking back, are you of the opinion that your numerous and often flamboyant affairs constituted a search, an unfulfilled search which led to your fascination with drugs and your eventual . . .

Je ne regrette rien!

My great-aunt, a senile Unitarian, once sent me a self-help book entitled *The Magic of Your Mind.* The book is filled with case histories of people who successfully applied Dr. Werner Longworth's ten-point program. Take Maynard Peters, now first vice-president of Leigh and Leigh, a company that handles huge financial accounts (that'll show all you doubters!). There was old Maynard hiding out from the "Japs" (his word, not mine) during World War II. But was Maynard worried? Oh no. He wrote down his problems on a piece of jungle bark, concentrated on various solutions, hit upon the one that served him best: hide out in a cave near a coconut grove, and if you see a Jap coming, let him have it. And Maynard survived. He made it! All I could think of after reading his revoltingly smug tale was that I was sorry those slanty-eyed little sons of bitches hadn't gotten their sadistic yellow hands on him. Dr. Longworth also advises a healthy return to religion. Consider the case of Albert Salomon, a down-and-out vacuum cleaner salesman who was so consumed with worry he weighed one hundred and twenty pounds, had a peptic ulcer, and shook all over. Well! One night in a dingy hotel room in Chikasha, Oklahoma, Albert uncovered a copy of the Bible (King James version), and from that day on, in Albert's own words, "I had more sales than I could handle. My health is excellent, I own a split-level ranch, two cars, a color TV, and a power lawn mower." I found Christ and made $20,000 a year. Poor Jesus. You really do get dragged through the knee-deep muddy every time, don't you? You must be twirling in your tomb. Or wherever it is you're twirling. In, at, above, or under.

Several months ago I wrote Dr. Longworth a vicious letter ending, "You know what you need, Dr. Longworth? A good kick in the ass." (I never sent it though.) But just thinking about him, my anger is back; I feel almost sane again. "Only till Christmas, only till Christmas," revolves in my head like a carol. The thought is somehow comforting;

I am breathing easier already. Death, the power to control my own death, consoles me. It outweighs the power I do not have to control my own life.

The telephone rings. It is Jory Levitt on two, asking if Danny can come up to play with Nicco this afternoon. I hear my voice, perfectly normal—my God, how normal I can sound—calmly saying, "yes." Saying yes is an act of mercy. Elly has warned me about Jory Levitt. None of the building children will play with Danny unless forced to, not that there's anything wrong with Danny except he's a spoiled, whining pain in the ass, but because Jory insists upon coming with him. She sits on the floor, crouched like a great duck, playing games, making sure the "friend" doesn't do or say anything to tilt Danny's psyche. The one time he came to our house, on Nicco's birthday, she played with Danny, alone, in our bedroom and dragged him off before the cake was served because the "excitement" was too much for him. After I hang up I realize the afternoon I've let myself in for, but then, remembering that I am to show up at Kate's school at ten-thirty, *dressed decently,* I manage to shower, find a pair of pantyhose, pull on a dress—black with a white collar; I look like an usherette—which almost fits, ease my feet into patent leather shoes with heels, transfer my wallet, keys, tissues, compact to a matching bag, take a Librium, cover all with my still-damp raincoat and walk shakily—I'm not used to heels and I'm shaking anyway—to the 79th Street crosstown. The question is, can I get on the bus? I'm late already, and it's one hell of a walk to East End, especially in these shoes. I decide to try it and manage to stay on until Third, which isn't a bad record and only leaves me a few blocks to walk, past rows of private brownstones with polished doorknobs. Through the ground-floor windows I can see starched maids washing dishes in shiny kitchens. The rain is letting up; a steamy smell springs from the pavement. I climb the stone steps of the school and am ushered into the auditorium by a sleek blonde in blue linen and pearls, wearing a plastic name tag. I am also given a plastic name tag. Every person in the room is wearing a plastic name tag. (Just like Marcus's convention; only the faces have changed.) I wish I'd gotten here earlier; I could have shuffled them all up—pinned Mrs. Upson Downwaith on Mrs. Downson Upwaith, Mrs. G. Cameron Ipswich on Mrs. C. Gameron Wipsich—oh Lord get me out of here except I can't because they're already leading me to the punch table, behind which, apparently, I am to pour, and I wish it were straight gin. What exactly happens when alcohol and plastic mix—interesting idea, I'll have to look that up in a chemistry book—maybe I could immolate the whole fucking bunch. Too late now, however, because the meeting is about to begin.

The meeting has been called to discuss the length of uniform skirts. There appear to be two factions: one group is militant about skirts reaching above the knee; the other equally militant about skirts reaching below the knee. The discussion goes on forever, getting nastier by the minute. An enormous woman in royal blue jersey stares down a jittery, dried-up redhead, saying, in a loud, flat voice, that others can do as they like; she doesn't want *her* daughter looking like a streetwalker. I am nauseous, falling asleep. Someone calls my name. I come up with a revolutionary suggestion: how about . . . *mid*-knee? The room is suddenly silent. I wait in terror for them to stomp me to death with the heels of their Gucci shoes or choke me with the chains of their Gucci bags. But no. My suggestion is greeted with praise, approval. Why hadn't anyone else thought of it? *Mid-knee*. Compromise. The American way. Several women clasp my hand warmly on the way out of the auditorium. I am a star! I see the headmistress bearing down on me. "Mrs. Calder," she says, all tweedy-beaming. (Fall, winter, spring she wears the same rump-sprung tweeds; probably sleeps in them.) "We are all so glad to see you still in*volved,* still conn*ected,* with The Houghton School. That suggestion was so innovative, so brilliant. Perhaps you might wish to consider re-enrolling Anna, I feel now that perhaps we made a mistake, perhaps now that she's had a respite, you might say, and there just happens to be an opening, just one, in the third grade next year." I do not wish. If I don't get out of that fetid building I'm going to start screaming, tearing off my clothes, and not only at mid-knee. The whole way. ("If you're going to do anything, Liza, do it right." That's what Daddy always said.)

Outside, after a few deep breaths, I feel better. The rain has stopped. I brave the bus, and when I get home, leave the breakfast dishes to soak and decide to take Max down; amazing he's held out this long—I forgot to leave paper for him. I am glancing up at the muggy sky, thinking positive thoughts about what I am going to do today—brush dog, food shop, vacuum, buy plant vitamins, date for Nicco—when a burly man with a long black beard and cut-off jeans hurtles toward me yelling, "So you're the goddamn bitch who's been letting your dog pee all over my tires!" Startled—I hadn't notice where Max was lifting his leg—I blink up at him. He is inches away but still yelling, spraying saliva in my face. "Your goddamn dog is ruining my tires. If you're dumb enough to have a dog in this goddamn city, at least don't let him pee all over other people's tires."

"But there's no other place," I say weakly. "I mean, all the curb space is taken up with cars and that's where dogs are supposed to go, on the curb."

"Shit. Take the goddamn dog to the park. If I ever see that goddamn dog peeing on my tires again I'll *kill* him. Understand?"

After this happy exchange Max drags me off and lifts his leg on yet another car. "Knock it off!" I shriek, yanking on his leash so hard the poor dog is nearly throttled. Two homosexuals passing by take this in. "Some people shouldn't be *allowed* to have dogs," one says to the other, glaring at me. "Some people should be reported to the ASPC*A*. Just look at that poor baby, Harold. Just *look* at him."

Shaking, I light a cigarette, wait until the block is clear, and furtively let Max pee himself out against a fire hydrant, half expecting the entire hook and ladder brigade to roar in and haul me off to jail, then head for home. By the time I do the dishes, make the beds, and take another Librium (which I desperately need at this point; things are not going as well as I'd hoped), it is time to go back downstairs and meet Nicco's bus. I meet Nicco's bus because the welfare hotel across the street houses a number of newly released mental patients, one of whom—an old woman with scraggly gray curls, sequined hair net, rolled down stockings and hoop earrings—also meets Nicco's bus. Daily. On several occasions she has threatened to "get" Nicco because she feels she can give him a better home. When I called the police about this, the desk sergeant informed me that there was nothing much they could do: "Lots of these nuts talk big, Ma'am, but they don't usually follow through; better watch out for her though. You never know." Damn right. I always go down fifteen minutes early.

For the first time in months, the old woman is nowhere in sight. I stand in front of the door for half an hour by my watch. Nicco's bus is sometimes early; never late. My neurotic mother image may be working again but hell, I *am* worried, even though it's only fifteen minutes. I am getting a familiar, painful sinking feeling in the pit of my stomach, so I borrow a dime from Stefan I and go to the phone booth on the corner where I can keep an eye on the street and call the school at the same time.

"Hi, Community School, what can I do for you?" says the bright young thing at the desk.

"Hi, this is Liza Calder. I know it's only quarter to one, but Nicco's bus hasn't come yet and I just wondered if you knew anything."

"Gee, Liza, maybe it broke down or something. Do you want me to try to get in touch with Tony? Oh gee, no, I can't do that, he's driving one of the buses himself today, Edgar's sick so Tony had to drive Edgar's bus. Listen, don't worry, what time does he usually get there?"

"Around twelve-thirty. But the thing is, he's never late and there's this sort of crazy old woman who waits for his bus. I mean, I'm sure everything is fine, but I'm, you know, kind of nervous because she really is crazy."

"Oh, don't be nervous. Gee, that's awful, having a crazy old woman wait for your kid's bus. They're probably just late or something. He'll be along soon."

I wait until one o'clock. Now even for me, the hell with neurosis, this is serious. Has he been abducted because the bus arrived early? Was he ever on the bus at all? Has the bus crashed into a car-truck-street light? Where is he? My palms are damp as I borrow another dime from Stefan I and dial again.

"He's still not there yet? That's funny. Wait a minute, let me ask around. Franny, do you know anything about Nicco Calder? He's not home yet and his mother's on the phone; she doesn't know where he is. Did you see him get on the bus? Well, ask Laurie if she knows anything." Pause. "Liza? Listen, Laurie says she's absolutely positive Nicco got on the bus. Maybe he got off with one of his friends; they do that sometimes, get off with one of their friends. Anyway, none of the drivers are back yet so I can't ask them. Why don't you call around?"

(This for $1,900 a year plus $250 for a one-way bus trip? I do love the school but this would never happen at Houghton—the mid-knee plaid uniform contingent knows exactly where it's at. I'm getting awfully Waspy all of a sudden.)

"I can't call around. I'm in a telephone booth on the corner and I'm afraid to go back upstairs because of the crazy old woman I mentioned. She just got out of a *mental* hospital."

"Gee. Well listen, don't get upset. I'm sure he'll turn up. Give me the number of the phone booth and I'll call you right back in case I hear anything."

I wait in the telephone booth for twenty minutes. It has started to rain again. I do not have any change, any money with me at all, and Stefan I is out of everything but dollars. So I dash upstairs, find the list of Nicco's classmates, grab my wallet (which, thank God, is filled with change), run back down to the phone booth, and start calling. There are fifteen names on the list. After call number four I locate a Spanish-speaking maid who, from what I can understand, has an extra child with her. I ask to speak to the extra child. The extra child is not Nicco; it is Paul Weinfeld who is crying because he wants to go home. I ask if he knows where Nicco might be. "I like Nicco!" he says, brightening. "Is he home?"

"No. No, he isn't. That's why I'm calling. I don't know where he is."

"Well," Paul says, beginning to cry again, "when he gets home can I come over to your house? I *hate* it here where I am."

I extricate myself from Paul Weinfeld and keep on calling until I am out of change. I call back the school with my last dime.

"Gee," says the bright young thing at the desk. "The line's been busy. I thought you gave me the wrong number; I've been trying to get you for half an hour. One of the teachers definitely saw Nicco leave with one of the mothers;

he's fine, he's probably having a great time at the zoo or someplace. It was a bus kid but the mother picked him up, and Nicco thought he was supposed to go with them, so that's where he is."

"Where. Which mother. Which kid. He did not have a note to go home with anyone. He is not supposed to go home with anyone without a note."

"Well, we're not sure about that, but look Liza, don't worry; don't get upset. I'm sure whichever mother it is will call you right after lunch."

Don't get upset. At this very moment my son is at the zoo, in the rain, being eaten by a lion. I go back upstairs, pour a martini—no ice, no vermouth. The six remaining people on Nicco's school list are not home, meaning that he could be with one of them. Or nowhere. Depending. As I am finishing my second martini and debating whether or not to call the police, Jory and Danny arrive.

"Where is Nicco? What do you mean, he isn't here?" Jory asks, looking worriedly at Danny. "We've come up four times already and you weren't here. Danny has been expecting to play with Nicco; he's been waiting all morning. Right after lunch, you said. Where have you *been?*"

Danny begins to whine.

"Yes, Jory, I know I said right after lunch, but the fact is, I'm a little upset. Nicco's bus never got here, and I still don't know where he is. I've been trying to find out where he is."

"But Danny has been *waiting*. You don't understand. He's been waiting all morning. You can't *do* this to him, disappoint him in this way. You don't understand what you're *doing*."

Saved, as often, by the phone. Saved?

"Hi, this is Ellen Barrett," says an unfamiliar voice. "I think we worked together on the school fair. Nicco seemed to think he had a date with John, and I called before but there wasn't any answer, so I just took him along. I thought maybe you'd gone out and there wouldn't be anyone home. We're at the aquarium now, just getting ready to leave; I'd offer to drop Nicco off but I have to get home in time to be there for the other two kids. I know it sounds crazy, going to the aquarium just for an hour in this weather, but what happened was, it looked like it was going to clear and I kept thinking today was Wednesday, Wednesday the girls both had dates and I'd promised John I'd take him, and then when we got here I suddenly realized it was Tuesday, and I have to get all three kids to the dentist by three-thirty, God I must be coming across like a lunatic, I get so mixed up lately. I haven't minded having Nicco at all, I've enjoyed it, the boys have had a great time, but if you could make it by three it would help."

"The aquarium. You mean the one in Brooklyn, out by Coney Island?"

"The aquarium!" Jory says. "You mean you let Nicco go to the *aquarium* when you knew Danny was waiting to play with him?"

"Yes, that's the one. There's the cutest little white whale out here, its eyes are just . . . I mean, it looks at you as if it were . . . anyway, do you think you could be at our house by three? It would really help a lot."

"Yes. I'll be there."

As soon as I hang up I remember that Anna arrives home at three and that if I leave to pick up Nicco, no one will be home. Danny is screaming at the top of his lungs, "you promised, you promised!" Jory has tears in her eyes. "I have never, absolutely never, heard of anything so unfeeling in my life, to do a thing like this to a three-and-a-half-year-old child," she says.

"Look Jory," I say with what's left of me. "It was all a mistake. Nicco went off with someone by mistake and until just this minute I haven't even known where he *was*. I'll keep Danny for the afternoon and *dinner* even, but right now I have to find a place to leave Anna until I get back from picking up Nicco. I don't like to leave the key with Stefan II; she's only seven and I don't trust Stefan II anyway. Do you think you could stay here until I get back? I don't like to ask, but . . ."

"Oh, I couldn't possibly do that. Danny cannot defecate in a strange toilet."

"Danny cannot *what?*"

"Defecate in a strange toilet. That's one reason I never allow him to visit other children without me. I have to be on hand to take him home in case he should have to defecate."

"Oh."

"I'd offer to wait for her bus and keep her in my own apartment until you get home, but Danny doesn't like girls; he doesn't like them at all. And he's so upset already that I don't want to do anything else to disturb him, he's upset enough. It will take me at least half an hour to calm him down as it is. Be sure to call me the minute you get back."

Jory and Danny, who is still screaming, leave. I call Elly, who should be back from nursery school by now, but both she and Jason must be out—no answer. I can only wait until Anna's bus arrives, rush over to the Barretts' in a cab, pick up Nicco, and rush back. Mrs. Barrett seems reasonable, but facing Jory won't be easy: even with cabs we won't make it home before three-thirty at the earliest. Cabs. I have forgotten to cash a check and after using up all that change, now have only two dollars in my wallet. I begin to cry, hang on, hang on, do something positive, while you're waiting you can do the laundry; you haven't for four days and everyone is out of underwear. I open the washing machine. Now it's true, for real. I really am going totally, irrevocably mad. Down the Rabbit-Hole, "EAT ME," Curiouser and Curiouser mad. The washing machine is filled with tiny organdy dresses, under infant-sized ruffled bonnets, inch-long socks. Then I begin to laugh. And laugh. Dolls' clothes. The load of dolls' clothes I promised Anna I'd wash and forgot to take out of the machine. Laughter somehow clears my head. New idea: I will dash up to Anna's school before the bus leaves, pick her up there, go straight to the Barretts' (they live way up on Riverside, in the hundreds) and take the bus home.

It is still raining. I get change at the drugstore and reach the school just as Anna's bus is loaded up and ready to leave, shouting, "Get her off! Get her off!" Several mothers look at me strangely as I grab Anna and ignore her requests for explanations until we are in the Barretts' elevator, drenched.

"What *is* it?" I snap. "Why do you keep *tugging* on me like that?"

"But Mommy," Anna says tearfully. "I'm just trying to tell you. Suzie Engle was supposed to come home with me. Don't you remember, I called her last night, you said I could, and now she's on the bus going home to our house and there's nobody home. That's what I've been trying to tell you all this time."

"Oh, God, Anna, okay, look. I'll call from the Barretts' and see if Elly's home. If she is, she can go down and meet the bus or see if Suzie's in the lobby or someplace. Don't worry, darling, I'm really sorry. I've just had my mind on a lot of other things and I wasn't listening. I'm sorry."

"That's okay," Anna says, squeezing my hand. "I forget things too." She looks mournful though, pale, big-eyed. Ellen Barrett a slim, freckled, sandy-haired woman, opens the door at the first ring. I explain my problem as quickly as I can, apologize for delaying her still further, and ask if I may use the phone. Elly answers breathlessly.

"Oh sure, babe, I'll go right on down. What does the kid look like, just in case she's wandering around the block or the building or something?"

I turn to Anna. "What does Suzie Engle look like?"

Anna hesitates. Down the hallway I can see Ellen Barrett, surrounded by children's raincoats and boots, sitting on a frayed velvet bench, looking at her watch.

"Well, her teeth kind of hang out in front. And she has funny fingernails. Mommy, can we go home soon?"

"What color hair does she have? What was she wearing?"

"Well, her hair is sort of like mine, but it's not really blond it's more like brown, not dark brown but sort of in between. But I know exactly what she was wearing. She was wearing a raincoat exactly like the one Roberta Keim has, the same exact one."

"But I don't *know* Roberta Keim. What *color* is the raincoat?"

"Green."

"Elly? Look for a kid with buck teeth wearing a green raincoat. I'll be home as fast as I can."

"Don't worry about it, babe, I'm stuck home anyway. I'm making bean soup and the goddamn stuff takes hours."

"I don't *want* to go home; I *hate* that dummy Danny!" Nicco screams when he hears the news. He and John Barrett run off and hide. It takes Ellen and me ten minutes to find them, hidden in a closet underneath a pile of men's suits that they have pulled off the hangers. "Maybe I'd better call the dentist," Ellen Barrett sighs.

"Nicco, get out of there *immediately;* I am getting very angry. You were not supposed to be here at *all,* you *know* you're not supposed to go anywhere without a note. Now help John hang up those suits. We are *late.*"

"No, no, forget the suits; I'll do it when I get back," Ellen says. "Maybe if we all leave together we can get everybody out of here." Her two girls, however, in their raincoats and boots, and sweating, are having a violent fight in the hall, so I apologize again, dress Nicco, and escape. The minute I get him downstairs I am shaking with such fury and relief at finding him alive and safe that I give him a smack on his behind that knocks him flat on the sidewalk. Three old ladies passing by under flowered umbrellas look on in horror. Nicco, face down, kicking his feet and wailing, refuses to get up. "Child beater!" hisses one, quaveringly converging on me, her doughy face so close to mine I can smell a stale odor, like death, on her breath. "I've *read* about mothers like you. I should report you to the SPCC."

"Or the police, Myrna. We should call the police," says the fat one in white vinyl. Her slitted eyes glitter. "You could go to *jail.*"

"Yes, *jail,*" says the third from a safe distance, waving her umbrella at me.

After a final "disgraceful!" the three totter off. Nicco still refuses to get up. I carry him, kicking and screaming, to the bus stop. "Anna, use my umbrella. I can't hold onto it. Where *is* your umbrella, by the way?"

"I left it at school. I can't get yours to work, Mommy. I can't open it," Anna sobs, by now completely done in.

The bus is mobbed, filled with the dizzying smell of sweat, wet clothes, old rubber. By the time we get home I am exhausted; I could lie down and sleep for hours. But of course, I can't. I tell the children to change their clothes and first call Jory, who arrives with Danny before Nicco is out of his raincoat, then Elly, who has Suzie. (She found her in front of the building, in the rain, trying to coax a spitting stray tomcat out from under a Volkswagen.)

"Yeah, she's here. Christ is she here. You'll see what I mean when I send her up. Good luck." Elly says.

"What would you like to play, Danny?" Jory asks, going into her duck crouch.

"That," Danny says, pointing to a plastic model woman—skeleton, internal organs, skin—unfortunately left on the coffee table.

"Uh. Dear, actually that's Kate's. I don't think she'd

like anyone to fool around with it. And anyway, it's really for older children, you know, it says on the box that it's for children over twelve and even for Kate it's . . ."

"Danny is very advanced; he was *reading* at the age of two," Jory says, sitting up straight. (As far as I know the kid can't read a word, he can't even put his own pants on but okay, let that one hang.) "Anyway, I wasn't *thinking* of letting him play with it alone; I will *help* him put it together."

I'm not willing to face Kate, however, and insist that the plastic woman stay in her box, untouched by under-ten-year-old hands. Danny immediately begins to cry. Nicco, still in his sopping raincoat, stares at Danny in disgust. "My Mommy knocked me down on the street before and I didn't cry that bad," he says loudly.

Jory looks at me, outraged. "No, no, of course not, he's just joking," I mutter, looking at Anna who is looking at me. And oh God do I need a drink but Jory doesn't drink and now it's time to pick up Kate at the 79th Street bus stop.

"Jory, this is absolutely the very last thing I have to do, but I just have to run down and pick up Kate at the bus stop. Do you think if Anna stayed in her own room Danny could hold out until I get back? It'll only take five minutes at the very most."

"Well, I suppose so," Jory says suspiciously. "I'll try to keep his mind off it. But while you're out—what were you planning for the boys' dinner?"

"Dinner?"

"Yes. You invited Danny for dinner. What were you planning to give them?"

"Spaghetti. I didn't have time to shop today and that's all I have in the house."

"Oh no, I don't approve of that. Danny always has a balanced meal—meat, vegetables, a baked potato. I couldn't let him eat spaghetti."

"Jory, I'm late; I don't want Kate standing there waiting. I really don't feel like shopping for something else right now, and besides, I don't have any money, I forgot to cash a check. Eating spaghetti once won't hurt him; all the kids love it."

"No. What I'll do is, when you get back, I'll take him downstairs while I fix his dinner, and bring him back up here with it when it's ready."

"Whatever you want."

On my way out I open the door on a buck-toothed, neuter-looking child with no-color hair, carrying a green raincoat. It stares straight at me, unblinking, jeaned legs wide apart, one hand on its hip. "Anna!" I call out over my shoulder. "Suzie's here." And before Jory can protest, run for the stairs.

Kate is standing on the corner of 79th Street in the pouring rain, shivering. "I'm so sorry I'm late darling; were you very worried?" I ask, seeing by her face that something, as usual, is the matter.

"It isn't that," she says.

"What then?" I put my arm around her.

"The cake. The cake for the book party that you made. They *hated* the cake. They *despised* it. They all adored Brooks Lambert's brownies and didn't even *touch* the cake. They said the icing looked like zinc *ointment.*"

"Oh baby, I'm sorry. Really I am. Girls are like that sometimes, you know; they can be awfully mean. Maybe they were just jealous or something."

"They *weren't* jealous. It *was* awful. The icing was all lumpy looking and ghastly. I don't *blame* them for not wanting to touch it. It was the most ghastly looking cake I've ever *seen;* it looked like those awful cakes in those cake stores on Broadway."

I remove my arm. "Why the hell didn't *you* make it, then? Jesus Christ, do I do *anything* right? I stayed up until ten to ice that goddamn cake. You chose what kind of cake to make, anyway."

Kate bursts into tears. "You don't have to swear all the time. None of the other mothers swear," she sobs. "Everybody can *hear* you. Everybody is *watching* us."

When we get back home Anna comes out of her room saying, "I tried to stop them, Mommy, honestly I did; do you want me to make you a drink?" Pieces of the plastic woman—intestines, womb, lungs, ovaries, heart, liver—are scattered all over the living room floor. Jory is explaining each organ and its function to Danny and a bored-looking Nicco (still in his wet raincoat). Kate beckons. She rarely misbehaves in front of others. "That is *mine,*" she whispers tearfully. "I *told* you not to let anyone touch my plastic woman. Grandmother gave it to me for my birthday. It is *mine.*"

"That kid sure is a brat," Suzie says, just missing us as she swings higher and higher on the indoor swing-gym set attached to Anna's doorjamb. "His mother told us we had to stay in here until you got back. Who'd want to come out anyway, with a brat like that around?" Anna's room isn't simply messy, it is chaotic—dress-up clothes on the floor, plastic jewelry, dolls, jump ropes tangled on the bed, a sheet thumbtacked to the wall and closet door, forming a sagging tent, Play-Doh, Magic Markers, crayons, and a mixture of what looks like talcum powder and water in a plastic pail on the table. I go back into the living room, prepared to do battle, and insist that all pieces of the plastic woman go back into the box immediately. Jory begins to argue. They are not hurting anything, she protests, and the boys are acquiring knowledge, they are learning something very important. What is upsetting Danny, however, is that he is very interested in looking at a vagina, and they are unable to find a vagina among the hundreds of tiny bones, skin and organs strewn across the rug. I explain that I have five children in the house, plus Jory herself, have not yet started dinner, and am not able to help her look for a plastic vagina.

"But you don't understand. Danny wants to see one *now*."

"Why," I say, throwing pieces of unmatched organs back into the box like a madwoman, "don't you take your goddamn pants off and stand on your head and show him *yours?* Why settle for plastic when he can see the real thing? That'll send him. That'll turn him on."

Well, at least that ends our dinner date with Danny. And all other dates. Hopefully for good.

"Can I see yours, Mom?" Nicco asks, smiling widely.

"*No*. Absolutely not. Take off your raincoat."

I feel terrific, full of energy. Later on I'll call Elly and tell her what happened; we'll have a good laugh. Right now, though, I'm so alive and up (and who knows how long the high will last, better make hay while I can) I think I'll get to some of the things on my morning list—brush dog, for instance.

To brush a dog you need two things: (1) a brush; and (2) a dog. I have the brush in hand, but as usual, the moment Max sees it (not even sees; that dog must have extrasensory perception—I was holding the brush behind my back) he snarls and, red-eyed, mean, and growling, disappears under the bed. I lift up a flap of bedspread and crooningly offer water, dog biscuits, a walk. Max stares at me with one eye, curls his lip—"I may be a dog but you've pulled this crap a million times; how dumb do you think I *am?*"—and gives me a nip on the finger that draws blood.

"You filthy little bastard!" I yell, still half under the bed.

"Hey, you have dust all over you," Suzie remarks as I'm in the bathroom, winding a Band-Aid around my finger. She has stripped to grimy flowered underpants and is wearing a wreath of large, dead leaves in her hair. "You know what? That big plant in your dining room is about to die. Its leaves are plopping down all over the place."

Plant vitamins. Another forgotten item. My avocado, my baby that I nursed from a pit five years ago, was fine yesterday. But this morning I noticed that it looked sad and withered; it had the dry, yellow look of a bedridden old man in a city nursing home. I call Elly, tell her about Jory, which makes her howl, and then ask if I can borrow some vitamins, even the human kind, but she is out of everything too. "But listen, I know this really great plant person; someone gave me his number," she says. "He's just starting up in business, he's going to do consultations and things, I'm sure he'd talk to you. Why don't you call him? My friend said he saved this *tree* she had, even bigger than yours, it went all the way up to the ceiling, just by *talking* to it. Give him a call, why don't you?"

I dial. Four-four-four, two-four-three-two. On the first ring a breathy voice drawls, "Yes?"

After explaining how I got his number and then going into my avocado and its problem there is a long, poignant silence.

"Plants don't just die over*night,*" says the voice. "It must have suffered some sort of traumatic *shock.* Have you shifted your plant arrangement in any way, moved plants from one room to another, acquired any new plants recently?"

"Well," I murmur guiltily, "I did move my kangaroo vine into the living room; the avocado and the kangaroo vine in one room together were kind of overpowering. And, oh yes. I had this other avocado pit rooting in the kitchen and it had quite a root formation, it was sprouting, so yesterday I put it in the dining room, on the windowsill. The dining room gets quite a lot of sun."

"Well for heaven's *sake,* there's your *answer,*" the

voice says accusingly. "You have not only taken away your avocado's best *friend,* you have introduced a new *baby* in the room. Your avocado is obviously dying of loneliness and jealousy. Your only hope now, and I must say, the chances seem extremely slim, is to move the kangaroo vine *back* into the dining room, keep the new baby out of sight, and above all don't let your avocado see you *hovering* over the new baby, acting as if you loved it more than you love your *old* avocado, and *reassure* your old avocado—talk to it, stroke its leaves, tell it you love it, make sure it knows you're *sorry.* I can't promise anything, of course, especially over the phone. I might be able to fit in a house call tomorrow morning. What's your address?"

"Uh. How much do you charge for house calls?"

"My minimum is fifteen dollars. Excluding extras—vitamins, special sprays, extended therapy, and so on."

"I . . . maybe I should just wait a day or so. That seems a little . . . high."

"Well! If you're going to think of money at a time like this I don't know why you bothered to call in the first place," the voice says, hanging up with a crash.

I take a Librium, make myself a martini, take several big sips, and get out the stepladder. The kangaroo vine is hanging on a chain from the living room ceiling above the window in a pot that must weigh at least twenty-five pounds; it took Andrew over an hour to drill the hole and screw in a hook. Its vines leap and fly in all directions. By the time I manage to get it down and half drag, half carry it back to the dining room—where, thank God, the previous hook remains; Andrew was going to unscrew it and replaster the hole tonight—my lower back is aching and I have broken two nails. I finish my martini, mix another, and am standing on the ladder, trying to fit the end of the chain into the hook when the telephone rings.

"Kate, get that, will you?" I shout. The telephone

continues to ring. "Kate. Anna! Get the phone." When there is no response I climb down from the ladder, put the pot on the floor and, swearing, head for the kitchen.

It is Suzie Engle's mother, a young divorcée whom I have never really met but only seen occasionally outside the school—tall, slim, attractive with long streaked blond hair and small pert breasts showing firm under her bright jerseys and embroidered Indian blouses. Rumor has it that she lives in a large, one-room studio apartment with sleeping platforms she built herself for the kids—there's a younger child, about three, named Robin—is a free-lance writer, and, as they used to say, swings. I've always liked the look of her: loose, lanky, not the Librium type at all.

"Hi Liza, could you do me a tremendous favor?" she says, speaking so quickly the words run together. "I just got home, I've got a date tonight, I have to shower, wash my hair and everything, and if I run down to pick up Suzie I won't have time, could you possibly put her in a cab, she's used to cabs, she takes them all the time, if you could just give her two dollars, I think two dollars should cover it, I'll pay you back tomorrow, would that be okay?"

A cab. I'm supposed to put a seven-year-old child in a cab? Alone? (Well, as one ex-shrink said, I can't take on responsibility for the safety and/or happiness of every single person in the entire world. That's known as an unhealthy need for power, caused by deep-rooted feelings of guilt and insignificance. That's what he said. So he did.)

"She could take the bus, she's used to the bus too, she takes the one-oh-four home from school, but I'm not sure she knows the way from your house, and I need her home to watch Robin, the sitter can't come until eight. So if you could put her in a cab, actually you don't even have to go down with her, if you could just give her the two dollars she can go down by herself."

I am not responsible for Suzie's safety. Repeat. I am

not responsible for Suzie's safety. My avocado is dying, dinner is not ready, my dog is not brushed, my apartment is not vacuumed. If Suzie is raped, mugged, murdered, it is not my fault.

"I don't mind at all, but I don't have two dollars. I forgot to cash a check and all I have left is about a dollar. But you could meet her down in front of the building."

"But if I meet her in front of the building I won't have time to shower and do my hair, see, that's what I meant."

"No, not in front of *our* building, in front of *your* building."

"Oh. Oh God. Yeah. Okay. I'll get right into the shower. Tell her if I'm not down just to tell the cab to wait. Or no, tell her to tell him to leave the meter running and she can come upstairs and get the money and go back down and pay him. That way I won't have to go down."

"Okay. I'll tell her to tell him that."

"I'm really sorry, I hope I'm not putting you out or anything, I know I was supposed to pick her up at five-thirty, but I got stuck downtown at an interview, I guess I should have picked her up on my way home, but it was getting so late, I hope you don't have theater tickets or people coming to dinner or something. Anyway, thanks an awful lot. See you!"

"See you."

It takes almost half an hour to find Suzie's clothes; Anna's room has gotten worse than ever. Since Kate refuses to stay alone in the apartment with Nicco, Anna wants to come downstairs with me to put Suzie in a cab (and I am not about to let Suzie go down alone), I am forced to take all four children over to Broadway, where the taxi situation seems better—West End is empty of cabs. As I case passing drivers, looking for a nice, fatherly type who can be trusted, Suzie shouts, "There's one!" and sticks up a skinny arm. A cab swerves over, bumping the curb and barely missing Nicco. The driver is wearing a shocking pink shirt unbuttoned to the waist, a leather wristband, and Indian beggar's beads. His hair, a lovely dark auburn shade, reaches below his shoulders. Suzie clamors in. "I *know* my address," she says scornfully when I go into a little speech about getting this child home safely, and to the correct address. "Quite a kid. How old are you, baby?" the driver asks, turning around to look at her as he depresses the gas pedal and careens off, forgetting to turn on his meter.

It is not my fault.

"When's dinner? I'm starved." Kate says as soon as we unlock the front door.

"When I get it ready," I say, between my teeth.

The avocado looks more mournful than ever. "Look, here's your friend!" I say brightly as I hook on the kangaroo vine and stand back to survey the jungle-like result. "And I'm going to get that nasty baby right out of here. You know I love you, don't you? I really do love you. As soon as I put the spaghetti water on, I'm coming right back to talk to you some more." I turn around just in time to see Andrew standing in the doorway, staring at me strangely.

"I wish you wouldn't come in so *quietly* like that," I say before he can say anything. "And if you're wondering why I'm talking to the avocado, it's because I spoke to this plant person Elly recommended who's supposed to be brilliant, and that's one of the things he told me to do. Do you know what it would cost to replace a plant this size? It would cost at least twenty-five dollars." (And I've got it too; found money, ferret money.)

"You should have waited for me; you shouldn't have tried to lift a thing like that by yourself. Anyway, I thought you wanted that other thing in the living room. What did you put it back in here for?"

"Because the plant person said . . . oh, never mind.

And they're not *things,* they're *plants,* that's part of the problem. You have to . . . look, do you think the two of us could sit down like other people and have a drink together, just for once, instead of me drinking in the kitchen and you sitting in the living room? And if you could *make* the drinks for once, you know, like Justin does, I promise, I absolutely swear that I'll only bore you for a few minutes and then I'll get up and get dinner."

"Liza, I'm not pushing you about dinner; I never do," Andrew says wearily, loosening his tie. "And you don't bore me. I'm tired, that's all. If you want us to have a drink together before dinner every night, fine. The only reason I don't usually make drinks is that you know I don't drink much, especially martinis, and I don't really know how to make them."

"You take a glass. You put some ice in the glass. You pour some gin in the glass. You pour a drop of vermouth in the glass. Is that too much for you to handle?"

He looks at me with those inscrutable gray eyes. "Do something," I want to scream. "Say something. Get angry. React. Anything but this terrible nothingness." But he doesn't, can't, won't; he simply takes two aspirins, gets out two glasses, and begins to make the drinks. We sit on opposite sides of the living room, not speaking.

"In thirteen years of marriage, you have never made me a drink," I say finally.

"I made you one tonight."

"I won't live this way anymore. I can't stand it. I can't live like this."

"Like what? Oh Liza, can't live like what?"

"We don't talk. We just live here together like shadows. We never say anything. I'm going mad and you just sit there, watching it all happen. You're watching me die."

"We're talking now."

He has not touched his drink.

"We're *not* talking. *I'm* talking. Oh shit, what's the use. I'm going to start dinner."

"Wait. Don't just walk off like that, that's what you always do. Let's talk then. What do you want to talk about?"

He takes a sip of martini, grimaces. I see his eyes straying toward the open *Time* magazine on the coffee table.

"Don't ask me what I want to talk about. What do *you* want to talk about?"

He looks at me helplessly; gray eyes as inscrutable as ever. "Well, what was your day like? What did you do today?"

My day. Suzie, Jory, Danny, the rain, buses, Nicco. An eddy. Circuity. Fragments. Without beginning. Without end. I do not know what my day was like except that somehow I lived it, and tomorrow can only hold more of the same. Amen.

"What a goddamn trite, stupid question," I say, slamming my drink down on the table so hard it sloshes all over *Time* magazine. " 'What was your day like?' If you can't think up anything better than that, it's no wonder you'll never be a partner in that goddamn firm."

"Maybe you're right. Maybe we can't go on like this. Every night. Every single night there's something. Can't we ever spend an evening in peace? Why do we have to fight all the time?"

"Peace. Peace is in a morgue. Peace is when you're dead. Why the hell don't you *move* into a morgue? You'd fit in just fine. And we *don't* fight; *I* fight. Oh fuck you. I have to go heat up the sauce."

After a dinner of spaghetti and canned sauce (which Andrew does not touch; he doesn't say anything, he just doesn't touch it, just as he will not drink domestic wine, just as he will not eat frozen stuffed peppers) I scream at the children to help me clear the table. Kate mutters something about homework and disappears, Nicco brings a single slice of bread out to the kitchen, and Anna, trying to carry three glasses at once, drops two and struggling to hold back tears, gets out the broom and dustpan, barefooted steps on a piece of broken glass and breaks down completely. I wash and bandage her cut toe and settle her sobbing in front of the television set with her foot on a pillow. Andrew is quietly stacking plates.

"I know, I'm incompetent, right? You don't have to say it," I say, snatching the plates out of his hands.

"Liza, for God's sake, I didn't say that, I'm just trying to help. Every time I try to help you you get angry."

"You don't try to help me. You never help me. If you wanted to help me where the hell were you all through this fucking impossible day?"

"I was working. What do you want me to do, stay home? Sometimes I don't know what you want; sometimes I think you don't know what you want."

"What I want," I yell, throwing plates, food and all, into the sink, "is for you to leave me the hell alone."

He stands there, watching me. A plate shatters; flowered jagged triangles fill the steaming soapy water. The sink is about to overflow. I am crying, searching for broken fragments, burning my hands in the burning water. Max, looking matted and unkempt, skulks into the kitchen, eyeing his dish. I have forgotten to feed him. Still crying, I reach into the cupboard for a can of dog food. The can slips out of my wet, soapy hands and falls to the floor. Andrew bends to pick it up and hands it to me gently.

"Why do you drink so much?" he asks.

The can just misses his chest and lands upright on the counter.

Much later, when the kitchen has been cleaned, Max has been fed and the children are sleeping, I remember the avocado. The baby I have not loved enough. Whispering words of love I stroke its leaves, kiss it, lay my cheek upon its drying stalk. A large dead leaf trembles, hesitates, then drops to the floor with a loud crunching sound. I am kicking the avocado, shaking it back and forth until a sole leaf remains at the top, beating it with my fists, screaming, "Fuck you, you bitch. If you want to die then go ahead. Drop dead. *Die.*"

I know Andrew can hear me. He is in the living room, listening to Mahler, but the noise I am making must be heard. He does not come in. I splash water on my face, brush my hair, go into the living room and face him.

"Not one more day," I tell him. "Tomorrow I'm going to call Nina Farrow. Tomorrow I'm going to start looking for a job. You couldn't pay someone a hundred dollars a week to put up with this shit. You couldn't pay someone two hundred. I have had *enough.*"

He switches off the record player. "But what about the children?" Who's going to stay with the children?"

"Fuck the goddamn kids! Hire a keeper. Send them to a reformatory. I'm tired of thinking of the goddamn kids. What about me for a change? What about *me?*"

"You don't mean that."

"I do mean it; I *do.* Tomorrow I am going to start looking for a job."

And having made this momentous decision, the next day after lunch I take Nicco to the park and watch a German nursemaid slap a two-year-old baby twice in the face and shake him back and forth until his teeth rattle. Because he got his cotton shorts dirty, playing in the sandbox.

VII

They found Mrs. Chisolm floating face down in the East River, her pink bow soggy. She was wearing a black silk dress, a feather boa, and all her rings. She had apparently mistaken a passing tugboat for the *Mauretania,* and after escaping from the hospital, hailed the tug and jumped (fell? was pushed?) from the dock. In the obituary column of *The New York Times* I learned that she had been a distinguished lawyer, had fought all her life for women's rights, and had been jailed at the age of seventy-one for obstructing justice when she tried to accompany two little black girls into a segregated school in New Orleans. Her son and his wife flew in from London for the funeral. There were no other immediate survivors.

I have just hung up from talking to my friend Lauren, who recommended me to Nina Farrow about a job. Lauren has a good deal of pull; she is vice-president of an ad agency that handles huge cosmetics accounts. "And for God's sake whatever you do, don't go on and on about Andrew and the children; Nina absolutely abhors kids," said my-friend-Lauren. "If she asks, tell her you have a nurse who's been with you for years. I mean, don't go into all your *problems,* a whole bunch of shit about what time you have to be home for dinner or Easter vacations or a bunch of shit like that. I've really given you a fantastic buildup. Don't fuck it up."

My mother always said that no woman in her right mind would marry, or if she were insane enough to do so, would never have children. Although at the time I thought it rather insensitive of her to tell David and me throughout our childhood that she had never wanted children, had only had us because my father insisted, now I wonder . . . perhaps Mother was light-years ahead of her time. It is a family joke that my father "rescued" her from pursuing her career. After the musical comedy in which she appeared folded, he talked her into turning down her next offer—a tour of southern Ohio doing a tap on toe routine while playing the trombone—and married her instead. My mother does not, and never did, know how to play the trombone, but the booking agent said it didn't matter. She would have followed an act in which two poodles in ruffled tutus stood on their hind legs and jumped through hoops.

"So look," continued my-friend-Lauren. "I'll call Nina right now to remind her about you and then you call her in about fifteen minutes. I know there's at least one opening, maybe two. At least there *was* an opening when I first called you. Why the hell didn't you call her right away?"

"I've been a little hung up. Uh. Lauren, it isn't that I don't appreciate what you're doing for me, I really do, it sounds terrific, I can't tell you how grateful I am, it's just that I was thinking, well, you know, here I am trying to get started again, and it's just that that kind of magazine, I happened to read through it last night, I was hoping maybe, I don't know, maybe for something a little more, well not fulfilling, that's a ridiculous word, I know that, but I just remember how I felt at the agency and . . ."

"Oh Christ. Not another one. Who the hell do you

think you are? Maya Plisetskaya? Picasso? Dostoyevsky? You want to sit home and write poetry or something? You don't know how lucky you are even being *considered* for an editorial job, you've never even *worked* in publishing. Nina hardly ever even *sees* anyone like this, you don't know what I've had to go through to con her into it. There are twenty-one-year-old girls just out of college who'd work for *nothing* to get this kind of experience. You know the kind of shit you'd have to go through if you went into an employment agency cold? You've been out of commission a hell of a long time, baby. Except for a few schlock free-lance jobs you haven't worked in ten years. It isn't easy, you know, getting a chance at a job like this at your age, when you haven't worked in ten years."

I know. Oh, how well I know. And true enough, I am not Picasso. Or Dostoyevsky. Definitely not Maya Plisetskaya. In my head I soar and leap like a boneless bird, but on earth I have trouble walking more than five blocks unless I'm wearing sneakers. I have no blazing talents. I do not want to be a teacher or a doctor or a psychiatric social worker. I could not dissect the pig in sophomore biology (they let me pass anyway; I turned the professor on). I spent three months working part-time at a foundling hospital when Kate was a baby and Mama Rosie, the cleaning lady, came twice a week instead of half a day, as she does now. (My mother also stayed with Kate on those days; I figured between the two of them Kate probably wouldn't suffocate in her crib or strangle on her pacifier, but I worried anyway.) I read to the foundling children, took them to the park, listened to their sobs of "mommy, mommy," at nap-time, pushed their clinging hands away at four, and finally went on a crying jag, slept fitfully when at all, and at Andrew's request quit after several weeks of nightmares in which starving babies screamed and bled as I hacked them off my body with a carving knife. I do not know what I want to do, except that I do not want to do what I am presently doing, which is going mad, and I have promised myself, before dying, to try playing by the new rules. Although going mad seems a lot more healthy at present.

I am good, really good, at only two things. One is Latin. Latin was my best subject at school. Very few people speak Latin. The other is taking Mensa tests. I am very good at taking Mensa tests. I always finish before the allotted time limit with a perfect score.

Nina Farrow is the beauty editor of a woman's magazine, one which helps women along by telling them to get their asses out there in the great big, real world and keep moving on, up, do, be, become. In leafing through the pages of this month's issue, which I ran out to buy yesterday, however, I find that most of the articles are concerned with either fashion, beauty, sex, or food. Sometimes a combination of all four. Here are three current titles: (1) "Seduce your man with this delectable little dinner: guacamole (made by your own well-manicured hands, of course), taco chips, chili (mmm! hot-hot!), and for a fabulous finale, lemon ice served in cut-out petaled lemons, each mound topped with a luscious blueberry (looking just like you know what!)"; (2) "Flabby thighs? Sagging derriere? Too much tummy? Consider—yes! —plastic surgery. (We assume you've already done *away* with those nasty little bags under your chipmunk-bright eyes or lopped a bit off that now-perky nose if nec.)"; (3) "101 ways to have an orgasm."

There is also a travel section. I do not know how many readers can afford to zoom off to Mozambique or Dubrovnik for the weekend. It sounds like fun though. They tell you just what to pack, too.

I pour a martini, wait fifteen minutes, and call Nina Farrow. Over the phone I get an instant mental picture—straight, short blond hair parted to one side, dangling chains, blue eyeshadow, melon lipstick. Tall. Bone thin. Brittle.

Wearing a hat. Her voice sounds like the clatter of electric typewriter keys. Ratata*tatata*tat.

"Oh yes, Liza Calder, Lauren just called, she's mentioned you before, I understand you did some agency work with her years ago, editorial work is different, quite different you know, but Lauren said, she really seemed to feel, let's see, my week's rather frantic I'm afraid but I think—*Marge!* Look up my schedule! Wednesday. Let's say Wednesday. For lunch. Meet me at the office and we'll head on from here. You have the address?"

"Yes. Yes I do. And thank you. Thank you so much. It will be a pleasure to meet you. And to get out of this madhouse. I haven't been downtown in so long except to Macy's to buy the kids jeans I . . ."

Wrong thing to say.

Deep breath. "I mean, I'm really looking forward to the possibility of working again; it's been really a long time since I . . ."

Wrong thing to say. Again.

"Yes. I *do* wonder about that *gap*. We'll discuss it Wednesday, however, I have a long-distance call waiting, twelve-thirty, 'ta," says Nina Farrow, hanging up.

Without mentioning children, whom I have mindlessly mentioned already, that *gap* is going to be awfully hard to explain.

Wednesday. At twelve-thirty. It suddenly hits me that tomorrow is Wednesday. Oh God. Did she mean this Wednesday or next Wednesday? If she meant this Wednesday wouldn't she simply have said "tomorrow?" But she also said "my week's rather frantic." Wouldn't that mean *this* week? Do I dare call back to make sure? No, I do not dare. I'll just have to take my chances and bet on tomorrow.

Tomorrow. Wednesday. At twelve-thirty. Wednesday is my day to take the children to school. Nicco's bus arrives at twelve-thirty. Who the hell am I going to find to babysit at that hour? Well, at least I didn't mention *that* problem. Before Mother's lockup, after I was sure the children had survived babyhood, I never needed daytime sitters. Although Mother steadily drank her way through my gin supply into a nodding buzz and the apartment wound up looking like the aftermath of hurricane Hannah, she was always ready to hop into a cab and arrived within the hour. The Barnard girls I use in the evenings are usually not available during the day, especially not on short notice, but I call anyway and of course I am right; no one is available. The only sure alternative is a child care agency that charges $2.75 an hour, four-hour minimum, plus cab fare. I once used the agency in desperation when Nicco was about two and my parents were off on a cruise. An old, dowager-humped woman wearing a leg brace and a red shawl arrived and hobbled directly into Nicco's room. "Don't you worry, dearie, I won't leave him for a minute, those girls are big enough to look after themselves, you just go on and have a good time," she said. When I returned I found an empty container that had held an entire Sara Lee chocolate cake on the kitchen table, ten Pampers, most of them dry, wadded up in the garbage pail, and the old woman flushed and in the middle of an erotic experience I still can't pin down. Why *was* she changing all those Pampers—could an inch-long penis be that much of a turn-on? And an entire Sara Lee chocolate cake—is there some connection I am missing? Hopefully I can avoid the child care agency and instead find Nicco a date. His penis is longer now. And he might cooperate. In fact, I *know* he'd cooperate. He's under everyone's skirts, including my own; he drives the girls wild—peeking through the keyhole when Kate's undressing, pulling down Anna's pants; last week he did something really terrible to a skinny spinster as she was climbing up onto the Broadway bus.

Hopefully I can also find something to wear. My mother, a compulsive shopper, always provided me with clothes, few of which now fit; during the past month I have gained another five pounds, not that I'm fat, just a little bit chunky, a little bit "chonky" like that waitress Jim Croce sang about in "Top Hat Bar and Grille." Chonky, funky Lil in her tight hippy-hugger slacks. Kind of honky-tonky too, just like me. Maybe I could get a job in a bar. Lil seemed to be having an awful lot of fun. I understand the pay is good.

Back to reality. What little I have that does fit is either not clean or does not match. I have the pants suit I wore on my last excursion with my father and ferrety old Marcus, but the jacket has a large wine spot on the lapel. One of my sole good pair of shoes is missing a heel; Nicco used it as a hammer the other day, the same day he borrowed Andrew's screwdriver and tried to pry the electrical sockets off the living room walls. My other pair of shoes, fairly presentable, is bright red. Bright red shoes will not match the green jersey shift that is clean and does fit. It is not Christmas. My black and white usherette outfit is all right for an uptown school meeting, but is five years old and seems dead wrong for a downtown meeting with the editor of a well-known magazine that advocates fashion as if it were a new religion. Anyway, the weather has turned cool again. I have an old pea jacket, forget that, and an orange wool coat, one of Mother's offerings. It is also not Halloween. Christ, I don't even know what they're wearing downtown anymore, it may really *be* Dalmatian shit for all I know, better look in the magazine to get an idea.

I notice that I come into style every ten years or so. I am not in style now. Well, that's not quite true. My eyes and hair may pass, but in the magazine's twenty-five pages of fashion, there isn't a dress in sight, only pants and calico-looking long skirts. Unless I can borrow something from Elly, and she's much taller, I'm finished. I panic in stores. Even if I could face Bloomingdale's or Gimbel's East, it's too late now, almost time for the girls to get home, and nothing ever fits. Who do they make clothes for, giraffes? I'm not *that* short. It's not simply a matter of turning up hems or cuffs; half a foot of material, minimum, has to be cut off, and I'm no tailor.

I call Elly. Before I can go into my clothing problem, she says: "Christ. Do you know what that bitch did?"

"Bitch? Which bitch?"

"Jory. Jory Levitt. She pulled the same thing on poor old Marcia Plunkner. Have your kids had chicken pox?"

"God no. Funny, they've been exposed at school and stuff but they never have. Why?"

"Because that's what Danny had the day she dumped him on you. Okay, accidents happen, you don't always know when your kid is coming down with something, but that bitch, that goddamn bitch, she *knew* he had it, I got the whole story from Stefan I. He had it all over his chest and back and in his hair, she'd already had him to the doctor, it just wasn't on his face yet, just a few bumps. Didn't you see them?"

"Oh God yes, now that I think of it, I did. But I thought they were just bites or a rash or something."

"Bites my ass. After Marcia found out Jory told Marcia she didn't know but she knew all right; what did she think a three-and-a-half-year-old kid had, acne? When they left your house she took him down to Marcia's and you know Marcia, she was all mixed up and in the middle of feeding the baby and cooking supper, so she let them stay. She got so screwed up listening to Jory she put a whole cup of salt in the meat loaf, she thought it was breadcrumbs. Jory told her all about that scene up at your house; she said you had no right to have children, that any mother who used language like that in front of children was unfit. Marcia sends her condolences, by the way. That bitch. She's probably exposed the whole goddamn building by now; my kids have had it, thank God. Better look up the incubation period in Spock. I think it's about two weeks but look it up to be sure. I hope you don't have anything planned for the next month or so because unless God is looking down on you grinning insanely you're going to have one hell of a month."

"Oh Elly, *Elly,* that's one reason I called. I have this job interview set up for tomorrow and I don't have anything to wear, I was going to ask to borrow something. Oh Jesus, suppose I get the job? I can't leave three kids with chicken pox with a new sitter, she wouldn't last a day."

"All right, babe, don't cry. Look, let's get the clothes thing settled. *Get* the job first. *Then* worry. I knew you were talking about looking for a job, but I thought you were just talking. I think it's great, terrific, anything to get out of the goddamn house for a change."

"Yeah. Sure. So I get out of the goddamn house and into a whole other bunch of shit. Who am I kidding? I worked before. I know."

"So you're exchanging one bunch of shit for another. What's so bad about that? At least the shit will be different."

"Yeah, it'll be different all right. Do you know where I'm going for an interview? *Free Woman.* Have you ever *read Free Woman?"*

"No babe, I play it safe. I stick to the one that teaches you how to make marshmallow Jell-O molds shaped like rabbits. You can even put some coconut on top, like fur."

"Play it safe. That's exactly what a shrink told me once when I was into Ouspensky and freaking out over the fourth dimension. 'Play it safe. Stick to the *Reader's Digest,'* he said."

"I didn't mean it like that. You know what I mean."

"Well, if you ever want to try a hundred and one ways to have an orgasm, read *Free Woman. Jesus.* Who *reads* this shit? Typists? Keypunch operators? Dirty old ladies? Housewives in Lefrak City? One hundred and one ways to have an orgasm. *Christ.*"

"Calm down, for God's sake, stop crying again, don't be such a snob. Not every keypunch operator has an orgasm every day, you know. Do you want to come down or should I come up? What exactly, if anything, have you got to wear, and then maybe I can figure something out."

"Red shoes. A green shift. The pants to a pale beige pants suit. A black and white dress. An orange coat."

"Oh boy, let me think that over. Red shoes. That's bad. What size do you wear?"

"Eight triple A."

"I wear a nine B. I have a great pair of beige shoes; they're brand new. Maybe we could stuff them with paper or something."

"I am not going downtown wearing shoes stuffed with paper."

"Okay, okay, I'm just suggesting. What's wrong with the top of the pants suit?"

"It has a big wine stain on it."

"Couldn't you cover it with a pin?"

"No, it's too big. You'd have to have a pin the size of a shield. Maybe I could start a new trend, a sort of Middle Ages look, I could carry a sword or a jousting stick or something."

"All right, take it easy. Pale beige pants. Red shoes. Red and beige. I think I have an idea. Hang in."

While I'm hanging in I call the five mothers on Nicco's school list that I know well enough to ask to take him for tomorrow afternoon. One child is sick with tonsillitis, three already have dates, and the fifth child's mother is in tears.

"That bastard, that filthy bastard, he hasn't sent a support check in months but like an idiot, like the trusting asshole I am, I sent B.J. off anyway, I paid for the plane fare myself, he was supposed to send him back the day before school started and now he says he won't send him back, that he doesn't want B.J. growing up in this filthy city, that he wants him out in the fresh air and trees and anyway, he has this new girl friend he's going to marry who adores children, and I don't, so why should he send him back?" sobs B.J.'s mother. "He said all I ever did when we were married was complain; I never said I didn't like children, I just used to be very tired. I'd get home from work and have to pick up all the toys and give B.J. his bath and get dinner ready, and he's always been difficult, very active, but I never said I didn't like children. I never said I didn't love him. My God I'm going mad without him; I'll die if I don't get him back. I get home and the apartment's so *empty*. I go into his room and look at his toys, I can't stand it anymore, he's all I've got."

"God, Barbara, that's awful. Couldn't you fly out there and get him? Maybe you should get a lawyer."

"I *can't* fly out there and get him. I'll lose my job. Anyway, I'm broke. I spent my last cent on his plane fare and I don't get paid until next week; I'm living on cottage cheese and peanut butter. You don't know the kind of place I work for, they'd never give me an advance. They'd never give me any more time off. I've already taken my vacation and I keep getting sick, I'm only home now because I have this terrible case of flu or something, I can't even get out of bed."

"Oh Barbara, I'm so *sorry*. I didn't even know you'd gone back to work full time."

"I *had* to go back to work full time. I quit my old job, a great job, because Larry said I should stay home with B.J. and then two months later he walks out. What are we supposed to live on, welfare?"

"Barbara, listen, I'll speak to Andrew tonight, I'm sure there's some way for you to get a lawyer. His firm doesn't usually handle this kind of thing but I'm sure he'll know of somebody. You should have told me before, you never mentioned anything, why didn't you call me? Please don't cry."

"If I don't get him back I'll die," sobs Barbara.

The incubation period for chicken pox, according to Dr. Spock, is between eleven and nineteen days after exposure.

I finish my martini. Elly arrives, a red silk blouse, a tan silk blouse, and a black wool jacket draped over her arm.

"Elly, you don't have any daytime sitters, do you?" I ask. "I'm having a hell of a time finding a sitter for tomorrow for Nicco; I can't find him a date."

"Gee, babe, no I don't. If I run into a problem Justin's usually around. What time do you need somebody? I'll be home around three; I have parent conferences until around three."

"No, that's no good. I have to be down there at twelve-thirty."

"Shit. And Justin'll be gone all day; he has a thing, auction, to go to or he could keep him. Isn't there an agency or something you could call?"

"I guess I'll have to. I don't want to but I guess I'll have to."

"You worry too much. Now. Put out the clothes you've got. I'd personally forget those dresses. Nobody wears dresses like that any more."

I get out my beige pants and red shoes and try them on with Elly's red blouse and black jacket. Elly stands back and looks at me, squinting.

"No," she says at last. "They fit all right but something's wrong. If we only had a red bag, maybe. Do you have a red bag?"

"No."

"Okay. Try on the tan blouse."

I try on the tan blouse. Elly backs off and squints again.

"That's better, much better," she says. It almost matches the pants. Now with the black jacket and a black bag, you have a black bag don't you, the whole thing hangs together, sort of."

"Sort of. Thanks a lot. And they don't fit all right. The sleeves are too long. You can't even see my hands."

"So you'll be carrying a bag, won't you? Just keep your arms bent up. They're not interviewing your body, are they? You look fine. Do you have any earrings or anything?"

"They hurt. All my earrings hurt. I never had the guts to have my ears pierced."

"How about beads?"

"Only green. And the clasp is broken."

"You're fighting me, baby. What about all that jewelry your father keeps giving you, that stuff you showed me once?"

"Oh Elly, come *on*. A pendant that says 'I love you' on it? A brushed gold bracelet with ninety-nine hearts?"

"Well, it looks expensive anyway."

"No."

"Okay, okay. Don't cry. Wait, I've got it. Red. Red beads. I've got some. That'll really pull the whole thing together. I'll go down and get them."

Elly returns with the red beads and two icy, brimming martinis. "Okay. *Now,"* she says, draping the beads over my head with a professional air and taking a final squint. "Terrific. You really look terrific. No, don't look at me like that, I mean it. Just like those ads and stuff. A little makeup on your eyes, a little, you know, color, and you'll be fine."

"Bullshit. I thought you were into no makeup and no bras and hair growing under your arms."

"Come on baby, grow up. There's a big nasty world out there that isn't liberated yet. Play the game if you have to. You know it's just this year they let me wear jeans to work? Here, have a drink. Let's celebrate."

"Celebrate what? I haven't even got the goddamn job yet."

"You will. I have a feeling."

"You have a feeling. Who the hell are you, Nostradamus? Krishnamurti? Madame Blavatsky?"

"Don't throw names at me, baby, I only went to a State Teachers' College."

"I don't even have a degree, you know. No one ever asked me, but I don't even have a degree, I only have three years of college. I've never been so fucking bored in my entire life; I only stayed up there to be near Andrew. The man at the agency, this great guy I worked for, just sort of pushed me through. He said I was too smart to be a secretary. Actually I was a lousy secretary. I took a shorthand course and I could write it down all right but I couldn't read it. Christ, I can't even read my *own* writing. Anyway, nobody ever asked me."

"So if they ask you tomorrow, lie. Anyway, they probably won't ask you this time either. You *sound* as if you have a degree, that's the important thing. What did you major in?"

"English. What else?"

"Yeah. What else is right. How does Andrew feel about this whole thing? About your going back to work I mean."

"I haven't told him yet," I say, staring into the depths of my martini. "I mean, I told him last week that I'd had it, but I haven't really told him."

"Jesus, baby," Elly explodes. "What's the matter with you? Haven't you ever heard of communicating?"

"We don't communicate. At least, he doesn't. He just sits there. Sometimes . . . you know . . . sometimes I think that kind of silence, oh he never criticizes or hardly ever gets mad, he isn't even demanding, but that silence, that awful silence, it's sadistic. I used to beg him, literally beg him, to talk to me, and he'd just sit there. He'd just stare at me and not say a word. Now I just . . . I don't beg anymore. Unless I'm really freaked out I don't beg. I don't say anything."

"Yeah. You freak out pretty often, you know. The poor bastard. I've seen you cut his balls off more than once."

"Fuck you too," I say. We laugh, clinking glasses.

"We are two bad-ass old ladies," Elly says, giggling. "Ballbreakers. Cock killers."

"You may," I say with semi-drunken solemnity, "have a point, baby. You just may have a point."

"Look. Tell him. Calmly. I mean, don't overreact; don't get threatening and pissed off. See what happens. Justin and I have really been doing better; sometimes I can tell him things now that I never would have been able to tell him before. And take off those clothes so they don't get messed up for tomorrow."

"All right. I will. I'll take off the clothes. And I'll try to tell him."

As soon as Elly leaves I call the child-care agency and book someone for tomorrow, explaining that it is absolutely vital that the sitter arrive by eleven-thirty so that I can meet her first and show her around the apartment. "And please, this time could you send someone not too terribly old?" I timidly inquire. "He's rather active and the last time . . ."

"By our records, I see that you are not a regular customer of Children, Inc.," a female voice with a faintly British accent says nastily. "We interview each sitter in depth. Each sitter provides *total* care: bathing, feeding, walking, creative play. You've hardly given us time to *find* you a sitter; it's also extremely difficult to find a sitter of our *cal*iber who is willing to *go* to the West Side. I can assure you that whomever we send is totally qualified and totally re*spon*sible. I shall call you back within the half hour."

In ten minutes the phone rings and Children, Inc. informs me that a Mrs. Morris will arrive at eleven-thirty.

This evening Andrew is late. In a fit of guilt I hurriedly dust, vacuum, pick up scattered clothes, settle Nicco in the bathtub with his boats, and fix an eggplant casserole Andrew especially likes. I am just getting Nicco dried and into his pajamas when I hear the key in the lock. My stomach muscles contract, a tense churning. Andrew brings with him a smell of cool air and leaves and a good clean smell of sweat. I lean against him for a moment, against the body I have known so long, and I am close to tears again. I want to hide within that body, barricade myself within its sturdy warmth. Nicco runs toward us and Andrew picks him up. For a moment the three of us are motionless, silhouetted by the shaft of light slanting down the hall. The light is dancing; fairy dust, my mother used to say, catch some fairy dust, and when David was a child she said the same. And David would run, grasping at the dancing air, crying when he opened his tiny hand again and again to emptiness.

"Fairy dust!" Anna cries as she flings herself at Andrew.

"There *are* no fairies," says Kate, giving Andrew a cool kiss. "Daddy! I got an A on my report. I want you to come into my room and see it. I brought it home especially to show you."

"That's wonderful, Kate. I'm very proud of you," Andrew says, releasing Nicco and Anna and me with a last hug. "I'll be in to see it in just a minute. Just let me wash up first."

"But Daddy, I want you to come *now*."

"In a minute, Kate. Just let me wash my hands. I wouldn't want to get the report dirty, you know."

"Your hands are never dirty," Kate says, looking at me with pure scorn. She did not tell me about the report.

"There *are* fairies," I say to Anna on the way to the kitchen to check on the eggplant casserole.

"I know," says Anna, unfazed. "There are three in my room right now; I just gave them dinner."

"What did you give them?"

"Eggplant."

Andrew comes into the kitchen, gets down two glasses and a pitcher, takes out an ice tray. Without saying a word he begins to mix a small pitcher of martinis, measuring carefully with a shot glass. I stare at him in amazement.

"What the hell are you doing?" I ask.

"I thought I'd make us a drink. Isn't that what you want me to do, make the drinks?"

"But you don't like martinis."

"I never really said that. And you're right, it would be nice to sit down before dinner, just the two of us. Maybe the children can watch television while we have our drinks. Is anything decent on?"

"I'll look," I say, too stunned to say more.

When we are seated in the living room, martinis in hand, we are going through the motions all right, but it all seems artificial, contrived, right down to the record playing in the background. A good setting, for what I have to say. I taste my martini cautiously. There is far too much vermouth.

"Andrew, do you remember what I was saying, when I was so mad that night, that I'd had it, that I was going to look for a job?"

Andrew finishes chewing his cracker and cheese, swallows, takes a sip of his martini and says, "I remember."

"Well, I am. That is, Lauren gave me the name of a person to call, a woman, an editor at *Free Woman,* it's a woman's magazine, and I'm going to see her tomorrow. It's not for sure or anything, I don't know if I'll even get the job or what kind of job it is . . . but I wanted to tell you."

Andrew looks at me, drinks half his martini in one gulp, stares down at the floor, gulps down the other half, and sets the glass on the coffee table. He does not bother with a coaster. "Well, you've told me."

"Don't you want to hear any more about it? Don't you even want me to tell you why?"

"No. No, I don't. I don't know what you think you're

doing. You have three children. Suppose you get this . . . job, or whatever it is? Are you going to leave the children with a total stranger? Or are they just going to come home to an empty house? Or perhaps a day-care center; there's a day-care center in the cellar across the street."

"It's been defunded. Of course not. Don't be ridiculous. I'm going to find someone, not just anyone, I'm going to find a very good person who'll play with the children and take Nicco to the park and everything. You don't think I'd leave them with just anyone."

"And what are we going to have to pay this very good person? Ninety dollars a week? A hundred dollars a week?"

"*We* aren't going to have to pay her; I'll pay her myself, out of my salary."

"Your salary. Have you ever considered the fact that if you're lucky enough to earn even ten thousand dollars a year, which I strongly doubt, between taxes, this person's salary, carfare, lunches, the clothes you'll need, you will clear something like two thousand dollars a year, if that? That you are leaving your children, one of whom is four years old, for two thousand dollars a year?"

"Andrew, I've thought of all that. I know that. But I'm not going back to work because of the money."

"Most people work for money. Do you know that almost any woman in my office would do anything to be able to stay home? If you feel you have to do something, why not take a part-time job in the mornings, or go back to doing some kind of volunteer work?"

"You *know* what happened at the foundling hospital. And part-time jobs are mostly typing envelopes. They don't pay enough."

"I thought you weren't going back to work because of the money."

"I'm not, not exactly, but I have to do something. I can't stay here anymore, day after day, just cleaning and picking up clothes. Something is happening to me; I'm dizzy all the time. I feel . . . I want to do something. I'll go mad if I don't do something."

"If you really mean that, you should go back to a psychiatrist. God knows you know enough of them; you must have been to at least half the psychiatrists in New York."

"I will not go back to a shrink; most of them are crazy. They're crazier than I am."

"That's interesting, considering all those years and thousands of dollars."

"Most of the time I went was when I was working. I paid for most of it myself."

"While we lived on what I earned."

"I made you a special dinner. I made an eggplant casserole for you."

"Sit down! You say I never talk. I'm talking now."

That's for sure. The words are hitting me like shotgun pellets. Andrew hasn't said this much in thirteen years. If this is communication, I'm not sure I like it. But I sit back down.

"And have you thought about vacations? And what about the summer? We've rented that house for seven years, we've put down a deposit. What did you intend to do with the children during the summer? Send them out to play in front of an open fire hydrant? Or will the fire escape do?"

"I thought I made it clear Andrew, I thought I told you, I would not spend another summer alone in that house with the snapping turtles in the bay and that crazy sniper last year so that I couldn't sleep, I slept with that awful gun under my bed and what's the good of that when we have to keep the bullets in a locked box in the closet because of Nicco and I don't know how to load the goddamn thing anyway and we had to lock all the windows every night and no other children around, just the children bored and fighting all day and afraid to go into the water out front because of the turtles, my God they were as big as Max, I didn't blame them, so we had to drive to the ocean every day, and one crazy mother's helper after another, the last one, I told you, the one whose father was a State Supreme Court Judge, that's all I needed, for him to find out, she went through all my gin, she'd come in after midnight with her blouse all ripped, I had to sit up waiting for her, all right, she helped, but she fell asleep all the time at the beach, I told you, I thought I made it clear, I would not spend another summer alone in that house. You never told me you sent in a deposit."

"You never told me all that. You never said the sitters were crazy."

"I did. I *did* tell you."

"You say so many crazy things I never know when you're serious. You're the original girl who cried wolf."

"Cried wolf. Oh, that's original. That's very witty."

"I don't even believe you about this job."

"This job is real. I am going down tomorrow. And by the way, you'll have to take the children to school. I need the time to get dressed and fixed up and organized. I can't take them tomorrow."

"What time do you supposedly have to be downtown?"

"Twelve-thirty."

"Twelve-thirty. You are actually telling me that you need four hours to get dressed? Has it ever occurred to you that I manage to leave the house fully dressed and intact by eight-thirty, eight when I have to take the children to school, every single morning?"

"All right. But you don't have the other things. You don't have to think about anything else. You don't have to remember about the children, or food, or dates, or sitters. All you have to do is leave. I have a sitter coming at eleven-thirty, a strange sitter from an agency, and I want to show her around and explain about Nicco's bus and everything.

I'm worried about leaving him with a strange sitter myself. You could give me a little support."

"Support. What support have you ever given me? I come home to a madhouse every night with you drunk or screaming and crying and the house a shambles."

"I cleaned the goddamn house today. You bastard. You fucking bastard. I hate your lousy guts."

"That's right, go out to the kitchen and make yourself another drink. That's what you always do when something happens, isn't it, make yourself another drink?"

"You bastard. I'd like to walk out of this house and never come back."

"I'm sure," Andrew says, pouring himself what's left in the martini pitcher, draining it and standing up, "that you would."

During dinner, which Andrew does not comment on, the children sense the tension, a new tension with rules yet unlearned. Without protest they help clear the table. Anna has tears in her eyes but says nothing. When I go to put Nicco to bed Andrew is already there, reading Nicco a story about a bear who sailed around the world on a raft he'd built himself from a magical tree, a tree that doled out daily rations of delicious honey just in time for breakfast, lunch, and dinner. Andrew and Nicco, intent on the story, do not see me.

"But then the little bear grew tired of being alone," Andrew read. "He grew tired of honey every day for breakfast, lunch, and dinner. He missed his mother. He missed his father. He wanted to go home. And so he did. When the little bear got home, his mother and father were so happy to see him. And the little bear told his mother and father all about the strange, exotic lands he'd seen as he sailed around the world. 'But,' said the little bear, 'the best place of all is' . . . where, Nicco?"

"Home!" Nicco yells.

I have read the story so often I know it by heart. Looking at Andrew and Nicco, so happy together, contained in their happiness, I feel lost. Perhaps no one really needs me as much as I think, but the thought, instead of reassuring me, is terrifying. Am I, then, expendable after all?

"I'll kiss you good-night," I say when Andrew has left the room.

"Daddy already did," Nicco says, snuggling down to sleep.

"Well, I want to anyway. Don't go to sleep yet, Nicco, I have to talk to you. When you get home tomorrow, I won't be home. I have to go downtown. A sitter will be here; she'll be downstairs waiting for your bus and then she'll take you upstairs and give you lunch and play games with you, maybe even take you to the park. Do you mind, darling? I won't be gone very long."

"I don't mind," Nicco says. "I like babysitters. Does she look like Zibby, with long hair?"

"I don't know, darling. I don't know what she looks like, but I'm sure she's very nice. Nicco, there's something else I want to tell you. You know there's often an old lady on the corner when your bus comes? Well, just in case the sitter isn't downstairs, I'm sure she will be, but just in case, I want you to go right into the building and ring for the elevator. Don't go anywhere near that old woman; don't talk to her or go near her. She's a little . . . crazy. I don't want to scare you but there are lots of crazy people, sick people, in this city and you have to be careful. Will you promise me not to go anywhere near the crazy old woman?"

"Don't worry, Mom, I'll karate chop her," says Nicco, clenching his fist and jabbing at the air.

"Good boy," I say.

"*Will* you take them in the morning?" I ask Andrew before I go to get ready for bed. He does not look up from the book he is reading.

"I'll take them," he says.

"And will you get rid of that goddamn *stalk* in the dining room? I can't eat, looking at that stalk. It's like eating in the middle of a funeral."

"Anything else?" Andrew asks.

I lie sleepless for a long time under the covers, waiting, but Andrew does not come.

In the morning, when everyone is gone, I feel more lost than ever. I fixed sausages and scrambled eggs for breakfast, but only Anna and Nicco seemed happy. The dead avocado stalk is gone. But I do not have much time. I have to make the beds, straighten up for the sitter, do the dishes, shower, take Max out, leave Andrew's and the pediatrician's number, damn, I should have asked Nina Farrow where we were going so I could have left that number too, fix myself up. By the time I get everything done and am fixed up it is almost eleven. All things considered, I don't look too bad. I took a lot of time with my makeup; my eyes look large and bright. My hair is newly washed and brush-dried; it fluffs out around my face. My samples, pitifully few—ads, a promotional piece for a deodorant, a few booklets—are dusted off and ready in one of Andrew's old attaché cases. But a resumé. They might ask me for a resumé. I rush to the typewriter, which needs a new ribbon, insert a blank piece of white paper, light a cigarette and sit there, thinking. Finally I type my name, address, telephone number, and work experience. The words barely take up a quarter of the page. I add: Personal data. Married for thirteen years. Three children. Thirty-four years old. My husband is a lawyer. I pull the sheet out of the typewriter, crumple it up and stuff it into the bathroom wastebasket. Then I rummage in my top bureau drawer for the blue velvet case that holds my engagement ring, the ring Andrew gave me when I was nineteen, the ring I almost never wear. It is a small, perfect diamond. I do not like diamonds, or at least feel that if you're going to wear one at all, it should be vulgar, enormous. But Andrew insisted upon a diamond, and insisted too that however small, it must be unflawed. I wear the ring only when I feel in need of security; it is a banner, like being pregnant or walking down the street hand in hand with a child. If Nina Farrow sneers at my clothes or puts down my lack of experience, the ring says "fuck you, world. I am loved." I slip it onto my finger over my narrow wedding band and feel like crying.

I would give my soul for a drink but do not dare—I have not had any breakfast—so I sip a cup of coffee, light another cigarette, and go over the reasons I will give to Nina Farrow about going back to work. I cannot at the moment think of any reasons. I can hardly tell her that I am going mad and contemplating suicide within the year.

At twelve o'clock, half an hour late, the doorbell rings and an elderly woman who looks exactly like the lunatic who waits for Nicco's school bus, right down to the sequined hair net, walks shakily in. "I'm Mrs. Morris, from Children, Inc., I hope I'm not too late, I had a terrible night, I could hardly sleep a wink," she croaks. "My arthritis is excruciating, it keeps me up all night; I wouldn't do this for a living if I didn't have to, you know, but my Social Security checks don't even cover . . . my legs are like toothpicks, they snap, all this running around after children, I'm not up to it, I can only accept two jobs a week, all this running, I hope you don't expect me to take him to the park or anything like that. Oh my sakes, I hate dogs, I'm allergic to them, they didn't tell me, does he bite?"

"No, no, he doesn't. He's a very old dog. Mrs. Morris, I'm rather late. The only thing I want to be absolutely certain of is that you meet my little boy's bus at exactly twelve-fifteen downstairs in front of the building. His name is Nicco, he has sort of fuzzy light brown hair and gray eyes, it's a small yellow bus, it stops right in front of the door. His sandwich is in the refrigerator, a peanut butter sandwich. You don't have to take him to the park or anything, just please be sure to meet the bus. It usually comes around twelve-thirty but I want you to go down at twelve-fifteen, we have a problem, there's a woman who . . ."

"I can't stand for fifteen minutes Mrs.—what's your name again?"

"Calder. Mrs. Calder."

"I can't stand for fifteen minutes, Mrs. Calder. Is there a place to sit in the lobby?"

"Well, the thing is, Mrs. Morris, if you stay in the lobby you can't really see the bus when it stops. The couch in the lobby is sort of to the side and you can't see the front door if you're sitting on it."

"Oh I'll see it all right. Don't you fret. Hadn't you better give me your keys?" Mrs. Morris asks, setting her spectacles aright on her squat nose, groping, unable to see the keys I am holding outstretched less than two feet away.

My heart is beating wildly as I ask Stefan I to be sure that Nicco gets into the building safely. "Yes, lady," Stefan I says, smiling. "But if I no down, I cannot, please. No if I up, only please yes if I down."

In front of the building sits a large black dog of indeterminate breed with soulful brown eyes and a pink, lolling tongue. He is wearing a leather collar and a license tag. He looks at me for a moment, then wags his tail and kisses my hand. Automatically, I pat his head. The dog follows me as I head for the bus stop, heeling neatly at crossings. "Go *home,*" I repeat futilely. "Good dog. Good boy. Go *home.*" The dog tries to board the Broadway bus with me, growling hoarsely and baring his teeth when the driver orders him off. I have only fifteen minutes to get down to Fifty-ninth Street, but I cannot leave this dog lost and alone on Broadway. In any case, he will not get off the bus. So I head quickly back to the building, followed by the dog, and ask Stefan I if the dog can sit in the lobby until I get back, hoping that his owner, who must be frantic with worry by now, will come along and see him. I haven't time to check out the license, but he definitely doesn't look like a stray; strays don't wear licenses. Stefan I smiles and semi-bows. He, unlike Stefan II, likes dogs and the dog seems to like him as he speaks to it in Polish.

"Yes please lady," says Stefan.

"Stay," I say sternly to the dog. "I'll figure out everything when I get back." The dog gives me another kiss that sideswipes my hand and leaves a slight but noticeable stain on my pale beige pants.

It is now exactly twelve-twenty. Mrs. Morris is not downstairs yet and the air is slowly moving as I head back for the Broadway bus to keep my appointment with Nina Farrow out there, somewhere, in the great big, real world.

VIII

Nina Farrow is exactly as I pictured her, right down to the hat which is felt and gray and slanted over one eye, except for the melon lipstick which isn't melon but a kind of silvery fuschia; it matches her pointed nails. Exactly. At least it matched her pointed nails when I last saw her today around three; she may be into a whole other color scheme by now. But I'm sure that no matter what color scheme she's into, her lips and nails will match. Exactly.

Sitting on a splashily flowered couch in the waiting room under a huge hovering plant (I was twenty minutes late but was kept waiting anyway), worrying about Nicco and the large black dog, wondering whether or not I would get home in time to meet Anna's bus, I overheard this conversation:

Female voice: "Frank wants to do an article on a nymphomaniac."

Male voice: "So? Find one and do it."

Female voice: "Not so easy. I've made about thirty phone calls, I've checked all the editors. No one *knows* a nymphomaniac. Frank doesn't want a psychiatric-type article; he wants a real, true-to-life, first-person account."

Male voice: "Balls. Don't tell me that in the entire city of New York you can't find a goddamn nymphomaniac. You're just not trying."

Female voice (trembly): "But a first-person account . . ."

Male voice: "Ghosted, for Christ's sake. He means ghosted. You think you're going to find a nymphomaniac who also *writes?*"

Female voice (tearful): "Well *I* didn't know; I've only *been* here three weeks. You don't have to *yell.*"

While I was thinking over this conversation, wondering if I would have the initiative, the aggression, the chutzpah to go out there and find a real-life, honest-to-goodness nymphomaniac and what I would ask her if I did—"Hey sister, so fucking's your bag, is it? Now that I've found you, tell me. Tell it like it is. Forget the tape. Open your heart. Do those multiple orgasms kind of lose their kick after the first hundred and one or so?" (Sobbing Nympho: "Multiple shmultiple. *What* kick? Don't you *read?* I'd sell my soul for *half* an orgasm, a *quarter* orga . . .")—a young girl with false lashes and tightly curled blond hair came out and announced, in awe, that Nina Farrow could see me now. Apparently I had lucked into the right Wednesday. I followed the young girl down a maze of cubicles, doors, and hallways through which sleek people, their arms piled high with papers, dashed busily around, and finally landed in a surprisingly small office. The only touch of elegance was a single rose, slightly wilted, in a slender vase. Photographs of models covered the walls. The metal desk was a wild litter of perfume bottles, lipsticks, blushers, and face cream. Nina Farrow, one ear to the phone, motioned me to one of two straight-backed chairs, riffling through piles of paper with the other hand. She shook her head, looked up at the ceiling wearily, rolled her eyes and finally shouted into the receiver: "What in the name of God do you girls *do* down there, sit on your fat butts polishing your fingernails? I sent those corrections down two days ago, Marge took them down herself and they aren't back yet, I could have typed them myself in ten minutes, what do I have to do to get some action, send a firecracker down the mail chute?"

Nina Farrow did not wait for an answer but slammed the phone down and swiveled around to face me. "Honestly," she said, her voice tap-tapping away as she lit a long, filter-tipped cigarette. "The cretins you have to deal with. They'd do better to pay them to stay home."

I nodded brightly in agreement, my eyes glazing over, wondering if I dared light a cigarette too. I was terrified. When I smiled I felt the corners of my mouth tremble, a fixed, loony leer. I was sweating inside Elly's black wool jacket; I could feel beads of sweat standing out all over my face. My stomach ached.

"We don't have much time, we have to meet Frank in ten minutes, Frank Johnson, our articles editor. Marge got my schedule fouled up, *naturally,* she forgot that I had a luncheon meeting with Frank, but Lauren's *such* a dear, *such* a good friend I didn't want to cancel out, I thought you might as well tag along, I'd just like to get a slight run-down first. You're a good friend of Lauren's I take it? Well. What have you been doing with yourself?" said Nina Farrow, glancing at the enormous black-faced watch taking up most of her slender wrist. The numerals looked like baby shark's teeth.

What have I been doing with myself. Cleaning up dog shit. Cleaning toilet bowls. Cooking dinner. Taking care of children. Do not mention children.

"I . . . well, as Lauren told you I guess, yes, I am a pretty good friend of hers, I did some work with her at the agency, at Martin, Minor, Fellow and Flynn. I worked at the agency for two and a half years. Actually, I started as a secretary but I was promoted very quickly, I became a junior copywriter in, oh, about seven months. I worked . . ."

"Aren't you a bit warm in that jacket? Why don't you slip it off?"

I slipped off the jacket, smelling the sharp tangy smell of my own sweat, plus a faint odor of Elly. I straightened the collar of Elly's blouse. It looked wrinkled. In the light that streamed in from Nina Farrow's window, I noticed that it really did not match my pants.

"Thank you. Yes. So I worked at the agency, on the . . . God, it's insane but I can't remember the name of the account, it was for a tranquilizer, isn't that insane? Anyway it was the one, you probably remember it, the one with the woman sitting on a flowered couch with her head in her hands, 'Are you anxious, bored, depressed?' the copy went, I remember that. Wait, I think I have a copy of it in my briefcase." I bent down and desperately grabbed a handful of papers. "I thought perhaps you'd like to see some samples of my work."

Nina Farrow held the samples between two fingers, looked at them for a moment, smiled, handed them back to me and said, "God. The things they used to do in those days. Sad, wasn't it?"

"Yes, yes it was. It was sad."

"Did you enjoy your work?"

"I . . . oh yes, very much. I've always been very active, very interested in working."

"But . . ." Nina Farrow tapped her gold pen on the desk, swiveled around so that she was in living profile, her nose narrow and slightly pointed at the tip, swiveled back again so suddenly I jumped. "That gap. That ghastly *gap.*"

"Gap? What gap?" All I could think of was the view my obstetrician-gynecologist must have at my Pap test.

"The gap in your *career.*" Nina Farrow said patiently.

"Oh. That gap."

"I understand that you have not worked in over ten years," she continued. "Why?"

"Why?"

"Yes. Why?"

"Oh. Well, actually I worked almost right through to the end of my first . . . pregnancy. I wanted very much to continue working but . . . perhaps Lauren told you, I've kept busy with various free-lance jobs, some of the same I just showed you . . . I found, I felt that . . . my husband wanted a family, you see . . . the demands of three children on top of a full-time job would be . . . a bit too much to handle."

"Ah." Nina Farrow looked at me, leaned back in her swivel chair, curled one corner of her silvery-fuschia top lip.

"Until," I hurried on, "until of course I realized how boring, how wasted my life was, and the moment I realized that, that all I wanted, all I needed, was to get back to work, I made all the arrangements, I have this fantastic live-in nanny who's totally taken over, taken total charge, and of course the two older children are older now, they're in school most of the day, I hardly even see them, all three children have dinner with the nanny and everything. My time is totally my own now and I want to use that time in a useful, fulfilling way."

The whole thing was beginning to come on like a soap opera; I couldn't believe the inanities that were spewing out of my crazed mouth until I remembered. I'd heard, word for word, the same lines while watching television with Mother in the loony bin. Nina Farrow, however, perked up, looked more interested.

"So you found, did you, that playing wife and Mommy wasn't all it was cracked up to be? You're sorry now that you married and had children?"

God forgive me.

"Yes."

"Well!" Nina Farrow said. "That's exactly the point

we're trying to get across to our readers. Freedom. Independence. Total autonomy. No ties. Personal fulfillment above all else."

"Yes. I noticed that in your last issue."

"You read our magazine then?"

"Oh yes, absolutely. Every month."

"Did you see my article on the now no-brow in the February issue? I thought that was rather superb myself. Silly little model, she didn't want us to shave off her brows at first but I talked her into it. And now the entire country is picking up the look! Superb, wasn't it?"

"Yes. Superb."

"And that title, the now . . . no-brow. It really caught the theme, the mood, didn't it?"

"Yes, it really did. It really caught the mood."

Nina Farrow laughed softly, a back-patting laugh. "But here I am, running on and on, and we're here to find out about you, aren't we?"

"Yes. I . . . yes, we are."

"Well then. *Let's* talk about you. Give me a little rundown on your talents, your interests. What do you like to do?"

What do I like to do. Eat. Drink. Laugh. Fuck.

"I'm . . . very interested in . . . well, I guess what you're trying to get across in *Free Woman*. Freedom. Independence. Total autonomy. No ties. I think that women have been put down too long, put themselves down too long too, actually. I'm very interested in getting that point across to other women. And I'm very interested in personal fulfillment, developing my own interests, putting myself first for a change."

"Could you be a little more specific?" asked Nina Farrow, checking her makeup in a large magnifying mirror.

"Oh yes. Yes of course. Well, I have many interests. I'm interested in beauty and fashion and art, I'm sort of a gourmet cook too, and of course I do have some copywriting experience. I think my interests and experience might be of some value to you. I think I could really be of some value to *Free Woman*."

"I wonder that you didn't call up your old agency. Is there any particular reason you feel that editorial work is more fulfilling than advertising?" Nina Farrow asked.

I did not call up my old agency because my ex-boss was fired a year and a half ago and is still unemployed, Willie is, as far as I know, still in Arkansas running the orphans' home, and the only other person I know well enough to call is drying out in a sanitarium. Except for Lauren, I have no contacts.

"Oh. Well, I didn't call up my old agency because I feel that advertising—of course, I know it's necessary; I'm not naive—but advertising is sort of, it can tend to be sort of a rat race, not that I mind hard work, I've always kept very busy, but it can tend to be, well, let's face it, a little . . . phony. I'd much rather be involved with something real, with a magazine like *Free Woman*, a magazine that is trying to help women fulfill themselves. I think *Free Woman* would offer much more scope for my interests, that I could help other women fulfill themselves and fulfill myself at the same time."

Working for *Free Woman* would also get me *out of the house,* away from the gin and peanut butter.

"The more I listen to you, Liza, I think so too," said Nina Farrow, checking her reflection in the magnifying mirror again, adding a touch of lipstick, standing and putting her hand on my shoulder as she firmly guided me toward the door.

"Thank you very much, Ms. Farrow."

"Call me Nina," said Nina Farrow.

"Thank you very much, Nina," said I.

Marge, Nina Farrow's tightly curled secretary, looked

up at me enviously as we passed. One of her false lashes was askew. Her long calico skirt seemed to be wilting, like a heat-drenched summer garden. She looked tired.

"Have those letters ready by the time I get back; they have to go out this afternoon," Nina Farrow said.

"Yes, Ms. Farrow," said Marge.

"And *try* to get my phone messages straight this time, will you, darling? I couldn't even *read* them yesterday."

"I'll try, Ms. Farrow," said Marge, her cheek muscles clenching.

In the waiting room we picked up Frank, the articles editor. Frank, unlike most of the staff, is not sleek. My first impression was of a short, fat obscene little man with darting blue eyes and white hair cut in a crew cut, almost shaved. He was wearing a dark red shirt, a floppy red and white polka-dotted tie, a light gray suit, and shiny shoes with buckles. When we arrived he was looking at his watch and tapping his foot.

"For Christ's sake, Nina!" said Frank, ignoring me. "It's one twenty-five already."

"Now Frank, darling," said Nina, bending down and giving him an airy kiss on top of his head. "Don't be nasty. We're only a few minutes late. I want you to meet Liza Calder. Liza will be joining us for lunch; she's a friend, a very *good* friend, of Lauren Isaacson's."

"Friend of Lauren's, huh?" said Frank, giving my hand a limp shake. His palms were unpleasantly damp. "You know who she looks like, Nina? She looks just like Karen Miller. Doesn't she look just like Karen Miller, Nina?"

"She doesn't look *anything* like Karen Miller," Nina said. "Come along, darlings, where *is* the elevator?"

In the restaurant, which was wooded, brightly lit, and jammed with people, we were whisked past the front door line-up and seated at a round table in the center of the room. I never sit in the center of any room. I always keep my back against a solid wall. Just in case. The waiter hovered.

"What would you like to drink?" Nina asked.

"Oh, thank you, but I never drink in the daytime, I'm not used to it, it makes me sort of drowsy," I said.

"Are you sure, darling?"

"Yes. Yes, really."

"Two martinis then, on the rocks, very dry," said Nina to the waiter.

My mouth was aching with saliva. I could hear those cubes rattling already. Juniper! My trusted friend! If ever I needed you, now's the time.

"Uh, actually, maybe I'll try one too," I said. "I don't want to make you feel uncomfortable. I don't want to be odd girl out or anything."

Nina and Frank laughed. I felt better, more with it, more like one of the crowd.

"What we need, what we are in desperate need of at *Free Woman,* are fresh new *ideas,*" Nina Farrow said after the martinis arrived. "Isn't that right, Frank?"

"Yeah, that's right," Frank said, staring lewdly at my breasts which, I noticed, were pointing like two unfurled flags through Elly's silky beige blouse.

"We *all* contribute, right down to the last little associate editor. We all sit down every Monday morning and talk over ideas. That's what's so fantastic, so marvelous about working for *Free Woman.* You, for instance, you, if you joined the staff, would have the same opportunity to use your imagination, contribute. Isn't that right, Frank?"

"Right," Frank said, still staring at my breasts.

"My, these are strong," I said.

"My God, this martini is ghastly, simply drowning in vermouth. Waiter!" Nina Farrow said.

"That nymphomaniac idea, for instance, remember, Frank?" Nina Farrow said when her new, drier martini had arrived and been tasted for approval, "that was so . . . so extremely creative, so fantastic. And *where* did it come from? Just guess."

"I've never had a drink this strong, in the daytime that is," I said.

"Go ahead. Just take a guess."

"From a nymphomaniac?" I asked. It just came out.

Nina and Frank roared with laughter. I even chuckled a little myself.

"A nymphomaniac! Isn't that a scream? This girl has real humor!" Nina said, rocking back and forth. "No, darling, it came . . . you absolutely won't believe this . . . from a nobody, an absolute nobody, an associate food editor, a silly little mouse with stringy hair and glasses. Incredible! Of course it's basically Frank's idea now, he's enlarged on the theme, outlined the approach, but from a tiny little mouse in the food department! Isn't that incredible?"

"Incredible," I said, finishing my martini and wanting another.

"All we have to do now is find one," Frank said, visually unbuttoning my blouse.

"I wonder . . . this would be rather unfair, right off the top of your head of course," Nina said, "but I wonder if *you* have any fresh new ideas along that line—you're up to date on what we've done recently; you're a regular reader of *Free Woman*—any ideas at all that would help *Free Woman*'s readers understand themselves just a teeny bit better, cope with the great big world."

Fresh new ideas along that line. My dog had an orgasm before I did? I was sucked to ecstasy by a werewolf? Fucked by Gentle Ben? My mind was a washed slate. The only picture that sprang to mind was sweet nude Willie atop the Plaza fountain, jerking off to infinity.

"Have you ever done a really comprehensive article on masturbation?" I asked wildly, sweating again.

"Do you know, incredibly enough, we haven't. That's an incredible idea, a fan*tas*tic idea; we could even work in the myth of the vaginal orgasm. All these *myths,* all these *sha*dows that keep women from fulfilling themselves. You really have the *Free Woman* feeling. Doesn't she have the *Free Woman* feeling, Frank? Darling, I know it's unfair, you'll want to trot on home and do a total outline, of course, but I wonder . . . what *are* your thoughts on masturbation?"

My thoughts on masturbation, right off the top of my head, were these: It is absolutely okay if you're anxious, bored, depressed and have nothing much else to do, or even if you have something to do—like going to the supermarket or defrosting the refrigerator—but aren't in the mood. It will not cause mental illness or complexion problems. It feels fine. It does not however, in most cases, measure up to fucking with a real live man. The feeling is simply not the same. In my opinion.

"Oh. Well, I think that . . . any kind of pleasure . . . I mean, total autonomy certainly entails . . . masturbation. And there you might be some night, I mean, I'm sure *Free Woman*'s readers are so attractive and sophisticated they can have a man any time they want one, but some night there you might be, home alone after work, totally free, without any ties, and your career might be so exciting and demanding that you might not feel up to going out and finding a man or it might be raining or something, so you could just . . masturbate."

"You look just like Karen Miller. Doesn't she look just like Karen Miller, Nina?" asked Frank.

"Darling, I *told* you, she doesn't look *anything* like Karen Miller," Nina said. "You know sweetie, while you were talking—you go ahead with a total outline; that was a fantastic presentation—I had this superb idea. I probably shouldn't speak out like this, it's only because I'm really becoming quite fond of you, but if you lost ten pounds, just ten teeny pounds, you'd be an absolute knockout. Maybe we could do a make-over, a total make-over, before and after pictures, makeup, exercise, diet, hair—we'd have to use a wig of course, your hair's too short to do anything *with*—your eyes . . ."

"My eyes? You want to make over my *eyes?*" I had a horrible vision of Nina cutting out my pupils and replacing them with something more knockout.

"Contacts, darling, contacts. With that hair you'd look much better in green. How do you photograph?"

"I photograph pretty well, I guess."

"I'll tell you what. Bring in some pictures, just snapshots will do, and then we'll see. I have a feeling it would turn out fantastically—housewife returning to work turns over a new leaf, et cetera, et cetera. That's actually a fantastic idea now that I think of it. Isn't that a fantastic idea, Frank?"

"Let's eat," Frank said, his eyes traveling below my belt.

Frank ordered beef Stroganoff and noodles. I followed Nina's lead and chose chef's salad with lemon juice dressing. There was a great deal of tongue in the salad. A ghostly, sad-eyed steer floated reproachfully before my eyes for a moment, stuck out its tongue, and disappeared.

"My *God,*" Nina Farrow said, slamming down her fork after one bite and signaling the waiter. "This salad is *ghastly,* it's simply reeking of oil."

Frank looked at me wearily. "Every time we have lunch, every goddamn time we have lunch, it's something," he said. "There's too much vermouth or the coffee isn't hot enough or the silverware isn't clean." He turned on Nina. "Can't we ever have lunch in peace?"

"Complaints, nothing but complaints," said Nina.

The conversation had a vaguely familiar ring.

As we were finishing our lunch Nina Farrow looked

at me intently. "I like this girl, Frank, I really do," she said. "I really think she might be an asset to *Free Woman.*"

"So where can we put her?" Frank asked, chomping away on pecan pie and bumping my knee with his own.

"Well, darling, there only *are* two openings, and I *do* think Liza might have a bit of trouble handling that do in the fashion department; we have to get her back in circulation first, give her time to get acclimated, find herself, find her niche. But I think she could certainly handle the 'Letters to the Editor' column; it's being passed from editor to editor, Susan left two months ago and *someone's* got to take it on. It's more or less your department, actually it isn't really anyone's department, but basically she'd be working under you. Don't you think she could work under you, Frank?"

"Yeah," said Frank, bumping my knee again. "Sure she could."

I edged my legs a little farther to the left. Frank glared.

It was by then almost three o'clock. My poor Anna. I didn't like the idea of her riding up alone with Stefan II and finding a strange sitter in the house. I also wanted to check up on Nicco, but didn't dare excuse myself to find the telephone. It seemed unprofessional.

"Well, what do you think?" Nina Farrow asked. "Do you think you could handle it?"

Handle it? Handle what? All I could think of were the gaily beribboned handlebars on Nicco's tricycle. How long had I been semi-comatose? I looked at Nina Farrow blankly, blinking, my mouth slightly open.

"The Letters to the *Editor* column," Nina said as if speaking to a small, not-too-bright child. "Answering letters that come in. On a variety of subjects that concern our readers: beauty, sex, various problems. Do you think you could handle it?"

"Helping solve other people's problems you mean? Yes, I think I could handle that. I think I'd like that."

"And on the side of course, as we've said, you could always try out article ideas. Most of our articles are assigned, but quite a few of our editors take on assignments successfully."

"That sounds great. I'd like very much to try that."

I was finding it difficult to concentrate due to a sudden sensation that something was happening down around my pelvis, a pinging twinge and then a faint wetness. I shifted my buttocks but the sensation continued. Yes, definitely, there went another one. I was bleeding, seeping clotted puddles. And Elly's black jacket barely reached down to the end of my ass. If I got up to go to the ladies' room, I would have to walk away from Frank and Nina, and I did not know the state of the seat of my pants. I wanted to cry. I wanted to go home. I could feel a drop of blood detach itself from a giant clot, hesitate, then trickle slowly down my right inner thigh.

"Marvelous!" said Nina Farrow. "Now. We don't want to rush you. You go home and think it over, *we'll* think it over, send us some more samples, work on your masturbation outline. Then we'll talk, what's today, Wednesday? Yes, we'll talk, say, Friday. Call me Friday. Not before ten, or between one and three, or after five-thirty. Of course the decision isn't mine alone, but most of the letters *are* concerned with beauty, and if you want a hint, just a teeny hint, I think everything will work out swimmingly. Don't you think everything will work out swimmingly, Frank?"

"You talk too goddamn much, Nina," said Frank, signing the credit card form, standing up and brushing pecan pie crumbs off his crotch.

I should have left my knee where it was.

"Which way are you headed?" Nina asked, applying

a new coat of silvery-fuschia lipstick, patting her nose with a puff, and also standing up.

"Oh, you two go on ahead. Actually, I have to make a phone call, I had another interview lined up but now that I've spoken to you I think I'll just call and cancel it," I said, pressing my legs together.

"But darling," Nina said when I made no effort to get up, "We can't just leave you *sitting* here like this."

"Yes. Yes you can. I often . . . just sit like this. Really."

"Well, if you're sure," Nina said doubtfully. On their way out Frank muttered something and I heard Nina hiss: "Don't be a fool, Frank. Last month Lauren's ads alone totalled . . ."

I tied Elly's black jacket around my waist by the arms, the way we used to tie our sweaters at school, and edged carefully toward the ladies' room. There was, thank God, a Kotex machine. The situation, though messy, was not as bad as I'd thought; there were only two stains on the upper inside of my pants—most of the blood had been caught by my underpants and girdle. Kind of a tie-dyed effect, just the touch of red Elly had been looking for until she found the beads. I wiped off as much as I could, sponged the blood off my thighs with a piece of wet toilet paper, peed, dried myself, got the Kotex into place, pulled my underpants, girdle, and pants back on, put on Elly's jacket and checked myself in the mirror. The evidence was hidden, almost. On my way to the door I glanced at our now-empty table. There was a tiny smear of blood on the white leather chair. My chair. I looked at my face in the mirrored wall.

"Who is Karen Miller?" I asked my face.

It was by then so late I hailed the first cab I could find. When I reached our lobby the large black dog was still there, waiting, guarding the door. Stefan II did not look happy.

"Lady, lady," he said. "Stefan tell me keep for you. I no keeper for nothing. Why you want dog like wolf? Black. Cheap. Cheapest building I ever work. Jews. Dogs. Hippies. Dirty hippies."

This last to the retreating form of a bearded man in denims from the eighth floor who is one of the foremost geophysicists in the country.

"I will tip you Stefan," I said with dignity as the dog took a loving sniff of my ass, followed me into the elevator, and gave Stefan II a vicious stare, "as soon as I get some change."

I opened the door on a frantic Mrs. Morris, minus her hairnet, a sobbing Anna and a red-faced, angry-looking Nicco. "My sakes, what's that, not another dog. What's wrong with this child, I've never stayed with a child like this, never in my life," said Mrs. Morris. "He keeps punching me, trying to trip me, he keeps sneaking up behind me and twisting my arm behind my back, once I fell down on the floor. But I fixed him all right."

"Fixed him? What do you mean?"

"I mean I spanked him. I had just about enough. That fixed him all right. You see how quiet he is now?"

"You spanked my child?"

"She did, Mommy, she hit him with Kate's ruler; I saw her do it myself," Anna sobbed.

My whole body shook with fury. I could have killed that old woman, strangled her with my two shaking hands. Although I have often been tempted to buy a bullwhip, nobody beats up my own kids but me. Andrew does not believe in hitting children. I do not believe in hitting children either; I just get intense personal enjoyment out of it sometimes. But only sometimes. And only open-handed. And only my own hand. For the first time in my life, I understood the concept of murder.

"Get out of here," I shrieked over the black dog's savage growls, flinging money and pushing Mrs. Morris out the door. "I'm going to report you to the agency. I'm going to call the police."

"No wonder," Mrs. Morris said, intimidated but not through yet as she beat a tottering path toward the elevator, "you have a terrible child like this. All these newfangled ideas. All these notions. Spare the rod and spoil the child, that's what I always say."

"Out, out, out!" I shrieked.

"You forgot to pay me my carfare," Mrs. Morris said as the elevator doors opened. I removed one red shoe and threw it at Mrs. Morris. The doors closed.

When Anna's sobbing and the black dog's growls had quieted down, I made myself a martini, swallowed a Librium, and took Nicco on my lap.

"Nicco, Mrs. Morris shouldn't have done what she did, it was an awful thing to do, but why were you trying to trip her, hitting her like that?"

"But Mom, you told me to," Nicco said.

"Nicco, I never told you any such thing."

"Yes. Yes you did. You said watch out for the crazy old lady. And I said I'd karate chop her. And you said good boy."

"Oh Nicco. Oh no. It wasn't *that* old lady I meant, it was another old lady. Oh God."

"It was awful, Mommy, awful, she just kept on hitting and hitting him; she must have hit him about a hundred times," Anna sobbed, wiping fresh tears away. "Where *were* you, Mommy? You never told me you wouldn't be home today."

"Not a hundred. More like three," Nicco said.

"It was at *least* five," Anna said.

"Nicco darling, tell me, did she hurt you very badly? Let me see. If she hurt you I'll call the police right now. I'll have her put away so far she'll never get out. I'll have her put in jail. I'll take her to court for a sanity hearing. Believe me, there are places for people like this."

"No, Mom, old bitch, forget it. Old fuckhead, next time I'll kung fu her," Nicco said. "What's that dog? Can we keep it?"

"I don't think so, darling, I think it's someone else's dog. I think it's just lost. I'll tell you what, when we walk over to the bus stop to pick up Kate, we'll take the dog with us, we'll stop for ice cream, that way maybe its owner will see it. I thought someone would come for it right away. Actually, maybe I should call the ASPCA first; its owner may have reported it missing."

As I bent down to look at its license tag, the large black dog wagged its tail. The date on the license tag was 1972. I called the ASPCA anyway. The ASPCA answered after nine rings. The voice on the other end of the line informed me that the license bureau was now closed; I would have to call back in the morning. I left my name and number anyway.

"I wouldn't count on anything, Ma'am," said the voice. "Most people, if they let a tag expire, they've just abandoned the dog. They've just taken the dog somewhere and let him go."

"But he doesn't look like a stray; he's so friendly," I said, already knowing, foreseeing, that the voice was right.

"Well, I'm just telling you from past experience, Ma'am," the voice said. "You've got an abandoned dog there."

"But what should I *do?* I can't keep him; I've already *got* a dog. I've got another male."

"Well, Ma'am, if you really care about the dog your

best bet would be to keep him overnight and check the license bureau in the morning. Or if you can't keep him you can turn him in here or at your local precinct and we'll pick him up there."

"My local *precinct?* What . . . would you put him in a cage or anything overnight? I don't think he'd like to be put in a cage; he's very large. Very friendly."

"As I said, Ma'am, your best bet, if you really care about the dog, would be to keep him overnight. Once we pick them up, we keep them forty-eight to seventy-two hours. You then have the chance to adopt the dog, if we can't find the owner and nobody's claimed him."

"And then?"

"Then we put them up for adoption; we keep them from three to five days, depending."

"Depending? Depending on what?"

"Let's put it this way, Ma'am. Your best bet, if you really care about the dog, would be at least to keep him overnight. Why don't you think about keeping him? You'd be surprised how fast two dogs, even males, take to each other sometimes. Why don't you give it a try?"

"It's really funny," I said to Anna when I hung up. "He doesn't look like a stray at all. God, maybe he is a stray, though; maybe he's starving."

"I wonder what Max will think when he comes out from under the bed," Anna said, her arms around the large black dog's neck.

As soon as I began to open a can of dog food Max darted out from the bedroom, took one look at the large black dog, and came to a skidding halt just outside the kitchen door. The two dogs eyed each other cautiously. Max entered the kitchen and circled the large black dog slowly. He went into a sudden yipping, snapping fit, making energetic jealous feints at the large black dog, who looked disdainfully down at him. One bite of those massive jaws, however, and good-bye Max. So I picked Max up, suffering a small nip in the process, and locked him in the bedroom. Max howled. The large black dog was right behind me.

"Come on, old boy, I bet you're pretty hungry," I said as he followed me back to the kitchen. The dog sniffed the dish of dog food, paused, took one bite, sighed and pressed his heavy body against me. He looked sad.

"Okay, baby, we'll get you home," I said.

"I am home," said those soulful brown eyes.

I quickly made up some posters describing the dog —large black dog, possible shepherd-retriever-collie mix; plumed tail; male—and giving my name and telephone number. As I was working on the eleventh poster, the doorbell rang.

"Isn't it time to pick up Kate?" Anna asked, patting the dog's head. His head was resting in my lap.

"Mother, where *were* you?" Kate said when I opened the front door. "I waited and waited. You *know* I'm afraid to walk home in this neighborhood; you said *yourself* it wasn't safe. One of your shoes is out by the elevator. Good God, what's *that?*"

"A dog. A large black dog that I found. And as soon as I change my pants we're going to take him out and walk him through the neighborhood and put up these posters."

"You might at least say you're *sorry,*" said Kate.

"Why do you have to change your pants, Mom?" Nicco asked.

"Because they're sort of messy. I had a slight accident downtown. I forgot that my period was due and I didn't have any Kotex with me so I have to change my pants."

"Period, comma, question mark!" said Nicco.

"Oh. *That,*" Kate said with distaste.

"Can I watch, Mom?" said Nicco.

"*No.* Absolutely not. Put on your shoes."

I slipped into the bedroom, almost closing the door

on the large black dog's nose, left my bloodied pants, girdle, and underpants on the bed, got out my sanitary belt and changed into clean underpants and jeans. I was, unfortunately, completely out of Kotex. The moment I closed the door the large black dog began to hurl his body at the door, scratching and crying. I could hear the sounds of falling plaster and paint.

"I'm sorry, baby," I said to Max as I slipped out the door into the waiting paws of the large black dog.

When we returned from Scotch-taping posters up and down West End and Broadway, with the dog tugging and dragging and Kate complaining all the way, Andrew was home, standing in the hall, still in his raincoat. He looked pale and terrified.

"Liza, where *were* you? I came home and went into the bedroom to change, I thought maybe you'd gone out on an errand or something, and I found this terrible bloody pile of clothes and Max had peed all over the floor. What in the name of God is *that?*" Andrew said, shaken.

"Just a dog I found. He was wearing a license so I thought I could find his owner right away, but actually the license is old, from seventy-two, so I have to wait until morning to call the ASPCA again, the license bureau was closed. He's only staying this one night. He's very gentle, very friendly. He doesn't seem like a stray. I was saying to Anna before, he doesn't seem like a stray at all."

Andrew just stood there, looking at me. The children were all tugging at him at once. The large black dog was guarding me with his body, looking at Andrew.

"It looked like an ax murder," Andrew said.

"What did?"

"Those clothes. That awful pile of clothes on the bed."

"Oh Andrew," I said, hugging him and laughing. "I had sort of an accident downtown, my period started downtown, that's all. Didn't you see, the blood was only in my pants?"

"No, I just saw blood," Andrew said, glancing at the children. "Couldn't you at least have put them in the laundry?"

I stopped laughing. "I *would* have put them in the laundry," I said, "except when I got home the dog was still here and I wanted to change and tape the posters up as soon as I could, so I just threw the clothes on the bed."

"Yes, you were so busy making posters about a *dog* you forgot to pick me *up,*" Kate said.

"Dad! A bad, crazy old lady beat me up with a ruler, but I won! I karate chopped her, just like on TV!" Nicco said.

"It's true, Daddy," Anna said, her eyes filling again. "And when I came home I didn't even know where Mommy was. I was scared."

"Who beat you up? Liza, what is this all about?" Andrew asked.

"Oh, actually she didn't really beat him up. We had this problem with a sitter, an old woman from an agency, and Nicco got her confused with another old woman, the crazy woman I told you about, the one who waits for his bus, so he acted up quite a bit, I guess, hitting her and tripping her, so she finally just hit him a few times. I've looked. There isn't a mark on him. He's fine. I mean, I was pretty upset myself when I first heard about it, but now I . . ."

"But she hit him with a ruler! Did you call the agency?"

"Well, no. No I didn't. I got a little mixed up over the dog and calling the ASPCA and everything."

"So because of a goddamn dog you forget to pick up your daughter, and in a neighborhood like this too! You forget to tell Anna you won't be home. And on top of it all you forget to call an agency that's sent you a sitter who beats up your four-year-old son. That's charming. You've done a lot of crazy things in your time, but today really tops them all."

"It wasn't only the dog," I said defensively. "I was downtown all afternoon at the interview, at my job interview, and . . ."

"Oh yes, the *job* interview," Andrew said, more furious than ever. "We musn't forget the all-important *job* interview. What will happen when and if you actually *work?* Will you forget you *have* a family?"

"Don't talk to me that way! I'm doing the best I can!" I yelled.

"Please don't fight, Mommy," Anna begged, really crying by then. "Why don't you sit down and have a drink with Daddy?"

"I will in a minute, baby," I said, struggling for control. "I just have to run down to the drugstore and buy some Kotex. I forgot to buy Kotex while we were out."

"You've forgotten so many things today," Anna said, giggling nervously, between tears and laughter. "Maybe you forgot to buy something to drink, too."

"That is one thing she never forgets," said Andrew, picking Nicco up in his arms and carrying him into the living room to search for bruises.

"Fuck you," I said to the closed door as I rang for Stefan II.

"You want to be dog keeper for nothing, okay. I no want to be dog keeper for nothing," said Stefan II the moment the elevator doors opened.

"I will tip you on my way back, Stefan; I'm on my way to the drugstore," I said.

"Fuck you too," I thought.

During dinner the large black dog sat politely in a corner, not even reacting when Nicco dropped a chicken leg on the floor.

"You see how well behaved he is?" I remarked to the company at large. "Max is always begging."

"Mommy, don't you think though, Max must feel

kind of sad, all locked up like that? He must think we like this dog better. Maybe he thinks we're going to give him away," Anna said worriedly.

"Anna's right," Andrew said later as were getting ready for bed. "It's ridiculous to lock Max up and let the other dog have the freedom of the apartment. I'm going to barricade him in the dining room for the night." I could hear the sounds of moving furniture and then the dog's cries and barks.

"Why are you so concerned about Max all of a sudden?" I asked when Andrew returned. "You don't like dogs. You've never liked Max."

"I like dogs."

"No. No you don't. You don't understand about dogs or people or women or love or . . . anything. How can you understand about love if you don't even like dogs?"

"I only know," said Andrew, getting into his pajamas, "that you have apparently devoted most of the day to a strange dog and forgotten about three children you supposedly love. It's something you do consistently."

"I do not. I never forget the children. I love the children. I'm going to call the agency in the morning, I nearly called the police, I nearly killed her, you're making me feel as if leaving them for a few hours amounts to child neglect, abuse, or something. And by the way, I called Barbara Schmidt, B.J.'s mother, before I called the agency I was trying to find Nicco a date, I called about ten mothers, and she wanted to know if you knew of a lawyer. She's broke and her ex-husband took B.J. for Easter vacation and won't let him come home."

"Maybe. I'll ask around. I don't mean just the children. On the outside you're the great humanitarian, the great lover of humanity, you want to help everybody, and you treat the people close to you like shit. You treat me like shit."

Shit? Andrew never says "shit."

"That's not true."

"Look at that dog. Why did you have to take in that dog?"

"And I did not devote most of the day to that dog. I told you, I went downtown for my interview today. I was down there being interviewed for hours. I'm exhausted."

"How did it go, your interview?"

"It went very well. The job sounds fantastic. I'm only one of a lot of people being considered of course, but I think it went well. It's a terrific job."

"Doing what?"

"Well, editing, sort of. Being in charge of a column."

"Why are you crying?"

"Because . . . I don't know why I'm crying. I don't *know* why. I want . . . I want . . . oh Andrew, I don't know what I want. Just hold me."

Andrew took me in his arms and gently stroked my hair. He wiped my tears away with his fingers, one by one.

"Not to make love. Just hold me," I said again.

Andrew tucked me into the curve of his body, pulled up the covers, and turned out the light.

"I want you to go to sleep now," he said.

But I could not sleep. At around one A.M. there was a terrible crash from the dining room. When we got up to investigate we found, in a sea of broken bottles spilling liquid, the large black dog. He had overturned all of Andrew's barricades—a heavy footlocker, Nicco's tricycle, a wrought-iron tea wagon holding six bottles of wine and my private hoard of gin—to go back home to mother. Mother me.

IX

That was yesterday. Or rather, early this morning. As Andrew flatly refused to sleep in the same room with a strange dog, we locked Max in and the large black dog out. He barked and cried until two when I got up, locked the bedroom door, got a blanket and pillow from the linen closet and went out to sleep on the couch, mumbling something about it only being for one night. Andrew said nothing but turned over and rolled himself into a tight, disapproving ball. It is now four and I am sitting in the kitchen, the dog at my feet, waiting for the coffee to percolate and the sun to come up. I could not get back to sleep. Anna woke once around two-thirty but after checking on me, fell asleep again. Alone in the grayish dawn, I feel strangely at peace. In the lighted square of a window across the street, a naked girl is dancing. Modern jazz. Silent drums. When the coffee is ready I pour a cup and scribble ideas for writing samples on a scratch pad. After the sudden cool of yesterday, the weather seems to be turning warm again; it smells of summer. I open the kitchen window, which Andrew always closes, hang my robe on the back of the chair and keep on writing. Until Nicco wakes at six there is no sound but the dog's regular breathing. He is tired; he sleeps with his head on one clumsy paw, his nostrils twitching.

As soon as I get back from taking the children to school (to make up, among other things, for not having taken them yesterday), stopping off for a new typewriter ribbon and a bottle of gin on my way, I call the ASPCA license bureau. There is no answer. I keep on calling. Finally a deep-down-Dixie female black voice, quite different from the male red-necked drawl I talked to yesterday, picks up. I hear funky laughter in the background. After a long wait the voice comes up with this information:

"De dawg register to a Mr. L. Rodriguez up on Hundred sixty-eight Street. De telephone number 567-0238."

"Oh thank God. Thank you! I'm so glad you still have it on record. That's wonderful!" Relief floods my soul.

"Dat don't mean nuthin'," says the voice darkly. "Seventy-two license, he probly not dere. Mens like dat, dey moves all de time. Dey on de run."

"Well, I'm going to try anyway; I'm going to call right now," I say, still undaunted. "What's the dog's name by the way? Just to be sure I have the right owner. Is the dog's name on the registration?"

There is a long, pregnant pause backed by heavy breathing.

"De dawg name Spook," says the voice.

I call Mr. L. Rodriguez. On the seventh ring, a woman answers.

"Hello, Mrs. Rodriguez?" I say brightly. "You and your husband will be happy to know that I think I've found your dog."

"Who you callin' Mizz Rodriguez, who you think I am you honky bitch, you think I give my body to some motherfuckin' *Spic?*" says definitely-not-Mrs.-Rodriguez, slamming down the phone.

Shaking but determined, I call every L. Rodriguez in the telephone book. There are eleven of them. Three telephones have been disconnected; the other eight L. Rodriguez' scream at me in vitriolic Spanish. From my minimal knowledge of Spanish, I think they are screaming at me for having woken them up.

I telephone my local precinct, ask if anyone has inquired about the dog, and then give a description of the dog, my name and telephone number to a bored-sounding desk sergeant. The only lost-dog inquiry, the sergeant says wearily, above screams and scuffling noises, involves a white standard poodle named Alfred. Distinguishing feature: one testicle.

When I hang up the large black dog stands, shakes himself, and kisses my knee. "Spook?" I say. "Spook?" The dog's ears shoot up, his eyes brighten, he hurls himself at me joyfully and buries his long wet nose in my armpit.

Yes, I've got Spook on my hands all right.

The telephone rings. It is my-friend-Lauren. "What the hell have you been *doing,* I've been trying to reach you for *hours,* I wanted to know how it went yesterday," says Lauren.

I crack.

"Oh Lauren, *Lauren,* I've got this enormous dog in the house, I found him yesterday and he was wearing a license, I thought I could track down his owner right away, but it's a seventy-two license, I put up posters and everything, I've called the police and the ASPCA, Max hates him, he's jealous, so I have to keep Max locked in the bedroom, and I don't know what to *do.* I *can't* turn him in, I just *can't,* but I can't keep him here either. I . . . Lauren? Are you still there?"

There is another long, pregnant pause.

"Jesus *Christ,*" says Lauren. "Every time I call, every

single time I call, you're into some kind of crazy mess. I've never *heard* of anyone who got himself into so many crazy messes. It's either one of your kids is lost or some maniac chased you down Broadway or the bathtub upstairs is overflowing or you're on your way to Roosevelt Emergency because Nicco cracked his head open; the last time, I remember, you were on your way out to feed some goddamn cat you'd found in a cardboard box on Columbus. *Jesus.* Your whole life reads like some insane *book* or something."

"That wasn't the last time, with the cat, that was the time before," I say defensively. "And anyway, this dog really wasn't my fault, he followed me, I just have to find some way to . . ."

"Liza, I have a client meeting in ten minutes. Could you possibly forget the goddamn dog for a minute and tell me how the interview went? I set it *up* for you, you know. I'd like to know how it *went.*"

"I'm sorry, Lauren, honestly I am. I'm just cracking up lately, I'm falling apart and now this . . . actually, I think it went pretty well. Nina and Frank, Frank the articles editor, they seemed to like me. Nina said if I wanted a hint everything would go—swimmingly—I think she said. I have to write up some samples and do an outline; I'm supposed to call her Friday."

"Terrific!" says my-friend-Lauren. "That's better. That sounds very hopeful. You're working on the samples now, aren't you?"

"Well, as soon as I get the dog figured out, I will. I can't leave Max locked up all the time, he pees all over the floor. And anyway, the other dog, the dog I found, doesn't like to be left alone. He cries, he howls if I'm not here. My neighbor told me that all the time I was gone, taking the children to school, he just kept on howling. So I have to get the dog thing settled first."

"Liza, *forget* the dog; turn him *in* for Christ's sake. First things first. Are you supposed to send the samples in or take them down or what?"

"She didn't say. Wait, yes, she said 'send us some more samples,' I think. But I know she said to call her Friday. Oh God. She couldn't have meant to have them in by *this* Friday, could she? I would have had to mail them last night; that's impossible. Oh God. I went through this whole thing before. Before the interview she said Wednesday, for lunch, and since it was Tuesday I didn't know if she meant yesterday or next Wednesday so I just . . ."

"Liza, calm *down*. Take it *easy*. Let me think. I guess she *could* have expected you to mail them off last night; you had the whole evening, after all. *Some* people would have gone straight home and banged them out. It does seem a bit much, though, especially with the mail what it is. But you should probably get them down there this afternoon just to be sure; it looks better. Have you done *any* work on the samples yet?"

"Well, uh, last night was a little hectic, but I've been thinking over ideas; I've got all the ideas in my head, I even wrote some down. All I have to do now really is type them out. I stayed up practically all night thinking . . ."

"Good. At least *that's* something. Now look, you *want* this, you *know* you want it, you've been bitching and bitching about how you're going out of your mind and here you've almost *got* what you want. Don't fuck it up. Just concentrate on those samples. Put everything else out of your mind."

"Right. You're absolutely right, Lauren. I will. I'll start typing them right now. I have about two hours until Nicco gets home, he's bringing home a friend and . . ."

"What do you *mean,* until Nicco gets home? Why the hell can't you work *after* Nicco gets home? Just put out some juice and cookies and tell them to go off and play. My God, Liza, what do you think all those *other* women, those writers and artists and all those other people who work at home do? *They* don't let their children rule their lives. Just tell Nicco you're busy, that you have work to do. Come *on*. Get your ass together. Get going. Think of yourself for a change. You'll never get anywhere if you don't think of yourself. You can't just live for the sake of other people. It's *sick.*"

"That sounds exactly like Ayn Rand."

"Anne . . . did you say what I think you said?"

"No, I'm just thinking out loud. And thanks, Lauren. Thanks for everything."

"Let me know Friday how things turn out. It sounds hopeful. I'm really happy for you, Liza."

"I know, Lauren. Thanks again."

How the hell am I going to get the samples downtown this afternoon? Maybe Elly can stay with the children and bail me out, but there's no point in calling now; she won't be home yet. The large black dog nudges my knee. Partly to avoid facing the typewriter, I offer him food, but he will not touch it. It occurs to me that perhaps he does not like canned dog food, so I cook some hamburger, carrots, and onions together and put down the dish. The dog falls to hungrily, licking up every last bite. When he is finished he seems more confident, more at home; he strides around the apartment sniffing furniture, lifting his leg here and there, circling four times before he lies down in front of the door. I mop up the pee—not streams, like Max, only dribbles—unlock Max and feed him, lock myself and the large black dog in the bedroom and try to type a rough draft of the samples I scribbled down in the early hours of the morning. But the large black dog does not like me to type. At the end of each line, as the bell rings, he gently takes my arm in his enormous jaws. Soon he is not quite so gentle. He barks loudly at the sound of the bell. His teeth leave faint marks on my arm.

This will never work out.

I have to think of myself.

I take the dog downstairs to wait for Nicco and his friend Chad, staring down the crazy old lady on the corner, letting her get a good look at Spook; the sight of those huge, slobbering jaws may change her mind about abducting Nicco. There's a silver lining in every cloud.

Nicco and Chad clamber out of the bus. Nicco is carrying a large rifle made of wood. Because I refuse to buy him toy guns he makes them every chance he gets in school—rifles, machine guns, pistols, all complete with moving parts—and brings them home. That's what you get for belonging to Another Mother for Peace. I decide not to mention the gun.

"Nicco darling, I know you and Chad are probably very hungry, but I have to get rid of this dog; I have to take him to the police station and turn him in. It's too far to take him to the ASPCA. I can't get any work done; I just can't keep him any longer. Do you mind walking over to the police station? It's only a few blocks, and then we'll come right back home and have lunch."

"No, I don't mind, Mom," Nicco says, crouching and taking careful aim at the crazy old lady on the corner. "Is that her?"

"Yes. But don't go near her. Put down that gun."

"What's the matter with her, Mrs. Calder?" asks Chad. He is a thin, knobby, worried-looking little boy with granny glasses and lank, almost white bangs that hang down to eyes the color of seashells. His parents are both child psychologists. Easily teased, quick to cry, he looks upon Nicco as a god.

"Oh, nothing much. She's just a little crazy. It's best to stay away from people like that."

"Is she in analysis?" asks Chad, looking more worried than ever. "She should be in analysis."

"I don't know, darling. I don't think so. But don't

worry, I'm here, she won't come near you. The main thing now is to get the dog to the police station. Won't that be fun, to see the inside of a police station?"

"Yippee! Hurray!" yells Nicco.

"I don't know," Chad says doubtfully.

Spook, locked into a primal sitting position, will not move.

"Get up, Spook," I say. "Get *up.*"

"Spook, that's a funny name for a dog," says Nicco.

We walk slowly toward Columbus. How am I going to be able to do it. I'll never be able to do it. I must do it. As we are nearing Amsterdam a black couple I recognize from the welfare hotel across the street heads toward us. The wife is dazzling, a symphony of red slacks, orange sweater, pink scarf, and dyed blond Afro. She stoops down to pat the dog. My heart leaps. I know a dog lover when I see one. Maybe I'm in luck.

"Marshall, just look at this good old boy," the woman croons. "Ain't he a good old boy?"

"He's a very good boy, very loving, very friendly," I say, trying for a soft sell and hoping to Christ that Nicco will keep his mouth shut. "I'm on my way to the police station to turn him in. I'd keep him myself but I have a male dog of my own. It's a shame to turn him in, he's a beautiful dog, very friendly, I hate to do it; I don't trust the ASPCA. They don't keep them very long, you know. A day or two at the most."

"That terrible, terrible," the woman says, still fondling the dog. "Marshall, can't we keep this good old boy? Ever since Franklin D. passed I been dying for a good old boy like this."

"I guess so honey," the man says. "You sure?"

"Sure I sure. My heart aching for a dog."

"Well, if you sure you sure."

Now I'm not so sure.

"I . . . are you sure you really want him? He's large, you know. He'll have to go to the park and everything. I want to be sure he'll have a good home. I mean, I'm sure you'll give him a good home, but he'll eat a lot. He'll need a lot of room."

"Oh, we got a *big* room, a great big room. He be fine. This good old boy be fine, won't you sugar?" The dog wags his tail and kisses her hand. A stab of jealousy shoots through my heart. Traitor. Turncoat. Canine opportunist.

"Well. That's great, I guess. Do you . . . would you mind very much giving me your name and telephone number? I left my name and number at the ASPCA and the precinct. I mean, I'm sure no one will claim him; no one has, but just in case I suppose I should know where he is."

"Why sure, honey, I give you our name. The phone in the hall. You call any old time. Just ask for Mr.-Mrs.-Brown."

The woman reaches elbow-deep into her shiny orange shoulder bag, takes out a pencil and a tattered piece of Kleenex, and laboriously prints her name and number on it. I pocket the information, give the dog a last kiss, and turn over the leash. The dog is looking at me. I cannot stand the way he is looking at me.

"He, uh, he ate this morning," I say, trying to prolong our moment of parting. "He doesn't seem to like dog food. He likes regular food—hamburger and things like that. Vegetables."

"He house-broke?" asks the man.

"Oh yes. Absolutely. But you should take him to the park regularly. And . . . you should really get a new leash. This leash isn't anywhere near strong enough. A strong chain leash, that's what you should get."

"Oh, I got a leash," says the woman. "Old Franklin D., he was a big old boy. I kept all his things after he passed."

"What happened to Franklin D.?" I ask, immediately wishing I hadn't.

"Poor old Franklin D., that poor old boy, run away in the park, run out on Riverside and got run over by a mail truck. I cried all night over poor old Franklin D."

Oh my God.

"Well. 'Bye baby. I . . . actually, I wouldn't let him off the leash in the park, at least until he knows you. And even then I'm not sure I . . . would you mind if I called tonight to see how he's doing?"

"No, honey, I don't mind, you go right ahead and call. What this old boy's name? What your name, sugar?"

The husband looms above me, ink black, bunching muscles, over six feet tall, topping three hundred pounds. I cannot do it. Nicco does it for me.

"Spook! His name is Spook. Like Halloween!" yells Nicco.

"I'm afraid of Halloween," says Chad, looking pale.

When we get home I feel light-headed; my whole body aches. I had no right to give him away, no right. One room. A welfare hotel. He'll probably pee on the floor and the husband will beat him with Franklin D.'s leash. They'll probably spend their welfare check on wine and sell him for vivisection. Save a life and you are responsible for that life forever; isn't that a Chinese proverb? I take a Librium, put two hot dogs on to boil, set out catsup, mustard, and a jar of dill pickles. Nicco chatters away happily as he eats, gulping milk which leaves a sweep of white moustache around his wide mouth, dipping a pickle into a splash of catsup on his plate. Chad sits with a paper napkin spread out on his knobby knees and another tucked under his chin, barely eating. He chews each bite about ten times before swallowing. When Nicco says, in a conversational tone, "Know what? Hot dogs is made from pigs' ears, right Mom?" he stops eating completely. For once, I am not hungry; I do not encourage Nicco to finish so I can get at the leftovers. I do not even want a drink.

"What's the matter, Mom?" Nicco asks, finally noticing. "Why do you have your head down in your hands like that?"

"I feel sad about the dog, Nicco. I'm worried about the dog. I don't know if I did the right thing or not, giving him away."

"Don't worry, Mom, you always worry," Nicco says, giving me a milky kiss and sliding off his chair. "She's a nice lady. He'll be okay. Come on, Chaddie! Let's play war!"

Where did he come from, this happy child, my child of joy, so simple, basic, unconcerned? A changeling? One of those hospital mix-ups you're always reading about? No, I saw him born. I think of my brother David as a little boy, sensitive, moody, hiding away with his books and crayons whenever my father was home. No, Nicco is not at all like David. Andrew then? I do not know what Andrew was like; I cannot picture him as a child. The little he has said of his New England childhood does not sound happy—barren fields, ground hard-packed with frost. They were always poor. One rare memory Andrew has shared: His father had lost yet another job. His mother woke him and his younger brother up one night and pushed them, shivering, down the stairs. Through the open front door Andrew could see his father's body far away in the winter night, outlined against a silvery cluster of pine. His father was looking at the sky. "Look at him," Andrew's mother said. "Look at him so hard you'll never forget it. Do you want to wind up like that, looking at the stars?"

Both Andrew's parents died before he was twenty. His mother never saw him graduate from college. Perhaps Nicco is what Andrew might have been. I do not know.

I pour some coffee and go into the bedroom to try to work. If I'm to get the samples downtown this afternoon I don't have much time, and I still don't know how I'm going to get them down there; Elly doesn't answer. Right under the card table holding the typewriter, soft, pungent, and steaming, is a pile of dog shit. Max. My fault again. And I have given away his leash. The shit, its presence, odor, convoluted shape, seems so fitting I almost hate to clean it up. But I put down paper for Max, clean up the shit, wash my hands, and start typing out a rough draft of the samples. As I am halfway down the first page it occurs to me that I really cannot work on samples without reading some back issues of *Free Woman;* with my luck I am liable to repeat something that's already been done. But I do not have time to go down to the back magazine store; better check with Lauren. She'll know. Nicco and Chad are shooting at each other in the hall. The noise is deafening. It is very hard to think.

"Boys!" I yell. "Please play something more quiet. Nicco, you know how I feel about guns. And Chad's mother would have a fit; she specifically told me that Chad was not to play with guns *ever*. You remember the last time. You know that, Chad. You heard your mother yourself."

"Chad's mother's an old bitch," says Nicco.

"Yeah, old bitch," says Chad, looking at Nicco for backup and giggling hysterically.

"Cut it out, Nicco, that isn't funny," I say, picking up the phone to call Lauren.

The boys switch to Evel Knievel and his motorcycle. They rev up the motorcycle. The motorcycle shoots over a plastic ramp, careens down the hall, and smashes into the wall. The revving noise is worse than the shooting, a drill on a tender tooth.

"Boys!" I yell again, hanging up in the middle of dialing. "I am going to give you some juice and cookies and then you must absolutely go off and play something *quiet*. I am *working*."

I set out the juice and cookies and go back to the bedroom. All is silent. Maybe Lauren knows what she's talking about; for a woman without children, she's certainly full of advice. I dial again. After explaining my ideas—a true-to-life, first-person account of a divorcée's fun new life after two stultifying years of marriage; hand language (a whole bunch of sexy gestures you can do with your hands); and, combining sex, fashion, beauty, and food in one knockout wrap-up, International Parties in your very own Pad (one week Japanese hair, gown, makeup, chopsticks, chicken mizutaki, paper lanterns, oriental erotica, the next a Roman orgy etc., just to keep your man off balance)—Lauren says:

"Not bad. Not bad. I don't remember anything like that being done lately. That last thing sounds sort of familiar, but it doesn't matter. I don't think *they've* done it anyway. All those magazines rip each other off. Go ahead. It all sounds fine. Stick in as much sex as you can; they even do it in the decorating section."

"I didn't see any decorating section."

"It's only about two pages; look in this month's issue. I think it was 'How to turn your one-room studio apartment into a harem'; it had tents draped onto the ceiling, paisley tents. A two-page color spread."

"Okay, I'll look. Lauren do you think . . . is a page or so on each idea enough?"

"Yes. They're just samples, you know. My God Liza, what *is* that noise? It sounds as if someone's hammering through your wall."

"Oh, that's just Nicco and his friend. They're playing with this motorcycle toy, with Evel Knievel, and after you rev up the motorcycle it smashes into the wall. I tried the juice and cookie idea, Lauren. It didn't work for long."

Lauren sighs and says, "Liza, really, you'd better pull yourself together; you let those kids get away with absolute murder. You let them walk all over you. But I'm going to mind my own business if it kills me. Which it *is*. Now look, don't forget, let me know what happens Friday. I think I'll call Nina again today anyway, give her a shove. It couldn't hurt."

"Thanks, Lauren. Thanks again. For everything. 'Bye."

I get out my copy of *Free Woman* and turn to the decorating section. It's true; there really is a two-page article on how to turn your one-room studio apartment into a harem. The article, which features a semi-nude model lying on silk pillows under yards and yards of paisley, is called "Waiting for Your Sheik."

Amazingly, although Nicco and Chad return to the guns, the words come easily. I am almost finished with a rough draft of my third sample and wondering whether or not I should include the masturbation outline in the package I am hopefully taking downtown when the telephone rings. "Be quiet, boys!" I shout. "It might be a call about my work."

"Mrs. Calder? My name is Sebastian," says one of the most high-flying homosexual voices I have ever heard, and not a pleasant one either. "I saw your name and telephone number on a *po*ster this insane utter *maniac* was tearing to *shreds* on West *End*. Now take this down. I have a friend named Desmond who . . ."

I knew it. I have given away someone else's dog. Mr. and Mrs. Brown will not give him back. I will be taken to court. I will wind up behind bars.

"Oh dear, Sebastian, I'm terribly sorry," I groan. "Oh God, I should have waited, I should have kept him, but I have a male of my own, he was jealous, I couldn't keep him, I've already given him to . . ."

"Will you *lissen?* Will you please let me *fi*nish? Will you do me that *fa*vor?" asks Sebastian.

"Yes. Yes of course. I'm sorry," I say, cowed.

"As I was trying to *say,* I have a friend named Desmond, a savior, an utter god, the entire city of New York should go down on its knees and kiss his *feet,* who takes homeless animals, animals that utter criminals leave to *die* in *agony* in the *streets,* into his apartment and keeps them until he finds a good home. He investigates each home personally, no children, no . . ."

"Sebastian, I really do thank you, I appreciate your concern, but the thing is I've . . ."

"Will you let me finish? Thank you. I'm in a phone booth on my way to my *flute* lesson. I've already spoken to Desmond about the dog and he's willing to accept it. The fee is only fifty dollars which is *insane,* but that's the way Desmond *is.* Now take this down. One oh one Riverside, Apartment E, 873–2110."

"Thank you. I've taken it down. But as I was saying, the thing is, I tried everything, I tried the ASPCA and the precinct and every L. Rodriguez in the phone book, that was who the dog was registered to, L. Rodriguez, except he wasn't there, there wasn't any L. Rodriguez, the license had expired, it was a seventy-two license, so anyway, I was on my way to the precinct to turn the dog in, the ASPCA is so far from here and I had two children with me, and this very nice couple, they live in the hotel across the street, real dog lovers, offered to take the dog and so . . . I gave them the dog."

"What do you *know* about this couple?" Sebastian asks, venom in his lisp.

How the hell did he know I have doubts of my own?

"Oh. Well, I've seen them around the neighborhood. They seem like a very nice couple. They seemed to really like the dog."

"But have you *investigated?* What *kind* of a hotel does this . . . couple . . . live in? A *hotel* is no place for a possible shepherd-retriever-collie *mix."*

"It's a . . . welfare hotel, actually. But the woman said they had a very nice room. A big room."

"I have never *heard* of anything so u-t-t-e-r-l-y out*rageous,"* cries Sebastian, enraged. "A *welfare* ho*tel.* The *precinct.* Two *chil*dren. Don't interrupt; just let me finish.

I have exactly one more minute to give you. I'm extremely busy. My flute teacher goes into a foaming de*press*ion if I'm so much as a second late. I feel, however, I have a *duty,* a human-to-human duty, to tell you that your irresponsibility is an utter *outrage.* No wonder this city, this entire *coun*try, is falling apart at its very seams. No wonder . . ."

Something deep inside me that has been there for a long time, perhaps forever, waiting, flickers, falters, then ignites.

"I'm extremely busy, too, Sebastian, I'm working," I hear myself saying loudly. "I'm finishing an important magazine assignment. I'm due downtown in about one minute. I've been listening to you. Now *you* listen. I'll give you the couple's phone number and you can go over there and investigate. You can take the dog and give him to Desmond. You can keep the dog yourself. You can take your flute and stick it up your ass. I did the best I could. Get the fuck off my back."

My, my, my. Excluding Jory Levitt and her aborted search for a plastic vagina, I have never before told anyone outside my own family off. I am polite even when listening to an obscene phone call or letting some aggressive matron push me out of the check-out line at Food City. I feel a little guilty, of course, but nice. More than nice. I feel, as I did after my confrontation with Jory, terrific, as if a small part of my ass has gotten back together, returned to the sagging fold.

I type up my rough drafts quickly and neatly, read them over, and find two decent snapshots of myself. (Taken two years ago, but so what. I was thinner then.) I am about to try Elly again when the doorbell rings and Elly, in a man's shirt with rolled-up sleeves, a velvet vest, and jeans, comes breathlessly in. She looks disarrayed; her hair needs washing.

"I tried to call first but the line's been busy. I meant to call last night but the old man and I were having a terrible fight," Elly says, sitting down, kicking off her clogs and lighting a cigarette. "We're cool now, we made up. That Justin, that old fuckhead, I love him, I really do, but Jesus, sometimes . . . sometimes . . . now he feels sorry, he said he's sorry he said why don't I look the way I did ten years ago, he's worried about my drinking, he said. Shit. What the hell am I supposed to look like at forty-one, Linda Lovelace? Okay, that wasn't all there was to it, I guess I started it, but Jesus. My God, the noise in here, it's worse than downstairs. Alex, the little shit, he has three friends over; maybe now Justin will see why I need at least two martinis to get through the fucking afternoon. I don't know why anyone has children. I hate children. I hate them almost as much as I hate people."

"Come on. You know you love Alex. You're crazy about him. Elly, I wondered if you could . . ." But Elly is off and running. All the signs are there. She has had one martini, maybe two. Her eyes are luminous darts. I see that she is wearing dark red nail polish. A concession to Linda Lovelace?

"Sure. Sure I love him. It's Marilyn I'd like to throw out and start over. Alex just drives me out of my mind, that's all. But I adore him. I was thinking the other day, what's so bad about incest? I mean, who better than your own mother to turn you on? It's just this fucking *culture* we're living in, these fucking *rules.* I bet in about fifty years kids will be screwing their mothers and everybody will think it's cool. Doesn't Nicco turn you on? Come on. Admit it."

"Yes. Yes he does sometimes. Elly, do you think you could possibly . . ."

"So? What's wrong with that?"

"Nicco turning me on? Nothing, I guess. It just seems kind of, I don't know, futile. I mean, what's the point of sleeping with him? I can't marry him or anything. Elly, I have sort of a . . ."

"Marry him. *Marry* him. Why the hell do you have

to *marry* him?" Elly says, pink with rage, tearing at her hair. "Jesus. That's what started Justin off last night. Can't you get turned on by somebody without wanting to *marry* them?"

"All right, I was just kidding, that was a dumb thing to say. Nicco and I will screw our heads off tonight after Andrew's asleep. But right now I have a problem. Do you think you could stay with the kids while I take some samples downtown? It shouldn't take me more than an hour; I'll take the bus straight down and . . ."

"Oh Christ," Elly says, "I don't know what the hell's the matter with me lately. That's what I came up to ask about, the interview, to see how the interview went. Jesus, I must be losing my mind."

"Well, as you said, at least the shit would be different. It certainly was. It was very different. Anyway, it looks as if I have the job if I want it; that's why I have to take these . . ."

"Terrific!" Elly shrieks, jumping up and throwing her arms around me, upsetting a full ashtray on her way. "That's terrific! Sure I'll stay; take your time. Justin can goddamn well stay down there until you get back. He can stay down there the whole fucking night for all I care."

"I thought you made up."

"We did. But I'm still mad. Not only that, he started pushing me around, he'd had a few drinks himself and he pushed me into the wall. He banged my head right into the wall. Bastard."

"Andrew did that once too," I say thoughtfully. "When I was late and he didn't know where I was."

"*Andrew* did that? I don't believe it."

"Yes. He did. Do you mind if I borrow your jacket again? I forgot to give it back yesterday."

"Sure babe. Jesus, I can't believe he really did that. Isn't it too hot for a jacket though?"

"Yes, but it'll cover me up on top. At least my jeans

are clean. I'm not going to go in or anything; I'm just going to leave the stuff with the receptionist. I'll be in and out in a minute; nobody will see me. I hope."

"What about the girls?"

"Oh God. The girls. I forgot about the girls. Well, Anna will have to come up by herself unless you feel like going down to meet her. She came up by herself yesterday, but I didn't tell her I wouldn't be down to meet her, so if you could go down it would help. The bus usually comes a little after three; it's almost three now. But if you go you better take the boys with you. And I can pick Kate up at the bus stop on my way back. Oh, look, forget it; you're doing enough. She can come up by herself. She'll be all right. I guess."

"You worry too goddamn much," Elly says. "I read a thing about that, about overprotective mothers. It said they basically hate their kids. I mean, I know you don't, but look at Jory. That kid's going to turn into a fag or a murderer. Let her come up alone. Christ, there they go with the guns again. Who's the albino with the skinny little legs?"

"Chad. His mother isn't coming until five, but just in case she's early, get the guns away from them before you open the door. She doesn't like him to play with guns. She's a shrink. A psychologist anyway."

"Shrinks are the worst," Elly says, grimacing.

That may be true. Chad's mother, although she has a maid and a nurse, is constantly calling to see if Chad can visit Nicco. The last time she also called in the middle of the afternoon to make sure he wasn't playing with guns or taking off his clothes. "What exactly are they doing?" she asked. "I'll check," I said. I went into the dining room. The boys were watching a sadistic, sexist, racist cartoon on television. I went back to the phone. "They're not playing with guns or taking off their clothes; they're watching a sadistic, sexist, racist cartoon on TV," I said. (I'd had a drink or two.)

"Oh fine, I just wanted to be sure everything was all right," she said. And of course when she arrived they *were* playing with Nicco's homemade arsenal, sedentary sadism having palled. And did she ever let me have it.

"All right. But just in case. I don't need any more problems. She's a big deal in the PTA besides."

"He looks like a myopic ant, do you know that?" Elly says, curling up in the living room with a magazine. "You don't mind if I have a drink, do you?"

"Of course not. You know where it is. Just hide it if she comes early. I'll hurry."

"Don't. I want Justin to suffer."

On the bus heading downtown I read over the samples again. (I decided not to include the masturbation outline; that will take some thought.) There is only one typographical error, which I carefully correct with a pen. They read well, I think, very *Free Woman*—colorful, snappy, knockout all the way. I have always been an excellent mimic. Riffling papers, my pen poised, I enjoy (what I assume to be) the envious glances of heavily teased shoppers on their way to Macy's and mothers holding whining children. I am a little worried about Anna, more about getting back in time to pick up Kate. But I am not dizzy.

The waiting room is completely empty. The flowered couch is empty, waiting too. Without thinking, I automatically make the sign of the cross on my envelope full of samples and place the envelope dead center in the middle of the reception desk. Since my confirmation in an East Side Episcopal church twenty-four years ago, I have never made the sign of the cross on anything, anywhere. I touch the envelope again with my left forefinger, touch my forehead, then my heart, and leave. Right foot first.

Kate is already at the bus stop by the time I get there.

"I thought you'd forgotten to pick me up. *Again,*" she says nastily, tossing her immaculate, combed blond hair.

"No, but from now on you're going to have to walk home alone. It's only a few blocks, all the other girls do it, if you walk on West End you'll be fine," I say firmly, although I'm not at all sure she'll be fine; I see the way men look at Kate, West End as well as Broadway. She is tall for her age, and beautiful. A hint of budding breasts. A curve of honeyed calf below her swirling skirts. My baby, my little girl who was never mine. I suddenly want to touch her, take her hand, but I know she will not let me, so I do not try. I have been hurt too often.

"All the other girls do *not* do it. Most of them are picked up in limousines right in front of *school.* It's only girls who live over *here* who do it," says Kate.

"Well, we don't have a limousine," I say grimly. "And we live over *here.* Hurry up now. Elly's staying with Anna and Nicco and his friend; I don't want to keep her waiting."

"Oh, not *Elly,*" Kate says, rolling her eyes.

"Shut up; I don't like your friends either," I snap.

We ride to our floor in silence.

Stefan II opens the elevator door and announces out of nowhere: "They should string up in streets."

"Who?" I ask. "Who should they string up in streets?" (Talk to an Eastern European long enough and you start dropping all but the most essential words; Hemingway without the style.)

"Criminals. Communists. Dirty hippies. Crime, dirt, rape. No want to work. Liberals. All liberals' fault. String up in streets, no more crime."

"I'm a liberal," I say, my head held high.

Stefan II stares at me in horror, his thick lips hanging down onto his neckless collarbone.

"You liberal?"

"Yes. Yes I am."

"Did you *have* to say that?" Kate demands as soon as the elevator doors close.

"Yes, I did," I say, unlocking our door. "I very definitely did."

"Well, if you want to *know,*" says Kate, "Stefan may be just an *elevator* operator, but Playton Hughes' father thinks exactly the same thing. He thinks the liberals who've infiltrated the government are the reason this country is practically in the throes of a *depression.*"

"I don't give a flying fuck what Playton Hughes' father thinks," I say. "Go do your goddamn homework."

Nicco, Chad, and Anna are watching television. Elly is still sitting in the living room, an empty glass in her hand. She has the manic, expectant look I have come to know means that she is in the middle of a lucid gin high, when thought is a cold blue irrefutable crystal, not to be tangled with. I say her name twice but she does not answer, so I sit down and wait. I do not have to wait long.

"You know, I've been thinking," Elly says. "What you've done, having the guts to go down and get a terrific job like that, a real job, made me think. I've had it with that little hole I'm in, nothing but old ladies and those crazy mothers and other people's fucking kids all day. I'm going to quit. Yeah," she says, seeing my startled face. "Really. I've never done anything but teach. I've never done *anything.* I want to get into something else, acting maybe, did I ever tell you, I always wanted to be an actress, or TV, educational TV. I'm going to go in tomorrow and tell them I've had it, that I'm not coming back next year. Fuck it. The old bat who runs the place, she must be about a hundred and two, she doesn't like the way I teach anyway. She wants the girls to wear dresses and play in the doll corner and the boys are all supposed to play with blocks and beat each other up on the roof. And the mothers, the fucking mothers that come to observe all the time, the *questions* they ask, I feel like I'm on trial. The last time this asshole, she's so uptight she sends the kid off to school in an organdy pinafore, a *pinafore,* for Christ's sake, like Rebecca of Sunnybrook Farm, she asks me, very haughty, 'What do you do about discipline?' Well, I was tired and I'd just about had it, so I said, 'Oh, I just hit 'em.' I was only kidding, of course, I'd just had it, but the word got back to old lady Mitchell and down she comes raving the other day, asking me what I think I'm doing, telling all the mothers I hit the kids. Shit. I don't need this shit for what I get paid. I get paid *nothing.* The janitor gets paid more than I do; I asked him. I'm going to go right in tomorrow and tell her I've had it."

When Elly's in this kind of mood, she requires careful handling. Or am I on guard simply because I am cold sober and she is not? For the first time I think I understand how Andrew must feel. It is not a pleasant feeling.

"But," I proceed cautiously, "teaching . . . as a teacher, you really have a lot going for you; you have vacations and summers free and all that. You clear everything you earn. Maybe you should think it over. If I get this job I'll have to hire someone full time; I'll be lucky if I clear anything. I don't like leaving the kids all day long anyway. And going down for this job didn't take much guts. I'm not at all sure I . . ."

"Liza, that's just what I mean. We're all so afraid. We're afraid to take chances. I don't *want* to think it over. Sure we need the money; it pays the kids' tuition. But if I'm going to work I want to do something I want to do, and I want to get *paid* for it. All these cop-outs—teaching, nursing, social work—they're all just a bunch of fucking cop-outs, they're not real. Listen, we all have to stop being so afraid. Unless we put up a fight, we're finished. Who was it, Edna O'Brien, said we should all be armed?"

"Yes, but . . . what are we going to do? I mean, you're right of course, but we can't just go out and blow up IBM. Until the system changes there really isn't much you can . . ."

"That's a lot of crap. Reactionary crap. *We* have to change the system. Why *can't* we blow up IBM? Look, they're doing it in, where is it, Sweden? Or maybe it's Denmark. Anyway, they have equal pay and day care and lots of couples both work part time and split the rest of the shit, the kids and stuff; they have open marriages. If they get turned on by somebody they don't have to sneak around. They have affairs all the time. I mean, it's *possible.* I just read an article. I think it was Sweden."

"Well, it hasn't happened here yet."

"So? That's exactly what I mean. We should be armed."

"Could you kill somebody, Elly?"

She looks thoughtful, bites her thumb. Her nail polish is already chipping. "Yeah, I think I could," she says finally. "Could you?"

"Only myself," I say softly.

"Do you mean it?"

"I'll try anything once."

We laugh nervously, not looking at each other.

"Yeah, that's the problem, isn't it?" Elly says. "We'd be the first to go. Oh Christ, that reminds me, I forgot to tell you."

"Tell me what?"

"For this I need another drink."

We go into the kitchen, Elly stumbling slightly, and I fix two martinis. I do not really want a martini, but I fix myself one anyway.

"Remember Natalie, Charlie's mother?" Elly asks when we are settled in the living room again.

"Yes. Sure. The Liberated Woman. Who had it made."

"Yeah. Get this. You know what she's done? She's selling her business, she's leaving New York, and going to marry this pig, this male chauvinist son of a bitch, a *banker* or something, I've met him, he's the most uptight, boring son of a bitch I've ever met, and live in *Detroit*."

"But why? *Why?*"

"I don't know," Elly says gloomily, staring into the depths of her martini. "I mean, she was free, she had money, that terrific job, a business of her *own,* for Christ's sake, a kid. Why is right. All she told me was that she was tired of screwing around, that she wanted to settle down. She said Charlie needed a father. *I* don't know."

"Maybe she was just ready to exchange shit too," I say. I feel depressed, depleted. Next Christmas seems a long way off.

"What do you mean?"

"That's what you said. You said if I took this job at least the shit would be different."

"Was it really that bad?"

"It was awful, Elly, *awful*. I'd rather clean out a toilet bowl any day. This woman, she . . . and on top of it all, I started bleeding in the middle of lunch, my period started right in the middle of lunch. I was bleeding all over the goddamn chair."

Elly laughs until she almost cries. Gin spills onto her velvet vest.

"Poor baby, does that ever sound Freudian," she says, between gasps. "You know what Justin's mother calls Freud? Frood. She told me her book club was discussing Frood and they got into this thing he wrote about his wife, about how he wanted to keep her sweet and innocent and safe at home in his ivory tower. Something like that anyway. Good old Mom doesn't remember the words exactly, but she said it was the *dearest* thing she ever read. Frood. *Christ*. Come on, baby. You know you really wouldn't rather clean out a toilet bowl. Women can bleed while they're working; there isn't a *law* against it, is there? Look at your mother. You said yourself you thought that ivory tower shit was part of what made her crack up. You want to wind up like that? I know that's a rough thing to say, but do you?"

I think that one over. No, I do not want to wind up like Mother. They have taken away her doll. The last time I went to see her I ran into my father in the lobby of the hospital. He was sitting on a green plastic chair, holding a bouquet of roses and a large box of chocolates. He was crying.

"She won't see me," he said, "she won't see me. A private room. Presents. Every other day I bring her roses. Yesterday I brought her a diamond, a diamond ring, and she won't see me. She threw the roses at me today. She says she wants her mother. Liza, please. Go up. Do something. This is killing me. I don't know what to do. Do something."

When I went up to my mother's room she was not wearing lipstick or a wig or a print silk dress. Her face and graying blond hair were washed clean; her short ruffled robe was fastened snugly at her chin with a wide satin ribbon. She put her arms around my neck.

"Feed me, Mommy. Feed me," she said.

And so at suppertime, although visiting hours were over, the nurses let me stay, and I held my mother's frail body in my arms and spooned chicken, rice, and peas into her open, waiting mouth. When I told my father she had eaten, he seemed happier. No. If it comes to a choice between death and madness, I will opt for death. But what I am thinking is, staying home, working, having an affair, not having an affair . . . what difference, in the end, does it make? Some things do make a difference; some things matter. Spook, for instance. Spook mattered a lot.

"Elly, just tell me one thing. Do you think writing an article on masturbation is more important than saving the life of a dog?"

"What?"

"Nothing. Never mind."

"Look baby, get your ass together. At least you'll be free. At least you'll be earning a living."

"I don't know about that. I don't even know what they're paying."

"Sure you will. It's a real job. All magazines pay a lot. It's not some lousy cop-out like me. You take it. Don't you let anyone stop you."

"But I don't even *want* the goddamn job."

"Then you go out and find something you *do* want. You're a smart woman. Anyone in their right mind would want you to work for them. Don't you *dare* be afraid; don't you *dare* put yourself down," says Elly, glowing pure with truth and fire. Her words are slurring.

Chad is picked up without incident. When Andrew comes home Elly goes to the door, stumbling again, throws her arms around him, kisses his neck and says, "Hi baby! Come on, loosen up. Have a drink. You know you've always turned me on." Andrew stiffens, smiles politely, and disengages himself. When Elly finally leaves he says:

"Couldn't you make friends with a normal woman?"

Spook, according to Mrs. Brown, is doing just fine.

The next morning I call three employment agencies. None of the people I speak to will give me any information whatsoever over the phone; I am brusquely told to come down and fill out an application. I then call a large advertising agency. The assistant to the personnel director, after finding out my age and minimal experience, laughs rudely and suggests I take a typing course and try Office Temporaries. My last call, before giving in and up to what

I already know, is to a militant feminist magazine. The laugh is almost as rude. There is one opening, in the typing pool. The pay is ninety dollars a week.

Not before ten, or between one and three, or after five-thirty, I call Nina Farrow.

"My, you are the speedy little one," says Nina. "I managed to read over your samples late yesterday afternoon. I didn't expect you'd have them in *that* quickly."

In spite of myself, I feel proud. My posture improves, even sitting down.

"Well, thank you. You did say Friday and I . . ."

"Did I say Friday? I don't remember saying that."

"Yes. I don't mean to contradict you or anything, but actually you did. You said Friday. Just as we were finishing lunch."

"Well, whatever. In any case, I found them absolutely fantastic. I discussed it all with Frank and several other editors this morning. We've decided, after a great deal of thought, that the job is yours. Isn't that fantastic? You can start whenever you like, next week if possible. The work *is* piling up."

"Well. That's . . . terrific. Thank you very much. I . . . you know, actually, we never exactly discussed salary." (Why the hell didn't I ask Lauren what, if anything, I'm worth? I could have called her last night at home. Shit.)

"Well, darling, of course you *are* just starting out. I don't know how much we could squeeze. What did you have in mind? Just a round figure."

"Oh. Well, uh, I . . . already have a nanny, as I said, but I feel that I should be contributing to her salary. I was thinking of, oh, as a round figure, somewhere in the neighborhood of . . . ten thousand dollars?"

Nina Farrow laughs softly, then sighs. I can see her wearily spreading out the lines between her brows with her silvery-fuschia-nailed fingers.

"But, my *dear,*" she says. "You have a husband. You are not the sole support of your family." It is not a question.

"No, no, of course not. My husband is a lawyer. But I do feel . . . I do have some experience, you know . . . well, of course it's just a round figure, but *Free Woman* does advocate independence, and I don't see how you can be independent if you . . . that is, I realize I'm just starting out again, but . . ."

"Let's say in the neighborhood of one fifty a week," Nina Farrow says briskly. "That *is* a bit higher than we'd planned, but I *do* see your point. We want all our editors, all our secretaries, right down to the teeniest little typist, to feel that their salary is commensurate with ability. Every woman who works for *Free Woman* deserves that right. Now. When can you start?"

"Oh. Well, next week is a little bit tight, actually. I realize the letters are piling up, but I do have a few commitments next week. Would two weeks be too long?"

"Two weeks," Nina Farrows says, sighing again. "*Not* ideal, but I suppose we can manage. Two weeks from Monday. Be here by nine and report to the personnel director on the second floor; he'll give you all the necessary forms to fill out. Then report up to me and I'll show you your desk and introduce you around. Meanwhile try to have that masturbation outline in; Frank's dying to see it. Those snaps are divine, by the way. Too divine. You photograph too well. We'll have to do something about that. Two weeks then. Congratulations. 'Ta."

Pain is shooting through my head. My teeth are chattering. What have I done? My children. No nanny. A job I don't want. Summer looming. Deposit on house. Masturbation. Frank. A hundred fifty dollars a week. Andrew. Andrew will leave me. I cannot support three children on $150 a week. I pour a waterglass full of gin, without ice, lie back on my bed, and stare at the ceiling. The cell is back. Its semipermeable membrane looks just as semipermeable as ever. If not more so. Nicco climbs into bed with me, touches each of my breasts, and says, "Ding dong. Ding dong." I fold him into my arms. We sleep.

X

"Andrew? Andrew, I took the job."

We are lying on a grassy hill in Central Park, overlooking the boat pond. Small white sails flutter in the distance. The remnants of a picnic—crumpled napkins, chicken bones, apple cores, an empty bottle of rosé—are scattered on the plaid blanket before us. Kate is roller-skating back and forth on a smooth area of pavement at the bottom of the hill; Nicco and Anna are playing house under a tree, reenacting our picnic with leaves for plates and twigs for chicken. I could not tell Andrew last night, he looked so drawn and tired that pity, the kind I felt for Spook, won out. Pity, and fear. I feel safer outside, amongst people.

Andrew looks at me. His hair is tousled, ruffled by the breeze; his eyes are pure gray, washed clear by the sun. I reach over and brush his hair off his forehead.

"Did you hear me, Andrew? I took the job. I start in two weeks."

"I never knew you'd been that unhappy," he says in a strange, dead tone. "All that time, I never knew."

Guilty, guilty, guilty.

"I haven't," I say quickly. "That is, if I have, it hasn't been your fault. It's just . . . staying home all those years I . . . when you think about it, I won't be gone that long. I'll be home just a few hours after the girls. If it were Anna I'd be leaving for the afternoon it would be different, but Nicco, if I find someone kind, someone who'll take him out, take him to the park, that's all he really wants. He's pretty independent. He doesn't really care who's with him. It's not like Anna."

"Why did we have them, then? Why did we have children?" Andrew asks in the same strange, dead tone.

"Oh Andrew, don't say that. You know I wanted children. You know we wanted children."

"But why have children to leave them? How can you leave them now, just before the summer? Why *now?*"

"Because I can't wait. I *can't.* If I don't take this job I'll never find another. I'm not *trained* for anything. I can't *do* anything. If it weren't for Lauren I'd never even have gotten this job. Look, if we can't get the deposit back, we could try to rent the house for July to someone else, couldn't we? We could put the children in day camp. And then in August I could come out on weekends and you could take your vacation there; you have three weeks, you'd still have the house for your vacation. And the children could be out there with you, they've never been alone with you before, they'd love it. And the maid or nurse or whoever we get could go out there and help you take care of things."

"I don't want to go without you."

"But Andrew, I've gone without *you;* I've spent seven straight summers out there alone without you. It's just this summer that will be a little hard. After the summer everything will settle down. Nothing will be so very different."

"Everything will be different," Andrew says, sitting up, hugging his knees and staring at the pond. "Everything."

And then on Monday afternoon the parade begins.

Nannies who don't do housework. Maids who don't like children. Kindly South Americans who don't speak English. Belligerent blacks who do speak English. Glazed young girls who want to live in. Shaky old ladies who want to leave by four. A warm, friendly Jamaican who seems perfect and never shows up the next day. A desperate unwed mother with an infant she'd have to bring along. Black women, brown women, white women, yellow women; short women, tall women, fat women, thin women. References that don't check out. Three drunks, one addict, and at least two sadists. Mama Rosie, the half-day-a-week cleaning lady, is out of the question. Although the children love and accept her for what she is, as do I, I have never left them alone with her. She is cranky, arthritic, doesn't want to work full time, and still believes that the best cure for colic is a grease-soaked rag. Which philosophy carries over into other child-rearing areas. Stop Nicco from climbing on windowsills? Hang him out by his feet. That'll stop him. Sure 'nuff.

And then on Friday, when I have almost given up hope, I find her. Dolores. A Colombian woman about my own age who speaks a pretty, broken English. (But at least it's English.) During our interview she sits, a little tense and shy, but fielding each question as it comes. When Nicco runs into the room she automatically holds out her arms. Anna hangs back but seems to like her too. Even Kate is charmed by her sweet face and deferential manner. (All of Kate's friends have maids; I suppose Dolores will be something of a social asset, which Kate needs badly. Her address is a sad minus.)

Dolores has two young boys of her own. Her husband left her three years ago; walked out. She does not know where he is. Her mother cares for the boys when they get home from school. She will clean, do the laundry, take Nicco to the park. No, she does not mind if the children have friends over; she loves children. I don't believe most people when they say they love children (usually the reverse is true) but I think Dolores means it. The summer will be a problem, especially those three weeks in the country (if Andrew agrees to go), but she will somehow arrange it. Her references check out. "She is an extremely responsible, well-trained maid; serves well, cleans well and is devoted to children," says Mrs. Reference in Park Avenue-Greenwich tones. "We were *distraught* at losing her, but the city just became too *much* for us to handle. And her mother, I believe she also has children—naturally we couldn't take all *that* on."

Naturally not. I don't give a shit about the serving well, cleaning well part, but the responsibility, the devotion, yes. And they're there. I hire Dolores. She will start Monday, a week before I begin working, so that the children will have a chance to get used to her. (And so that I can double-check; I trust my instincts, but I haven't trusted them in so long I want to be absolutely sure.) Once the children start camp, and during the school year, she will work from ten to six, earlier or later in emergencies, which we both hope won't happen too often. I am to pay her one hundred dollars a week, more when her hours are longer, plus carfare and half her Social Security, which will probably leave me nothing at all left over by the time I get through, but does not seem outrageous for taking care of an apartment and three children. Seems, in fact, outrageously low. I should know.

On Monday and Tuesday I watch Dolores closely with the children. I like what I see. She is efficient, careful, loving. If anything she is too careful, too permissive. When Nicco scrapes his knee she picks him up in her arms and dashes off for Mercurochrome and bandages, cuddles him, fixes a special drink of ginger ale. When he decides he does not like the sandwich she has prepared for his lunch, she immediately replaces it with another. But I talk to her about Nicco and each of the children. She may not understand all of my theories, she may not handle everything exactly the way I would—who would?—but she listens. She tries to understand. She makes tiny clothes for Anna's fairies. Anyone who makes clothes for fairies can't be all bad.

By Wednesday I feel secure enough to leave Nicco with Dolores while I go to Bloomingdale's to buy myself some new clothes—shoes, a linen skirt, some tops, a summer pants suit, two dresses. I am back into a size eleven for the first time in months; I must have lost a few pounds. It is the first time I have shopped for myself in years. I leave the clothes at the tailor to be altered, make an appointment to get my hair cut, stock up on staples, clean out closets.

When I tell Mama Rosie that I cannot afford to pay both her and Dolores, we both cry. I hug this old black woman, my second mother, who'd kill me if she ever heard me call her black, and tell her that I will try to find her another job. She does not have enough to live on, I know. Even my half day made a difference. But who will take on a black woman of sixty-eight who is only able to do superficial cleaning, often forgets a toilet here, a sink there, and cannot work more than four hours a day? It will take me a while to get over Mama Rosie.

The house is spotless. The children do not get chicken pox. Maybe God is looking down on me, grinning insanely, for once.

Andrew keeps an eye on the changing scene, but says nothing. Having for a short time chosen anger, he retreats into silence.

I finish my masturbation outline and mail it in to *Free Woman*. I hope Frank eats his fat heart out. The old fuck.

My father calls. He and Andrew have apparently been in contact. He is very upset. "How do you think it makes Andrew feel, having his wife go out and get a job?" he shouts into the phone as soon as I've said "hello." "That's a terrible thing, Liza, to do to a man. It's like cutting off his balls. All right, if you have to do it you have to, but a Spanish person! A maid! How can you leave your children with a maid? A nurse at least, a white human being, someone from England or Scotland or Germany even. But a maid! A Puerto Rican maid! That shows no sense at all."

"Dolores isn't Puerto Rican, she's Colombian."

"Colombian, Puerto Rican, it's all the same. What a thing to do to your husband. What a thing to do to your children. If it's a question of money just tell me. I'll pay. Who else should you be able to come to if not your own father? But what a thing! Do you think I'd ever have let your mother work? Do you think I'd ever have let her leave you with a maid?" shouts my father.

"Speaking of Mother, will she let you visit her? Or does she still tell the nurses not to let you in?" I ask from between clenched teeth. My sarcasm goes unnoticed, as usual.

"And that's another thing," says my father. "I did what you said. I stopped bringing her presents. I stopped bringing her flowers. I don't understand, I thought, but all right, anything, I'll try. And now. Now! She lets me in, yes, but you know what she calls me? Daddy. Daddy! She thinks I'm her father. That drunken no-good, that poet, that Episcopalian bum. She thinks I'm him."

On Saturday night after dinner I call a family conference. They troop into the living room, dragging their feet. But nothing can stop me now. I may not know where I'm going, but I'm on my way. Bodies in motion stay in motion.

"Sit down. I have something to say," I announce.

They sit in a row on the couch, looking unpleasant. I sit facing them, in a chair. Like a shrink.

"You know I am going to start working on Monday," I say.

They nod. In unison.

"All right. Here is what I want to say. Dolores is a very

fine person. She's going to have a lot to do; she's going to be working very hard. And when I get home I'm going to be tired. Things are going to have to be different around here; everybody is going to have to start taking care of themselves for a change. That means not eating and dropping clothes all over the house. It means straightening up your own rooms, making your own beds—at least you, Kate, and maybe Anna—taking the dog out once in a while, helping set and clear the table. Without arguing. I think maybe I'll make up a schedule so that everybody will know what to do when. And Kate, I meant what I said. You're absolutely going to have to walk home from the bus stop alone and really help out around the house. You're certainly old enough. We can't expect Dolores to do it all."

"Why not? She's a maid, isn't she, that's what maids are for," says Kate. "I don't see what you're making such a big fuss about. *You* did it all. Why can't *she* do it all?"

Before I have time to stop and think, I get up and slap Kate in the face. Kate bursts into tears and leaves the room.

"I'm glad you won't be here anymore, *glad,*" she sobs. "I hope you *never* come home."

"You had no reason to slap her like that," Andrew says, getting up to go after her. "You can't blame the children for being upset."

"Do you think it's pleasant to hear that for ten years your only relationship with your family has been that of a maid?" I call after him furiously.

But he is gone. He does not answer.

"I don't, Mommy. I don't think of you like a maid," says Anna, on the verge of tears.

Later, after the children are asleep and I am in bed, reading over back issues of *Free Woman,* which I went downtown to buy on Thursday, Andrew comes into the bedroom. He is holding two glasses of wine.

"I shouldn't have said that, in front of Kate," he says. "I know you've had too much to do. It's true, she's very rude sometimes. I can see why you got upset."

"Don't worry. It doesn't matter."

This is no time for a fight.

"Would you like some wine?"

"Yes. I'd like some wine."

In spite of myself, my body tenses. When Andrew switches out the light and I feel his naked body against me, every nerve is jumping. He makes good love, better than ever before; there is a new intensity to it, fierce, that shatters me. I am drowning. Nothing else is real. Nothing. Not death nor life nor work nor love nor friendship nor laughter. This is all there is. I am crying, my teeth in Andrew's shoulder. I am crushed by his weight. Still inside me, he raises himself on his arms and looks down into my eyes.

"Please don't do it," he says. "Don't go. I love you. I'll lose you. I know it."

"You won't lose me. I don't know what you mean; I don't know what you're saying." (But of course, I do know what he's saying. I just didn't know that he knew.) "Andrew. Andrew, listen to me. I didn't know. I didn't know it meant that much to you. Andrew, don't turn away. Look at me. I won't go. I'll call Monday and say I can't come in. Please. Please look at me."

He turns back, holds me so tightly I cannot breathe. He is crying. I have never seen him cry before. My body is alive again. How many women have this? It occurs to me that I am having an affair with my husband. Pure and simple sex. The kind other women seek elsewhere. Well, I have always done everything ass-backwards.

The next day, Sunday, all of us drive to the suburbs for lunch with business friends of Andrew's. The parkway is lined with varying shades of green; on the left the river shimmers. When we reach the town in which the Fosters live, Andrew looks around at the neat village green with its small white church, rows of quaint shops, clean empty streets and says, "It's so clean here, isn't it? So quiet. The air smells different. It's good to see trees."

To me a tree is a tree is a tree. I can't get all that excited.

"Yes," I say warily. Andrew has tried to convince me to move to the suburbs more than once.

"And the children are safe. Look, they can ride their bicycles around and visit their friends. You don't have to worry about them all the time."

"Mm."

From what I've heard, you worry plenty. Especially after they hit thirteen or so. There is a sole child in sight riding a bicycle. He is blond, freckled, gap-toothed, and looks like a Norman Rockwell version of Tom Sawyer.

"No wonder the Fosters moved," Andrew says. "Lots of families are moving out of the city. Even the ones with a great deal of money. Maybe it's something we should think about."

"I don't want to leave the city, Daddy," Kate says. "It's just because of where we live that you feel that way. If we lived on the East Side you wouldn't feel that way. People out here are so different. The girls my age act retarded. And the mothers look so old."

That's my girl. For once.

Andrew puts his arm around me. Unusual. He is an extremely cautious driver. Since last night he has been very loving.

"Your mother will never look old," he says firmly.

Kate makes a throwing up noise from the back seat.

We turn into the Fosters' driveway. The house is square and white with black shutters. Off to one side is a badminton court and a small pool. There are flowers everywhere. No one is in sight. In fact, aside from Tom Sawyer, no one has been in sight on any of the lovely winding lanes or bright green lawns we have passed. Where are all the happy children, breathing in that safe, clean, quiet air?

Elaine Foster, a pretty blonde, comes out to meet us, her footsteps crunching heavily on blue-gray gravel. She has put on weight. Her face looks strained. She is holding a cigarette in one hand and a glass of wine in the other. I've always liked her; she is a bright, warm, funny woman—when her husband isn't around.

"God, come in, I'm so glad you could come," says Elaine. "Most people won't come up; they act as if we lived in *Alaska*. My God is that *Kate?* God, she's grown. The children are inside. Somewhere. I don't know why they're inside all the time; in the city they were always whining to go to the park and now that we've moved they spend most of the time in the closet, it seems to me. Come in. Or rather, come out. We're having lunch on the back patio. Donald's idea."

We walk through the house and onto the back patio. The sun is streaming down; a fat bee is buzzing sleepily over a vase of tulips. Donald, in a sort of tan safari outfit, is mixing drinks.

"Your house is just beautiful," I say politely. I have never known how to talk to Donald Foster.

"Terrific, isn't it? Of course, it isn't finished yet. We're adding a new wing, a children's wing, upstairs, and putting in a completely new kitchen for Elaine," says Donald. He is pink with healthy sunburn, freshly shaved; his hair is damp. Probably played golf this morning, came home and took an ice-cold shower. He-man. Rugby-like. I hope, for Elaine's sake, the shower did its job. "But I'll take you on a tour as soon as you've had a drink," Donald continues heartily, slapping Andrew on the back. "I can't tell you, I honestly can't tell you, old man, what this move has done for us. I don't know how we ever stood the city, we never go in anymore, never, I can hardly stand leaving all this every morning and going in to work but of course I . . . Elaine. Elaine, uh, don't you think you've had enough wine? You're supposed to be . . . sort of taking it easy, aren't you, darling? Why don't you check on that fantastic quiche?

"Elaine's become a fantastic cook since we moved; she's taking lessons from a woman out here, someone who studied at *Cercle des Gourmettes,*" Donald says to Andrew, sotto voce. "Well now. Let's take that tour."

I put down my one-quarter-finished Bloody Mary. Why do new homeowners always want to take you on tours? I never take anyone on a tour of my apartment. God forbid.

We walk dutifully through room after room of expensively furnished, immaculate rooms. Not a book, toy, ashtray, or pillow is out of place. Do people actually live in these rooms, living, breathing people? The answer, I discover later when I escape and go to the kitchen to help Elaine with lunch, is no. In at least one case.

Elaine is taking a crabmeat quiche out of the oven. Salad, homemade bread, radishes, and curls of butter lie in wait on the butcher-block table. Tears are running down Elaine's cheeks into the quiche. She is drinking straight vodka. When she sees me, her head jerks up and she frantically wipes her eyes with a dish towel. "Oh God, please don't say anything," she whispers. "I'm not supposed to be drinking, especially vodka. I'm only allowed to have wine. One glass of wine. For God's sake, don't say anything."

"Of course I won't. But why can't you . . . is there some special reason you're not supposed to drink?"

Elaine laughs, stops abruptly, laughs again. She is still crying. "Oh Liza, I'm so glad you came. The women out here are incredible. What am I saying, I don't even *know* any women out here; I only see them at the supermarket or at that fucking cooking course Donald made me sign up for.

I don't know what they *do* all day behind all those shut doors. You could go for weeks without seeing a soul. *Anybody*. Yes, there's a reason I'm not supposed to drink. I cracked up. I mean really. I was in the hospital for a month; I went totally out of my mind. In April. Ever since then I've been on Thorazine or some goddamn thing, I don't know, I can't think straight, I have to go to a shrink twice a week, I hate him, he's the most stupid asshole I've ever met, his socks keep falling down. I don't know what happened; the kids were in school all day and I just sat here alone, I kept on cleaning, I'd even clean things I'd just cleaned, just to have something to do. And I started drinking. Really drinking. I'd start at ten in the morning. And then one night we had some people over, awful people, the first people from here we'd ever had over, Donald met the husband playing golf, the wife looked like Eleanor Roosevelt but younger, you know, her mouth went all over the place, she kept wanting me to *join* things, some committee to plant tulips in front of the ladies' village improvement society, some fucked-up thing about getting *Catcher in the Rye* banned from the library, and Donald said something like, I don't know, yes I do, he began making fun of my work. He called it my therapy. 'Yes, Elaine worked in the city, it was good therapy for her, she ought to find something out here to keep her busy too,' he said. Therapy. I put him through law school. I loved my job. I was really helping those children. But then when they made him a partner we had to move. We had to buy this fucking house. I *hate* this fucking house."

"But . . . couldn't you find work up here, Elaine? I mean, what you were doing was so important, it's ridiculous for anyone to put it down, call that kind of work your . . ."

"There *aren't* any retarded children up here. They must kill them at birth or hide them in the attic or something. Every kid up here has straight blond hair and little blue eyes, they all look alike, every goddamn one of them, they're so fucking normal it makes me sick. Everybody up here makes me sick. Sometimes I look out the window and I'd give my life to see a dwarf or a degenerate or somebody with one leg or . . . anyway, after the people left I went into the bathroom and swallowed a whole bottle of sleeping pills. They pumped my stomach; they said I nearly died. So I'm not supposed to drink; that's what they say brought it on. Drinking."

Elaine is really crying now, barely able to control the sound of her sobbing. I pull her head to my shoulder and stroke her hair. "The quiche," she says, gesturing feebly. "It's getting cold."

"Forget the quiche."

"But it wasn't drinking that brought it on. It was Chloe. Remember Chloe, that little dog we had? Donald hated her; he was always asking why we couldn't get rid of her and buy an Afghan or a Briard or something, but I really loved that dog. And then in March she died. She ran out into the road and a car ran over her and she died. She died in my arms. Oh God, he's calling me. Go out there and tell him lunch will be ready in a minute, will you? I can't go out there looking like this. He thinks I'm better. Better. Believe me, the next chance I get I won't fuck it up. The next time I'll die. Like Chloe. She was the only damned thing in the house that cared about me."

We are snug in the car, driving home. It is almost dark. Nicco is fast asleep in my arms in the front seat. Anna's head is lolling. Kate is staring out the window, counting trees.

"They really have a lovely place," Andrew says.

"Did you know Elaine tried to kill herself?" I ask.

At the wheel Andrew's hands tense, then relax. "Good God, no. Why? What happened?"

"Andrew, I want to try this job. I want to take it. I have to take it."

"What does Elaine have to do with it? I thought we decided you weren't going to. You said you weren't going to."

"I shouldn't have said that. I have to."

Andrew's eyes are straight ahead, watching the road. He suddenly accelerates. He knows I am afraid of speed.

"I guess that's that, then. I can't stop you," Andrew says.

The speedometer wavers at sixty-seven miles an hour.

The next morning I am up by six. By seven I am made up, perfumed, dressed, and terrified. By eight the breakfast dishes are in the sink, Max has been walked, and I am ready to take the children to school. I would like to ask Andrew to take them on this, my first day of work, but if I'm going to play by the rules, it's my day. So I'm playing.

"You'll check, won't you, that Dolores got here all right?" Andrew asks as we are standing by the door.

"I'll check."

"Are you at least going to earn enough to pay her? You never told me what you're going to earn. I can't afford to pay a full-time maid."

"I will pay her."

"And you mentioned day camp. Are you also going to earn enough to pay for day camp? I can't afford to pay for that either. That and the house. Suppose we can't rent the house?"

"I'll find a way. I'll write an article. They said I could do articles on the side. Andrew, please. Do we have to talk about it now?"

"Articles. You've never written an article in your life. What in the name of God are you going to write an article about?"

"Masturbation."

That should hold him for a while.

"Jesus Christ," says Andrew.

"Wish me luck."

"Good luck," says Andrew, not meaning it.

I point Kate in the direction of the 79th Street crosstown and on impulse, kiss her cheek. "Keep an eye on things, will you baby?" I murmur. "I left the office number by the phone. I'll be home by six at the latest."

Kate pulls away. Her eyes are pure ice.

"I don't care what time you get home," says Kate. "And I will *not* walk that dog."

In front of Anna and Nicco's school, I go over the instructions again. Stay with Dolores in the park. Come right up in the elevator. Do not leave clothes and food all over the house.

"Don't worry, Mom," says Nicco.

"I'll miss you Mommy," says Anna. "And Kate will too. She just doesn't know how to tell you. But she will."

Thinking over this flash of seven-year-old insight, I dash for the bus.

I arrive at the office a little before nine. The personnel director is not in yet. The downstairs office is enormous. Row upon row of gray metal desks. Only two are occupied.

"Nobody gets in on time except the pool; you might as well relax," says a heavy, dark-haired girl wearing a miniskirt that shows off thighs like columns. "You're going to work upstairs, right? I can always tell. You want some coffee? Who're you going to work for?"

"Yes, I'd love some. I don't know exactly who I'm going to be working for, Frank Johnson, I guess. And Nina Farrow."

"Oh boy," the girl says. "You want regular? A Danish or something?"

"No thanks. Just coffee. Regular."

The coffee arrives. It is much too sweet but I drink it anyway. The office is rapidly filling up with girls, girls who slap heavy imitation leather shoulder bags onto stained blotters, remove covers from typewriters, order coffee, munch Danishes and doughnuts. By nine-thirty the room resounds with the clatter of keys, the bumping of tabs, the grinding of margin releases. My head is throbbing.

At ten the personnel director arrives. I spend over an hour filling out a sheaf of forms that ask questions going back to elementary school and continuing right on up to the present. Thirty-four years old. Three children. My husband is a lawyer. Suppose I didn't have a husband? My diamond ring catches the light as my hand fills out form after form. Used to snacking all morning, I am already hungry.

By the time I get upstairs to Nina Farrow's office it is after eleven. Her door is closed. Marge, dressed this time in yellow bell-bottoms and a paisley top, asks me to wait; Nina is in conference. By twelve I am still waiting and starved. I am so hungry I feel shaky and weak; I feel like crying. Finally the door opens.

"Liza. Darling!" says Nina. "*So* sorry I got tied up." (Through the open door I can see that her office is empty. It is, however, redolent of nail polish.) "Well. Let's get you settled. Let me show you your desk."

My desk is at the end of the corridor, outside Frank's office. The secretaries' desks descend in a straight line down the left of the corridor. My desk is on the right. I am not, then, considered a secretary. But as all the editors have offices or cubicles of their own, I am apparently not considered an editor either. On my desk is a pile of papers.

"Are those the letters?" I ask, trying to sound intelligent. (And to cover the roaring growls emanating from my stomach.) "I can't wait to get a look at them, to see what the readers' problems are."

Nina sighs. "No darling. These are samples of what's already been done. Carbons."

"Oh. Well, should I go over the carbons and then look at the letters?"

Nina sighs again.

"Darling. There *are* no letters."

"No letters? I'm afraid I don't understand."

"Let me explain. Sit down."

We sit.

"Letters come *in,*" says Nina, "but we do not *use* them. Most letters from readers are totally unusable. They do not fit in with the concept we want to get across during any particular month. Say, for example, we are running an article about diet. We will then run a letter that asks a *question* about diet, a question, that will, of course be answered in the *article* about diet. Or say, as in the September issue—we work three months ahead you know—we have several fantastic full-page ads on blush-on. Dear Lauren. We can't mention products by name, obviously, but what we *can* do, *did* do, was run a letter from this poor little extremely no-color salesgirl from Butte, Montana, begging, absolutely begging, for advice, her entire life was in shreds, she sat home night after night, and the advice of course was, guess. Just take a guess."

"To use blush-on," I say. Listen, I'm no dummy. Growl, growl.

"Exactly! I knew you'd catch on quickly," says Nina Farrow. "Oh, it doesn't hurt to *read* the few letters that come in, of course; oc*ca*sionally a letter will come in that will give us a new idea, but basically we give you ten ideas a month, and then you write each letter and answer it. Do you see?"

"You mean . . . I'll be writing to people who don't exist? I'll be writing the letters myself and answering them myself?"

"That's the idea!" says Nina gaily. "As you'll see, geographic diversity is vital. We balance our letters geographically. There is an atlas in the file cabinet at the other end of the hall. Each column should reflect diversity—North, East, West, Midwest, Southwest, South—and balance: small towns, large cities, small cities, suburbs, teeny little towns. And as you'll see from the carbons, the readers' names must vary ethnically; it makes the letters seem more real, more authentic. We wouldn't want to have six Italians and four

Lithuanians—second generation of course—have their letters appear the very same month, now would we?"

"No. No, we wouldn't."

"Of course not. We'd have every group in the country after us."

"Yes. I can certainly see your point."

Nina Farrow looks at me intently. She is always looking at me intently; maybe she's myopic and refuses to wear glasses. Or maybe her contacts are slipping.

"There is another point, a vital point, I'd like to make before you begin," says Nina.

"Yes. Anything. Any help at all you can give me."

"We are always totally *honest* with our readers. We never talk *down* to them. If we are anything, we are sin*cere*."

Right on.

"I think I get the idea."

"Fantastic! Now. Let me take you around, introduce you to the staff. I'm sure you'll make many friends. We have a delightful staff. A fantastic staff."

Frank grunts. Marge smiles feebly. The rest of the staff does not appear to notice me one way or the other. We return to my desk.

"I *must* dash," Nina says, looking at her watch. "I'm *hours* late. Oh yes. Your lunch hour is from one to two. We're not fanatics about it, this *is* 1974, but we *do* like our girls to be responsible about keeping to their allotted hours. You *were* here by nine, weren't you?"

"Yes. I was here by nine."

"I *knew* you were that type of person. Now before I dash off I'll just give you our current list of ideas and you can go through the carbons. There are reference books on beauty, popular psychology, and so on in the bottom drawer of your desk. Then why don't you try out a few letters? Just a trial run, of course, we don't expect you to pick it all up your very first day, but perhaps you'll surprise us. Wouldn't that be fun?"

"Yes, it would be. Fun."

"Fantastic. I'll just leave you to your own devices until one and then you trot on off for lunch. Remember—total honesty. No phoniness. 'Ta."

I look through the carbons. But what interests me most are the letters I find by accident while looking in the middle drawer for a pencil. Real letters. Here is a real letter from a real reader in Mayfield, Georgia:

> "Dear *Free Woman,*
>
> Please help me. I am thirty one year old. I have three little kids under age of five. They are all over the house which cuts in to my grooming time a grate deal. I would like to look nice like those wonderful ladies in your magazine. My husband is a good man although he has a drinking problem, he drove me in to town last week and bought me many nice gifts a new dress, a lipstick red, some rouge to match as you say, and an eyebrow pensil black. I have aplied these cosmetics for two weeks now and a rinse on my hair, blond, but my husband's problem is not better. He leaves me alone at nite with the kids or if he stays home sometimes he beats me up. But the worst is he will not talk to me, even when I am waring the cosmetics and the new dress he acts just like I were not their. I am so lonely sometimes I want to die. Do not think because of this letter I do not beleive in God, I do, I know it is sinfull to want to die, but I don't have anyone to tell my problems too. I am 5 5 weight 140, do you think if I lost weight down to 120 as your diet guide suggests to be my proper weight my cercumstances might improve?
>
> Very truly yours,
>
> Mrs. John Thomas O'Malley
>
> P.S. Please whatever you do, if you print this letter, do not use my name."

Dear Mrs. O'Malley,

I too have a weight problem. In fact, we have many problems in common. My husband does not drink or beat me up, but I agree with you; the loneliness is the worst, unbearable. I do not, however, feel that dieting or applying blush-on—we call it blush-on now, not rouge—will solve our problems. If you are seriously contemplating suicide, as I am, would you consider leaving your husband and moving to New York? (I would offer to move South, but I do not think I could live in the South.) We could share an apartment. One of us could care for all six children—I also have three children; the similarities are amazing—while the other sought a meaningful career. We could switch off every six months. I understand all kinds of revolutionary arrangements are being worked out in Sweden. Or perhaps it's Denmark. No matter. We must not be afraid. We must not be reactionary. It is up to us to change the system. Or if you feel a move is totally out of the question, why not contact your local parish priest? Unfortunately I am not a Catholic and do not have this type of option, but I noticed your name sounded strongly ethnic, so I . . .

Another real letter from a real (very real) reader. Fine geographic diversity. Brooklyn, New York:

"Dear *Free Woman,*

If you want my personal opinion, your magazine is the biggest bunch of shit I ever read. I hope you print this.

Sincerely,
Bunnie Nussbaum"

Dear Bunnie,
I'm with you.

* * *

I replace the real letters in the drawer and look over the carbons and reference books until one. No one invites me to have lunch with them. The secretaries go laughing off in clannish clumps; the editors go laughing off in clannish clumps. I am not laughing. I am not part of a clump. I am all alone. I go into a steamy luncheonette on a side street and order a hamburger, French fries, and coffee. I am starving; I have never been so hungry in my life. Before I am finished with the hamburger I order another. In the mirror behind the counter I see that I look exhausted; there are dark circles under my eyes; I am very pale. I finish the second hamburger, buy some aspirin and cigarettes and, seeing the telephone booth, remember that I have forgotten to be sure that Dolores arrived on schedule. Knowing Dolores, I am ashamed to call, but do. Dolores and Nicco are on their way to the park. No, she will not forget to be back in time for Anna. Yes, she will make sure Nicco does not ride his tricycle down the hill. Her soft sad voice soothes me.

I walk slowly back to the office, smoking a cigarette. It is only one-thirty, but I have nowhere to go, and the sun's harsh glare hurts my eyes. In the ladies' room I splash cold water on my face, brush my hair, and swallow two aspirins. By two o'clock I am hard at work at some letters. By four forty-five the people I have made up have become very real to me. I am wondering whether or not to tell a balding woman in Waco, Texas, to seek professional help—the problem sounds really bad; her hair is falling out by the handfuls; I'm not at all sure the article on carefree hair care offered by *Free Woman* will answer her questions—when Frank comes out of his office, puts his fat hand on the back of my neck, and unzips the zipper of my brand new top.

"Knock it off!" I yell before I have time to think.

If looks could kill. Perhaps by Christmas I won't need a gun. Frank will more than do.

"I'm sorry, I didn't mean it quite that way. You just . . . sort of startled me," I mumble. "I'm sorry."

Frank picks up the letters I am working on, reads them quickly, throws them back on my desk and says:

"That sucks."

"Excuse me?"

"I *said,* that sucks. It's crap. Shit. No good. Do it over."

Frank goes back into his office. I go into the ladies' room, lock myself into a cubicle, and cry. I do not come out until five-fifteen, when hopefully most of the staff will be gone. My eyes are still red.

A man I have not seen before is coming out of the art department. He has very dark brown curly hair, big brown eyes, a large nose, and a bushy moustache. Thin. Not too tall. About forty. He looks at me.

"Hey, what's the matter? Are you crying or something?"

I shake my head.

"Yes. Yes you are. At least you were. You're new, aren't you? What's the matter? Did somebody say something? You can't take this group seriously; if you take them seriously you're wiped out, dead. I saw you sitting outside Frank's office. You're not taking over as his secretary, are you? I hope not. You don't look like a secretary. Here. Take this."

I take the handkerchief he is handing me and blow my nose.

"No, I'm not a secretary. I don't know what I am. I'm supposed to write letters to people who don't exist."

The man laughs, showing beautiful white teeth. I want to touch his dark-eyed face.

"Who are you?" I ask. "You don't look like anyone else around here. You don't look sleek."

"I'm an art director. I mean, that's what I do here, for a living. I paint on the side. What do you mean, I don't look sleek? Who's sleek, Frank? Hey listen, please don't cry. Do you . . . which way are you walking? Would you like to stop off for a drink? You could, you know, tell me what happened. I'd really like to know what happened, what made you cry. Just for a drink."

Involuntarily, I stiffen. I am afraid. This man, whoever he is, will not be just for a drink. Whatever is going on between us is so powerful vibrations are bouncing off the walls in waves.

"I . . . thank you, I'd really like to, but it's my first day, the children . . . my children and husband will expect me to be home on time. The maid leaves at six and I'm not sure what time my husband will be home. So I suppose I should really get home."

"Sure, that's okay, I should get home too," says the man. "My kids, the two little ones, they like to come meet me in the car; my wife picks me up at the station. And if I miss the early train they're already in bed; they can't come. But maybe some day we could have lunch. We could have lunch, couldn't we? That would be okay, to have lunch. I'd like to take you to lunch. Just, you know, to talk. Would you like that?"

"Yes, I'd like that. That would be fun."

(Husband, wife, children at home, kids in the car. Now we know, as if we didn't know it already. We are both married.)

In the elevator, we do not speak. When we reach the lobby I walk quickly toward the door. I am out in the street, almost running toward the bus stop.

"Wait. Hey wait. What's your name? You have a name, don't you? What's your name?"

"Liza."

"Liza. Don't you want to know my name?"

"What's your name?"

"Joe. My name's Joe."

XI

Joe. I do not have lunch with him that week, or any other week in June, although he often asks me. But I sense his presence all around; I wait at the water cooler to catch sight of him through the art department door, his sleeves rolled up to the elbows, his hair wild and fuzzy as he bends over his drawing board. He is funny, the office clown. He makes everyone laugh. But like all clowns, he emanates sadness, a quiet, desperate sadness that makes me want to hold him, touch him, take his hand. At night, alone in my bedroom, when I am sure that Andrew is in the living room reading or listening to music, I look at my body, the body I have not looked at in so long. I want it to be beautiful again, thin, a young body.

"Why are you doing exercises?" Andrew asks, coming in on me as I'm touching my toes.

"It's good for you. Exercise is good for you."

I am losing weight, down to a hundred and twenty-five pounds. My skin looks different, too, younger. I keep forgetting my age; twice I give up my seat to startled young women on the Broadway bus. I feel about seventeen.

"You look pretty, Mommy," says Anna. "You look happy. Is it your work office that's making you so happy?" She is constantly reassuring me that she is glad that I'm happy, that she is happy, that everything at home is fine.

"Thank you, darling. But I'll never be as pretty as you."

"If we don't make you over soon, there won't *be* anything to make over," Nina Farrow says, laughing, but not nicely. "Darling! You're positively glowing. You look like someone in love."

Andrew reluctantly agrees to spend his vacation in the country. We manage to rent the house for the month of July. I enroll the children in day camp.

"What will you do with your boys in August?" I ask Dolores, knowing that I should offer to let her bring her boys to the country; knowing too that there is no point; Andrew would say no.

"I don't know, Mrs. Liza. Last year playground, city had day program, but no more. My mother take to playground, I guess. But she is old, so old. Three weeks long time for her alone," says Dolores.

But I am not paying attention. I am not listening. I cannot think of Dolores, or the children, or Andrew. I cannot think of anything. I am waiting.

"You realize that this camp will cost over nine hundred dollars for the three of them, just for one month?" Andrew asks one evening after dinner. (The house and mother's helper cost more, just for one month, but I do not feel like arguing.)

"I'm working on the article."

But I am not working on the article. I sit in front of my typewriter and write Joe's name over and over. Joe. Joseph. Joseph Rossi. Mrs. Joseph Rossi. I rip the papers into tiny pieces and flush them down the toilet.

Everyone looks like him. Everyone. The delivery boy,

bus drivers, strange men on the street. When I see curly dark hair and a bushy moustache, my heart stops. Late at night, very early in the morning, I lie in bed thinking about him. My body is a burning wire; every muscle, every nerve, every brain cell is screaming toward him. Just like in all the songs. But I thought this sort of thing only happened in songs. Or bad movies. I cannot believe this is happening. This is crazy.

"Are you ever going to have lunch with me?" says Joe one morning toward the middle of July, sitting on my desk, legs dangling. "You don't have to sit through a whole lunch if you don't want to. A meatball, maybe. A biscuit tortoni. Would you rather I'd just stop asking?"

We have lunch in a small Italian restaurant, dim and noisy, with wine bottles dripping multicolored wax onto checkered cloths. Although he made me laugh as we walked over from the office, clowning, talking—he never stopped talking—I think he is as frightened as I am.

"They have great spaghetti here. Would you like some spaghetti? With clam sauce?"

"I'm supposed to be on sort of a diet."

"Come on. You're too skinny. I like my women chunky. Have some spaghetti with me."

"I'm not one of your women. But I'll have spaghetti. With you."

"Are you Italian? Your eyes look Italian."

"My father is. Half Italian anyway."

"Hey, that's great. I'm Italian too. Two Italians."

"Why? What difference does it make?" My hands are ice cold. I cannot stand the table separating us. I cannot breathe. I am dizzy. My heart is beating triple-time.

"I don't know. Have some more wine. You started to say something. What were you going to say?"

"Sorry. I was going to say . . . did you ever . . . when you said chunky it made me think of a song I like, a song Jim Croce sang. Do you like Jim Croce? You look sort of like him. Older, but . . . you know."

"I do? Nobody ever said that before. What do you mean older? I'm just a kid. That's funny, your saying that; I just bought a new album. Yes, I like Jim Croce. 'Lover's Cross,' do you like that one? And Crosby, Stills. Even Bob Dylan. I still like Bob Dylan."

"So do I. My . . . husband doesn't like that kind of music. He likes classical music. Good music."

"My wife doesn't like that kind of music either. My daughter does but my wife . . . I guess she really doesn't like any kind of music. She watches television a lot. I don't watch television much. Do you like the spaghetti?"

"Yes, it's great. Neither do I. I felt so terrible when he died."

"Who?"

"Jim Croce. Everyone good seems to die."

"Young. Like James Dean. Remember James Dean? *Rebel Without a Cause?* I was kind of like that when I was young."

"Yes. And *East of Eden.* I loved James Dean. John Steinbeck died too. He wasn't that young, but he was young to die. What I said before . . . when I said you looked older, I just meant you looked young for your age. You do, you know. Look young for your age."

"How old do you think I am?"

"About forty."

"Forty-two. How did you know?"

"Because of your eyes. You have bread crumbs in your moustache."

"Brush them off then."

"I can't."

"Why not?"

"I . . . can't touch you. I don't want to touch you."

Joe puts his hand over mine. His hand is ice cold too.

We have lunch, and lunch again, every day for the next four weeks. And we talk, my God do we talk, about everything: music, people, life, death, work, children, his wife, Andrew. Everything but bed. Within a month I know more about him than I know about Andrew. Does anyone know anything about Andrew?

"What's your husband like?"

"I don't know. Quiet. What's . . . what kind of person is your wife?"

"She's . . . it's not her fault. We married young. She was only nineteen. We had kids right away. She's good with children, she's a good cook, a good wife. We were very young. She . . . I don't know, she . . . just stayed the same."

"How old is your daughter?"

"Sixteen. Real trouble. The boys never gave us this kind of trouble. She's wild. I'm afraid for her. I can't get through to her."

"My oldest daughter, she's only ten, but I have a lot of problems with her too. She . . . it was wrong from the beginning. I couldn't love her. She hates me. She really hates me."

"Nobody could hate you."

"Kate does."

And so on.

Well, crazy or not, here it is. A man who talks. And listens. The American Dream. Or in this case, the Italian Dream. A little battered, a little rump-sprung, more Sancho Panza on Dapple than prince on white charger, but Dream all the same. I know. Love is blind. But damn it, he *is* my dream—bright, funny, vulnerable, verbal, gentle, loving. Everything I've ever wanted all rolled up into one. How could we have missed each other so very long ago?

He is always touching me—holding my hand, patting my ass, ruffling my hair. He kisses me everywhere—my nose, fingers, face. Used to affection simply as a prelude to fucking,

I now know how much I longed for a man's careless, animal touch, for tenderness without the automatic assumption that bed would immediately follow. And of course the fact that this particular touch is unsanctioned adds to the total whatever-it-is I am feeling. Which is a lot.

"Someone will see us."

"No one will see us."

We are sitting on a bench near the Plaza fountain, eating sausage and pepper heros and drinking Coca-Cola out of a single can. Two straws. "I was thinking," Joe says, his mouth full. "I mean, here we are kind of . . . your husband, my wife, they don't seem to be . . . enough. And I was thinking, maybe we could, you know, fill in where they . . ." He stops chewing, swallows, takes a sip of Coke and looks down at his hands. When he looks up his brown eyes are sad. "I'm not very happy, Liza."

"I'm not either, Joseph."

I call him Joseph, not Joe. It makes him more my own. No one else calls him Joseph.

"What I mean is," Joe goes on, "oh, I kid around a lot, I come on like a swinger and everything" (he doesn't; hasn't since our first fumbling lunch, but I say nothing), "but this whole thing I . . . do you think we can handle all this?"

There is no need to ask what he means by "all this." I have been thinking the same thing. Two families. Conflicting allegiance. Time. Involvement. Complications. Pain. Probably more pain than pleasure in the end. Am I unconsciously seeking out pain? I don't think so. Doesn't any last, desperate grab at joy involve the risk of pain? How can an end be weighed against a beginning, or the time between? I can no longer make a rational decision. I am, as they say, hooked.

"Well, do you?" asks Joe again.

"I don't know, Joseph. There have been people who . . . I've heard about people who . . . they seem to be able to handle it. We can try. As long as we don't hurt anybody."

"As long as we don't hurt anybody."

The next day we are playful, determinedly gay. We are going to show each other that we can handle it.

"Let's go to the zoo."

"Okay. Why not?"

We buy hot dogs at an outdoor stand and wander hand in hand past cages filled with exhausted-looking gorillas and sleeping lions. In the damp heat Joe's hair is curlier than ever.

"My God, that looks like the biggest rat in the world," I say, pausing before a cage filled with tapirs and a huge, heavy, brownish something sitting on its haunches staring at me.

"Let's see." Joe reads from the sign above the cage: "The largest rodent in the world is the Capybara (family Hydrochoeridae) which frequents wooded areas close to streams, rivers and swamps. Groups of up to twenty individuals are active at dawn and dusk, but in areas of human settlement they tend, as some other normally diurnal mammals do, to become entirely nocturnal. These are quiet, rather dignified animals, entirely vegetarian and a little more intelligent than most rodents. They are hunted by Jaguars, by Alligators and by Man."

"The largest rodent in the world! Hey, Mama! You've got extrasensory perception!" He calls me Mama sometimes. Or old lady. Just two overaged teen-agers in love. Silly, somewhat sad, but I like it. We laugh helplessly, leaning on each other. As we are laughing a tapir separates itself from the crowd and approaches the Capybara. The Capybara just sits there, staring straight ahead, as the tapir begins salaciously to lick its haunches. Still ignoring the tapir, it shifts its weight, sighs, and slowly lies flat on its back. The tapir then begins to lick the Capybara's stomach. The tapir has a hard-on the likes of which I have never seen.

"That's us," says Joe.

"What's us?"

"The tapir and the capy-whatever-it-is. The big rat."

I pull my hand away.

"That's not funny."

"Why are you crying? Don't cry; I didn't mean anything. Jesus, you sure know how to cry. Why are you crying? What did I do?"

"Because I thought this was different. I thought you were different. I thought . . . oh, it doesn't matter what I thought. It's all the same. It will never be any different. God damn you, let me *go*."

But Joe does not let me go. He forces me to face him. He is holding onto me so tightly his fingers are biting into my arms.

"Don't you give me that," Joe says angrily. "I want you. All of you. For God's sake, Liza, don't you know that? Don't you want to go to bed with me?"

"Oh my God, yes. Yes I do."

I never knew how much I wanted it until the words were out.

Joe's fingers slowly release their grip. He looks at me and touches my face.

"I don't think it's going to work out quite the way we planned, is it old lady?" Joe says sadly.

"No. Maybe we better stop right here."

"I can't. Can you?"

"No. I can't either."

"Think they tryin' to tell you something, baby?" asks the pretty black teller, grinning widely. I have just come up against my third blank wall. Workmen are attaching entrance and exit signs, connected by wide red ribbons, to different areas of the bank; the check-cashing lines have become too long to handle. But the sweating, swearing workmen cannot figure out the maze of ribbon. The entrance signs are affixed to the proper metal posts, but the passages between the wide red ribbons lead to nowhere. There is no way out.

"Oh fuck the goddamn signs and just go up to a teller," says one of the workmen, seeing my problem. A loop of ribbon dangles over his left ear; he looks like a furious Christmas present. "It's going to take the whole goddamn day to figure this out. Why the fuck didn't they give us a blueprint or something? How the fuck are we supposed to figure this out by ourselves?"

Good question.

I have come to the bank to cash a check so that I can pay the obstetrician-gynecologist in cash. I do not want Andrew to see the bill. I am on my way to the ob-gyn to be fitted for a new diaphragm.

In the ob-gyn's waiting room two pregnant women, one holding a squirming toddler, are talking. The toddler is wearing a pink smocked dress, white socks with lace edging, patent leather shoes, and a frilly bonnet. It arches its back, trying to escape from its mother's firm clutches, and screams loudly. The mother sighs and tightens her grasp. "She's so active; she never stops moving. It's a shame she wasn't a boy," the mother says.

The other pregnant women nods in wise agreement. A copy of *Free Woman* lies open in her lap.

"Liza!" says Dr. Weiss. "How good to see you! How are the babies? What do I mean babies, I haven't seen you in two years, you should come in at least once a year for a Pap test, I told you that the last time. I know, I know, don't tell me, the house, three children, you forget. What's the problem? Out to overpopulate the world again?"

"No. Actually, I'd like to be fitted for a diaphragm.

I just can't take those pills, and the last diaphragm I was fitted for was right after Anna was born. Seven years ago."

"Seven years! Would you wear the same dress for seven years? So. You can't take the pill. Too bad, but it happens. Come into my fitting room. I'm doing a Pap on you today whether you like it or not." He slaps my behind proprietarily in passing, but I don't mind. I like Dr. Weiss.

The diaphragm does not seem so difficult to insert this time; once it is in place I cannot feel it at all. I am fitted, Papped, dried, powdered, and out of Dr. Weiss's office by two-thirty.

When I return to *Free Woman* Nina Farrow is waiting at my desk, looking at her watch. Tiny lines furrow her brows. She looks annoyed.

"Liza. *Darling,*" says Nina. "It's almost *three.*"

(What the hell is she doing back from lunch so early? Who's on her tail all of a sudden?)

"I know. I'm sorry. I had a doctor's appointment."

"But you are *consistently* late back from lunch, I hear. It is an *ongoing* problem. I thought I made it clear that we expect our girls to keep to their allotted hours. During the past two weeks you have not been back on time *once.*"

Someone's been squealing. Frank's secretary? She doesn't like me. And if she's been squealing on that, how much else has she been squealing on? Do people know about Joe and me?

"I'm really sorry; it won't happen again. I didn't realize I'd been late that often."

"Just because your work is becoming noticed upstairs doesn't mean you have the right to take such flagrant advantage of the situation. You're not an editor *yet,*" says Nina Farrow, turning on her heel and slamming the door to her office.

Who's upstairs? I thought *we* were upstairs. There's more? Although I have been churning out letters to nonexistent readers everywhere from Sioux City to San Diego, I didn't know anyone had been noticing my work. I thought everyone thought it—in Frank's words—sucked.

Hmm.

XII

"Joseph, where are we going to go? I won't go to a hotel. I don't want to go to a hotel."

We are sitting on a bench in the park. Or rather, I am sitting with Joe's head in my lap, idly brushing his nose with a small leaf.

"Oh my God."

"What?"

"Oh Joseph, I know that woman, it's the mother of one of Nicco's school friends. Oh God, she saw us; I know she saw us. Sit *up*."

Joe sits up. "Even if she did see us, what do you think she's going to do, call your husband? Come on, old lady. Calm down," says Joe. But he seems nervous too.

"I am so fucking sick of people telling me to calm down," I almost yell. "It's all so easy for you. You've got a wife thirty-five miles away. You don't have people walking all over town who know you."

"I know people."

"It's not the same. It's not the same for a man. Everybody expects a man to screw around."

"Screw around? Is that what we're doing?"

"No. Yes. Not yet. Anyway, it's not the same."

"You have some fucking temper, you know that?"

"You'd better believe it."

"Are we having a fight?"

"Our first fight."

"I don't feel like fighting."

"Neither do I."

"Let's go to bed instead."

"Where?"

"Anywhere."

But I know we are both thinking the same thing. Andrew and the children leave for the country in just two days.

My own bed? Make love to another man in my own bed? Somehow the idea doesn't seem so outrageous anymore. But how the hell would I get him upstairs? The downstairs gate to the stairway is locked at all times. The elevator, considering Stefan II—and it would be Stefan II unless we dashed up on our lunch hour—is out of the question. Pass him off as my brother? He doesn't look like my brother. Could he carry a doctor's bag or a pail and squeegee? Too dangerous. And anyway, that would be a one-shot deal. Elly? I could go upstairs and Joe could pretend to be a guest of Elly and Justin's, get off at their floor and walk up the stairs. But what would Justin say? Men stick together in these things, don't they? Or do they? Give in and go to a hotel? *No.* Not only because of my memories of old Marcus, but because I know Andrew will call each night from the country. He worries if I'm not exactly where I'm supposed to be; one night when I had a drink after work with Joe he was frantic. I'd called to be sure he was home and then told him I had to work late, but Andrew, being Andrew, called the office and of course I wasn't there. When I got home I mumbled something about the phone on my desk having been out of order, but Frank's secretary had picked up and (naturally) told him I'd already left. I then mumbled something about Frank's secretary being a jerk and that I'd probably been in conference with Nina. Andrew accepted this explanation, but just barely; I can't risk it again. Besides, I'm a terrible liar. Thinking over and rejecting all these possible arrangements, I'm getting madder by the minute, mostly at Joe. Why do *I* have to figure it out? Why can't *he* figure it out? What am I *doing,* I, Liza Thulin Calder, who wore white gloves and curtsied to dancing teachers, even contemplating such a nasty, evil, low-down thing as adultery? And then I suppress a lusty giggle. I seem to alternate between Waspy disgust and Rabelaisian delight which, considering my conflicting background, comes as no surprise. Why can't I make up my fucking mind? But I want him. God, how I want him. As I am pondering these imponderables, I bump into Elly in the lobby of our building. I have only seen her twice since June; I have not called. How could I have forgotten her so quickly?

"Elly! Why don't you come up for a drink? I haven't seen you for ages; I've been so hung up with this fucking job. Can you come up now?"

Elly smiles wanly and shakes her head. She looks tired. New lines crinkle around her eyes. "Thanks babe, but I'm just on my way home to change; I have to go right out again; I'm late already. But maybe next week. I'd like to talk to you; I really would. Andrew will be gone next week, won't he? I didn't mean it like that, but you know what I mean."

"Yes, they'll all be gone. We're leaving Friday but I'll be back Sunday night. How did you know?"

"Kate told Marilyn. Believe it or not, those two little shits are finally making friends. How's the job?"

"Pure crap. I'll tell you more when we see each other. How's . . . did you find anything yet? For September?"

"Not yet, but I'm looking around. I'll find something," says Elly. Her face brightens with a sudden, wicked grin; she looks more like the old Elly. "Hey, guess what I got from good old Mom Buck in the mail this morning? A recipe for Coca-Cola cake. Coca-*Cola* cake. *Christ.*"

Still laughing, we ride up together. Stefan II looks at us disapprovingly.

"I'll call you Monday night," I say when we reach Elly's floor.

"Terrific, babe. It's been too long."

Stefan II slams the door shut and says:

"No lady."

"Why?" (When will I ever learn?)

"Black people. Hippies. All time black people, hippies, in, out, in, out."

"Yes, they have many black friends. And artists."

"No lady have black friends. Why you friend with hippy like that? You no lady too?" Stefan II asks slyly.

"She's my best friend," I say. "And you're right, Stefan. I'm no lady. Good evening."

I open the door on confusion. Suitcases and straw bags are lined up in the hall, Dolores is mopping up something in the kitchen, the television is blaring, and Nicco is pointing what looks like a stick at Anna's head. Dolores speaks first.

"Mrs. Liza, dog throw up, vomit all the time, also pipi. Very hard, all the time cleaning up, trying to make clean house, with dog throwing up, making pipi so much," says Dolores, reaching for another piece of paper towel.

"Bang!" Nicco says. "Bang Bang!"

In the dimness of the hall, what I took to be a stick turns out to be Andrew's rifle.

"Nicco! Oh my God. Give that to me. Put it down."

"Don't worry, Mom," Nicco says calmly as I grab the gun out of his hands. "It isn't loaded."

"How do you know whether or not it's loaded?" I say, shaking, holding the gun gingerly and pointing it toward the empty living room, ready to knock him flat.

"Because. I already shot the trigger at Anna's head and nothing happened. Dummy old gun. Doesn't even work."

This time I do knock him flat. Open-handed, but flat all the same. Nicco yells. Dolores looks shocked and moves to pick him up, but, seeing my face, stops.

"Dolores, this is a *real gun.* Where did he find it?"

"I don't know, Mrs. Liza. Very busy with dog vomit, pipi. I no see. He say Daddy's gun, Daddy say can play, when I try to take he cry, so I think all right to let him have if Daddy say can play," says Dolores.

"But Dolores, of course his father wouldn't let him . . . good God, he might have . . ."

Sensing her terror, watching her hands nervously clenching and unclenching her apron, I decide to vent my rage on Andrew instead. He must have taken the gun down from the closet or wherever the hell he keeps it–I've never even *known* where he keeps it; he hides everything–to pack for the country. Even unloaded, he should have known better.

"Dolores, I know you don't like to see Nicco cry, but please, the next time, don't let him play with anything dangerous. We've talked about that," I say, struggling for control and not succeeding very well.

"Yes, Mrs. Liza," says Dolores, still terrified.

"Don't you think it was pretty stupid to leave that gun where Nicco could get at it?" I ask Andrew later when I've calmed down and we have finished dinner.

"It wasn't loaded. Anyway, isn't that why we have Dolores? To keep an eye on Nicco?" Andrew throws back. He seems nervous; he has been pacing around all evening checking suitcases, looking through his wallet, writing, then tearing up, lists. "What time is she coming tomorrow morning anyway?"

"Early. Around eight. He might have found the bullets though. He's gotten very good with locks. Andrew, you'll watch him, won't you? I mean, Dolores is fine, she's very good, but sometimes she can be . . . that is, she spoils him sometimes; she gives in to anything he wants. With the water and cars and everything I'm . . . you'll watch him, won't you?"

Andrew sighs, shuffles his credit cards, looks at the checkbook, then at me.

"I'll watch him. But it will seem funny out there, without you," Andrew says.

In the morning, after the frenzied tie-ups of Nassau and parts of Suffolk county, when we are almost there, Andrew's face relaxes. He asks me to light him a cigarette. I light one and place it between his lips. He pats my knee, draws on the cigarette deeply several times, then flips it out the open window.

"I'm glad; I don't like you to smoke, Daddy," says Kate from the back seat where she is cramped between Dolores and Anna. Dolores cuddles Nicco absently and stares out the window, unseeing.

The country. The house seems different this year, smaller. Or perhaps it is simply that the children are bigger, and that Dolores is with us. But the bay is the same, calm and blue; the pine trees still cluster near the shabby white fence; the air still smells of salt and wet, rotting wood, and flowers. We unload suitcases, toys, boxes of groceries. Dolores fixes sandwiches for the children. While they are eating, I make two Bloody Marys and carry them out onto the breezy deck. Andrew is looking at a distant sailboat through a pair of binoculars. He puts the binoculars down when he sees me and reaches for my hand.

"You know, I was thinking, maybe it *will* be good for them, to be alone with me," he says. In his voice there is a question, a plea. I sit down in a canvas chair and gaze at the water. For the past month it has become increasingly difficult to look at Andrew. He, who rarely touched me, who never liked to be touched except in bed, now reaches out for me often. But now it is I who cannot bear to be touched. At least by him. I squeeze his hand and gently withdraw my own.

"Drink your Bloody Mary," I say.

On Sunday night Andrew and the children come to the station with me. The platform is filled with people—lean, bronzed women with sun-bleached hair; small children in summer pajamas; men carrying overnight bags and attaché cases; young groupers, their jeans still damp and sandy from a last-minute run on the beach. It is a summer ritual, waiting for the train. Friday nights are festive; mothers check their makeup in shining car mirrors; dashboards hold pitchers of martinis. Children run up and down the platform; they dance with excitement. But this is the train that carries fathers back to the city, the train for saying good-bye. And this year I am going back to the city, not Andrew. I am going back alone.

The mournful whistle wails down the track; I can see its searching beam. A small boy in blue and white striped pajamas darts forward and places a penny on the rail. In his father's arms, a baby cries. I kiss the children quickly; Andrew presses a square package into my hand.

"Call me as soon as you get home, no matter what time it is. I won't be able to sleep without knowing whether or not you got home safely."

"Don't worry; I'll be all right. What's this?"

"Nothing. Something. Don't open it until you get home."

The train is hot and stuffy; it smells of soot. The

package lies in the palm of my hand. Idly, I undo the strand of yellow ribbon. Inside the white tissue paper is a small box. I open it and from the soft cotton draw a narrow gold bracelet and a card that says: "I know you won't believe me. I know I don't say it very well or often enough, but I really do love you. Happy Birthday. Andrew."

My birthday. I had forgotten. My birthday is this coming Thursday. I will be thirty-five years old.

Goddamn it, Andrew, why do you have to turn around *now,* now, on the very eve, as it were, of my infidelity? Why can't you shut up and let me hate you in peace? Shit. Shit shit shit shit shit.

But when I arrive home at midnight and call, I tell Andrew that the note and present made me happy. He tells me that the children are planning a gala birthday celebration for Friday night. He says he loves me. I say I love him. We say good-bye.

On Monday, when I turn my key in the lock, the apartment is so silent. I have never, in my entire life, really been alone before. I pour a drink, put on a record, and look through the refrigerator. It is half empty, stocked with food for a woman alone: yogurt, individually wrapped chops and chicken breasts, small cans of tuna fish and salmon. I take out a container of yogurt, then put it back again. I am not hungry. After Andrew calls, I pour myself another drink and sit, listening to music until, with a start, I realize that it is dark outside; it is ten-thirty. But I cannot get up; I do not even have enough energy to fix myself a sandwich. Joe. I am willing Joe to call me. The telephone rings. But it is not Joe. It is Elly.

"You sound weird, babe," she says. "Why didn't you call? Are you okay?"

"Oh Christ, I meant to call, I was thinking about it and . . . Elly, could you . . . why don't you come on up tonight? Are you doing anything tonight?"

"Gee babe, I can't. The house is full of clients; Justin's giving this thing, party sort of, for clients. I'd ask you down but it's such shit you wouldn't believe. How about tomorrow? Would tomorrow night be okay?"

"Yes. Sure. Don't worry about it."

"Are you sure you're okay? You sound weird."

"I'm okay."

The evening is filled with hours I have never before noticed. I want to call Joe; I dial five times and hang up before anyone answers. I could not bear to hear his wife's voice. Or worse, the voice of a child. Very slowly, I remove the makeup from my face, shower, wash my hair. When I finally turn out the lights at twelve, night sounds surround me: creaking doors, keys, latches, footsteps. My bed is empty; when I reached out to touch a familiar body, it is not there. So this is what it's like, to be alone! To long for a man, to wait for a telephone call that does not come. No dishes to wash, no clothes to mend, no sleeping children to check on. Free. Totally free. He could have called me. He could have found some excuse to get out of the house and driven to a gas station and called me. Perhaps he will still call.

By one o'clock he has not called. I dial the country house. Andrew answers on the first ring.

"Liza! Is anything wrong?"

"No, Andrew. I couldn't sleep, that's all. I felt lonely and I couldn't sleep."

"I can't sleep either. I miss you, Liza."

"I miss you too. I . . . I just wanted to tell you again, I really liked the bracelet. I liked it a lot."

"I'm glad."

"You'll be sure to watch Nicco in the water, won't you? He runs in; he thinks he can swim. You have to watch him."

"Don't worry. I will."

"And the gun. You put the gun where he can't get at it, didn't you?"

"Yes. Don't worry."

"Well. That's all I wanted to say, I guess. That I missed you."

"I miss you too. Call me later if you can't sleep."

Not until two, after downing three shots of straight gin, do I finally fall asleep. But I do not call Andrew again.

"Why didn't you call me last night; you knew I'd be alone," I hiss at Joe when we meet at the water cooler.

"I couldn't. My wife stayed up until three watching some goddamn talk show," Joe hisses back.

What is this, a French farce? Why is it so easy for everyone else? I've seen movies; I've read a lot. I know what's going on. The whole world illicitly fucking itself to death and I can't even get one lousy phone call.

On the way home I pick up an extra bottle of gin. Elly arrives early, around six.

"My God, it's so neat in here it makes me sick," says Elly, collapsing on the couch. "You're goddamn lucky, you know that? I haven't been alone for one fucking minute since I got married."

"I don't know. It feels kind of creepy."

"Creepy. I should only feel so creepy."

We're going through our routine, but we are uneasy with each other; the jokes, the teasing lines are forced. It is only when we are finishing our second martini that I find the courage to ask Elly what I have been wanting to ask all evening: can Joe take the elevator to her house, stay there for a few minutes and then, when the coast is clear, head on up to me and my bed. I don't like it (neither does Joe) but it seems the only possible solution. Elly listens to my pressing problems involving the mechanics of lust, throws back her head, and laughs. And laughs.

"What the hell are you laughing at?" I ask, trying not to laugh too. "It isn't all that funny."

"Oh baby," Elly says, between gasps. "If I'd only known. Sometimes you come on so goddamn uptight I didn't dare . . . I mean, you aren't really but sometimes . . . no, I'm only laughing because . . . Jesus, both of us, that's wild, and here I've been going out of my mind not having someone to talk to, another woman to talk to. . . . I've been having this thing, affair, with a man I met when I was taking a course, a communications course. He's . . . Hispanic. Well, he isn't really Hispanic, he's part black, his father was black, but he thinks of himself as Hispanic. He's sort of a revolutionary; he's got this storefront school, for one thing, and he helps Hispanic kids get free lunches and stuff. You know what he did once? He told me. He went into the executive office of this big food company, A and P I think it was, or Shopwell, anyway he went in and told them that if they didn't donate food for his kids, he'd blow them up. Yeah. He'd start planting bombs in all their little branches and work his way up to the biggest fucking branch they had. And he got it! He got milk and bread and all the stuff he needed. Can you imagine having the guts to do a thing like that?"

"He sounds . . . young."

"He is young. Twenty-nine. Luis. He's beautiful; he looks like coffee. The whole thing is beautiful. Christ, I should have told you before. If we can't even talk to each other . . ."

"Luis? His name is Luis? Not Rodriguez, I hope."

"Why should his name be Rodriguez? That's like saying every Jew should be named Schwartz. Anyway, I told you, his father was black. From Mississippi."

"Forget it; I'm just kidding. This dog I found belonged to someone named L. Rodriguez. Just a joke. How long has this . . . uh . . . thing been going on?" (Somehow

I cannot picture Elly in bed with a coffee-colored, twenty-nine-year-old, semi-Hispanic revolutionary.)

"Over a year now. Since last June. On and off. I mean, he's busy; he's got a lot of projects. But we see each other whenever we can. He's got a place near here, a studio, where he lives and holds meetings and everything. I go over sometimes to help out. We're lucky, to have a place of our own. Anyway, sure your guy can come to our house first. But why do you want to put yourself through all that shit? Why don't you just tell Andrew? I told Justin."

"You *told* Justin?" I ask incredulously.

Elly finishes the dregs of her martini. "Yes, yes I did," she says defiantly. "Fuck it. What's marriage if you can't be honest? What kind of a relationship is that, to go sneaking around? I did that at first; it's shit. That's what I told Justin. I respect him too much to pull that kind of shit. Do you know, I'm the first woman he ever had a real relationship with? I mean, we didn't get *married* until he was thirty-*three,* for Christ's sake; we've been married for twelve *years.* How can you expect two people to just lie around fucking each other for all those years, I said. Just because I care about someone else doesn't mean I don't care about *him.* That whole Freudian thing about limited love, it's just a bunch of shit. Sure I do; I tell him everything. And listen, it's not just one-way. I try to get him to do things too. So far he won't; he says he doesn't want to. But at least he knows he's free."

"But . . . doesn't it hurt him? To have you sitting there, telling him all about it?"

"Why shouldn't I hurt him? He hurts *me* all the time," Elly bursts out. "He's always after me about my drinking, about my legs; when he's drunk he even criticizes the way I hold a fork, just because of that middle-class asshole of a mother he's stuck with. Why shouldn't I hurt him?"

I have no answer.

"You can't live just not to hurt other people," Elly adds absently, chewing on the edge of her glass. "Anyway, what's his name, Joe? Sure he can come."

"Don't you think you should check with Justin?"

"I don't have to check with anybody; it's my house too. But I still think you should tell him."

What *would* Andrew do if I told him. Divorce me? Beat me up? Take the children and run? Kill himself? Kill me? The possibilities are interesting. And endless. But I'm not about to explore them, at least not now. I've got enough problems as it is.

The next evening I ride up in the elevator with Stefan II and Joe follows twenty minutes later by the stairs.

"I don't like this," he says, panting. "I feel like a goddamn Russian spy. Who are those people anyway?"

"I told you; she's my best friend. Don't worry."

"They're nice. They gave me a drink. The guy patted my shoulder on the way out, like I was fifteen and on my way to the local cathouse for the first time. That's just how I feel, too. Christ."

But the moment I put my arms around him, kiss him, I feel his body relaxing against mine. Holding his hand, I lead him to my husband's bed.

"Why are you pulling down the shades?"

"I don't know. I'm used to the dark."

"Pull them up; I want to look at you," says Joe.

The sex is both good and not good. Nothing like old Marcus, but certainly not as good as it is (or was; Andrew and I have not made love in over three weeks. I'm running out of excuses.) with Andrew; how could it be? We do not know each other's bodies. We tentatively touch each other, ask questions. Just being this near him is enough. Joe runs his hands down my hips.

"What are you doing?"

"Learning you. Looking at you. I like to look at you. Every chunky inch."

"I thought you said I was too skinny."

"Skinny, chunky, it doesn't matter. I want to know every inch."

"Do you *ever* stop talking? Or eating? Or touching?"

"Never," says Joe, cupping my breast in his hand and kissing it. The gesture is both lewd and achingly tender. I am close to tears.

Afterwards he rests his curly head on my stomach and we lie there in happy silence, breathing slowly together, at peace.

"It will be better next time," Joe says after a while.

"Yes. It will."

Joe slaps me lightly. "Don't put me down. That's a put-down, you know that?"

He pushes the pillows up against the headboard, shifts his weight, reaches behind the pillows, pulls out a teddy bear and says: "Oh Jesus. What's this?"

"Oh. That's . . . my little girl, Anna, she . . . was afraid I'd be lonesome at night so she . . . I should have put it away; I forgot. Oh Joseph." I am somewhere between tears and laughter.

Joe puts the teddy bear carefully on the night table and looks around the room. "I feel like the police are going to break down the door any minute. Jesus, Mama. I'm nervous."

"Don't be nervous. Do you want some wine? I'll make us some dinner soon. Steak. I bought some steak."

"You're pretty cool. Do you do this often?"

"No. I do *not* do this often. Why are you holding the sheet up around you like that?"

"Don't be nervous. I *am* nervous. What the hell have you got against hotels anyway?"

"Wait, let me get the wine first."

When I return Joe is smoking a cigarette, looking at the teddy bear. I climb back into bed.

"I want to know," says Joe. "What have you got against hotels? Why are you smiling like that?"

The urge to tell him is irresistible. "Oh Joseph, it was so funny. A couple of months ago, I don't know, I was drunk and miserable and I met this man at a restaurant, my father and I were having lunch, and after my father left this man, Marcus was his name, *Marcus,* he asked me to have a drink. And then somehow we were in his hotel room, it was awful, all orange and plastic, and we made love, if you can call it that, he had a . . . uh . . . he was very small, and afterwards he paid me. *Paid* me. He thought I was a prostitute. Isn't that a riot?"

"JESUS CHRIST!" says Joe, exploding sheets and reaching for his pants.

"Joseph, wait. What is it? What's the matter?"

"What's the *matter?* How the hell do you think it makes me feel to hear a thing like that?" says Joe furiously, looking as if any minute he's going to slap me in the face. "What the hell's the matter with you, to tell a man a thing like that after he's just made love to you? Lady, you have a lot to learn. About men. And about me. Especially about me."

"I didn't mean . . . I was just talking. Trying to talk. Joseph, honestly, I didn't mean to hurt you. I just thought . . ."

"Well, don't think" Joe says, still looking as if he's going to hit me. "I don't want to hear about anything like that. Ever. DO YOU UNDERSTAND?"

Oh yes. Indeed I do. Quite clearly. *Le plus ça change* . . . But at least this time it's clear. All laid out. No shit. Not veiled, as with Andrew.

Later, over dinner, Joe cools off.

"Look, I didn't mean to yell at you," Joe says, cutting

his steak. "It's just that . . . I can't stand the thought of you doing anything like that. I don't want to know. You aren't like that, to me."

"What am I then, to you?"

"Everything," Joe says softly. "Everything."

The telephone rings, shattering the mood. Joe jumps a foot, drops his fork, and drains his wine in a single gulp. It is Andrew. But of course. All we need now is a surprise visit from dear old Dad.

"Hi," I say, trying to keep my voice calm. Unconsciously I tighten the thin cotton robe around my waist.

"Is everything all right?" asks Andrew.

"Yes, everything's fine. I'm just having something to eat. Why? Did you try to call before?" (When we were in bed I'd taken the phone off the hook.)

"No. Why do you ask?"

"I don't know. I just thought you might have. Well. How are the children?"

"Are they always like this?"

"Like what? Isn't Dolores helping?"

"She's helping but . . . anyway, they're fine. We went to the ocean today. Anna went right in; she wasn't afraid. We all miss you. Wait, here, I'll put them on the phone."

"Mommy, Nicco killed a clam. It was on the sand still breathing and he dropped a rock right on it on purpose. It was all smashed," says Anna sadly.

"Darling, I'm sorry. Little boys sometimes . . . try not to be upset about it."

Anna's voice brightens. "I'm not anymore. I gave it a wonderful funeral. With a cross on top," says Anna.

"Hello! Hello! Hello!" shouts Nicco.

"Mother. We are all fine. I'm taking care of Daddy," says Kate busily.

Andrew comes back on the phone.

"Would you like me to call later, after you've finished dinner?" he asks.

"Well, actually I think I'll go to bed early tonight; I'm really tired. But I'll speak to you tomorrow. Have fun."

"I love you, Liza."

"Me too."

"What did you say? You're talking so softly I can hardly hear you."

"I said, 'me too.' "

When I go back into the dining room with its flickering candles and blinds wide open to purple rooftop shadows and the lights along Broadway, Joe has stopped eating; he is smoking a cigarette. I put my hand on his fuzzy hair.

"Joseph, I'm sorry." (Andrew, I'm sorry too. And Kate, Anna, Nicco, Mommy and Daddy, Joe's wife and children, late grandparents, ex-Episcopalian-god, I'm sorry. I ask forgiveness of you all.)

"Couldn't you have left the goddamn phone off the hook?" asks Joe stabbing out his cigarette and lighting another.

"Look, you have a wife. You have children. That's why you can't stay here all night, remember? Because you have a wife. And children. *Five* children. Who the hell has five children anymore? Do you think I like the thought of how you *got* those five children?"

Joe's expression changes; he looks at me with those eyes.

"All right. It's just . . . Liza, listen to me. Listen. I've never felt anything like this before. Never. Don't laugh. I think about you all the time. Every goddamn woman I see looks like you. I can't stand the thought of you with anyone else. I can't stand being away from you. I don't know what the hell I'm doing anymore."

"I'm not laughing, Joseph. It's the same for me. Never before."

The telephone rings again.

"Don't answer it," says Joe, kissing my eyes and mouth.

"I *have* to; it' ll be worse if I don't. Once when I was in the shower and didn't hear the phone Andrew called the *police*. Can you believe that?" I murmur, between kisses.

"At this point I can believe anything," says Joe, meaning it.

Surprise. Dear old Dad. But at least he's on the phone, not at the door.

"Liza! I tried to get you before; the line was busy. Alone like that, I was worried, you shouldn't be alone. Have you eaten? I'm right across town, I could stop off and pick up some things at Zabar's, I could be there in twenty minutes. Some nice smoked salmon, maybe, you like smoked salmon. Black bread. A little Brie. Don't talk about money, I want to do it for you."

"No!" I shriek. "I mean, thanks Dad, but I've already eaten. I was planning to go to bed early."

"I know you, it's the salmon, isn't it? The price. All right, tightwad, forget the salmon. How about sausage?"

"No, Dad, really. I'm really tired; I want to go to bed."

"All right. I understand. The job, you're busy, of course you're tired, you're doing too much, how much can a woman handle? But tomorrow, remember, we have a special date, I'll pick you up at work, you'll bring some clothes to the office and change, you won't have to go all the way home first. My baby! Thirty-five tomorrow! I can't believe it."

"That's right. Lovely. Tomorrow. Great."

"I'll pick you up at five-thirty."

"Five-thirty."

"I have something really big planned. No, I'm not going to tell you, you'll have to wait. But I can tell you this:

after champagne, dinner at Lutèce, you're going to open a tiny little box and you're going to see the most beautiful . . . no, I'm not going to tell you. Do you want me to give you a hint?"

"No, Dad. I think I'd rather wait."

"The best things come in small packages, you know. You don't want to take a guess?"

"No. Really. I'll let you surprise me."

I hang up and go back into the dining room. Joe and I look at each other. Joe's moustache starts to twitch. The corners of my mouth turn up. We both begin to laugh, belly laughter that leaves us shaking, tears in our eyes.

"Your father?" asks Joe, choking.

"My father."

"Oh man," says Joe. "Oh man. This is too much."

"Too much.

"Oh man."

We wind up back in the bedroom. Joe turns on all the lights. The air-conditioner is rattling orgasmically away.

"Don't you have to catch a train?" I murmur from somewhere beneath his curly chest.

"Shut up, chunky," says Joe.

Chunky?

Discovery. I am really good in bed.

XIII

"Jump! Smile! Lean forward! That's it! Hold it! Now. Jump again! Smile! Laugh! Let's see those teeth!"

They are photographing me for the make-over article. For my "before" pictures they made me take off all my makeup, combed my hair straight down over my eyes, and dressed me in a kind of smock that made me look pregnant. We are now hours into "after." It seems as if I have been jumping forever; the hot white lights are blinding me. The photographer is darting, kneeling, shooting up, shooting down. I am wearing a pale blond shoulder-length wig, painstakingly arranged by Carlos-the-hair-stylist. Whenever the photographer stops shooting, Carlos hops forward, sticks the end of a rattail comb straight into my scalp, lifts the wig, which is secured by over thirty bobby pins, half off my head, and jams in some more pins, teasing as he goes. Andreas-the-makeup-man spent over an hour highlighting, shadowing, hollowing, brightening, deepening, and removing. I have on: two pairs of false lashes; brown eyeliner; brown eyebrow pencil; gray, blue, and green eyeshadow; white eyegloss, Erase; blush-on; bisque and beige foundation; brown contouring shadow; translucent powder; highlighting gloss; pink, red, and taupe lipstick. Joe looks on nervously; as the art director he was forced to come to the sitting. "Jump!" says the photographer again.

"Oh God," says Nina, cool and sleek in red plaid and a green felt hat. "Her wig is falling off again. Carlos!"

"Hey, uh, Nina, don't you think we should take a break?" Joe asks. "She's been jumping all afternoon. She must be dead on her feet."

Nina turns to glare at him. "What are *you* so concerned about, darling?" she asks. "Why, you'd think you two had something going *on*. Wouldn't you think they had something going on, Carlos?"

Carlos, busy with the rattail comb, smiles but does not answer. Joe's fists clench. I shut my eyes, willing: *no. Don't.* I know his temper. (I should; it's a hell of a lot like my own.)

"Do you think they all know?" Joe asks a few days later while we're having lunch. We are at the zoo. We return to the zoo often. The zoo; our natural habitat. Balloons and the shrill voices of children float above us in the cold air; the leaves are yellow, red, and orange, dazzling against the bright fall sky. But we do not see the leaves or hear the voices; we do not notice. My love. The man I love. He is sad and I am sad and I want us both to be happy. I touch the silver ring he gave me, a simple band, almost a wedding ring.

"Know what?"

"What. You know what. About us. That bitch. That dried-up bitch. I'd like to knock her phony teeth down her throat one by one. Do you think they all know?"

"I don't know. What if they do? Does it bother you? I thought I was the neurotic one. I thought we said we weren't going to let it bother us."

"Just thinking. Sometimes I get so goddamn sick of sneaking around; I wonder . . . I think . . . Liza, what the hell are we doing? We can't even spend a weekend alone.

We can't even spend one fucking *night* alone. Sometimes I . . . oh shit. No, don't say anything; I know that look. Let's go see how the capybara's doing."

We always check on the capybara; when we're down it makes us laugh. But the capybara is not in its cage. The tapirs, snouts to the ground, still fill the rocky enclosure with primeval, bulky grace, but the capybara is not there. It is not anywhere in the zoo. I am pulling Joe's hand, almost running, as we peer into cage after cage.

"Where's the, you know, capybara?" I ask a keeper frantically.

"The what?"

"Capybara. The thing that was in the cage with the tapirs. Where is it?"

"Calm down, missus. You mean that big brown thing that looked like a rat? A big rat? She's gone. Got married, she did."

"Married?"

The keeper grins and grinds out the stub of a cigarette with his well-worn boot.

"That's right. Got married and moved to Chicago. Rat over there was pining for a lady friend, so off she went. Miserable she was here anyway with the tapirs at her all the time, a regular, forgive me missus, gang bang of sorts it was. Needed one of her own kind, she did. The animals went in two by two, that's what the Bible says, and truer words were never spoke. Funny what animals will do when they're penned up; they'd never carry on like that in the wild. Whole cage in an uproar, lady tapirs all riled up; jealous as fiends they were. Just like people."

Just like people.

After three painful visits to hotels, we now have a place of our own, an apartment belonging to a divorced friend of Joe's; he lets us use it when he doesn't have plans of his own. Which he often does. The first time we were as excited as two children let loose on the main floor of Schwarz: Joe led me to a small brownstone and, three flights up, unlocked the door to a one-bedroom apartment with exposed brick walls, an Indian rug, a black leather couch, and a huge rubber plant taking up half the living room. But he was so at ease, pouring wine in the minuscule kitchen, showing me the way to the bathroom, carefully turning down the suede bedspread, putting a towel on top of the beige sheet that I wondered: Had he ever been here before with a woman? Another woman? And although I loved the warmth of his body against mine, his tender hands, the long lean muscles of his legs, I kept thinking about the (maybe) other woman. About his wife. About every other woman he's had since he started screwing at the age of sixteen. Kept thinking how much I'd like to kill, kill, kill them all.

Just like people.

One evening a few weeks later, while trying to finish the masturbation article (Andrew keeps bringing up the camp bill, and Frank's getting impatient), I receive a telephone call from Justin Buck. Surprising. Justin never calls; all arrangements are made through Elly and myself.

"Hey. I was thinking," says Justin, full of confidence, except he isn't; it sounds as if he's laboriously rehearsed every word, "we never have a chance to talk, you know? All you hear about is what a bad-ass old man I am, secondhand. Why don't we have a drink down at the bar tonight? Are you doing anything tonight? It would be fun, just the two of us, to have a drink. Down at the bar. Tonight. If it's okay with Andrew, I mean."

It takes me a minute to get my thoughts organized. I had wanted to finish the God-awful article—I'm having a hell of a time with it—and hand it in tomorrow. I have a free evening; Andrew is in Boston and although I could have gotten a sitter, left a message that I'd gone to a movie, and spent the evening with Joe, *Joe* couldn't disentangle himself. Something about a school conference. His sixteen-year-old daughter, apparently, has not been attending school very often. But my evening is turning out not to be free. The children have been at me from the moment I sat down at the typewriter. I've always noticed that as long as I'm doing nothing, no one bothers me, but let me try to work, read, even brush my teeth, and I am instantly surrounded. Right this second Max is throwing up and Anna is standing on the neat pile of finished copy I've carefully placed on the floor saying, "See, Mommy? I don't bother you. I let you work."

"Oh. Sure. That sounds like fun. Excuse me just one minute, Justin. Anna, could you please get off that work? I'll have to retype the whole thing now; just look at your slippers, they're soaked. What the hell have you been into? *Christ.* Sorry, Justin. Sure. I guess Kate could babysit; Andrew won't be home tonight; he's away. In Boston. She doesn't usually want to sit, she never *has,* but it's just down on the corner, I could leave the number. She might. That sounds like fun. Does . . . uh . . . Elly know about this? I mean, is it all right with her?"

"Sure it's all right. Why shouldn't it be all right? Why don't I pick you up around seven-thirty?"

"Okay. Seven-thirty. Great. If Kate will sit."

Oh God. Now what. Am I to be a guinea pig for Justin's first try at open marriage? Sexual freedom? How much, as dear old Dad said, can a woman handle? And is it really all right with Elly? I can just see her, up to her elbows in bean soup, watching Justin take off. I can just hear her too. Are you supposed to have a drink with your best friend's husband? Or maybe she just wants to get him out of the house so she can see her revolutionary? But no. Justin and Elly have a marriage involving honest communication. Or so Elly says.

"I didn't *know* my slippers were wet, Mommy," sobs

Anna. "I didn't *know* that was your work. I must have stepped in that big awful puddle in the bathroom."

"What puddle? Oh Jesus."

When I go to investigate I find, not dog pee or an overflowing bathtub as expected, but a cracked pipe beneath the sink, spewing water. After endless ringing of the back elevator Handy Stefan arrives, drunk as usual.

"Ah lady," says Handy Stefan sadly, reeking of rye, bending heavily and coming up with a piece of rusty pipe that crumbles in his hand. "Ah lady."

By the time Handy Stefan has bandaged the pipe and promised to return tomorrow with a new section (that'll be the day), it is almost seven-thirty. I go to tackle Kate.

Her room, as usual, is immaculate. She is sitting at her desk, the lamp throwing a stream of light onto her beautiful hair. She is reading a book. *The Little Princess.* Something in my heart catches. When Kate sees me she hastily turns *The Little Princess* face down and picks up a school book, pretending to study it industriously.

"Couldn't you at least *knock?*" asks Kate.

"I'm sorry, you're right, I should have. Kate, uh, I wondered if you'd like to babysit for about an hour tonight while I go out, just down to the bar, Mr. Buck wants to talk to me about something, I'd pay you the regular rate, of course, I've been thinking, now that you're almost eleven you might like to sit sometimes, just for a short time, you're very capable, you could save up for, you know, special things you might want, Daddy told me how good you were with Nicco, how you helped watch him out in the country." I run out of words and wait. Useless. She'll never agree to it.

"Yes Mother, I'd like that. Should they go to bed by eight?" asks Kate, shocking me into catatonic silence.

"Yes, please," I say, still unable to move. What the hell is going on?

Justin rings the doorbell on the dot of seven-thirty,

just as I am writing down the telephone number of the Elysium bar for Kate. He is all dressed up: checked slacks, turtleneck, blue blazer with shiny brass buttons; the one thing missing is a slightly wilted gardenia in a white box. First date. Too bad I don't have a strapless net formal with small fake flowers strewn across the skirt.

"Hey, you look great, terrific; how much weight have you lost?" asks Justin jauntily.

"About twelve pounds. I don't know why, I didn't try, I just lost it."

"That's great."

Kate eyes Justin up and down, but says nothing. Justin begins to hum. After reminding Kate to lock the door and not to open it to anyone, we ride down in the elevator with Stefan II and head for the corner, stepping over two sleeping drunks and an overturned garbage can on our way.

When we are settled on bar stools, martinis in front of us, Justin stops humming and says: "I guess you wondered why I asked you to have a drink. Alone like this, I mean."

(Yes.)

"No, not really. We're friends after all."

"Right. That's just it. We're friends. I think . . . you know . . . like . . . it's good to be able to talk. Talk to a woman. Another woman besides your wife. We're all so hung up. Men don't just have to have men friends and women have women friends; men should have women friends and women should have men friends; it doesn't always have to be loaded. I mean, shit. Why shouldn't you and I have a drink? There's nothing wrong with that."

"No, there isn't."

(Is there?)

Justin sips his drink thoughtfully, his stubby, wide-nailed fingers drumming on the dark, scarred bar.

"Forty-five. Man, that's old."

"Not so old. Why do you say that?"

"Shit. I don't know. I *feel* old, that's why. Elly, she . . . like . . . she's into so many things and I'm . . . I feel like . . . I guess she told you about the thing she has going. With that guy."

"Yes."

Justin dips absently into a bowl of salted peanuts and eats one. Without joy. "Well, you know, she's right. I mean, why shouldn't she if she wants to? Have something else going? Like, just you and me sitting here talking, even that means something, right? Man, life is short. And you know, I'm glad she can talk to me about it, I really am, I'm really with her on that, it's just that . . . Jesus. Hey. Do you want another drink? I want another drink. I want about twenty more drinks. I want to get so fucking drunk I . . . oh shit. You know, sometimes it's rough sitting there listening to the whole thing. I mean, man, she doesn't just *tell* me about the guy; she *tells* me. Everything. What they do in bed. The whole thing. And . . . like . . . I'm worried about her, you know? I really am. Okay, so that job she had wasn't the greatest, but man, since she started staying home she drinks from morning on; she's got me really worried. An actress. How the fuck did she think she was going to make it as an actress? And teaching's tight. She can't find anything. She doesn't even send out resumés anymore; she just sits there and drinks. And when she drinks the thing is she . . . do you want a peanut?"

"No thanks."

"You should try one. They're good. So anyway, she's really hung up on this guy, and when she drinks she gets way down, she really freaks out, she cries and . . . did you know he had another girl? No, she didn't tell you that, did she. So when she's down, I have to sit there and comfort her. *Comfort* her. Tell her sure he loves her. Like, she's got me; why shouldn't he have somebody else? Okay, so I'm middle-class, I'm uptight, that's what she says, but man, sometimes, sitting there, listening to all that shit, getting my balls cut off by the inch, saying things I don't mean, saying sure he loves her, go ahead, see him, when what I'd really like to do is kill the son of a bitch, I wonder what the fuck I'm doing."

"So you get mad," I say, not asking a question but stating a fact.

"Yeah, I get mad. Once or twice I even hit her. Pushed her around. Man, that makes me want to die, that I did that. But Jesus, sometimes I get so mad. So fucking mad. Jealous. That's it. Jealous. She says I have no right to be jealous, that nobody should own anybody else. Man, I'm not for owning anybody, but *she's* jealous of that bastard's girl; why don't *I* have the right to be jealous if that's the way I am? But she doesn't see that. She won't listen. She talks all right, but she won't listen. Not to me."

I search for words.

"Justin, Elly's going through something right now. Thinking things through. I mean, I can see that that must be really rough, having to listen to all that, but it's happening to all of us in a way. I mean, she may not be handling it very well, but I can see what she means. It is kind of crazy just to stay locked up with one person for the rest of your life. Jealousy isn't necessarily . . . maybe it's only because we've been taught to think that . . . I mean, there are places where . . ."

"I know. Don't tell me. Sweden. Denmark. She's way beyond all that now. She read a new article. Now she's into Eskimos and Lobis and some bunch of assholes in Bolivia. Her favorite right now are the Toda. Jealousy doesn't *exist* in wherever the fuck the Toda hang out, she says. Shit, I told her, I live *here;* I'm not a Toda or a fucking Eskimo. Oh man, I love her, I really do, but . . ."

I see the tears in his eyes and put my hand on his arm.

"It'll all work out, Justin. Don't . . . she loves you too."

"I know. I just wish she wouldn't talk about it all the

time. But . . . you know . . . I hate lies. I'd hate her to feel she couldn't talk to me about it. I . . . oh shit. I don't know what I think. Have you . . . does Andrew know about you and that guy? Joe?"

"No. I haven't told him. I can't. He isn't . . . we don't have that kind of a marriage."

"Sometimes it takes more guts to keep your mouth shut," says Justin, ordering two more martinis.

"Not guts exactly. I just can't tell him."

"What about him? He's in Boston now, right? How do you know he's in Boston? Or what he's doing in Boston?"

"Because. He'd never do anything. He's not the type."

"You love the other guy, don't you? Really love him. I can tell. Jesus, I must be drunk, I shouldn't say this, but I never have understood what you and Andrew have going. Elly and me, at least we . . . but you and Andrew. I don't get it. Have you ever, you know, thought of splitting? Just taking off?"

I look into the swirling depths of the martini I do not want, stirring it round and round with my finger. Of course I have thought of it. Just taking off. Just saying, "fuck everything" and grab, grab, grabbing at happiness. But divorce. The thought fills me with terror. Andrew, whatever he is, is a man I have slept, eaten, fought, lived with; a man I once loved. Am I happy with Andrew? No. Would I be happy with Joe? Yes. But the catch is, I want it all simple: no Andrew, no Joe's wife, no children, no hostile parents. And because it can never be simple, would we be happy? We have never talked of marriage, but the thought is always there. Marriage. Why marriage? Why can't I take my chances? Because I do not want to be alone. Because I am afraid, so afraid. I love Joe, trust him, but late at night as visions of marriage dance in my head (Joe and I having breakfast, dressing for an evening out, walking hand in hand by the river), I wonder: what are the current rules for a two-way split? Would he tell his wife first? Would I tell Andrew first? Would we pick a day and time and tell them simultaneously? Suppose at some point in the proceedings Joe changed his mind? Could his daughter's tears, his sons' outrage sway him? Suppose Andrew wouldn't take me back. What then? I would be alone. Thirty-five years old. Three children. Alone. And why *hasn't* Joe ever mentioned marriage?

"I've thought about it, but . . . I don't think it's as easy as it sounds. I'm so mixed up I . . . oh Justin, I'm too old to believe in fairy tales."

"Come on, baby. Other people do it. You ever read the statistics? Shit, people split all the time. You're no masochist; you're a goddamn strong woman. Stronger than you think. Why *not* you?"

Why not me. It is an interesting question, one that I'd better start exploring. Fast.

A couple from the building enters the bar. I wave but they skulk past us, eyes downward.

Back upstairs, Anna and Nicco are in bed and Kate, incredibly, has washed the few dishes in the sink. I thank her, pay her, and watch her carefully place the six quarters one by one in the blue and yellow ceramic piggy bank my mother gave her last Christmas. Her small hand rests upon the pig for a moment and she looks up at me.

"Mother," says Kate. "Do you think Grandmother will ever get well?"

I hesitate, hardly knowing how to speak, having almost forgotten how to speak to this child except in anger.

"I don't know, Kate. I hope so. We have to go on hoping."

"You must . . . it must make you sad. I guess that's one reason you went to work. To keep from thinking about her too much."

"Partly, Kate."

"Is that what you were talking about with Mr. Buck? With Justin?"

"No, we were talking about other things. Other problems."

Kate sighs and drops the last coin into the bank. It lands with a shallow clink. There is something like pity and a strange understanding in her eyes.

"Anyway, don't worry, Mommy; I won't tell Daddy you went with Justin to the bar," says Kate, shocking me into catatonic silence for the second time in one evening.

I keep dreaming that Andrew is dead. But I am not sure. I dream that he is lying in a large coffin banked by flowers. Joe, Kate, Anna, Nicco and I, and a blurred group of other people, stand in front of an altar. We are all crying, but somehow we are happy too. I am wearing a wedding gown. Just as the minister opens a worn black book embossed with the words: "Dear *Free Woman,* I have a problem," Andrew opens his eyes, slowly rises to a sitting position, looks around and says dazedly: "What am I doing here?"

Right now I am sitting outside Frank's office, waiting. He and Nina are in conference, discussing the masturbation article I handed in this morning. After what seems like hours Nina comes out, smiling brightly. "Liza. Darling!" says Nina.

I follow her pointed jeweled finger into Frank's office and sit in a chair facing his desk. Nina sinks into a leather couch and disappears in a cloud of cigarette smoke.

"Not bad," says Frank gruffly, as if he'd rather be saying the opposite. "Few cuts here and there, few changes—I think that bit about the woman jerking off after her lover leaves sucks; shit, what dame like that wouldn't be glad to have a man at all, but—not bad. We're taking it."

"You're . . . taking it?"

Somehow this possibility never crossed my mind.

Nina reappears. "Of *course* we're taking it. Silly girl. You see, darling?" says Nina, turning to Frank. "I knew it all along. I told you, didn't I? I knew she'd find her niche. I knew she'd be an asset to *Free Woman."*

Frank gestures impatiently. "I'm putting through a check; five hundred, that all right? High for a first article but they like it upstairs, so five hundred. Now. We want you to try another."

"Still on spec, of course," says Nina, lighting up again, "but we have this superb idea, this fan*tas*tic idea. Remember at the last meeting when that little Nora somebody from Decorating—God, I think it's the first she's spoken up since she's *been* here, and she's *been* here for *years*—mentioned a friend of hers, a young girl who's managed, against the most incredible odds, to fulfill herself, get out there in the great big world and fight, absolutely battle for personal fulfillment? Well, after the meeting I sounded her out a bit further, got the total story. This friend—the story is incredible—was orphaned at the age of six. And . . . she's black and handicapped! In a *wheel*chair or something insane like that. Yet she put herself through college. Has an exciting career. Many lovers. Well, actually. I don't know if they're *lover* lovers, considering the fact that she's almost totally *paralyzed,* but the point is, she's *surrounded* by men. Stunning too, from what Nora says—always up to the minute, fashion-wise; always totally groomed. Now *there's* an example to offer the readers of *Free Woman!* And darling, we want you, yes *you,* to interview this girl and write the article! What an opportunity! Isn't that incredible?"

"Incredible," I say, already dreading it. "If you'll give me the information I'll get onto it right away."

"Darling," says Nina, looking at me intently, "I shouldn't say this; I should let it come straight from the horse's mouth, as it were, but . . . they adore you upstairs. They really do. And if you want a hint, just a teeny hint, I think you might just be due for a raise after Christmas."

"Time enough to talk about that later. She's gotta really produce first," grumbles Frank.

"Oh, and darling," Nina says, ignoring Frank, "Surprise! Here are the proofs back from the photographer. He blew up a couple of eight-by-tens for you, too. Nice of him, wasn't it?"

I look at the girl in the photographs, a slim girl with huge eyes, hollow cheekbones, and long silky hair—smiling, laughing, bending seductively toward the camera. A beautiful girl. Me.

"Oh God, Joseph, they want me to go interview some paraplegic who's got it made, they gave me her address, she lives way up in the Bronx, I don't *want* to go, I *hate* the Bronx, I've never *been* to the Bronx, I *hate* interviewing people, I *hate* people who've got it made, I *hate* writing," I wail over wine and spaghetti carbonara at our first lunchtime haunt.

"Calm down, old lady. You could use the money, couldn't you? You think I like my work? You think I'm in this for the fun of it?" asks Joe, tearing off a chunk of bread.

"Don't be so fucking simplistic. And stop *eating* for a minute. I'm trying to talk to you and you're not listening; you're just handing me a bunch of lousy clichés."

"Keep your voice down, for Christ's sake. What did I do? What's the matter, Mama? You premenstrual or something?" asks Joe, calmly digging into his side dish of fried eggplant.

"Goddamn you, I could kill you for that; if we weren't here I'd break this wine bottle over your head. That's just what my father used to say."

"Yeah. From what you've told me, your father had his hands full."

"Very funny."

I look at Joe. He looks at me. After a minute we both begin to laugh.

"You know, it wasn't really so much my father. It was Mother. She'd always use that as an excuse. Whenever I was upset or nervous she'd say to my father—they thought I couldn't hear; my mother didn't like to talk about things like that, especially in front of me—'It's best to leave Liza alone at the moment; she's . . . uh . . . having female problems.' And my father would say, '*When* can I talk to her then? Tell me. *When.* She's always either *having* her period, or just *had* her period, or just *about* to have her period. Jesus Christ, that leaves me about one day a month I get to talk to my own daughter.' 'Don't be vulgar,' Mother would say."

"The poor guy," Joe says, still laughing. "He must have had a hell of a time."

"I'm just beginning to see that. I always thought he was awful. He's still awful, but I think you'd like him."

"I think so too. Too bad I'll never get to meet him."

"Never?"

Joe stops laughing.

"Well, what's your plan? Do you want me to drop in while you're in the middle of Thanksgiving dinner? Introduce myself as your lover? Or why don't you haul him up to my house?"

"You shift moods almost as fast as I do. Now you're mad. You premenstrual or something?"

"All right, you don't want to talk about it. *I* want to talk about it; we *have* to talk about about it. Jesus Christ, old lady, we have Friday off next week, four straight days free and I'm going to have to sit there—*her* relatives, *my* relatives, and kids all over the place and the boys coming down from college with their girls. Christ. Four days, and you and I could have . . . oh shit, what's the use, four days wouldn't be enough anyway . . . Oh Liza, Liza, goddamn it, why are we playing games; what are we doing? I can't take any more of this. I'm forty-two years old and I've never done one single fucking thing I wanted to do. I want to be happy, I want to be happy, I want to be happy."

Joe's fist slams down onto the table, scattering crumbs; heads are beginning to turn.

"I want to be happy," Joe says again, like a small boy who has just been told that there is no Santa Claus, but still cannot quite believe it. His eyes are so sad, he looks so miserable that I would, at this moment, leave everything and everyone, do anything to make him happy. He is about to cry.

"Oh Joseph. Darling, darling, don't. Not here. We'll talk, we'll think about it, we'll work something out. I've been thinking. Maybe . . ."

Joe sniffs and puts his head in his hands.

"Oh shit," says Joe.

Oh shit is right.

Several days before Thanksgiving, out of nowhere, Andrew suggests that we have dinner out. As I do not like to leave Kate that long, and Barnard sitter service is closed, I finally tell a fourteen-year-old in the building to come up in about an hour.

"Where are we going?" I ask as I'm pulling on my boots.

"I want to surprise you," Andrew says.

As we are riding down in the elevator, Stefan II leers and says: "Lady. Glad to see you back with old husband."

My heart comes to a total halt. He knows. He's seen me with Joe. Downtown, maybe, or walking in the park. Oh God. Andrew looks at me quizzically.

"I see you have date with 3B," says Stefan II slyly. "After I take you down in elevator, I go for coffee, see you walk on Broadway, go into bar. I see you." He stands there, slit-eyed and smiling, waiting for the thrill of seeing Andrew beat me up in the elevator. That's what you do when your wife fools around with another man, isn't it? Beat her up? Cut off her head? Tie burning hot stones to the backs of her knees? (A fairly successful solution in Africa at one time, I think: "That'll teach you to run away again, Wangu!" "Running, who's talking about running, I can't even *walk*. *Now* see what you've done." "Well, you should have stayed home like I told you.") Some tribe or other. No matter. They all look alike anyway, as my father would say.

Andrew says nothing at all in the elevator, but when we're out on the street says, "What did he mean? I didn't know you'd had a drink with Justin. I assume that's what he meant by '3B.' *Did* you have a drink with Justin?"

"Actually, yes. Yes I did. He called that night you were in Boston and asked me to go down to the bar. To the Elysium. Just to talk. He's very worried about Elly; she's going through a lot lately and he just wanted to talk to someone about it. A friend."

"A friend," Andrew says. "That's interesting. I wouldn't have thought he lacked for friends."

"You don't have any friends; why is that? You're not close to one single man. Or woman."

"Let's stay on one subject. Why didn't you tell me you'd gone out with him?"

"Because I thought you might not like it; I thought you might think . . . I don't know. I don't know what I thought you'd think. It just didn't seem worth it to tell you."

"Worth it?" Andrew says, getting angry. "What *is* worth it? We hardly talk anymore. We hardly ever go to bed anymore. You act as if I'm not even there. What are you doing, sleeping with that son of a bitch? Am I supposed to take Elly on? Is that the plan you two have arranged? That's the new thing, isn't it? Switching?"

"Hardly. That was a new thing in the fifties. You have a fifties' mentality, do you know that? You should have a picture of Eisenhower hanging over your dresser."

"And what kind of mentality do you have. Elly's, that's whose. Every word she hands down is your Bible, your daily guide to live by. You damn well don't need to set me up. If I want to have an affair I can do better than that. Maybe I *should* have an affair."

"Maybe you should."

"Maybe I will."

"Go ahead. You're free."

"Nobody's free."

"I always thought you were a good person. But you weren't good. You were just quiet."

"I don't know what the hell I am anymore," says Andrew, hailing a cab.

But in the cab his mood changes; he puts his arm around me. I feel guiltily unfaithful. To Joe.

"Where are we going?" I ask again.

"I told you, I want to surprise you. We'll get out at Fifty-seventh Street and walk. Remember how we used to meet after work before the children were born? I'd pick you up at your office and we'd go out for a drink or for dinner. Do you remember?"

"Yes." But I do not want to remember.

At Fifty-seventh Street Andrew pays the driver and we walk down Fifth Avenue in the cold night. The store windows are already ablaze with Christmas decorations. When we turn East on Fifty-third Street, I know where we are going—to our favorite restaurant of long ago, a small French restaurant we have not been to in years. Andrew holds my hand more tightly; his wide mouth is smiling boyishly as he looks down at me with Nicco's gray eyes.

"Do you know where we're going now?"

"To the restaurant? The one we used to go to so often?"

"Yes. I thought it would be . . . I wanted to take you there."

But in place of the restaurant is a gaping hole and dark piles of boards and bricks. Incredulously, we retrace our steps.

"I'm sure it was here; I *know* it was here," says Andrew.

"It was here. I guess they've torn it down. Oh Andrew . . ."

"I should have called. I should have called first. Why didn't I call?"

"Don't look like that. It doesn't matter. We'll go someplace else."

Andrew stands there, looking at the emptiness. It takes several minutes before I'm able to lead him away.

When we are settled in a different restaurant, drinks in hand, Andrew lights a cigarette and says: "That was awful, to see that."

"A little bit funny, too."

Andrew tries to smile, but his eyes are sad. As sad as Joe's. Sad, desperate eyes.

"I didn't mean that before, about having an affair. I was just angry. You know I'd never look at anyone but you."

I sip my drink, not knowing what to say.

"That's nice to hear," I say finally, "but if you ever wanted to . . . I'd want you to feel . . . that you could."

"You say that, but how do you know how you'd feel? That sounds like Elly. I shouldn't have said what I did, but Liza, some of her ideas are, I don't know, take a couple, a man and a woman. A marriage. You try to build something together. If you love someone, how can you help but hurt them if you're involved with someone else?"

"There are a lot of ways of hurting people, Andrew. I'm not sure that being involved with someone else is the worst way."

"But marriage, a marriage . . . to make it work, you

have to save your energy for it. Your time. You have to put a lot into it, to make it work."

"Are you putting a lot into it, Andrew?" I ask, very quietly. "Our marriage?"

"But what have I *done,* to make you this unhappy? I've worked; I've supported a family; I've tried. Some of the things you've said to me . . . I've tried not to get angry, to keep things calm. I know I should talk more, that you wanted me to talk more but . . . sometimes I . . . you get so angry, you used to get so angry, I was afraid. Now when I try to talk half the time you don't even hear me. Oh Liza, Liza, what's happening to us?"

"I hear you but . . . Oh Andrew, why talk about it now? It's been so many years. So many years of loneliness."

"But I've been there. I've come home every night. I've been *there.*"

"That's just it. You haven't. Not really. I know you've tried to keep things quiet; I know you've supported us. But . . ."

"All those years," Andrew says, draining his glass. "You talk about so many years. Well, I'll tell you something I never thought I'd tell you. I *hate* my job, do you know that? *Hate* it. Do you know what it's like to go into an office day after day, doing work you despise?"

"I know what it's like. Why didn't you tell me? I wish you'd told me."

"But you don't have to work. I do, but you don't. At least when you were home I felt . . . but now . . . why are you doing it, then?"

"I don't know why, Andrew."

"I don't want to go on like this, working, getting up every morning, going to work, coming home. Maybe we should move. Maybe we should get out of the city. Move to the country, real country, where things wouldn't be so complicated. What kind of life do we have here?"

"That's not because of where we live."

"Look at us. Look at Kate, coming home alone. Look at Anna. Don't you think she feels it, that you're not home anymore? She cried every night in the country. She was crying for you."

"It isn't just my working, Andrew. It's us. Don't you think she knows about us?"

"Knows *what* about us?"

"That . . . you're right. We don't have any kind of life together. We never did. We never had anything but sex."

"Sex. Doesn't sex matter? It mattered before with us."

"It matters, but . . . it's not enough. Not anymore."

"Maybe we should go away, just the two of us. We've never been away alone. We have four days. We could take a trip, a short trip. Just the two of us."

"I don't think . . . Andrew, that's not going to help."

"What do we do then? Do we just give up? After thirteen years and three children, do we just give up? Liza, I want you to tell me the truth. Is there someone else? If there is I'll handle it somehow. I want to know. I have to know."

It takes me minutes, hours, years to answer.

"No, Andrew. There's no one else."

"Then somehow," Andrew says shakily, "somehow, we'll be all right."

I cannot look at Andrew's face.

"We'll go away for those four days, over Thanksgiving; we'll take a trip, a short trip," Andrew says again.

But we do not go away. Dolores cannot stay with the children; her mother is weak, too weak to handle her boys alone. And Mother is worse; my father is desperate. I cannot go away with my lover; I cannot go away with my husband. On Wednesday, at lunchtime, I ask to leave early (Nina disdainfully consents; I am terrified—what am I so terrified about when I'm prepared to die) and dash uptown to watch Anna play a turkey, and Nicco an Indian, in the Community School Thanksgiving program, just as yesterday evening I dashed home to change in time to watch Kate play Priscilla Alden. Yesterday, today—time I could have spent with Joe. We have a quick drink after work, but we are both distracted. Joe sighs, looks at his watch, and signals for the check.

"Happy Thanksgiving, old lady," says Joe. "Good luck."

"Good luck to you, too."

Thanksgiving. I get up at seven-thirty and start chopping, boiling, stuffing, and mashing so that I will be able to get out for a few hours to visit Mother. I leave Andrew instructions for basting and heating and ride the bus across town to meet my father at the hospital. There are very few people on the bus. The few that are are separating as of old—one octogenarian head rolls straight down the aisle like a bowling ball and lands between two lavender-gloved hands—but somehow, since I notice that my own hands have left my body and nestled in a navel resting on a sign that reads: "A High School Diploma in Three Easy Weeks! Only $10 Down!"—I feel reassured.

The sight of my mother's body curled in a fetal position on her narrow bed, her untouched holiday dinner on a tray, however, is not so reassuring. My father is crying. All the men I know seem to be doing a great deal of crying lately. Whatever happened to "boys don't cry?" Or maybe I'm just hanging out with the wrong boys?

"Come on, Dad," I say helplessly. "There's nothing more we can do here. The children are waiting; I have a lovely dinner all ready; we'll open the champagne you sent. Come on. There's nothing more you can do."

"My God," my father says. "My God."

Dinner is tense. There is a great clinking of glasses and silverware, but little conversation. We are all painfully conscious of the two empty places. It is the first Thanksgiving we have not all been together in years. Do they celebrate Thanksgiving in the Hare Krishna temple? *Prasadam* in a turkey mold? I glance at my own turkey, its legs vulgarly spread-eagled. (In the rush this morning I forgot to truss it.) Andrew stands to carve.

"Where is Grandmother and Uncle David?" Nicco asks. "Did they get a divorce?" Nicco's friend Chad's parents have recently gotten a divorce—a separation, anyway. The topic fascinates Nicco. My father begins to cry again. I pass filled plates around the table, trying to think of something, anything, to cheer my father up. Then it comes.

"Dad! I didn't tell you, but they're going to have my picture in the magazine. In the February issue. Isn't that exciting?"

My father drops his forkful of apple, onion, and bread stuffing, looks at me in ecstasy and says: "My baby! My little girl! On the cover of a magazine! A famous magazine!"

"Well, no Dad. Not on the cover. They have . . . uh . . . you know . . . very young girls on the cover. Models. Professional models. I'm . . . actually on page eighty-one."

The table droops into heavy silence once again. After the pumpkin pie, coffee, and brandy, the children, Andrew, and Max go downstairs to see my father off in a cab.

I look around me. Dishes. So many dishes. Dishes full of leftover food—turkey, stuffing, creamed onions, sweet potatoes, mashed potatoes, turnips, peas, cranberry sauce, gravy, celery, olives, raisins, pie. Our traditional Thanksgiving dinner; from the time I can remember it has always been the same—cooked and served by maids during my childhood, since my marriage cooked and served by me. What would have happened if this year I had done something really daring—left out the peas, forgotten about the mashed potatoes? I know what would have happened. The Finger of God would have reached down and killed me on sight, that's what would have happened. And my death is my own affair. No interfering fingers, God's or anyone else's.

Wearily, I begin to stack plates; it will take me hours to clean up. Joe. I don't care, I don't care, I'm going to call him; I can always hang up if someone else answers. I dial and luck is with me. Joe answers on the first ring.

"It's me. Can you talk?"

"Right now it's clear. They're all still in there, eating, stuffing themselves sick. It's murder, Mama."

"It's murder here too. I love you."

"I love you. Maybe we could murder them all."

"Too risky. Maybe we could do a blind date thing. Does Carla like gray-eyed, quiet, lawyer types?"

"Depends on how many TV sets he has. Very important to Carla, TV sets."

"I'd better hang up."

"Don't hang up, not yet. Did I tell you I love you?"

"Yes. Only three more days."

"Three more days. Jesus, it already seems like . . . Carla? No, wrong number. Some jerk asking for a funeral parlor."

Even I could have thought up a better one than that.

I pour myself a glass of brandy, my third, and begin to stack plates. By the time Andrew, the children, and Max return I have worked myself into a blind, white-hot rage. The type that needs a target. Four, discounting Max, are presently available. Another quick glass of brandy. Good. Now I'm ready.

"Let's all help your mother clean up," says Andrew, picking up the platter holding the battered turkey carcass.

I snatch the platter from his hands and smash it to the floor.

"*Help* me. *Help* me," I yell. "You'd think I cooked this fucking mess for myself. It's always *my* dinner, *my* dishes, *my* laundry, *my* dog, and if someone actually condescends to *help* me I'm supposed to be so fucking *grateful,* I'm supposed to screw my fucking guts out because you folded a pair of your own goddamn underpants. Well, you're not *helping* me, no one's *helping* me, I'm going to break every fucking dish in this shit heap, I'm going to . . ."

I am throwing dishes, glasses, silverware, candlesticks; a bowl half full of peas trembles in the air, then lands. Peas shoot across the room like nauseous bullets. The children are huddled in a corner, terrified, watching me. Suddenly Andrew moves forward and slaps me so hard I trip and fall. He is on top of me, holding me down with arms like steel.

"You lunatic, you bitch, you maniac," says Andrew. "I'd like to kill you."

In a flash Kate leaps on his back like a small tigress, digs tiny nails into his shoulders. "Leave her alone, leave her alone, leave her alone," gasps Kate, her blond hair flying. Andrew turns and slaps Kate full in the face. It is the first time he has ever slapped Kate, or any of the children, or, for that matter, me. Anna screams in fright, a thin, piercing wail, a wail I have often heard before, at Mother's hospital. Andrew shakes his head in shock and stands up slowly, staring at his hands as if he had never seen them before.

"Dear God," he says, sitting heavily down at the table. He looks around the room, at the broken dishes and glasses and Kate lying crumpled and sobbing near an overturned chair, buries his head in his hands and begins to cry, great relentless sobs that shake his whole body.

I crawl over to the crumple that is Kate and fold it in my arms.

"I love you, Kate. I love you," I say, without caution, gently smoothing hair from her wet face.

Kate's eyes widen. She sits up and looks at me, stunned.

"You do? *I never knew that,*" says Kate.

Oh my God.

"I love you too Mommy; I love you so much," sobs Kate as her arms go around my neck.

Kate loves me.

Anna is still standing in the corner, unblinking, trembling. I help Kate up and, with my arm still around her, hold out my hand to Anna.

"Come on, baby; it's all right now. I want you to get ready for bed, I want both of you to go to bed. Everything will be all right. Anna. Anna?"

For a moment she does not move. Then she shudders and leans against me; her body relaxes. With my arms around both girls, I take them off to bed.

"Mommy, could . . . would it be all right if Anna slept in my room tonight?" asks Kate. "I want her to. She can sleep in my bag, my new sleeping bag. If she wants to."

"I want to," says Anna, in a whisper.

I leave my daughters, one in a flowered sleeping bag, the other snuggled under a soft yellow quilt, to solve their own mysteries and head back for the dining room, to solve mysteries still pending.

Andrew and I pick up the pieces of glass and china in silence. Nicco, wearing the Indian suit and headdress he has worn all day, happily carries out bags of garbage. His headdress is askew on his fuzzy head.

"I'm a good boy, aren't I, Dad, I'm helping," says Nicco. "Dad, when you were little, did you fight with the Indians? Did you go out with the men and fight the Indians when they tried to get your wagon train?"

"No, Nicco, I'm . . . that was very long ago."

"I'm glad; I like Indians," says Nicco. "Dad, when you were little, were you a good boy too?"

Andrew hesitates, then smiles his funny smile.

"Yes, Nicco," says Andrew. "When I was little, I was a very good boy."

When Nicco is finally in bed we sit in the darkened living room, not speaking, enveloped in our separate thoughts.

"Can you ever forgive me?" Andrew says at last.

"Come on, I was going crazy; I was angry too. Being angry is better than . . . nothing. We'll be eating off paper plates for months."

But this is not Joe, it is Andrew. And Andrew does not laugh; he does not even smile.

"And Kate. How could I do a thing like that, to a child? What must she think of me. What I did makes me sick. I feel sick."

"I forgive you, Andrew. And Kate will too. Let's go to bed. We've both had enough for one day."

In the bathroom, I undress and insert my diaphragm, small boxed treasure that I have kept hidden in a locked jewelry case, that I have never used with Andrew. We hold each other tightly and make love for the first time in a very long time. It is the way it used to be. I had all but forgotten the tender, open, loving man of my nights.

"I don't have to use anything? Are you sure?"

"Yes; I have something now. I got something from the doctor."

"Pills?"

"No. Something else. Are you happy?"

"Oh God, yes, yes. It's better, so much better. Is it better for you?"

"I think so. Yes. It's funny, it was awful before. When I used one before. Do you remember?"

"I remember. Are you sure you're all right now?"

"More than all right. This is the first time we've ever talked in bed, do you know that?"

For a long while I lie awake in Andrew's arms, thinking. "I love you; I want to change," he said. "I'm so mixed up. I feel as if I've been sleepwalking; I've been sleepwalking all my life," he said.

So he loves me. That I knew. That's the worst of it. And he's been sleepwalking; he wants to change. I don't think he will change, can change very much, but because he has asked for a chance I cannot leave him. But I cannot break with Joe either. And I cannot live that way; I cannot handle that. Dear old Dad was right—how much can a woman handle? So let's sum up. I've tried it all; you can't say I haven't. Fuck liberation. Also fuck the opposite. Fuck everything. It is almost Christmas, time to begin looking for a gun. I keep my word. Why look for a gun when we have a gun? Ah. Because Andrew's rifle is too big, too powerful for the neat bloodless hole I have my heart set upon. Because, no matter how convincing the suicide notes I leave—three sealed for the children to open when they reach the age of eighteen; one for Andrew, one for my father, one for David, one for Joe if I can figure out a safe way to get it to him—the police may find out about my bout with sexual freedom and decide that Andrew has murdered me in revenge. And that's not playing fair. No it's up to me to find my own goddamn gun. Four weeks to go. I wonder if there's room in the great big Inn in the Sky. Christmas and a man named Joseph; all I need are a full, bulging belly, three Wise Men and a couple of camels. Pretty liberated of Mary, when you think about it—that immaculate conception business; even more with it and now and lib than being the adoptive single parent of a Third World child. But Mary was way ahead of me. Christmas, here I come.

XIV

Finding a gun in New York City, I find, is not all that easy. For one thing, I am not gun-oriented; although I know enough to know that a rifle is not what I'm after, I am not sure what kind of gun I should be trying to find. Andrew would probably know, or Joe, but I do not want to involve either of them in my coming demise. (Justin received a psychiatric discharge after three traumatic months in the Marine Corps—no help there.) Two visits to the public library were not fruitful. I did manage to unearth a copy of something called *The Soldier's Guide,* circa 1952, but most of the guide deals with personal hygiene ("brush your teeth; change your socks; keep your brass bright"); more explicit advice ("FIND 'EM, FIX 'EM, FIGHT 'EM, FINISH 'EM!") or my personal favorite: *"You must obey the orders of your leaders.* This does not mean that you are a slave or that you can't stand up for your rights. It does mean that you are a member of a military team and, like any successful team, it has no place for the temperamental 'star' who wants to play the game according to his own rules. Your duty as a soldier means that you will give up some of your personal freedoms for the good of the whole team—and for the greater freedom of your country."

There are several pages of photographs of guns at the back of the guide, but the photographs are either of submachine guns, rifle grenades, rocket launchers, mortars, or enormous things called howitzers. The 240-mm howitzer, M1, on carriage M1, for example, weighs 64,700 pounds; weight of projectile—360 pounds. Rather hard to kill oneself with *that.*

I did find out one thing, though. I would not have made a good soldier, circa 1952 or any other circa.

Anyway, on with the search. One freezing Sunday afternoon as I'm coming back from the store, Super Stefan drives up in his battered blue Chevy. His wife and babies are sitting in the back seat smiling fixed, fearful, female Slavic smiles. Tied to the trunk of the car is a deer, a beautiful dead deer with soft staring eyes. Sudden idea:

"My," I say fighting nausea, trying not to look at the eyes, the lolling neck, the bloody, gaping hole, "that's quite a deer you've got there. Are you . . . do you hunt a lot?"

Super Stefan grins broadly, his beefy red face beaming.

"Yes lady. Hunt, kill. Deer, rabbit, squirrel, duck; hunt, kill, kill them all."

"I guess then . . . you know a lot about guns. About different kinds of guns, I mean."

"Gun is gun."

"Yes, but, there are different kinds of guns aren't there? I mean, you wouldn't use a very small gun, a gun, you know, that could fit in, oh, say, a pocketbook or something, to kill a deer with, would you? I mean, I was just wondering what kind of gun you'd use to kill something smaller, a squirrel or a rabbit, something like that. Without so much blood, I mean. A smaller hole."

"Use same gun. One gun for all."

"Oh. Well, how did you pick out the kind of gun you

have? Did you just go into a gun store and ask someone or what?"

Super Stefan laughs and slaps me on the back so hard I almost fall down on the icy pavement.

"You make joke," says Super Stefan.

After some hurried lunch-hour telephone calls to gun shops (I look in the Yellow Pages under "G,"; "Come on, old lady, I'm hungry; what the hell are you *doing* in there?" mouths Joe through the glass door of the phone booth), I find that the type of gun, or rather pistol, I'm looking for is either a .22 or .25 (both "ladies' pistols," a kindly old gun seller with an office on Fifth told me). Yes, he has them in stock. But to buy a pistol you need a permit. And to get a permit you have to apply for one at your local precinct. And that's only the first step; something about sponsorship and the Firearms Control Board. Funny, I don't remember Andrew having had to go through all that when he bought the rifle in the country seven years ago; perhaps the rules have changed. Or perhaps the rules for pistols and rifles vary. Or maybe he just didn't tell me. But I can hardly ask for the details now.

"Getting a permit, my dear, is a fairly difficult procedure," the kindly-old-gun-seller said. Was he ever right. At the local precinct, under the pseudonym of Laura Jones, I am shuffled from one officer to another, each nastier and more impatient than the last—"Look, Laura, you don't need a gun;" "Whadaya mean, a gun? Ya outaya mind?;" "Forget it; get outta here; go home;"—but I am determined: "All right, all right, don't *cry* for Chrissake; I'll let you talk to the Company Commander."

The Company Commander sighs, folds his hands, shakes his head, smiles at me from across an acre of desk and says:

"Now what would a nice little lady like you be wanting with a twenty-two?"

"Oh. Well, with the city being so dangerous and all,

rape and all that, and muggings; sometimes I don't get out of work till late, after dark; I have young children; my husband is away a lot; I thought, my husband thought . . . that I should have a gun. A small gun. For protection. I mean it doesn't *have* to be a twenty-two. It could be a twenty-five."

The Company Commander sighs again. "Laura, you don't need a gun for protection. The *police* are here to protect you. That's our job. Do you know what might happen, what happens all the time? Say a rapist breaks into your apartment. Overpowers you. You play it smart. Pretend to give in. While he's engaged in the sex act you reach for your gun. You struggle with each other for possession of the weapon. He grabs the gun away from you. Shoots you. With your own gun. If you hadn't had a gun, he couldn'ta shot you, right? Now you're dead. And Laura, it would be your own fault."

I sit there mesmerized, my mouth open, my eyes never leaving his face. I see it all—the rapist, gun, struggle—I hear the shot, feel the pain.

"Bunch of animals out there, shooting it up, killing innocent people," the Company Commander says, standing up. "Friday, Saturday nights banging away at each other okay, let 'em kill each other off, but innocent people! Law-abiding citizens! They should all get the chair. Every animal out there should get the chair."

I come out of the rape-murder saga haze.

"Yes, I see your point but . . . if *they're* all out there shooting it up, killing people, if *they* all have guns, why can't *I* have a gun? I don't want to kill anyone. I just want a gun. For protection. A twenty-two. Or a twenty-five."

The Company Commander sighs for the third time and sits back down.

"Sweetheart," he says, "let me tell you another story. We had a guy coming in here every day, begging for a permit. Faggot afraid of his own shadow. Said he needed a pistol for protection. Just like you. Protection! Bastard wanted to kill himself. You get depressed, gun around the house, you never know. Suppose we'd given him the permit. We'd have been aiding someone in committing a criminal act."

"How . . . uh . . . how did you know he wanted to kill himself?"

"Got a call a few weeks later. Neighbor said terrible moaning sounds were coming from the next apartment. So over we go and there's the bastard faggot all doubled up, so we rush him to Roosevelt. Died the next day. Mushrooms. Ate a whole bunch of poisonous mushrooms. Hell of a way to die. But at least our conscience was clear."

"But I don't want to commit suicide. I just want a gun!"

"You're a hard little lady to convince, aren't you, Laura. Okay, let me lay it on the line. There are only two ways to get a gun permit these days. Either you're in a retail business where you can prove you carry large amounts of cash, or you enjoy shooting as a sport."

"Oh. Well, I don't get much exercise. I think I might enjoy that. Shooting as a sport."

"Then you'd have to join a gun club. But you have to be a member for a year before you get a gun."

"A year! But what's the point of belonging to a gun club if you don't have a gun? I mean, what would I do there, while everyone else was shooting?"

"Make friends, meet people, socialize. Get out of the house. But take my advice, sweetheart. Find another sport. Bowling, maybe. Great exercise. My wife bowls twice a week and you should see her—fifty-five years old and a figure like a teen-ager." He stands, all three hundred pounds of him, in final dismissal. "And don't try to get a gun illegally up in Harlem or from a street kid; believe me, you'll get in a pack of trouble. White woman goes into a bar, goes up to a bunch of kids on the street asking questions, and she's liable to wind up in the river. And if we ever caught you we'd throw the book at you. Don't go out alone at night, watch out for side streets, don't carry more than five dollars, keep away from the animals, don't open your door to strangers, buy a police lock, call 911 if you run into any problems, and you won't need a gun. You'll do fine."

On the way home from the precinct I go over so-far-rejected suicide possibilities. Drowning? I'm told it's euphoric once you give in to the experience, but I'd never have the guts to give in. Pills? Too trite, and never certain. Poison? A mess. A jump off the George Washington Bridge? Another mess, and with my luck I'd probably land on a passing yacht and break up a beautiful people cocktail party. Gas? Might blow up the whole building. Hara-kiri? Forget it. Mushrooms? Too exotic. Which leaves Andrew's rifle. No, absolutely not; I've *got* to find a gun, and I don't have much time. I want to leave everything in order—house clean; refrigerator defrosted; Christmas presents bought and wrapped; tips for Super, Handy and Elevator Stefans; black paraplegic interviewed and article written (the article should cover my funeral expenses; I have nothing fancy in mind). And on top of everything else, find another maid. For Dolores, in an agony of embarrassment, has just informed me that she can no longer work; her mother is so feeble she cannot care for the boys. So Dolores will have to go on welfare. In two weeks.

The interview with the paraplegic is scheduled for tomorrow, at five-thirty; they will not let me interview her during office hours. They also will not send a photographer with me—"get the total story first; check it out; just hop on the tube," said Nina airily. (I'd like to see *her* hop on the tube. To the Bronx.)

When I called to make the appointment, the paraplegic's voice sounded strange; a light, faraway voice that left sentences dangling and questions unanswered. "I wonder why she wants me to meet her in the Bronx; I mean, I wonder why I couldn't have met her at her office after work, or for a drink or something," I said to Nina.

"Darling, *I* don't know; I can't be *every*where, do *every*thing," said Nina. "Perhaps she's on vacation, getting ready to jet to the Islands; winter vacations are very *in*. Or maybe she simply feels more comfortable being interviewed at home. Heavens, it's up to *you* to delve; that's what working your way up is all *about*."

The next day I spend $7.50 on a cab to the Bronx. The streets are empty—no traffic, no people, only broken windows, garbage and a chilling, all-pervasive silence. Block after block of abandoned buildings; another city, another world. We pull up in front of a six-story tenement; it looks abandoned too. But I check the address and yes, this is it. On the top floor I see a window hung with tattered cloth.

"You're crazy, lady; you'll never get a cab out of here," says the driver.

"Could you, do you think you could come back in about an hour? I can't afford to pay you to wait, actually I can't even afford the ride home, I had no idea . . . but my husband could meet me downstairs in front of our building with some money and . . ."

"Come back? Here? You think I'm crazy? I was crazy to come up here in the first place," says the driver, punching on his off-duty sign, accepting a two-dollar tip, locking his doors, and racing off.

I look at the twisted mailboxes in the entryway. There are only two names, Williams and Baker. Baker. 6A. I start to climb the six narrow, dim flights. Graffiti in luminous colors crowd the peeling walls. FUCK YOU, BABY. KISS MY ASS. JUANITA AND RAY. KILL THE PIGS. FIRST STREET DEVILS. There is not a light, not a sound, only the clatter of my boots on the rotting stairs. A pungent smell of urine and damp plaster; on the sixth floor landing a leaping pair of yellow eyes. A cat; only a cat. I knock at the door to 6A, and when no one answers, push it open. In a small front room an old black woman sits rocking back and forth. She says nothing but points down a long, dark hallway to a closed door.

"Come in, sister," says a voice.

In the tiny room, even smaller than the first, is an enormous young woman, so fat her eyes disappear into bulging cheeks. Her hair is filthy, her body wrapped in a torn flowered robe. She is sitting in a wheelchair.

"Are you . . . Jeannette?" I ask.

The mass of flesh nods slowly.

"I am Jeannette. But I am called by other names."

"You are called by . . . I . . . oh . . . Well, I . . . I'm Liza Calder from *Free Woman*. Have you seen Nora Davis recently? I mean, has it been a long time since you've seen her?"

"There is no time. There is no past or present or future. There is only the everlasting One. The One."

Oh boy. I have an immediate impulse to get the hell out of here as fast as I can, but instead sit down cautiously on the unmade cot. The sheets are gray with dirt. A long black hair coils like a snake upon the pillow. Beneath the cot, a bedpan reeks.

"Well, on the phone, when we talked on the phone, I explained the article they want to do. Are you able to . . . can you talk? Are you still working? You were, you had something to do with fashion, didn't you?"

The mass shakes with silent laughter. There is a gleam of wild, maniacal intelligence in what I can see of its eyes.

"You gave up your career then? You're not working? I understood . . . I thought . . . they told me that you'd done some really great things, put yourself through college, had lots of friends, lots of dates, that you had a lot of great things going considering your . . . excuse me, I didn't mean it that way, but . . . I was told that you were very active. Very busy."

The mass speaks. "Oh yes. I was busy. *Very* busy."

"But you're not working now?"

"No."

"Or dating?"

"No."

"Or going out? Getting around?"

"No."

"Well, would you mind telling me, could you tell me, what *do* you do?"

"Nothing."

"Nothing? Nothing at *all?* But . . . you're laughing; why are you laughing? Are you laughing at me? I'm afraid; you're frightening me. Why did you let me come here?"

"I did not let you come. You were sent. Sent to see."

"See? See what?"

"See God. I am God."

"You are . . . God?"

"I am God. The One. The everlasting One. Come. Come to God."

In a trance, I move toward the wheelchair. Jeannette, with a surprisingly strong hand, pulls my head to her breasts; I can smell her hot funky smell of grease and sweat and breath. She is whispering quick short words in my ear, words that have no meaning, no connection—voices, tits, yellow, cello, sky, toilet, crack, fuck, cock, blood, fur, piss, roses—words that build into a crescendo of shit, one word, shit, over and over, shit, shit, shit until she is screaming, her pupils dilated; there are bubbles of spit at the edges of her mouth. Terrified, I pull away.

"Carry the word! Carry the word!" The sound of her screams follows me down the stairs.

Shaking, I search the street for a taxi. There is nothing, no one in sight. I feel suspended in air, in time; I start to walk aimlessly, turn one corner, then another. On the corner lounge a group of boys, young black boys in jeans and leather jackets. Tarzan's Raiders, studded letters, jackets hazy, undulating eyes, quivering concentric circles of teeth. I am so dizzy I sit down on the curb. One of the boys turns, looks me up and down, then comes toward me. He is a tall boy, handsome, with smooth tan skin and a slow, sensuous gait. "Kinda far from home, ain't you Mother?" asks the boy. "What you *sittin'* here for like this? Good way to get your white self dead. Hey, what is it? What's the matter? You hurt? You shakin' all over. Shotgun!"

Another boy, shorter, darker, with an ugly scar that runs from his splayed nose up into his Afro, leaving an inch-wide path of white, hurries over.

"Shotgun, this lady not feelin' good. Get those motherfuckers over here. Let's get her inside."

"Inside" is a basement room in an abandoned building a half-block away. The room is very dark. Shotgun lights a candle.

"We got any whiskey around?" asks the tall boy.

"No, just Thunderbird. And the last of that gin."

"Well, *get* the gin, man. Move your *ass*. Can't you see this lady not feelin' good? You are a dumb nigger, man. A dumb *nigger*."

After a shot of gin, I look around me. Pallets on the floor. On the walls, posters of Malcolm X, George Jackson, Castro, raised black fists. Gun-hunting country if I ever saw one. My head is clearing. I should be frightened, but I'm not, not at all. Happy, warmed by gin and companionship, I feel as if I have known Tarzan's Raiders all my life.

"Are you Tarzan?" I ask the tall boy.

"Right on, baby. You feelin' better now? *Yes* you feelin' better. Man, you scared the shit out of me back there; what happened? Here, have another shot. You get yourself mugged or somethin'? Somethin' worse? What you *doin'* up here; you crazy? You walk around on the wrong turf up here and you get yourself in trouble. *Real* trouble. Anyway, we goin' to walk you to the subway. Once you get on your feet *all* of us goin' to walk you to the subway."

"You shouldn't have called him that," I say from somewhere in the far recesses of my programmed brain.

"Call who what? What you talkin' about?"

"Nigger. You called Shotgun a nigger. You shouldn't use that word; it's awful. It's an awful word."

Tarzan slaps his thigh and laughs so hard he falls to the floor and pounds his fist on a pallet. The other boys are laughing too.

"Man, you are somethin' else," says Tarzan. "Have another shot."

I accept a third shot of gin. They are all drinking Thunderbird; they are giving me the last of their gin. Yes, I think I can trust these boys. What have I got to lose? (My life. So what.)

"Tarzan, I'm already in trouble. Real trouble. I need a gun. I *have* to find a gun. A twenty-two. Or a twenty-five."

"A *gun?* What you need a *gun* for, baby? You want to eliminate somebody? Shit, only us *niggers* do that. *White* folks don't do that; oh *no*. You ever read the *News?* You ever do a study of the prison population? We animals, baby. *Animals.*"

More beautiful black laughter.

"Tarzan, I'm not kidding around. I may be a little high right now, a little mixed up, but if it wouldn't get you in trouble, if there's any way you could get it for me, I need a gun. A pistol. A small gun."

Tarzan looks at me closely. "You not jivin' me?"

"No."

"You know what you doin'?"

"Yes."

"Okay."

Tarzan sits there on the floor, thinking.

"What we got in the way of small weaponry, Shotgun?" he asks.

"Nothin' much. Maybe one twenty-two, but I got to dig for it."

"So *dig*, man. You heard the lady. She in *need*."

Shotgun lifts a piece of canvas in the corner of the room. Underneath are portable TV sets, radios, watches, and a small arsenal: shotguns, rifles—there must be fifteen of them. After much rummaging around, Shotgun comes up with a small pistol, dusts it off on his shirt carefully, and hands it to Tarzan. Tarzan looks at it critically, turning it back and forth in his hands. He points it at me playfully, takes aim, and pulls the trigger. Click. Nothing. Not that I expected anything. Trust is trust.

"Can I have it? Is it a twenty-two? How much do you want for it?" I ask eagerly.

"Hold on, baby," says Tarzan. "*Yes* it a twenty-two. And we friends, right? You not goin' to run off and *talk*. But I still takin' a *chance*. You not my regular-type customer. Also I got to keep us in chittlins and hominy grits. So I got to charge you somthin.' Like fifty dollars. Cash."

"I agree with you, Tarzan; I understand absolutely. You have your own worries, your own responsibilities. But I don't have that much money with me; I only have a few dollars; I didn't realize how much it cost to take a cab to the Bronx; I didn't even know where the Bronx *was*, so all I have is a few dollars. But I'll get the money together and we could meet somewhere downtown. When could you meet me? Monday? Tuesday? I could call you first and you could come right down."

"Baby, how you goin' to call me? We don't have no phone, we don't have no electricity, shit, we don't even have no *water*. We make a definite date now, say Monday, eight o'clock, corner Forty-second and Ninth. 510 West. Hotel there, brother a friend of mine, run the place. We meet inside. Eight o'clock. And baby, I be glad to lend you money for a cab, I see you a cab-type person, but we never goin' find a cab up here. So we goin' get you to the subway; it gettin' late. No sense *askin'* for trouble."

"Oh God. All right. But listen, Tarzan, could you possibly load the gun for me? I'll never be able to load it by myself. And could you . . . this might sound silly, but do you think you could . . . wrap it so, you know, it looked sort of like a present? A Christmas present? That way it wouldn't be so hard to get it into the house."

"A *Christmas* present? You mean with Santa Claus paper and ribbons and all that? Shit baby, you sure want a lot for your money, don't you? Okay, okay, I gotta be outta my head, but I'll do it. Let's move now; have a quick shot before we go. *There.* You steady now? You walkin'? Come on, you motherfuckers, let's get this girl on her way."

So for the first time in almost ten years, since Manny Gerber's manicured hand landed at my feet, I take the subway. And I am not afraid. I am not even dizzy.

"You're so late, I was worried, thank God at least the photographer was with you, did you have trouble getting a cab?" asks Andrew.

"No, not really; the interview just lasted a little longer than I expected."

"That *cretin,* that utter *cretin,*" says Nina of little-Nora-somebody-from-Decorating, when I explain that the black paraplegic hasn't quite got it made after all. "Oh well, no matter, you go ahead with the article and we'll simply take some snaps of some model or other sitting in a wheelchair. God. What a cretin."

"Make the whole article up, you mean?"

Nina sighs exaggeratedly. *"Yes,* darling," says Nina. "Make the whole article up."

"I won't do that," I hear myself saying. "I'll try to

find a real girl in the same situation, or I'll do another article, but . . . I won't do that. It's dishonest. It's phony. I won't do it."

Nina looks at me, astonished. I look right back at her, eye to eye.

"Well!" says Nina finally, stalking off. But that's all she says. And that's all that happens; I do not have a sudden heart attack or stroke; the ceiling stays in place; no body-shattering bombs go off.

Surprise.

Everything is in order. Everything. The house is shining, the tree up and decorated, the presents bought and wrapped, the new maid hired and ready to start a few days before Dolores leaves, an article called, "Italian Lovers . . . are they or aren't they?" finished and ready to be handed in. (Yes, they gave me another assignment. The topic, of course, was their idea, not mine. An unfortunate choice, that topic, but I need the money and it's nice, even for a short time, to know that I'm still popular. Upstairs.)

The gun is hidden deep in a giant-sized box of Kotex, high up in my closet behind a row of pocketbooks. (Tarzan did a fine wrapping job—fluted green ribbon, bright red paper.) All week long I have been conscious of its silent presence. I look at my children, at Andrew; I have a drink with Joe, but I feel nothing. I am beginning to view my actions with a detached interest.

"I have to get away for a few hours, I have to be by myself, I might not be back till late tonight, I can't explain. Can you understand that?" I ask Andrew the afternoon before Christmas.

"But now? On Christmas Eve? I . . . I think so. Yes, I think so. Go ahead," Andrew says.

I still feel nothing.

The train to the country is cold, almost empty. The pistol's light weight rests comfortingly on my lap. A friend.

My only friend now. Suburbs, small towns flash by in the dusk—houses, fences, red shutters, doorways framed in Christmas lights, reindeer prancing on shingled rooftops, a young child playing sadly, alone, by the side of the track. My stop. A voice is calling my stop. I get off the train and, guided by the salt, the sound, the sound I cannot hear but it is there, walk slowly toward the ocean, past boarded-up cottages, boats moored in icy yards. There are more houses now, many more houses. But I see my house, the summer home of my childhood, wedged between two houses that were not there before. The trim is blue now, not green; a front step is missing a support; there is my window, my old window, at the gabled top. I look at the house for a long time, then walk down the beach toward the area of dunes and tangled grass where the Italian boy and I first entwined.

There is snow on the sand; it crunches under my feet. All around me is an unearthly silence except for the beating of the ocean, calm tonight but beating still. It is almost dark. When I reach the dunes I sit down and unwrap the pistol. It feels cold, so cold in my hand. I hold the barrel to my left temple, release the safety catch as per Tarzan's instructions. No time now, no time for waiting, thinking; my whole life is racing through my head, fast, too fast: a blue and white dress I wore at six; my father lifting me onto a Shetland pony; pushing David in a carriage; bedtime poems; the day Nicco was born; Kate on a swing in a yellow snowsuit; Anna asleep; Andrew's face; the Italian boy's blue eyes; Joe, Joe laughing; an amusement park, a carrousel, "Earth Angel"; pull the trigger, pull the trigger.

But I cannot pull the trigger. I cannot die. Andrew, Kate, Anna, Nicco, Mother, my father, Joe, Elly—people who love me, need me—all reasons for living. But not the main reason. No, I cannot, *cannot* kill myself over two men, a set of rules that didn't work out, and a personal suicide pact that began as a half-joke, slowly crystallized, and now finds me sitting on this frozen sand. Death for myself, perhaps, for my own sake, some day, but not today, not now. Why? No reason really. At the moment I just feel like staying alive. I think I will give myself until Easter, see how things turn out. Easter seems like a good time limit. Maybe my affair with Joe will die a natural death; maybe we'll both learn to be happy with things as they are; maybe I will divorce Andrew and marry Joe; maybe Andrew will change; maybe I will say "fuck everybody" and move into a sleek, plant-filled studio apartment; maybe I will find some kind of work that means something . . . then again, maybe not to all six maybe's. Does any of this matter? Of course not. But somehow the absolute knowledge that none of it matters, that nothing matters, makes everything matter, and I care even more.

I walk down to the ocean's edge and am about to toss the .22 as far as I can into the water, but suddenly stop. It might be thrown back onto shore and found by a child or picked up by the police and traced to Shotgun. I must still think of these things. I rewrap the pistol carefully and head back for town. I am very hungry. In a deserted restaurant I order clams on the half shell. The clams taste good, cold and salty. I order another dozen and a glass of beer. Sipping beer, eating clams, watching the sleepy waiter wipe plates on his apron, I feel happy. More than happy. I feel, at the moment at least, at peace.

It is very late by the time I get home. Andrew has already arranged the presents under the tree. He asks no questions but opens a bottle of champagne; our usual Christmas Eve ritual has begun.

"You look better; you look happy," Andrew says, touching my face.

"Yes. I am happy. Oh God, I forgot the curry; I forgot to make the curry. How can it be Christmas Eve without shrimp curry?"

"Don't worry. You said you'd be home late so I picked up some bread at Zabar's, some French bread. And I made us some soup. It's not shrimp curry but it's something to eat. It's still Christmas Eve."

"Are you sure? Anna will like that castle thing, won't she? She's wanted it for months. Did you remember to help them put out something for Santa Claus? The oranges and cookies?"

"I remembered. Nicco and Anna remembered, too. See, it's all right next to the tree."

"You really made soup?"

"Yes. Clam soup. I bought some clams, fresh clams. I tasted it; it's not bad. What's so funny?"

"Nothing. Everything. Are you sure you don't mind about the curry?"

"I don't mind. I said so. I just hope you like the soup."

We stay up until midnight, drinking champagne, listening to the *Messiah* in the darkened living room. The phone rings and it is Joe, who whispers, "Merry Christmas, old lady."

"Wrong number?" Andrew asks.

"Yes. Wrong number. Merry Christmas."

"Merry Christmas."

We sit for a while longer, staring at the twinkling lights of the tree.

"Coming to bed?" Andrew asks finally, switching off the lights.

Well, why not? His hand is warm, his eyes are kind. Andrew made soup, I do not drink in the morning, have lost twelve pounds, taken the subway, told Nina Farrow off, made the beginnings of peace with my eldest daughter . . . small things, small steps.

I look behind me. My ass may not be together but it is still intact, hanging there like a slightly shriveled, overripe pear. I hear a faint rumble in my descending colon. Could it be . . . yes! . . . could it be . . . my ass is . . . laughing?

Epilogue

She got out. Mother. On New Year's day, after her thirty-second shock treatment, she awoke, showered, dressed, made herself up carefully, consumed half a grapefruit, a boiled egg, and a slice of wholewheat toast, called my father, and asked him to make a hairdresser's appointment for her at Saks.

"This is absurd; I look an absolute fright; whatever am I doing in this place?" she said.

She is now at home, busy buying bathing suits, skirts, dresses, and evening clothes for their upcoming trip to Acapulco.

None of this makes any sense.

I am sure of only two things.

The cell was really there.

Manny Gerber, D.D.S., should have stayed alive. He might have had the greatest fuck of his life the next day.

You never know.